BEAUTY SLEEP

Also by Daniel M. Klein

Embryo
Wavelengths
Magic Time

BEAUTY SLEEP

by Daniel M. Klein

St. Martin's Press • New York

KLEIN

This novel is a work of fiction. All of the events, characters, names, and places depicted in this novel are entirely fictitious or are used fictitiously. No representation that any statement made in this novel is true or that any incident depicted in this novel actually occurred is intended or should be inferred by the reader.

Editor: Jared Kieling
Design by Anne Scatto

Library of Congress Cataloging-in-Publication Data

Klein, Daniel M.
        Beauty sleep / Daniel M. Klein.
            p.   cm.
        ISBN 0-312-04264-7
        I. Title.
    PS3561.L344B4   1990
    813'.54—dc20   89-78094
                                          CIP

First Edition
10 9 8 7 6 5 4 3 2 1

For Samara and Freke,
beauties both

Beware of what you desire,
for you will surely get it.
—Bedouin Proverb

BEAUTY SLEEP

P R O L O G U E

....

Kelly could hear the Channel surf pounding against the cliffs outside her hotel-room window. Pulling aside the curtain, she gazed out at Dover Castle, floodlit sharp and bright as a stage set in the moonless night. Tomorrow, that's exactly what it would be—the set for her Saint-Laurent autumn coat shoot. The agency wanted Kelly surrounded by spume and spindrift, a windswept, gothic look for the collection. On the Concorde flight from New York that morning, the agency art director had offered her a copy of *Wuthering Heights* to read for atmosphere.

Kelly released the curtain, turned, and went over to the dresser. She had to be up and ready for makeup in less than seven hours, but she didn't feel at all tired yet. It wasn't even dinnertime in New York, closer to late lunch in Los Angeles, where she'd been on a *Vogue* shoot only three days ago. She glanced at herself in the dresser mirror and smiled. Still gorgeous after all these miles. Travel didn't even make a dent in her beauty: Her rose skin glowed and her violet eyes shone as if she'd been lounging at a spa all day. Still, she needed her sleep. She reached for her toilet bag, unzipped the side pocket, and removed a plastic prescription bottle labeled Quaalude—the model's friend, beauty sleep in a bottle. She opened it and shook a single large white tablet into her palm.

1

Kelly's pulse suddenly accelerated. Something had fluttered behind her—something she saw reflected in the dresser mirror. She remained motionless, studying the mirror; all she could see was a window, a framed oil painting of Dover Castle, and the open bathroom door. Slowly, she turned around, her eyes scanning the room. Nothing. She saw nothing out of the ordinary. It was a standard-issue international hotel room, little different from the one she'd occupied in Los Angeles earlier that week or in Rio the week before. Obviously all she'd seen in the mirror was the curtain rippling in the draft. Kelly took a deep breath and blew it out slowly. Too jumpy. She was far too jumpy these days; all her friends said so. Too many 'ludes in too many cities, that's what her problem was. What she needed was two weeks in a row in the same place.

Kelly walked to the bathroom, the pill still clutched in her hand. She turned on the cold water and let it run against her wrist for a few seconds before filling a glass, then popped the pill onto the back of her tongue and washed it down. Then she saw it again—a little ripple of curtain—but it was the shower curtain, not the window curtain. And there was definitely no draft in here. Kelly began to tremble. She suddenly raced back to the bedroom and headed for the door, but as her hand closed around the door handle, she stopped.

This is totally ridiculous, she told herself. What was she going to do—ask the night clerk to send somebody up at midnight to peek inside her shower? Madness! Too many 'ludes in too many cities. Kelly spun around, marched back into the bathroom, and stood in front of the shower. She took a deep breath, reached out her hand, and yanked the curtain open.

"Oh, God!"

A tall blond man stood inside the shower, pointing a black revolver at Kelly's head.

"Scream and you're dead," he whispered with a soft accent.

Kelly fell back against the tile wall, gasping for air. She couldn't have screamed if she'd tried.

"Now, please, stay just in front of me . . . we are going for a walk, my beauty," the man said.

PART

1

··

From Amy Martin's **"Beauty Bytes"**
FEMINA MAGAZINE, March

... but Albrye's mouth-watering photos in "Last Chance Desserts" are proof positive that a low-cal patisserie doesn't have to look like a microwaved sponge. ... And speaking of dehydrated sponges, have you ever taken a good gander at your skin after jetting to a conference in Cleveland? Flying on high in the sky is my idea of a reverse facial. That dry cabin air just leeches the moisture right out the old pores, leaving my skin dry and pasty-looking. Well, that tuned-in cosmetics company, Medmetics, has just launched Frequent Flier, a skin hydrater and toner specially formulated for the high-flying woman. I tried a dab on my hop to L.A. last week, but can only give the cream a 6.5 on the A.B.Q. (Amy's Beauty Quotient). True, that overbaked sponge look had vanished, but I deplaned looking like a glazed doughnut. (Why does *everything* make me think of pastry these days? It must be this damned diet!)

... I promised myself I wasn't going to write a word about Kelly Keane in this month's column, but only a few moments ago I was leafing through The Times Magazine *and suddenly there Kelly was staring back at me from the Bergdorf spread with those hypnotic lavender*

eyes. I can't really believe that we'll never see that heavenly face again, those eyes, those lips, those incredible Kelly Keane cheekbones. She was one of the chosen—a Perfect Beauty. In a way, I guess I think it's best that they never recovered her body from that awful accident in the English Channel. Alive, Kelly Keane was the very Ideal of Beauty and that's the way I want to remember her. . . .

—Amy

1

....

"Make me beautiful and I'll make you famous." Amy laughed, settling back into Cal Clay's chrome and leather makeup chair.

"Just make me rich, darling," Cal crooned, touching the back of her neck with his soft hands. He switched on a ring of high-intensity lamps and began gracefully circling her, pausing here and there to swing a video minicam over a section of her face and scrutinize it in blowup in the overhead monitor.

"You really should come in for a honey-almond scrub every week," he said, lightly tapping her cheek. "Just look at your pores... they're positively delirious."

"I'm so happy for them." Amy sighed, closing her eyes. She never liked watching the steps of a makeover. That spoiled the magic. The fun was in the before and after, the presto-chango. Anyway, she had gone through this so many times before, she could always reconstruct the makeup artist's techniques for her readers afterward.

Amy calculated that this would be her seventh makeover this year alone—all of them in the line of duty. Her readers adored these transformations: Amy with her natural light brown hair soft and loose in the "undone" look, her round cheeks given definition with sheer, luminous "no color" makeup, her close-set eyes widened with copper-colored triangles on the outer corners of her upper eyelids. Then a month later, *voila!*—a brand-new Amy with a dramatic sweep of straight black hair from a side part, her cheekbones highlighted with coral-pink blusher, her lips provocatively contoured to look twice their normal size. Amy Martin made over and over and over again.

"Dear Amy," her readers would write in. "Your Michael Maron makeover is absolutely *it!* Don't change so much as a hair ever again. You must feel like a new woman!"

And then, when the next set of before-and-after photos appeared alongside Amy's "Beauty Bytes" column, a hundred more readers would write in assuring Amy that this makeover was "absolutely it," that the True Beauty that had been lurking inside her all these years had finally emerged. Amy's power in the beauty world derived directly from these readers: They identified completely with her. Amy had a face like the women who read *Femina,* not like the women who smoldered on its covers or struck elegant long-legged poses in the layouts inside. In fact, Amy had the ideal face for cosmetic products: She was eminently *pleasant*-looking. Often, she looked quite cute and, in certain moods and from certain angles, even a bit sexy, but Amy just missed being genuinely pretty, and she had known that ever since she was twelve and shared her bedroom with her gorgeous fourteen-year-old sister, Molly.

"But doesn't it ever get a wee bit confusing?" her recently lapsed lover, Peter, used to ask as he inspected Amy with his dark sensual eyes when she arrived at his loft sporting yet another radical makeover. As their affair ground to its finale, Peter had adopted a maddeningly solicitous tone toward her. "I mean, doesn't seeing someone different in your mirror every month give your persona sort of a slippery feeling?"

"I don't have an identity problem, love; I've got a job," Amy would reply, her flushed cheeks prickling under fresh foundation. "And this—what I get done to my face—happens to be a regular feature of that job."

But that, of course, was ultimately what Peter couldn't swallow: Amy's job. She should have realized that when she discovered that he barely even glanced at her articles. And certainly she should have gotten the message from the way he would introduce her to his colleagues at screenings—as a writer or even reviewer but never, God forbid, as beauty editor of *Femina,* that glossy women's magazine. Peter Myers, producer of compassionate documentaries about exploited coal miners and beleaguered farmers, had turned out to be a job snob.

"If I still worked at *Ms.*, he probably would have asked me to marry him instead of backing out the door," Amy had told her therapy group. "That would've been perfect for Peter. There's nothing like a certified feminist on your arm to give you status at a documentary film festival."

"But what about *you?*" her therapist, Mary Goldfarb, had asked. "Why did you so desperately need Peter's approval?"

"Approval has nothing to do with it," Amy answered, shaking her head. "I just got sick of always making up excuses for his hypocrisy."

"I'm talking about all these makeovers," the therapist cut in firmly. "That's the cry for approval I hear, Amy. These makeovers are saying, If you can't love this face, then love that face, or that one, or that one. For you, it's a cycle. Until you feel worthy of love as yourself, you'll be trying on these faces endlessly—and you'll never be able to accept any man's love."

"The makeovers are part of my job, Mary."

"I think they're more than just that, Amy."

Why was it so damned hard for people like Mary to believe that Amy found the beauty world utterly fascinating in itself? In Amy's experience, that world ranked right up there with the worlds of politics and art in the consciousness of most of the population, female and male alike. When she was still at *Ms.* magazine and wrote articles about women's body issues—like her famous "Earthy Pits" piece in praise of underarm hair—no one had accused her of having some hidden neurotic agenda. And yet the day she accepted *Femina*'s salary-doubling offer to write a no-holds-barred, consumer-oriented beauty column, old friends were suddenly urging her to analyze her motives carefully. In the years since, of course, *Ms.*'s pages had begun to overflow with ads for eyeliners and rinses, even bras, while the new feminist role models like Cher began appearing on its covers. Somebody at *Ms.* had finally had the honesty to admit the simple proposition that looking good helped enormously in the fight for equality in this world. If Amy's passion for the beauty beat was neurotic, she was apparently in good company. Last year, she had confessed in her column that beginning when she was nine years old, she would secretly rifle through her sister's vanity case, trying on all her makeup, and that ever since, whenever she found herself alone in a beautiful woman's bathroom, she would snoop around like a burglar, trying on every cream and powder, every blush and eyeliner. "I'm the Goldilocks of the vanity closet," she wrote, and a record seven hundred readers wrote back admitting to the same sneaky vice. Did Mary Goldfarb think every one of them had a pathological repetition compulsion, too?

"I think you're going to be very, very happy," Cal Clay was murmuring above Amy, his boyish voice blending with the piped-in New Age "waterfall" music.

"What time is it?" Amy whispered, her eyes still closed.

"Just past three."

She must have dozed off. A faint dream presence of Peter still hovered over her, caressing her brow. God, she missed that man's touch, his long elegant fingers tracing slowly from her neck to her clavicle to her breasts. In the final analysis, did it really make any difference whether Peter liked introducing her to his friends as a reviewer? Cal Clay finished blotting along Amy's hairline.

"It's magic time," Cal sang.

Amy snapped open her eyes.

"Oh!" She sucked in her breath. She felt her heart accelerate, her face grow warm. She gaped at herself in the video monitor. God, she looked fabulous! Her eyes were large, dark, and smoky, the eyes of a nightclub chanteuse. Yes, there was definitely something Parisian about her entire face, a knowingness, a fragility. It was in the deep hollows beneath her cheekbones, the delicate molding around her brow. This face had elegance and mystery, a secret life behind it. Amy stared at herself, transfixed.

"Don't you just love it?" Clay said. He touched a switch and the lights around the mirror in front of Amy blinked on.

Amy slipped her gaze from the monitor to the mirror. The image was brighter here, clearer. Suddenly, she drew in her breath and held it; she was trying to stave off the familiar dull ache that was welling in her throat. But it was too late—that wonderful moment of perfect illusion was already vanishing. For all their lovely lavender shading, Amy's smoky eyes were still too close together, forever just missing the right balance; for all Cal's artful blending, those hollows beneath Amy's shallow cheekbones were still an obvious trompe l'oeil; and for all its aura of fragile translucence, the skin on Amy's face was still too sturdy, too thick. She might look marvelous in a quick glance, stepping from a taxi, or in a well-composed photograph for *Femina* magazine, but not in a careful once-over. Then she would look false, plastic—an unnatural beauty. Amy let out her breath in an audible sigh.

"Call in the photographer, would you, Cal?" she said, all business again. "I'm supposed to be at some press do in exactly twenty minutes."

"Yum, yum, look at you. You're going to have all these little doctors wagging their stethoscopes at you." Pamela Ross, Amy's editorial assistant, grasped Amy's arm as she came through the front door of the St. Mary's Hospital medical school annex. "Do you know where we're supposed to go?"

Amy pulled her official Diagnostique press invitation from the side pocket of her Filofax: Dr. David Copeland, Director of St. Mary's Department of Endocrinology and Research Consultant for the Hormone Products Division of Diagnostique, would lecture on the latest advances in hormone treatment for the skin surrounding the eye in Theater B on the third floor of the Catholic teaching hospital's annex. Amy led Pamela to the elevator, where their colleagues from *Vogue, Glamour,* and *Gloss* were already waiting along with Midge Krieger, president of the Marquessa Model Agency.

"I wonder what they're serving for munchies," Amy quipped as they all entered the elevator. "Thyroid in aspic?"

Only Pamela laughed. Dot van Deusen, the beauty editor of *Gloss,* averted her eyes; heaven forbid that even the elevator operator should think she was amused. Amy turned to wink at Pamela and in that instant caught Midge scrutinizing her face in the cold fluorescent light of the elevator.

"Cal Clay, right?" Midge asked, smiling.

"Aren't you clever?" Amy forced a broad grin. "How'd you ever guess?"

"It's those mysterious French cheekbones . . . they do look marvelous on you, darling," Midge said. The agency executive then leaned toward Amy and said quietly, "By the way, thanks for the kind words about Kelly in your column. We do so much want her to be remembered for her beauty and not for all that messiness at the end."

"No thanks needed," Amy replied. "I was a great admirer of Kelly."

As they walked out into the hallway, several smiling young men and women in pleated shirts and black bow ties proffered trays of wine spritzers and assorted sushi. Amy grabbed a fat tuna, mouthed the word *thyroid* to Pam, and popped it in her mouth. At the door to Theater B, a pretty Hispanic woman in a white medical coat handed them black loose-leaf binders that looked remarkably like doctors' casebooks: It was the press kit for "Mona, The Medicated Hormone Eye Gel, by Diagnostique."

"Think they're going to give us diplomas on the way out?" Amy shook her head incredulously as she and Pamela made their way down the steep stairway of the lecture hall. Blackboards covered with chemical symbols alternated with digitalized blow-ups of eyes on the cinder-block walls. "Totally shameless, aren't they?"

Of all the hype and hokum in the cosmetics industry, there was nothing Amy railed against more than this business of packaging makeup as medicine. Sure, the super vitamin Retin-A really did smooth out wrinkles, and the blood pressure medication minox-idil actually had turned out to sprout hairs on an impressive percentage of bald pates, but for every legitimate medical claim in cosmetic ads, there was a truckload of pure bullshit about "procollagen molecular restructuring" and "liposome regenera-tors," ads filled with inscrutable scientific reports from Swiss labo-ratories and glossy photos of men and women in lab coats swirling test tubes over Bunsen burners. A few years back, when the celebrated heart surgeon Christiaan Barnard appeared in a skin-cream ad that claimed he had discovered a formula that "stimu-lates cell proliferation" and "increases DNA synthesis," Amy had been one of the first journalists to investigate, and when it turned out that the good doctor actually hadn't even worked on the product but had merely offered his endorsement in exchange for a fee, Amy wrote a scathing exposé in *Femina*. Within weeks, Barnard's cell proliferator was practically off the shelves. Not everybody in the cosmetics business loved Amy Martin.

"Help, I think I'm having palpitations," Pamela twittered as she gazed at the tall black-haired man with deep-set blue eyes who was striding to the lectern, his medical coat fluttering be-hind him. "Is there a doctor in the house?"

Amy hadn't had time to put her contact lenses back in after her makeover, so she pulled her glasses from her bag and peered through them at the dark-haired man. He certainly was a sexy

12

specimen. He had a lean face with muscular creases on either side of a wide sensuous mouth, but above all, his eyes had it: Blue and lucid as sapphires, they beamed humor and confidence and virility. "Obviously they hired this guy from central casting."

"I don't care"—Pamela giggled—"As long as he takes Blue Cross."

"Good afternoon," the man began, smiling up at his audience. "I'm Dr. David Copeland, and on behalf of Diagnostique cosmetics, I'd like to thank all of you for joining us today."

Amy put away her glasses and flipped open her press kit. Sure enough, on the first page there was an eight-by-ten glossy of the gorgeous doctor, with his curriculum vitae listed below: Harvard College, A.B., Physicians and Surgeons, M.D., two years in the army and two more with the World Health Organization, followed by a residency in endocrinology at Mt. Sinai. He had joined St. Mary's Hospital four years ago and had begun consulting for Diagnostique a year after that. It didn't mention whether the prince was married or not.

"As I'm sure all of you know, eye creams have traditionally served as emollients and hydrators for dry skin around the eye, particularly the lower lid," Copeland went on, his eyes flashing. "But this was often only maintenance work that never dealt with the fundamental problem—the breakdown of the basement membrane, the skin's support structure."

As Copeland continued, Amy pulled the research and test-study sheets from her press kit and flipped through them. According to the release, Diagnostique's breakthrough was an androgen-derived enzyme dubbed elactase, which Copeland had synthesized himself in his laboratory here in St. Mary's Hospital. The test studies looked legitimate, complete with double-blind controls, but the numbers were less than overwhelming—some marginal skin pliability and membrane-density increases.

"It took the discovery of Retin-A for us to realize that an eye cream could actually rebuild skin tissue around the eyes," Copeland was saying. "Now, with elactase, Diagnostique has created an eye gel that ensures that all tissue will be soft, pliant, and young-looking."

Does it now, Doctor? Amy peered around her. What a rapt group of honor students this Dr. Copeland had today. Dot van Deusen, God love her, was even taking notes in her "casebook," obviously bucking for teacher's pet. Copeland continued speaking fluently without glancing at his notes, just the hint of a confident smile on his full lips. Now he paused to moisten those lips with his tongue, and Amy suddenly felt her cheeks grow warm. Dr. David Copeland was looking at her, yes, definitely looking directly at her, and there was something, well, clearly admiring in that look. What was it? The cheekbones? The smoky eyes? The translucent skin? Copeland smiled, nodding to her ever so slightly, and Amy felt herself irresistibly smiling back, barely listening as he went on about amino-acid strings and the role of cholesterol esters in penetrating all four layers of the skin.

"Well, well, the patient certainly seems to be responding to treatment," Pamela whispered in Amy's ear. She gestured toward the side door of the lecture hall where a willowy, raven-haired woman in a Donna Karan bodysuit had suddenly appeared and began striding toward Dr. Copeland. It was Francesca Levesque, top model from the Marquessa Agency.

"You're right on cue, Francesca," Copeland said, smiling with obvious pleasure as he took the model's hand like a dance partner and brought her up next to him at the lectern. "I'm sure all of you know Francesca. She's our Mona Girl."

Mona Girl? *Mona,* as in hormone? Amy felt a sudden stab of disgust for this whole phony setup, especially for this TV doctor with his Harvard degree and World Health Organization credentials. She was beginning to seriously wonder whether Dr. David Copeland really had anything to do with the development of this eye cream or whether he was pulling a Christiaan Barnard and just lending his name and handsome head to the product for a fat fee.

"I think we're ready to try to answer your questions," Copeland said, beaming up at the assembled beauty experts.

Dot van Deusen raised her hand and asked how frequently the doctor suggested applying the gel. What a truly interesting question, Dot . . . go to the head of the class. Karen Bergman, from Cosmetic Careers, asked whether there would be standard discount rates for the department-store chains. Another good question . . . sure glad we have an M.D. on hand to answer that one. Amy couldn't stand it any longer. She shot up her hand.

"You had a question . . . Ms. Martin, is it?" Copeland flashed his deep blue eyes at her.

"Yes," Amy said, rising. "It says here that you discovered elac-

14

tase right here at St. Mary's. Exactly what kind of research is it that you do in this hospital, Doctor?"

Copeland stroked his jaw a moment, then stepped in front of the lectern and gazed up at Amy.

"Actually, I was investigating the skin-coarsening mechanisms of hypothyroidism when I discovered the skin-softening properties of elactase," he said, looking warmly into her eyes. "In medicine, you see, it's not unusual to go looking for one thing and to come up with its opposite."

Appreciative murmurs all around. Copeland raised his eyebrows and smiled at Amy with obvious self-satisfaction. Amy remained standing.

"But it's precisely those skin-softening properties that puzzle me," she went on, pitching her voice a notch louder. "Your test results for skin pliability and membrane density don't show any significant gains over the eye creams already on the market. So what exactly is Mona Eye Gel's 'breakthrough,' Doctor?"

Copeland's shining eyes turned cold. Amy found it difficult to keep looking directly into them.

"It's a combination of factors, Ms. Martin," Copeland began deliberately. "Not the least of which is Mona's capacity for hydrating the lower lids. Dry lower lids, I assume you know, are a major problem area in today's environment."

"Dry lower lids?" Amy repeated, arching her eyebrows incredulously. "Are you speaking as a former member of the World Health Organization when you say that dry lower lids are one of the major problems in the world today?"

Copeland glared at Amy a second, then shook his head and strode back behind the lectern next to the magnificent-looking Francesca Levesque.

"Does anyone else have a question?"

2

....

"Who the hell does she think she is, Mother Teresa with a make-over?"

David Copeland pulled off the linen medical coat he'd worn for the press conference and threw it over a chair. The back and underarms of his shirt were sopped with perspiration and he could feel his pulse still throbbing in his temples, a sure sign that his volatile diastolic blood pressure was squeezing up toward one hundred. Somehow he had gotten through the remainder of the question and answer period, smiled famously with Francesca for the photographers, even personally handed out a few sample jars of Mona Eye Gel—all without letting his fury show. He didn't know what pissed him off more, that supercilious Martin woman—a beauty gossip trying to pass herself off as a medical ethicist—or the fact that he'd allowed himself to be talked into hawking his eye gel from a hospital lectern in the first place—not that it had been that difficult to convince him to put in his per-formance. Last week, *Hospital Journal* had listed ten more small teaching hospitals that had gone into bankruptcy; in today's fi-nancial climate, hawking some eye cream to ensure the survival of St. Mary's felt like a higher calling.

Not only did Diagnostique endow David's chair in St. Mary's

16

department of endocrinology, but in an arrangement worked out by Art Malley, St. Mary's chief financial officer, the cosmetics company had already contributed three tax-free half-million dollar gifts to the hospital based on projected earnings. Diagnostique's generosity had begun when Malley brought them elactase, the enzyme David had synthesized under a hospital grant in his cramped St. Mary's laboratory. Since then, David had been spending half his eighty-hour week in Diagnostique's spacious Brooklyn laboratories developing hormone-based beauty products and, starting today, he'd added "official spokesman" to his duties. No, it wasn't exactly an arrangement covered under the Hippocratic oath, but the survival of one of the last small compassionate hospitals in New York City *is* a major health issue, damn it, Ms. Martin!

"Don't take it personally, David. Amy's been a little brittle with everybody lately," Francesca said with a wide smile that displayed her perfect ivory teeth. "She's sexually undernourished, I hear."

David winced.

"Really, darling, don't let her ruin it for you. You were an absolute smash—everybody said so—and now it's time to celebrate." Francesca held up David's tweed sports jacket for him to put on. "We don't have to go out if you're too exhausted. We can get something Chinesey to take to my place, a little dim sum in the Jacuzzi. That should get the kinks out."

David took his jacket from her outstretched hands and put it on himself. He checked his watch—5:55. He could still make six-o'clock rounds if he left right now—not that he was expected on the ward tonight. His department colleagues knew he was taking care of business.

"I have a patient to see upstairs," David said impulsively.

"Oh, David, can't it wait until tomorrow? You look positively wrecked."

"No, it can't wait," David snapped. "She's having surgery in the morning."

Francesca lowered her green eyes in photogenic sympathy and David felt his temples pound again.

"Why don't you come along, Francesca?" he blurted. "You can see what I endured this torture down here for."

It was an absurd offer, absolutely adolescent, and David regretted it the moment he made it. Was he actually trying to prove his professional integrity to Francesca? She looked silently back at him, a rare and appealingly vulnerable expression on her patrician face. David reached out his hand and gently touched her cheek.

"Sorry," he said softly. "Look, why don't you run ahead and I'll bring you dinner in an hour. Home delivery."

Francesca slipped her hand under David's arm and squeezed his biceps.

"No, you're quite right," she whispered. "It is time I saw what you do here, darling."

David's senior associate, Raymond Kenworthy, was ushering half a dozen rumpled residents down the corridor when David arrived with Francesca Levesque in her clinging bodysuit.

"Evening, David. Joining us?" Kenworthy's sonorous West Indian basso resonated against the tile walls.

"Just looking in on the preop, Ray," David said. "Have you worked her up yet?"

Kenworthy hesitated. He, like all the residents, female and male alike, was unabashedly gazing at Francesca.

"Forgive me," David said. "This is Francesca Levesque, a, uh, colleague of mine."

David couldn't resist tossing out the word *colleague* as bait for the inevitable ironic smiles that appeared on the residents' faces. These young doctors reminded him of an old Harvard classmate who had spent four years pretending his merchant father was actually an aristocrat: They hated to acknowledge who was really paying the bills.

"Ms. Levesque expressed an interest in our work here," David went on coolly.

"David's told me about you," Kenworthy said, offering Francesca his large hand. "A pleasure."

One of the residents handed David a copy of the patient case summary. Her name was Moire O'Brien and she was a twenty-two-year-old Caucasian with a two-year history of amenorrhoea. When she was first seen in the unit three months ago, she had presented a classic clinical picture of Cushing's syndrome. Cortisol and ACTH tests had confirmed the diagnosis, so David and Ray had put her on hefty doses of cytadren and cortisone acetate, but her condition continued to deteriorate. A cranial CAT scan proved ambiguous at best: no obvious masses or lucencies. Nonetheless, both doctors had concluded that there was enough corollary evidence of a pituitary tumor to recommend a transphenoidal hypophysectomy. The surgery was scheduled for nine o'clock the next morning.

"Are there any questions before we examine the patient?" Ray asked.

Ever courteous, Francesca shook her head no. David followed down the corridor behind her, pausing a moment at the third door to wave in to the Webber boy, a fragile six-year-old amyotrophic diabetic who was staying overnight for his monthly glucose-uptake test. David caught up with Francesca just as Ray led the residents into a private room at the end of the corridor. Moire O'Brien was awaiting them in a fresh, pink-beribboned nightgown.

Francesca turned white the second she walked through the door. Then her knees buckled under her. David caught her, slinging his arm around her waist and bracing her against his hip.

"Just breathe deeply," he whispered. Francesca's body trembled against his. "Close your eyes."

Francesca nodded, but she clearly couldn't take her eyes off Moire O'Brien.

The patient had a red beard that stretched from ear to ear, dropping a good two inches from her chin to the first button of her nightdress. Her fleshy, florid face was moon-shaped and there was a pronounced "buffalo's hump" just below her neck. Garish purple striae radiated from under her sleeves down her arms. Only a few stray yellow hairs remained on her ulcerated scalp. Moire O'Brien was a grotesque, a freak. She was a perfect specimen of advanced Cushing's syndrome.

David checked to see whether anyone had witnessed Francesca's near-faint. Apparently not, thank God. All eyes were on Ray Kenworthy as he launched a textbook-perfect workup. While Ray spoke soothingly to the patient, he lifted the sheet and gently elevated her wasted legs with his large hands.

"Note the mild edema of the ankles," he said softly. His voice had the lilt of an admiring lover. "We've seen increased polydipsia and polyuria just in the last three days. That goes with the calcium picture."

At their Wednesday-night basketball games at the Y, Ray was the most aggressive man on the court, the total opposite of this bedside tender heart. That was the secret of Ray's happiness: He gave himself range. No blood-pressure problems for Ray Kenworthy. David played pickup basketball as if an intercollegiate referee was still calling fouls.

David looked quickly over at Francesca. She had recovered and was leaning against the wall just inside the door's shadow, but her eyes were still fastened on Moire O'Brien. David had positioned himself halfway between Francesca and the patient. What an odd and perfect symmetry, he thought: Beauty behind him, Beast in front of him. These were the familiar extremes in his life, but he could not remember ever having them so close to one another before. The two women were even about the same age, but the worlds they walked in were light-years apart. And David, of course, was smack in the middle. He was ineluctably drawn to the bizarre mass of flesh lying on that hospital bed, forever fascinated by the subtle changes of internal chemistry that had so ghoulishly distorted the Cushing's and acromegalia and Elephant Man's Disease patients he saw on the wards every day. And he was magnetized by the glowing, tender flesh of the ravishing model behind him whom he would take to bed tonight. He had always been bewitched by the look, the touch, the feel of a beautiful woman.

"Dr. Copeland?" Lisa Chou, a senior resident, handed David the large glossy color photograph Ray was circulating. It was a picture of Moire O'Brien taken at her graduation from Sacred Heart College less than two years ago. There was no point in even attempting to compare the beaming, blond woman in the photograph with the patient in front of them. She was literally beyond recognition.

"Clinical symptoms of Cushing's remained undetected by anyone until fourteen months after onset of the disease," Ray was saying. He gazed warmly into Moire O'Brien's eyes before continuing. "When did you first notice your body was changing, Moire?"

"It was my shoes, I guess," the patient answered, her voice as thick and deep as a man's. "I couldn't get in them anymore. I went from a four triple-A to a six D in just a couple months. I had to get new jeans, too, and new dresses. My mother thought it was from all the junk I was eating, so I went on this very strict diet, but that didn't help, either."

Ray nodded. "And then?"

"Then it was my rings," the patient went on. "I had to have one sawed off because it pinched so hard. And then I had to get new glasses because they didn't fit right anymore, either."

"What about your skin?" Ray asked softly. "And your hair and facial hair? When did you notice those changes?"

Moire O'Brien lowered her eyes.

"I don't know. I noticed all of that, of course. Everybody did. But I guess I thought it was just a temporary thing . . . you know, like all the acne and stuff I went through during adolescence. I figured if I took better care of myself and prayed real hard, it would all go away."

Ray nodded. "And when did you finally consult a doctor?"

"After I'd missed my period for a year."

Ray scanned the faces of the interns and residents before taking the patient's hand in both of his.

"But by that time, your body's endocrine system had totally run amok, Moire," he said, his voice pitched low, resonant as an actor's. "Your hormone messengers were carrying contradictory messages to your organ cells in a frenetic effort to regain your body's equilibrium. And all . . . all because your pituitary gland was producing a few micrograms too much of a single hormone that, like a false note at the start of a symphony, had thrown everything which followed into disharmony."

David had heard Ray recite this particular piece of original poetry to patients a hundred times before, but it was as impressive as ever. He felt Francesca grasp his arm. She had crept out of the shadow and stood beside him in the bright light.

"Moire, tomorrow morning at nine o'clock, we are going to remove part of your pituitary gland," Ray was saying. "I can't make any promises, but I'm positive that in less than three months you're going to be—"

Suddenly, Moire O'Brien uttered a sharp cry of pain as if she'd just been cut by the surgeon's knife. Tears flooded her eyes and she yanked her hand away from Ray.

"What is *she* doing here?" she cried, pointing at Francesca. "What is that beautiful woman doing here?"

21

* * *

They never stopped for dinner.

Driving uptown, David suddenly reached across the front seat and slid his hand inside the top of Francesca's bodysuit. He pressed hard against her left breast, felt the nipple swell quickly under his hand. He squeezed it between his thumb and forefinger, tugged on it. Neither of them spoke. They both stared straight ahead through the windshield.

In the elevator up to her apartment, David pressed Francesca into a corner, his hands tight on her hips. He ran his tongue along the side of her face, following the arabesque from her brow to her cheekbone. Her scent pulsed up at him. Francesca smiled, her eyes half-closed.

The moment they were inside her apartment, Francesca unfastened her bodysuit and stepped out of it. It took her five seconds at the most. All she wore now were bikini panties, a red triangle at the top of her long, golden legs.

David dropped his coat on the floor, pulled his shirt over his head. Francesca was in front of him, unhooking his belt, unbuttoning his pants, unzipping his fly. Her hands cupped the front of his briefs, squeezed him through the cotton, then she stretched the elastic waistband over his bulging penis and closed her warm hands around it. David slipped a finger under the side of her panties, yanked. They snapped clean like a rubber band. Francesca parted her legs. She pulled David to her, slipped the tip of his penis just inside the moist outer lips of her vagina, held him there as she rotated her pelvis against it.

Suddenly, David grabbed her buttocks in both hands and lifted her off the floor. He backed her against the wall and drove his penis deep inside her. Francesca's legs locked around his waist. David pushed deeper, ground into her. Francesca's mouth was open, sucking in air, a rasping sound. David slammed against her, smacking the backs of his hands against the wall. He drove himself into her as if he were impaling her to the wall.

Francesca gasped, stiffened, her thighs wrenching his waist in an enormous spasm. Seconds later, David climaxed, too, groaning, gushing, emptying himself into her. Then, finally, he was at peace, blessed peace, the first peace he had felt all day. Barely a word had been spoken since they'd left the hospital.

They disengaged, untangled, walked to her bedroom and

stretched out on the mink spread on top of Francesca's brass bed. David gazed at the wall across from them and the familiar silver-framed photographs of Francesca on the covers of *Vogue* and *Elle* and *Femina*. She nestled her smooth elegant body against his.

"We're lucky, aren't we?" she murmured.

3

. . . .

"So here is this woman out cold on the operating table with her bare tush propped up in the air like two huge scoops of mashed potatoes and this five-thousand-dollar-an-hour surgeon has his scalpel poised, ready to make an incision, when he suddenly turns to the nurse and says, 'What size dress does she have to get into? A *nine?*'"

Amy threw back her head and laughed deliciously.

"You're making this whole thing up, right?" Pamela said, grinning. She was leaning against the doorjamb of Amy's open office.

"I'm giving it to you verbatim, Pam, I swear to God," Amy said. She was sitting on the front edge of her desk, leaning forward. "Fifty years ago, this guy would have been a poor tailor, cutting clothes to fit this woman. Now he's a seven-figure liposuction specialist who cuts the woman to fit the clothes. But listen, at this point the nurse looks very seriously into Dr. Rothstein's eyes and says, 'A *small* nine, Doctor. And it's not just a dress—it's her wedding gown.'"

"Unbelievable."

Maude Jackson, assistant to the publisher, had drifted in beside Pamela, and now Jenny Massini, *Femina*'s picture editor, paused at the door, too. Amy waved them in. She loved telling a story out loud when it was absolutely fresh; it helped her find the right details for when she sat down to write it later. She was just back from spending the morning at Dr. Herbert Rothstein's Park Avenue clinic, where she had sat in on a liposuction consultation and then, scrubbed and outfitted in a green operating smock, had stood next to the plastic surgeon while he vacuumed a thousand grams of fat from the bride-to-be's size-twelve buttocks.

This year, liposuction had nosed out nose jobs, face lifts, skin buffs, wrinkle fills, and eyebag removals as the most popular knife style of the rich and famous. It was the unique cure for that condition from which every American woman was convinced she suffered: trochanteric lipodystrophy—saddlebag thighs. The "beauty" of this surgical procedure, Rothstein had explained to Amy, was in its simplicity. He merely had to make a half-inch incision on the perimeter of the offending area, insert a small hose called a cannula, and root it around for about a quarter of an hour. Then, when enough fat cells had been dislodged, he "Hoovered" them out.

"I almost lost it when he stuck that hose under her skin," Amy went on. "It made this horrendous slurpy sound, like a baby eating Jell-O. Rothstein started working up a real sweat whipping that hose around in there. And he kept stopping to let the nurse mop his forehead. Honest to God, it was straight out of some fifties movie. *Magnificent Obsession,* right?"

Amy slipped off her desk and assumed a mock-heroic expression. "Dr. Rothstein! Dr. Rothstein! Wanted in surgery," she intoned in an old-time movie voice. "We've got a tush in here that just won't stop."

Amy's colleagues burst out laughing.

"It gets worse," Amy went on, riding the laugh. "This little gnome is panting with exhaustion from wriggling his hose around when he suddenly stops, turns to me, and says in utter seriousness, 'This procedure has totally ruined my backhand.'"

"Quelle shmuck," Jenny said.

"I just don't get it," Maude said, shaking her head. "So this woman gets down to a nine and looks stunning in her Halston, but underneath it, she's now got skin like an elephant, right? From the liposuction—what do they call it—corrugated skin? Doesn't the lady care what she looks like in bed?"

"Bed?" Amy repeated, deadpan. "She doesn't have to worry about bed, Maude . . . she's getting *married.*"

Again, Amy's colleagues roared.

Of course, Amy had questioned Dr. Rothstein closely about how his procedure affected skin and then she had run by him the same list of questions she always put to plastic surgeons. Haven't you yet discovered a way to alter the basic texture of skin? The way it drapes? Its feel? The answer, after some hemming and hawing about stretching and buffing and wrinkle filling, was always, No, cosmetic surgery still cannot fundamentally improve skin tissue. It cannot change sturdy, porous skin like Amy's into soft, delicate skin like, say, Francesca Levesque's. Just as it still cannot do away with a too-round or too-narrow skull, a protruding windpipe, or, alas, still cannot reposition a pair of eyes that are set too close together.

"Rothstein's just another snake-oil salesman peddling dreams," Amy said. "These ladies lie down on his operating table convinced they're going to wake up looking like Michelle Pfeiffer, but they wake up looking like themselves, only a couple sizes smaller."

"Oh God, I hope you're not going to skewer this doctor, too," Maude said, smiling nervously. "Our legal department has a few other matters to attend to this week beside fending off another Amy Martin slander suit."

"Tell it to circulation," Amy replied. It seemed every time somebody threatened to sue over one of Amy's articles, *Femina* gained five thousand new readers and the magazine could hike its ad rates. Not a bad deal, considering none of the suits had stuck—yet, anyhow. But that didn't prevent *Femina*'s management from relentlessly trying to bridle Amy's stinging prose.

"I saw in layout this morning what you put in your column about that Dr. Copeland," Maude went on. "Poor boy, he'll never know what hit him."

"That poor boy happens to be one of the sexiest men I've ever seen in or out of a medical coat," Jenny said.

"He takes a good picture," Amy said coolly.

She wouldn't deny that Copeland seemed to bring out the lascivious wench in the ladies. When Pamela saw the picture proofs from the Diagnostique press conference, she had let fly some teenage comment about the doctor's "gorgeous buns." God knows, Amy's own shameless id wasn't any better. Never mind that Copeland was a self-satisfied hack, Amy's unconscious had gone right home from that awful press conference and dreamt up one whopper of a pornographic—and ridiculously corny—

scenario. In it, Amy lay spread-eagle on an examination table, Copeland hovering over her, studying her naked body with his deep-set, serious eyes. Really pathetic once you thought about it, but she'd woken up all hot and sweaty. The only thing encouraging about the dream was that Peter wasn't in it.

"I think Dr. Copeland will survive," Amy said, walking around her desk and sitting down in front of her computer. Of course, it wasn't David Copeland that Maude was worried about; it was the ad department's relationship to Diagnostique. "Beauty Bytes" had a way of making the job of selling ad space more difficult at times—not Amy's problem, as she informed them all at least once a week. She hit the floor switch and drilled her access code onto the keyboard. "Got to get cracking."

Maude and Jennifer started out the door, but Pamela lingered.

"I left your call list on my desk," Pamela said. "The usual suspects. Plus some miserable-sounding guy who wouldn't leave his name. Said he was a loyal reader of yours. And Bonnie from Pick called twice. She sounded totally hysterical."

"Models' agents are always hysterical, Pam. It's part of their job description."

"I promised her you'd call back this afternoon. It has to do with that 'New Latin Bombshells' piece you're doing. She's Carmina del Ray's agent, you know."

"Yes, I know." Amy sighed. "Okay, get her for me."

A minute later, Bonnie Bonfiglio was on the line and she did indeed sound hysterical the moment she said hello.

"Bad day?" Amy asked, the phone cradled against her ear so she could type her liposuction notes onto her PC while she talked.

"Worse than bad, Amy. Horrible," the agent moaned. "Sometimes I actually forget what sickies models are and then something like this happens."

"Something like what?"

"Like Carmina, you know. Christ, she was hot—I got her hourly to double in just six months and had her booked solid through December. We put everything we had into that girl and then—poof—just like that she's gone. Takes a swan dive into a bottomless pit."

"Carmina's dead?" Amy lifted her hands from her computer keyboard.

"Didn't Pamela tell you?" the agent asked. "It happened yesterday. Charlie Seppo called us from Nairobi this morning sounding absolutely crazy. It was his shoot, you know . . . Intrepid Jeans, a terrific account. He said they had a great first day up there in the Serengeti. He got some fabulous great white hunter stuff. Then that night, they all had dinner together in the hotel and that was it; they never saw her again. Just her shoes on the slate ledge next to this mile-deep canyon."

"She jumped?"

"I guess, or slipped. We'll never know. Apparently there's no way to get down there to pick up the pieces, that is, if anything's left after the lions have lunch. And she didn't leave any note. But Charlie says she'd been acting spacy since their layover in Italy. Boy troubles. She'd been moaning about some Milanese asshole who was doing a number on her. And between you and me, they found a whole pharmacy in her makeup bag. That part's not for publication, okay? Charlie's really bummed out. I mean this isn't the kind of shoot that looks good on your resumé."

"No, I suppose not," Amy said coldly.

For a second the agent was silent.

"Listen, Amy," she went on abruptly. "Are you still going to do that 'Latin Bombshell' piece?"

"I hadn't really thought about it, Bonnie."

"Well, if you do, we've got this real comer from São Paulo that you've just got to see to believe. Betina, her name is. We call her the original 'Girl From Ipanema.' Can I send over her comps?"

Amy shook her head incredulously.

"Jesus, Bonnie, you don't miss a beat, do you?" she said, and slammed down the phone.

Amy turned back to her computer, hesitated a second, then quickly opened up two windows on her screen. The one on the left was a file headed "Models and Drugs"; the one on the right, "Models and Suicide." She typed in Carmina del Ray's name, the date, and a brief description of what Bonnie had just told her, then closed both windows and began writing her article about the size-twelve tush on Dr. Rothstein's operating table.

4

Light beaming through the flask cast an amber circle on David's sleeve. He brought the flask closer to his eyes and gently swirled it. Not a speck of the brown fluid stuck to its sides. Ten days and not a clone in sight. The culture medium was wrong. Or maybe it was the "climate." Or most likely what was wrong was the very notion that the pheromone, alpha copulin, could be synthesized. Returning the flask to a wire rack on his bench, David noted in his lab book that as of April 20 at 11:15 P.M., A-C Culture #395 remained inert.

David unscrewed the top of his thermos and poured himself a cup of Columbian espresso, then leaned back in his chair and planted his feet on the side rung of his laboratory bench. Outside his window, a tugboat was passing under the Brooklyn Bridge behind the festive pinpoint lights of the River Café. There was a time-warp feel to the view at this time of night, a sense of Edward Hopper simplicity and isolation. David never felt so whole and peaceful as when he worked by himself at night in his Diagnostique laboratory. That feeling alone seemed to compensate for the little compromises he made for the company. There were no arrogant residents to contend with here, no tormented patients with their lives slipping away, just cosmetics research, pure and inconsequential. David held no illusions about the ultimate importance of eye gels or artificial fragrances in the grand scheme of things. Their relative insignificance was part of the solace he felt here. It gave his life balance.

Not that life at Diagnostique was pressure-free. Far from it. Mitch Papechki, the company's aggressive young CEO, was constantly reminding everybody who worked for him that Diagnostique could be crushed in a day by Estée Lauder or Revlon. "The painted ladies," he called the old, established cosmetics companies; among them, "the painted ladies" controlled more than two-thirds of the market. Mitch's competitive strategy was to position Diagnostique as the cosmetics line for single professional women in their thirties—women who wanted quick results, women who didn't have time to touch up their faces three times a day, women who got caught in the rain now and then. "Estée Lauder is for the woman who wants to look good in her mirror," Mitch would say. "Diagnostique is for the woman who's out in the world marketing herself."

At this point in his career, David found Mitch's rousing "Let's take on the big guys" pressure refreshing. It certainly beat hell out of the precious, hypocritical pressures of academic research. David had had enough of that at Mt. Sinai to last him a lifetime. There, under the auspices of the celebrated Czech endocrinologist Josef Siok, David had spent four years monitoring the effects of dopamine on luteinizing-hormone secretions in female mice. It was a painstaking but engrossing project with important implications for infertility treatment of humans, but the ultimate goal of the research became abundantly clear to David on the day Siok called him into his office and told him that a competing laboratory in Cambridge had pulled ahead of them and would be submitting their results to the *Journal of Reproductive Endocrinology* by the end of the month. Siok's solution was for David to "extrapolate" the remainder of his data immediately—in other words, fake it and beat them out. David had obliged; it would have been sheer career suicide to refuse the inestimable Josef Siok. A few years later, that experience had made it easier for David to offer elactase to Diagnostique. Although he had discovered the enzyme by accident, he'd seen its commercial possibilities immediately. And after Josef Siok, the world of commerce seemed very pure indeed.

"Can I bring you a sandwich, Dave?" Mitch Papechki craned

his boyish blond head inside the lab door. He was wearing his after-hours sweat suit with the Diagnostique "beaker" logo on the sleeve. In the evenings, Papechki often worked in what he called "the tank," a small windowless room down the hall from the research lab.

"No thanks, Mitch."

"Sure? I've got an extra tuna made with safflower mayo. Keep your lipids in shape."

David smiled. "Not tonight."

Papechki started out, then turned back.

"We had another go-around in sales this afternoon," he said. "Built a few fires. We're going to see some movement in Mona soon."

David nodded and Mitch jogged off down the hallway back to the tank. There were pictures of Mitch's mousy-looking wife and their four children all over the walls of his executive suite upstairs, yet the man never seemed to go home. David wasn't much better.

Although he'd only met Francesca three months ago, she was already complaining that David didn't spend enough time with her. Early that afternoon, she had telephoned from Aruba, where she'd been on a two-day bikini shoot for the Saks catalogue; she said that she had twisted a few arms and booked an early flight back. A limo was picking her up at Kennedy, so why didn't she swing straight over to St. Mary's and pick David up?

"Afraid I'll be in the lab tonight," David had replied automatically. He'd been looking forward to the recuperative solitude of the laboratory since morning, when he and Ray Kenworthy had spent three heartbreaking hours in a vain struggle to keep a little Korean child from slipping into diabetic coma.

"Then I'll just have to wait up for you, darling," Francesca said warmly.

"Listen, do you think we could make it another night?"

Francesca had remained silent for several seconds, then uttered a sexy "Who cares?" laugh.

"Well, I guess I might as well stay down here overnight then," she said. "Dangle in the pool."

"Lucky pool," David had replied seductively, suddenly longing for her. He'd flashed on Francesca in her string bikini lounging beside the Novatel pool and he'd felt a sudden intense pang of desire for her smooth-skinned body. Push, pull. Hello, good-bye. Good-bye, hello. When would this lover finally tire of his compulsive yes/no games?

David lifted A-C Culture #396 from the rack and held it to the light. His lust would be safer trapped inside a flask, he decided. That way, he could keep it under control. Hell, wasn't that what this alpha-copulin project was really all about—synthesizing a controllable sex urge? A survey by Mitch's consumer-research people had determined that if his target consumer had her druthers, she'd take an instant aphrodisiac over a subtle romantic perfume. She wanted a product that could give her sex she could count on. Dependable, schedulable sex for the Filofax woman. Mitch Papechki was convinced that if they could synthesize the sex-attractant pheromone, they'd have the ideal Diagnostique product. He'd already decided on a brand name for it—Heat.

"The painted ladies wouldn't put out a hormonal aphrodisiac perfume if their lives depended on it," Papechki had said when he presented the project at a research and development meeting. "Too sexy for them. Too honest. Afraid some healthy down-and-dirty sex will smudge their eyeliner. No, Heat is for the Diagnostique woman, the woman who's liberated enough to be able to say, 'Let's get down to it right now because I've got a meeting at three o'clock.' This is the product we've been looking for, gentlemen, the one that's going to position us for the next decade. Give us the edge we need."

Even though Mitch had admitted to David that he knew how little substantial research had been done on human pheromones, he'd committed $2 million to developing synthetic alpha copulin. His goal was to have atomizers of the airborne hormone on the shelves in less than two years. He told David it was the biggest gamble of his career.

"But I know you're going to do it for me, David," he'd said, smiling broadly across his desk. "You're the most talented endo-crinologist in the industry—and you're all mine."

Mitch had apparently read everything written about phero-mones in the professional journals. A biochemistry major at Cornell before his flair for marketing led him to Wharton for his MBA, he was a quick study. He told David he was impressed with how swiftly biologists had been able to isolate and synthesize a female moth pheromone that was now used to attract lusty male moths by the millions into commercial traps.

"What we're looking for is the human equivalent, right?" Mitch had said, winking at David.

Mitch was even more impressed with new research on a pheromone in human male perspiration that affected menstruation; a group of Philadelphia endocrinologists had demonstrated that a daily dab of the pheromone on a woman's upper lip could normalize her cycle. Now trade journals reported that pharmaceutical laboratories across the country were competing to be the first to clone and market this by-product of manly sweat. That was what had convinced Mitch that the alpha-copulin project was timely and doable. Alpha copulin had been discovered by a Dutch endocrinologist last year in the fatty acids of women's normal nocturnal vaginal secretions. Preliminary studies demonstrated that the pheromone discharged a "subliminal odor" that turned men's thoughts to sexual intercourse. How to produce the pheromone in a laboratory was another question.

David and his research associates had been working on the alpha-copulin project for six months now, ever since Mona eye gel had gone into production. It was a far more complex and engrossing project than the elactase eye cream had ever been. Alpha copulin was the result of six short-chain aliphatic acids naturally combining, but David still did not have a clue as to how to get any of them to combine inside a laboratory flask. After six months, all he was certain of was that human pheromones were infinitely more complex than moths'.

David swirled A-C Culture #396 in front of the light. Again, nothing stuck. Nothing growing inside. He started to return the flask to the rack when he heard a squeak directly behind him— sibilant, like a rat's hiss. David spun around in his chair. A blotchy-faced man in a ragged raincoat stood just outside the laboratory door. The man's head was tilted back, his mottled face pointed toward the ceiling. He had one hand poised over his nose.

"Can I help you?" David stood.

The man did not move. Another hiss.

David started for the door. Abruptly, the man yanked his hand away from his nose and thrust it inside his pocket. In that instant, David saw the purple and white plastic squeeze bottle in the man's hand, just a bottle of nasal spray.

"Lousy cold," the man said, his rheumy eyes turning toward David. "Can't shake the motherfucker."

33

With that, the man scurried on down the hallway, the tails of his raincoat flapping behind him.

"What are you doing here?" David called.

The man didn't stop. David started to race after him.

A click. Suddenly a frame of yellow light flashed onto the hallway floor. Mitch Papechki stepped out of the tank into the light. He grabbed the man by the sleeve of his raincoat.

"It's okay, Dave." Mitch smiled, waving dismissively. "Just a delivery."

··

5

Memo from Amy Martin to Harriet Schwartz, Editor in Chief:

Re.: Allergic reactions to Briley's Cold Cream.

Item stands as written. Enclosed find copies of two indepen-
dent lab reports corroborating 7+ percent incidence of skin
rashes with prolonged use of Briley's. Reports were obtained
through reliable sources.

Amy smiled to herself as she typed the words *reliable sources;* she
had pulled the lab reports directly from the Briley Corporation's
data bank by fiddling a password through their computer security system. Amy continued typing her memo:

I also have it on good authority that Jane Brody at the *Times* is
preparing a piece on hyperallergenic over-the-counter skin products and undoubtedly will eventually gain access to the same test
results. Let's not get scooped on this one, Harriet. This story is
going to break anyhow, so I want 100 percent backup from editorial when Maude and the ad people start crawling all over my
back. . . .

Amy's phone rang and she looked up from her computer screen. The button next to her direct line was flashing. She automatically looked at the digital clock on her desk: 6:56. No one else in editorial remained in the office tonight. She picked up the phone.

"Working late, Amy?" A man's voice, warm, intimate.

"Who is this?" Amy found herself smiling expectantly.

"I used to work late, too. Round the clock, day in and day out. Sure can screw up a fellow's personal life, if you know what I mean," the man went on.

"Please." Amy leaned forward in her chair. "I don't know who I'm talking to."

"Sure you do, Amy," the man went on. "You know me. Everything about me. Even what I used to play with as a kid, right?"

"I'm sorry. It doesn't ring a bell."

" 'Beauty Bytes.' January."

Amy sat up straight, her heart accelerating. She remembered the column, knew what he was talking about: It had been a short item near the bottom of the page about a new clay skin cleanser she'd tested and found sorely wanting. She'd made some joke to the effect that whoever developed the product must have been inspired as a child by Silly Putty. That was all there was to it—three lines at the most.

"I'm paid to make critical evaluations," Amy began her stock response; she'd had to use it more than once in her career. "And I certainly—"

"I haven't worked in two months," the man cut in, his voice now flat, ice-cold. "Instead of working night and day, I don't work at all. I've got nothing left. Nothing. Silly Putty, huh? Silly, silly."

"I'm afraid I'm going to hang up now," Amy said.

"Who the hell do you think you are, Amy Martin? I saw your fucking picture. I know who you are—"

Amy slammed the phone back onto the cradle. She was trembling. She snapped off her computer, stood, put on her coat, and stalked out, leaving the light burning in her office. There was no one else in the elevator when it arrived. She got on, pushed the button for the ground floor, then pressed her forehead against the cool wall panel inside the car. The elevator dropped fifteen floors, then slowed to a stop at the third. Automatically, Amy took a long step backward to the rear wall. A thin, unshaven man in a blue raincoat got on, nodded to Amy. She didn't respond, stared straight ahead, her heart pounding. Who the hell knew where her clay cleanser man had phoned from? He could be inside the building. He'd seen her picture, knew her face. Amy held her breath, watching the man in the blue raincoat from the corner of her eye. At the ground floor, she dashed ahead of him through the opening elevator doors. She headed straight for the front door of the building, then hesitated a second as she gazed out through the glass doors. Shit, he could be any of the men out there. Tomorrow, she'd have Pam find everything she could about him, dig up a picture of him. If he knew Amy's face, she sure as hell wanted to know his. Amy pulled up her collar and strode to the curb, waving for a cab. Christ, the amount of craziness in this business boggled the mind.

6

....

"Your limo's here, Miss Le Fevre," the doorman said on the house phone.

"Limo? I ordered a cab," Monique answered. She glanced at her watch. "And not even two minutes ago."

"What can I tell you? He's double-parked and he says he's supposed to take you out to the airport," the doorman replied. "The elevator's on its way up."

"Hey, thanks," Monique said, shaking her gold mane and smiling as she hung up.

She slipped on her suede jacket, lifted her red parachute-cloth overnight bag from the couch, and walked out her apartment door. Downstairs, the doorman opened the door for her with a flourish.

"You sure lead the life, Miss Le Fevre," he said.

Monique peered through the glass front door at the white stretch limousine with silvered windows that was double-parked in front. The chauffeur, a tall blond man in full livery and wire-rimmed glasses, was standing beside the car and now, as Monique stepped outside, he pulled open the limo's back door.

"Who sent you, the agency or the client?" Monique asked blithely as she entered the car.

"Excuse?" The man had a soft German accent.

"Who's paying for the ride—Zena or L'eggs?"

The driver got in behind the wheel and put the car in gear before replying.

"The client," he said over the limo's intercom.

"Well, isn't this loverly," Monique murmured to herself as she settled back into the sumptuous leather seat. She could barely believe how fast she was rising in the modeling world. Almost every week now she got a new client, and with each new client a new perk. But this was her first complimentary limo, a major step up. Nice the way they'd surprised her with it, too. Not bad for a girl from Copake Falls, Pennsylvania, who'd only been in New York City for five months. Monique gazed through the window at the people in the street and mused again, for perhaps the ten thousandth time, how marvelously lucky it was to be born gorgeous. The limousine turned and pulled onto the FDR Drive. Monique pressed her forehead against the window and squinted. They were on the northbound side. She abruptly slid forward on her seat.

"Driver," she said loudly, "I'm flying out of Newark, not Kennedy. We're going the wrong way."

The driver glanced at Monique in the rearview mirror and continued driving without a word.

"Hey, can't you hear me up there?" Monique rapped on the Plexiglas partition between the front and back seats. "Get off at Seventy-second and turn around. South, go south. Newark Airport."

This time, the driver did not even acknowledge her with a glance. Monique slammed the partition with both her open palms.

"Hey, you! Wake up!" she yelled. "You're going to make me miss my plane!"

A faint smug smile appeared on the driver's thin lips in the rearview mirror.

"Jesus Christ!" Monique screamed. "What the hell do you think you're doing?"

She spun back to the window beside her and saw a cab speeding parallel to them in the next lane. She motioned frantically to the cabdriver for help, then remembered that the windows were mirrored on the outside. She stabbed the button to open the automatic window. It didn't move.

"Please, you must relax, Miss Le Fevre," the driver intoned over the intercom.

"Fucker!" Monique screamed back at him. "Fucker!"

Suddenly, she heard a hissing sound directly in front of her. A split second later, she smelled the pungent, dizzying odor of the nitrous oxide that had started to fill the back of the car.

"Please, just relax, my beauty," the driver repeated.

7

. . . .

"We took her out of kindergarten when her—you know—her chest got too big. Like up to then we'd kept everything else a secret, but you can't hide these, can you, Doctor?"

"I guess not," David replied softly, not looking up at the patient's mother.

The patient, Lisa Carlosso, age five, sat on the examination table in a pair of Wonder Woman Underoos, a fuzzy stuffed bunny clutched to her full, plump breasts.

"What's this little guy's name?" David asked. He tweaked the bunny's nose.

"Bobo," the child whispered, pulling back from David. "He doesn't like it when other people touch him."

"I'm very sorry, Bobo," David said. "It's just that you remind me of a little guy who lived with me when I was a kid. His name was Mr. Wigglesworth, but I don't think he was anywhere near as fuzzy as you are."

For an instant, Lisa Carlosso's face lit up with a five-year-old's smile, but just as quickly it lapsed back to a teenagelike pout, petulant, almost sultry. David had seen this look before on other little girls suffering from the hormone disorder known as precocious puberty. When these four-, five-, and six-year-old children suddenly began developing women's bodies—not just breasts

41

and pubic hair but mature uteruses and ovaries—they also developed the facial expressions of pubescent women, the alternately arrogant and defensive look of ripe sexuality.

"Has Lisa menstruated at all?" David asked, glancing at the girl's mother on the other side of the examination table.

"Five times already. She's real regular, just like me," the mother answered, a hint of pride in her voice.

David rubbed his hands together to warm them, then reached out and cupped the little girl's head, gently probing under her jawbone as he worked his way around to the upper tip of her thyroid gland. Hypothyroidism was sometimes the cause of premature activation of the hypothalamic–pituitary–ovarian axis.

"I took her off chicken right away, of course," the girl's mother said matter-of-factly.

"Excuse me?" David lightly palpitated Lisa's thyroid gland. Density appeared normal.

"You know," the mother went on, "I read about it in a magazine. How these little girls down in Puerto Rico started growing up too fast just like Lisa. Some of them not even four and wearing brassieres and all. It turned out to come from the chickens they were eating. The chicken feed was loaded up with hormones. So I took Lisa off poultry first thing, but it didn't seem to make any difference."

David looked at the girl's mother.

"It was worth a try, at least," he said kindly.

David never ceased to be amazed by how quickly sensational medical news filtered down to his patients. The Puerto Rican cases of chicken-feed-induced precocious puberty had been reported in the *Journal of Clinical Endocrinology* only a year ago; now it was in the supermarket tabloids, no doubt replete with photographs of busty five-year-olds.

"Why don't you help Lisa back into her smock," David said. "I'm going to send Sister Berzins in to take blood for a hormone assay. She's very nice. Then she'll take you downstairs for a sonogram. We'll want a picture of Lisa's ovaries before we start treatment. If all goes well, that will be next week."

David checked his watch, then tucked his examination notes into Lisa Carlosso's folder and started for the door.

"Hey?"

David turned. The child was gazing back at him, her hands straight up in the air as her mother slipped the examination smock back on her. A sudden, awful, automatic erotic sensation passed through David. For just one instant, with her firm new breasts slightly elevated, the five-year-old looked like a model posing for a *Playboy* layout. Half baby-skinned child, half big-breasted woman, she was an exaggerated image of that combination of helplessness and bold sexuality that men desire in spite of themselves. David lowered his eyes uncomfortably.

"What is it, Lisa?" he asked.

"Do you still have your bunny?" the child asked. "You know, Mr. Wiggle?"

"Mr. Wigglesworth." David looked up again, relieved; the child was a child again. "I don't know. Maybe my mother kept him. I'll ask her."

"He could play with Bobo," Lisa Carlosso said.

"Yes, he could," David said softly. He opened the examination room door. "See you next week."

It was a few minutes to closing time for the Thursday-afternoon public clinic in child and adolescent endocrinology, yet the hallway remained crowded with mothers and children. David knew a good dozen of them by sight. Teddy Pallazo, a bright, spidery-looking boy suffering from Marfan's syndrome, waved at David and David waved back as he made his way to the nurses' station, where he handed Lisa Carlosso's file to Sister Berzins. The nurse was one of the last nuns still on staff at St. Mary's.

"Draw for TH3, GN, and oestradiol concentrations, please, Sister." David nodded respectfully. Even though he was a Jewish boy from Queens, he felt reverential in the presence of the gray-eyed nun. "And maybe you should call radiology right now and let them know you'll be taking the child down for an ovarian S.G."

"Of course, Doctor."

David glanced at the wall clock. It was just past five; he was already late for his appointment in the blood bank. He tapped the nurse in charge on the shoulder.

"I'm out of here," he said. "Tell Dr. Chou she'll have to cover the stragglers."

David was halfway to the elevator when he heard Ray Kenworthy's booming baritone call his name. Ray was standing outside Examination Room D, surrounded by young black boys in vivid satin athletic jackets. Every Thursday, scores of black children thronged to the clinic and waited hours to see their Dr. Kenworthy, even if other physicians were available. The Bahamian was one of only a dozen black endocrinologists in New York and it seemed that every black mother in the city had heard of him. David smiled. Ray's loyal following was one of the things David loved best about St. Mary's Hospital. You didn't find that kind of devotion in the megahospitals where the doctors had to have a merchant's preoccupation with patient volume and turnover to support their Mercedeses and second homes in the Berkshires.

"You're looking surprisingly fit for a dude who got his ass whipped last night," Ray said, clapping David on the back. At last night's game at the East Side 'Y', Ray had played particularly well, grabbing more rebounds than all the other players combined. "And then you went home and got it whipped all over again, am I right?"

"I don't know what you're talking about, Ray." David laughed. After the game, he had excused himself from drinks to race up to Francesca's for the rest of the night. The indefatigable St. Raymond had gone on to Harlem to coach his bantam-league basketball team for three hours.

"I'm scheduled to bleed now, too," Ray said as the elevator doors separated in front of them. "I went down yesterday, but they said my platelet count was too low. Glenda gave me chicken liver and johnnycake for breakfast. Now my blood's thicker than mud."

The elevator stopped at the second floor and Ray gestured for David to precede him out.

"By the way, thanks for doing this, my friend," Ray said. "Little Wayne's temperature still hasn't dipped below one-o-four."

"Glad I can help," David replied.

Little Wayne was an eight-year-old black child with sickle-cell anemia who had arrived in St. Mary's emergency room in shock four days ago. The boy's temperature was then 106 and rising. The emergency doctor had immediately IV'd 500 cc's of sodium salicylate in high-protein fluid into the boy's limp arm in an attempt to cut his fever. He had then called down Ray, the resident expert on sickle-cell anemia. Ray's diagnosis was swift and certain: The child was in aplastic crisis. Hemoglobin was crystalizing inside his red-blood cells, choking off oxygen. He could die in a matter of hours. Little Wayne needed all the fresh platelets he could get and would continue needing them until the crisis passed. But St. Mary's blood bank only had enough fresh platelet concentrate on hand for two transfusions—blood components were in short supply in this age of AIDS—so Ray had personally asked his hospital colleagues to make platelet donations.

"Seat's still hot, gentlemen." Art Malley was rolling down his sleeve when David and Ray entered the blood bank. Malley was a short, balding man with a florid face and red handlebar mustache. His voice was high and reedy, like a tenor in a barbershop quartet. Malley picked a rolled-up copy of *The Wall Street Journal* off a chair and tapped David on the shoulder with it. "The big 'D' took another dip today. Down three point six. Nothing to worry about, is it?"

"I'm not worried," David replied tersely. Malley routinely tried to engage him in discussions of Diagnostique's day-to-day finances but never once inquired about life on the ward upstairs. Who could fathom what quirk of fate had made this little man end up in health care instead of investment banking or aluminum siding.

"I talked to Mitch on Monday," Malley said, leaning toward David. "He thinks it's just a market adjustment until Mona gathers momentum. That jibe with your take on it?"

"I don't have any 'take' on it, Art," David replied. He could already feel a familiar throb in his temples; Malley was bad for his health.

"You're there every day, David," Malley went on, "I just thought you'd have some feel for where things are heading."

David took off his jacket before he replied.

"I don't have the fucking faintest idea where things are heading, Art," he said evenly. "That's why I went into research."

Malley stared coolly at David for a second, then touched his *Wall Street Journal* to his forehead in an absurd salute and walked out.

"That man," Ray intoned in broad Bahamian dialect, "there still be too much blood left in him."

David laughed and both men sat down in the vinyl plasmapheresis-donor chairs. The setup down here always reminded David of Fay's Beauty Parlor in Queens, where until he was ten he used to accompany his mother every Friday afternoon—the soft padded chairs, the pile of ragged magazines on the low table, the ominous-looking steel-gray machinery behind the chairs.

A pair of Filipino phlebologists immediately began hooking them up to the plasmapheresis separators. David's found an artery in the crook of his left elbow, drew fresh blood two inches up the inlet-flow tube and clamped it, then found a vein in his right arm and introduced the return-flow needle and tube. The phlebologist pressed a key and the separator began humming like an old refrigerator. She unclamped the inlet tube and David's blood began pulsing up into a plastic blood bag, then looped down into a centrifuge where the solid particles were separated from the plasma, then looped back into a separation container and fed again into the centrifuge for a second spin to remove the platelet particles; finally, David's blood minus platelets circulated back to him through his right arm.

"Think I'll grab a few winks," David said.

"Me, too," Ray answered. "Got a long night ahead of me. Glenda's coming in to straighten up the books. Every man should be married to a CPA. Sweet dreams, my friend."

David closed his eyes. He'd had less than three hours sleep last night. After a late supper, Francesca had led him into the long dressing room behind her bedroom to show him a gown she'd modeled at the de Ribes show in Paris earlier in the week. David had sat on an ottoman by the wall while she stood in front of an illuminated tripartite mirror and pulled her T-shirt over her head, then unbuttoned her jeans, slid them down her long legs, and kicked them away. She wasn't wearing a bra. She rolled her cotton panties over her hips and let them fall to her feet. David gazed at her magnificent body from four perspectives simultaneously: the high, red-nippled breasts facing him were perfect pointed pear halves in the side mirrors; the small delicate curve of her labia echoed in the bold mounds of her buttocks reflected in the mirror behind her. He'd wanted all of her at once and immediately, but Francesca raised her hand for him to remain seated. She slipped the pink silk satin dinner dress from its hanger and stepped into it, reaching behind her to zip up the back, and then, as if on the Paris runway, she began a slow balletic promenade toward him, turning the shiny skirt in her hand, beaming a regal, haughty smile over his head to invisible buyers from Saks and Ultimo and Boutique Montaigne. When she arrived directly in front of David, the epitome of fashion elegance, he suddenly reached out his hand and slipped it under her dress all the way up her bare legs. They made love right there on the carpet in front of the mirror, Francesca's three-thousand-dollar gown hiked to her waist. Later, they'd made love again in her bedroom, less urgently this time, more sensuously. David had had to leave her bed at five in the morning in order to put in a ten-hour day at Diagnostique before going to St. Mary's for the afternoon clinic.

"Dr. Cope-o-lan, we saw your pitcher."

David snapped open his eyes. The symmetrical smiles of the two Filipino phlebologists hovered in front of him. One was holding an open magazine out to him; she was pointing at a black and white photograph in the bottom right-hand corner of the page. David squinted. It took him a moment to recognize his own smiling face next to Francesca's in the photo. He narrowed his eyes and read the caption. It read, "Is there a doctor in the house?"

Jesus Christ! It was that Martin woman's column.

Across from him, Ray opened his eyes and smiled.

"May I see that, please?" David said.

"Sure, sure, Dr. Cope-o-lan."

The young woman placed the open magazine in David's lap. He drew in his breath and looked down at "Amy Martin's Beauty Bytes." At the top of the page was a photo of the Martin woman herself. She looked considerably less painted-up and done-over than she had at the press conference; in fact, she looked quite intelligent and mildly attractive in an intense, bred-in–New York sort of way. David began at the top of the column. The lead item was about some new nail-conditioning protein drops from Revlon that Ms. Martin had tried herself and found to be perfectly wonderful. "My only worry," she wrote, "is that these little drops are bringing out the tigress in me. I'm starting to leave these embarrassing scratch marks behind me everywhere I go." David somehow doubted that Ms. Martin led the wild and rampant love life at which she hinted. The next item was about a new low-protein diet that she had tried for a week; she said she had lost a pound and a half but she kept having obsessive daydreams about steak tartar. David smiled in spite of himself. He scanned down the column to the last item, the one right next to his and Francesca's picture.

That young, aggressive cosmetics company, Diagnostique, pulled out all the stops last month to launch their new hormone eye gel, Mona. Not only did they hire top Marquessa Agency model Francesca Levesque to play their Mona Girl (and Francesca needs more hormones like Manhattan needs more sushi bars), but they got themselves a genuine blue-eyed, Columbia-cum-Harvard medical doctor by the name of David Copeland to play their director of research. (Why do I keep thinking of that old commercial, "I'm not really a doctor, but I play one on TV"?) But whether he's for real or not, Dr. Copeland has come up with a real loser for Diagnostique. Mona made my eyelids feel like dumplings that had been left in the wonton soup too long. I give the gel a low 1 on Amy's Beauty Quotient. And by the way, Mrs. Copeland, wherever you are, is this really what you sent your little boy to medical school for?

What a bitch!

"Dr. Cope-o-lan, please!"

David jerked up his head. One of the phlebologists was leaning over him, a worried look on her oval face.

"Christ, what is it now?" David snapped.

"Your blood, Dr. Cope-o-lan," the woman said gently. "It does not flow good if you do like that."

David looked down at his hands: Both were clenched so tightly that the veins stood out on his wrists. Was it any wonder he'd become hypertensive before he was thirty-five?

"I'm sorry," he said.

"Nothing can be that bad, David," Ray said across from him. "Not in a magazine like that."

"You're right," David answered. "You're absolutely right, Ray."

He gestured with his head for the phlebologist to take the magazine from his lap. Then he closed his eyes again and tried to think tranquil thoughts. What the hell did he care what some wiseass beauty columnist thought of Mona Eye Gel, for Christ's sake? She was so obviously defensive, another member of that "target group" of single New York career women whose cleverness never quite disguised their unremitting bitterness. Of course, Mitch won't find any comfort in that. Ms. Martin's snide review certainly isn't going to boost sales. David shook his head. Forget it. Tonight was his one night off this week, no evening rounds, no Diagnostique, no Francesca. He would go straight to his apartment alone. Make a pitcher of vodka martinis, order in from Chicken Kitchen, have a quiet supper with his tropical fish. Maybe there would be some bucolic French film on Bravo to watch in bed. The solitary ecstasies.

"Dr. Cope-o-lan?"

Once again, David opened his eyes to see the young Filipino woman hovering in front of him. This time, she had a portable phone in her hand.

"For you, Doctor," she said, and she held the phone up to his ear.

"Dr. Copeland here."

"Yes, Doctor," the switchboard operator said. "I'll put your caller through."

"David?" It was Mitch Papechki. Christ, that hadn't taken long. When had Mitch gotten his copy of *Femina* magazine?

"What can I do for you, Mitch?"

"We've got a problem here, David. Things kind of came to a head this afternoon. You and I need to talk. Can you be here by seven?"

In spite of himself, David clenched his hands again. Mitch sounded like more than just a worried man. He sounded scared.

"I'll be there," David said. He looked down at his hands and saw the veins bulging at his wrists.

8

....

Standing in the middle of a room full of gorgeous women always made Amy's face ache. Probably because I smile too hard, she thought, surveying the glamorous guests at Tony Amato's gallery opening. Not that Amy wasn't feeling particularly attractive tonight. That afternoon André Sybert himself had given her a three-hour makeover in his downtown studio. The man's reputation was well deserved. For once, someone had let Amy's face speak for itself instead of trying to turn it into somebody else's.

"You have a fiercely intelligent face, Aimée," the Belgian makeup artist had told her as he combed out her hair. "A face full of wit, full of irony. It would be a crime to hide that face with cheap glamour girl tricks."

Sybert had proceeded to cut her dark brown hair close at the sides, leaving it full and fluffy on top, then shaped her eyebrows in playful arches, outlined her brown eyes in broad, Chaplinesque midnight mascara strokes, and covered her lips with a rose tint under a silvery gloss.

"You are sassy, so you should look sassy. It's as simple as that," Sybert had told her with a flourish of his hands as he turned up the mirror lights when he had finished.

Penny Twang, the new Guess Girl, brushed by Amy with a plastic goblet of champagne in her hand. There was a huge sepia-tinted Tony Amato photograph of Penny at the gallery entrance. In it, Penny was naked to the waist, her long torso arched, the nipples of her small firm breasts erect, her hands raised and spread wide at the sides of her head, the look of a startled doe on the teenager's jaw-achingly beautiful face. Amy decided she could do with a glass of champagne herself. She searched for the bar. More smiling to do. She knew most of the guests at this opening, certainly every model, model's agent, magazine editor, and glamour photographer present. There were other familiar faces too: Alice Farber, the gallery owner; Liv Titus, a popular model's lawyer; and Sylvia Kronberg, a research chemist whom the new management of La Douce Cosmetics had imported from Switzerland last fall to direct development of new products. Actually, Amy had never seen Kronberg in the flesh before, only her photograph in one of the trades, a photo that had hardly done justice to the thirtyish Swiss scientist. Kronberg was a tall regal-looking blonde in the Catherine Deneuve tradition, as beautiful as any high-priced model in the room. More so, actually. Kronberg possessed something in her face that most of the professional beauties were sorely lacking: intelligence. It was especially evident in her powerful green eyes. Kronberg returned Amy's smile and now walked toward her, her hand extended.

"I'm Sylvia Kronberg," she said with a slight accent as she took Amy's hand. "And you must be that makeover authority I've heard so much about."

"It's not much of a distinction, but it's mine," Amy said. Kronberg's hand was soft, her grasp firm.

"But you're really quite lovely," Kronberg said, openly studying Amy's face. There was something deliberate about her scrutiny—like a doctor's examination—that made Amy feel vaguely uncomfortable. "You do have the perfect face for it."

"So I've been told," Amy said. "Almost but not quite, right?"

Kronberg laughed quietly.

"Our entire industry is built on the notion of 'room for improvement.' For everyone, no matter how lovely." Kronberg looked intently into Amy's eyes. "But there's so much that passes for cosmetics that's no improvement at all, don't you think?

Quite the opposite, in fact. Paint overlays. Faces superimposed on faces that only call attention to what's missing from those faces in the first place. Eye shadows and blushes and lipsticks that have a life of their own, like Zulu war paint. Masks, really."

"I've always been of the opinion that whatever makes a woman feel beautiful is all right with me," Amy said coolly. Kronberg's line sounded suspiciously like the snobbery of a natural beauty, all the more condescending because she was in the cosmetics business herself.

"Is that truly what you believe?" Kronberg said, cocking her head to one side and revealing a brilliant amethyst pendular earring. "I rather thought you demanded quite a bit more than that from beauty products, judging by what I've read in 'Beauty Bytes.' I find your writing so refreshingly honest. And well researched. We don't have anything remotely like it in Europe, nor in other American magazines, as far as I can tell. They're all cover-to-cover puff and hyperbole. Not a critical word. It's virtually impossible to tell where the ad copy stops and the editorial copy begins."

Kronberg suddenly stopped talking, shook her elegant head, and smiled.

"Do excuse me. All I really intended to do was come over here and tell you in person how very much I admire your work, Ms. Martin," she said. "I hadn't intended to go on like that."

"Well, thank you," Amy replied, smiling graciously. She felt genuinely flattered. Of course, PR reps often chatted her up at functions like this in the naïve hope that they'd be rewarded with high marks for their clients' products in Amy's column. But Sylvia Kronberg was obviously too sophisticated to believe that could work for her—even if it was well known that the overextended La Douce organization was going to need all the help it could get once it finally came out with Kronberg's new cosmetics line. "Compliments are always welcome. I'm not universally loved in the industry, you know."

Kronberg laughed again.

"I can quite imagine," she said. "I don't suppose you endeared yourself to Dr. Copeland at Diagnostique with your latest column."

Amy felt her face prickle under André Sybert's rose-colored foundation.

"Your criticism was well founded, by the way," Kronberg went on, her green eyes sparkling. "We tested Copeland's gel in our lab—one is obliged to keep up with what the competition is doing—but this so-called elactase enzyme isn't anything of consequence. It's actually rather peripheral to the basic skin-altering hormones. No surprise, of course. And no surprise that it's failing. I'm afraid David Copeland isn't as grand a force in this business as some of us might have expected him to be."

Amy smiled. It sounded like Kronberg had a lot more on her mind that just putting down the competition's product.

"You know Dr. Copeland, then?" she asked.

"In passing," Kronberg replied. No smile back this time. She abruptly took Amy's hand and shook it again. "It's been a genuine pleasure. I do hope we can talk again sometime."

Kronberg stepped away and Amy found herself still smiling. There was always a perverse pleasure in hearing a great beauty get bitchy about a man; Amy took it as a sign that there was some justice left in the world. She again peered through the crowd searching for the bar. Where were the men tonight? As she'd left Sybert's studio this afternoon, she'd had a premonition that she'd meet somebody sexy and available at the gallery opening. Mary Goldfarb maintained that premonitions were only wish-fantasies that you willed to happen. But no fantasy was about to happen willfully or otherwise with only seven men in the room and probably not one of them single *and* straight. Four months had passed since she'd slept with anyone—"anyone" being Peter, of course. How long could this go on? A year? Two? The rest of her life?

Amy spotted the champagne bar under a pair of full-color Tony Amato portraits. One was a three-quarter face, high drama photo of Aida, the stunning Italian model who'd suddenly appeared on the scene with her picture on the cover of *Vogue.* The other was a dreamy profile of Kelly Keane. Jesus, maybe that was why Amy found this opening so depressing. Too many gorgeous ghosts on the walls. Kelly there, a long black-and-white nude of Monique Le Fevre in the middle of the far wall, and a rose-tinted photograph of Carmina del Ray in an Edwardian corset only a couple of pictures down from that one. All three of them gone from this world within the past half-year.

"Champagne, please." Amy nodded to the barman. He was tall

and blond and wore an expression that was obviously meant to convey that he was not really a bartender at all but was just filling in until his acting career began. A better actor would make a more convincing bartender, Amy thought.

"Amy, I almost didn't recognize you. You've been to André Sybert, am I right?"

Amy turned her head. Francesca Levesque was smiling down at her. The model wore a black Romeo Gigli suit with the jacket completely unbuttoned, revealing a swath of soft golden skin from her clavicle to her navel.

"Hello, Francesca. You're looking well ventilated tonight," Amy said. "Really, you look marvelous as always."

"You're kind." Francesca pursed her lips. "But not very."

Amy arched her freshly-shaped brows.

" 'Mona made my eyelids feel like dumplings.' " Francesca went on. "Honestly, Amy, I think it's your prose that's gone limp."

"It's not the prose, it's the product," Amy retorted.

"You really don't care who gets hurt as long as you get off a good gag, do you?"

"Come on, Francesca, I'm sure you'll survive," Amy said.

"Midge got me a good buy-out clause in case Mona doesn't make it, if that's what you mean," the model said ingenuously. "But I was thinking about David . . . Dr. Copeland. I haven't had the heart to show him your column, but I'm sure someone will and he won't take it well. He was already in a rage after your little remarks at his press conference."

"Oh, really? Is he dangerous?" Amy said caustically, but as she reached for her champagne glass, her hand was trembling so hard that she grasped the edge of the bar table instead. *In a rage?* Like that sickie who'd threatened her on the phone two nights ago? *Who the hell do you think you are, Amy Martin?* She'd had Pamela ask around about him the next day—his name was Anderson—and the word was he was a bit unhinged but probably harmless. In fact, someone had heard that he'd already been offered a new job, with a deodorant company in Toronto.

"David happens to be a dedicated physician who works very hard," Francesca said, tilting back her sculpted head. "Most of the time in a hospital with children, as a matter of fact."

"Francesca, I just test beauty products," Amy said, this time managing to pick up her glass, ready to move on. She'd already had one too many discussions about Dr. David Copeland tonight; she didn't even know the man. "It's a humble calling."

Amy was all set to make her escape when Tony Amato suddenly appeared and pointed his Hasselblad at the two women.

"Say *formaggio,*" Amato said, and he flashed a picture of Amy and Francesca standing next to one another with their champagne glasses held high.

"Francesca Levesque and friend"—Amy saw the caption in her mind, even as her smile froze for the camera.

"Congratulations, Tony," she said. "It's a marvelous show."

"Thank you for being here, darling."

Fine. Amy's presence had been duly noted, even recorded on film. Now she could get out of here. She made her way to the cloakroom and handed the attendant her coat check. She was putting on her coat when just ten feet away Peter Myers came sauntering through the gallery door. Jesus Christ, the erstwhile lover. He looked too damned jaunty for words.

"Hello, Peter," Amy said, managing to sound casual. "What a surprise."

Surprise, indeed. Peter had always detested Tony Amato, always maintained that the glamour photographer was the very antithesis of a genuine photo artist. Last year, Amy couldn't have dragged Peter to one of Amato's openings.

"Amy!" Peter strode up to her with an easy smile on his lean face. He kissed her cheeks one at a time European-style—also new to his repertoire. "I almost didn't recognize you. You've done something new to your face, haven't you?"

Amy felt her cheeks flush. Peter was still tossing out the same old *zets.* Some things didn't change.

"Oh, this?" she said lightly, touching her cheek. "It's for a story."

Christ! Was she actually still trying to explain her job to him? Still apologizing for wearing makeup, for God's sake?

"You look terrific," Peter said.

"It's supposed to make me look fiercely intelligent," Amy said with an ironic little laugh. "Full of wit and irony." '

Unbelievable what was coming out of her mouth. Mary Goldfarb was right about her: When she wasn't fighting men, she was putting herself down in front of them. "Different sides of the same coin" department. Lose, lose. What a damned shame it was. What a waste. Amy pulled the sash on her coat and took a step toward the door.

"Lovely to see you," Peter said. "Maybe we could have lunch sometime. I think it's time."

"Yes." Amy felt her pulse accelerate. Oh yes, indeed, premonitions were just wish-fantasies waiting to be willed. "Yes, it is time, isn't it?"

Suddenly a slender hand reached across Peter's shoulder from behind and touched his cheek. Peter made a half-turn.

"Peter, love. I almost gave up on you."

Holy God, it was Penny Twang! The teen model threw her long arms around Peter's neck and kissed him.

Peter started to make some absurd gesture of introduction but Amy was already out the door. Her heart was hammering and her eyes were burning. Unbelievable! Penny Twang? The goddamned Guess Girl? An eighteen-year-old model for the Prince of Substance? For the lover who'd broken off with Amy because he couldn't bear the fact that she worked for a glamour magazine? The fucker! Amy suddenly remembered seeing Peter talking with Penny at the video-awards dinner she had dragged him to kicking and screaming last spring. But just what the hell did Peter Myers talk about with Penny Twang? Euro-socialism? The plight of the sugar farmer?

A sharp gust of wind shot across Madison Avenue and stung Amy's eyes. Reflexively, she turned away and suddenly found herself peering back into the gallery window. Peter and Penny had disappeared into the crowd, thank God. Amy started to walk on but impulsively stopped again to gaze through the window. She was staring at Tony Amato's ethereal photograph of the late Kelly Keane.

That was what inspired it, she told everyone later. That mesmerizing image of Kelly Keane that seemed to glow through the gallery window like a specter. It flared in her mind's eye for the entire cab ride back to her West Side apartment, accompanied by flashes of Monique Le Fevre and Carmina del Ray, the two other beautiful ghosts on the gallery wall. By the time she had unlocked her apartment door, put on the kettle for tea, and sat down at the kitchen table with her lap-top computer, most of the article was already written in Amy's mind.

She called it "The Perils of Pulchritude."

And it began: "Why do the glorious young beauties keep dying? Is there something dangerous about having a gorgeous face?"

···

9

"Miss Cascades" Presumed Dead
In Airplane Accident

Spokane, May 11—Emily Pederson, nineteen, last year's "Miss Cascades," was reported missing and presumed dead in an airplane accident in the North Cascades today. Miss Pederson, daughter of Mr. and Mrs. Eric Pederson of 2123 Willow Drive, East Spokane, was a student at Spokane Community College, majoring in broadcasting.

The aircraft, a brown and tan single-engine Cessna tour plane, was last seen departing Bellingham County Airport at approximately 10 A.M. yesterday. Bellingham traffic manager, Ted Van Tine, said the plane, which had a New York State registration, was headed for Roosevelt Airport here. A radio response to a Missing Aircraft Bulletin issued at 6 P.M. reported seeing the plane over the North Cascades around noon. State Police report that efforts to locate the plane in the mountains were hampered by extreme fog. The plane was piloted by a woman carrying an international pilot's license; her name was not released pending notification of next of kin.

Miss Pederson had been the winner of many beauty and talent awards in the area in addition to the "Miss Cascades" title. Miss Pederson's mother said that after graduation, Emily had planned to pursue a career in television and modeling.

10

"Mona is dead, David. She has no legs. Never did. She didn't move from day one."

Mitch Papechki hadn't sat down since David arrived. He kept pacing back and forth behind the narrow worktable in the center of the tank, periodically stopping to pull a sales printout or marketing report from his open attaché case.

"We projected thirty to thirty-five thousand units retail for April. Look at this. Not even eight thousand. Less than twenty-five percent. First week in May? Under twenty percent. Last week? Nothing. Zilch. The chains dropped us before we got started. It's all over, my friend. We're pulling it. I'll make it official tomorrow. One page release . . . 'Diagnostique regrets. . . .' We'll drop ten points on the market by the end of the day."

"I don't get it, Mitch." David shook his head. "Two months and you're throwing in the towel?"

"It's called euthanasia, Doctor." Mitch flashed a grim smile. "A painless death so we can focus our resources on healthier prospects. We'll save half a million in advertising costs alone in the next three months."

"I can't believe that elactase isn't a viable product, not if you give it a chance," David said. "It tested beautifully."

"Tell me all about it," Mitch said, clapping his palm on the top of the table. Perspiration had darkened the neck and shoulders of his open oxford shirt. "We simply didn't step into the market the way we should have. I knew that in my gut that first day. It was a bad idea to pitch Mona at the hospital. A bad start. It came back and hit us smack in the face. You could tell the whole story from the way that Martin woman reacted."

"It sure as hell wasn't my idea," David retorted. He'd be damned if he was going to take any of the blame for that part of Mona's failure.

"Hey, I know that, David. My responsibility completely. I let publicity talk me into it." Mitch abruptly stopped pacing and looked down at David with his lucid, boyish eyes. "You've given us everything you had on this, David. I know that and I appreciate it. That's why it's so difficult for me to talk about how all of this is going to impact our relationship with St. Mary's."

"Somehow I knew this was coming," David said. He'd already started adjusting to the idea. He figured a cutback in this quarter's gift from Diagnostique would probably mean having to drop one bed on the ward immediately, maybe two, and probably going back to sharing Sister Berzins with children's pulmonary diseases.

"I haven't come up with any figures yet," Mitch went on, roving again. "And I'm sure any adjustments are only going to be temporary—you know, until we can get things back on track here. But I haven't said a word to Art Malley about any of this, so I'd appreciate it if you didn't talk about it with him for a couple of days."

"I've never had a problem not talking to Art Malley," David said. He found himself looking past Mitch to the blowup on the wall of the full-page ad introducing Mona Eye Gel that had appeared in all the major women's magazines two months ago. It showed the Mona Girl in a black crepe pants suit executing a *grande jette* over a Fifth Avenue puddle: Francesca's first and last leap for Mona Eye Gel. David wondered how she was going to take the news of Mona's demise. She probably already knew. David rubbed his hand across his forehead. All he wanted to do now was go home and crawl into bed. Commune with his tropical fish. Alone, he'd be able to remind himself again how little any of this mattered.

Mitch Papechki suddenly sat down.

"David," he said quietly. "It's funny, but there's part of me that sees all of this as a blessing in disguise. I mean, I always had a great deal of faith in Mona, but I never saw it as the kind of product we could build our identity on."

Mitch paused and leaned forward. Instinctively, David pulled back from him.

"Heat is that product, David," Mitch said, enunciating each word precisely. "I think we've both known that all along."

David gazed steadily back at Mitch, trying to ride past the sinking sensation he felt in his guts. The pheromone project remained stalled at the same point it had been six months ago and Mitch knew it. Was David supposed to offer his resignation? Is that what this was about? Abruptly, Mitch was on his feet again, smiling broadly.

"You know, I must have a screw loose or something," he said brightly, "but this is the kind of back-against-the-wall situation that brings out the best in me. It makes things simple: sink or swim. Gets my epinephrine flowing. An MBA's natural high, huh?"

Mitch laughed as he reached into his attaché case, withdrew a manila folder, and set it down on the table.

"By the way, have you had anything to eat?" he asked, striding to the corner of the room and hunkering down in front of a small refrigerator. "I've got some soya cheese in here. Couple of nonfat yogurts. Some ginseng cola."

"The cola sounds fine," David said.

Mitch set an open bottle of the ersatz cola on the table in front of David, then pushed the manila folder next to it.

"I was wondering what you make of this, David."

"What is it?"

"Just take a gander. Give me your impressions."

David took a long swallow of the cola and opened the folder. A stack of seven or eight poorly Xeroxed handwritten pages was inside. Laboratory notes. Just sketches, really. The kind David made himself late at night in the lab when his left brain was floating free. He recognized the scrawled protean guesswork that precedes the precision of experiment. David pulled his reading glasses from his breast pocket and began to read:

Corpus luteum > collapsed antrum of Graafian follicle. LH steroidogenesis?

61

Granulosa cell proliferation . . . Rate-limiting demolase >
AROMATASE PRODUCTION?
Possible androstenedione precursor of alpha copulin?

Alpha copulin? David took another long swallow of the health
cola before turning to the next page. The notes here were even
more difficult to make out. They seemed to have been scribbled
down faster, the letters and chemical symbols spiking above and
below the lines. There was no mention of alpha copulin on this
page, but the basic focus remained the same—speculations about
missing links in the endocrinology of female puberty. Incredible,
fascinating stuff.

A sudden sibilant wheeze behind him made David pull up his
head and twist around. Standing at the door with a bottle of nasal
spray in his hand was the acne-faced man David had seen loiter-
ing in Diagnostique's hallway several weeks ago.

"You really ought to kick that stuff, Armand," Mitch said, rising. "The more you use, the more you need, you know. David
Copeland, meet Armand Diltzer."

David neither stood nor offered his hand to the repellent-
looking, rheumy-eyed young man.

"Armand's going to lend us his expertise on the Heat project,"
Mitch went on as the young man walked past David to the other
side of the worktable. Mitch clapped him on the back and smiled.
"In fact, Armand is going to save our collective asses."

Mitch laughed, and reflexively David closed both hands into
tight fists.

"Are you an endocrinologist, Mr. Diltzer?" David asked, keeping his eyes on Mitch's face.

"Armand is a lab assistant," Mitch said flatly, his smile gone. He
turned to the young man. "Let's see what you've got."

"Now?" Diltzer asked nervously.

"Yes," Mitch said. "We're all going to be working together on
this from now on."

Diltzer reached inside his coat pocket and withdrew a clear
plastic food bag. He placed it on the table next to David's half-
empty cola bottle. The bag contained three stoppered vials of
what was clearly whole blood.

"Great," Mitch said. "I assume these are from the same test-
subject group she made such a row about?"

"From the same rack in the same cold room, that's all I can tell you," Armand Diltzer replied dully. He brushed the cuff of his coat under his nose.

"Very good. We'll be in touch, Armand." Diltzer scurried out the door and Mitch turned back to David. "Which blood lab do you think we should use for the RIA's, David? Obviously we'll want one from out of state."

David was already out of his chair and he was livid.

"What the fuck do you think you're pulling here, Mitch?" he cried. "You don't actually think you can sucker me into some industrial thievery scheme, do you?"

"I'm not trying to sucker you into anything, David," Mitch said evenly, not taking his eyes from David's. "I'm just trying to shake you loose. Open you up a little. Get you back on the creative track again."

"The fuck you are!" David snapped. "You're trying to turn me into a goddamned thief."

"Wait a second, will you, David? Just think a minute." Mitch gestured with his head in the direction of David's lab down the hallway. "Ideas have been a little scarce in there lately, we both know that. No blame. We all run hot and cold. It's just that we don't have the luxury of running cold right now, not at this point in the game."

"Listen, Mitch," David said, trying to hold down his voice. "I'm very sorry that Mona didn't work out. Very. But this doesn't work for me, get it? You'll have to get somebody else. There's no way I can stay here under these circumstances."

"David, please, we need you here," Mitch said, wagging his head. "I have complete faith in you. Your brain, your creativity. Your understanding of what we're trying to do here at Diagnostique. Come on, don't make this bigger than it is. We have an opportunity here to compare our work with what they're doing in another laboratory. That's it. These are far from unusual circumstances. Not in this business."

"Sorry, Mitch, I don't steal other people's work."

Mitch suddenly walked around the table until he was right next to David.

"I don't get it, Doctor. I don't understand what you think is at stake here? Who's going to publish first in the *Journal of Clinical Endocrinology?* Who's going to win the grant from NIH?" Mitch put his hand on David's shoulder. *"Perfume,* David. *Ladies' perfume.* That's all. Bubbles and bangles. The important stuff is what you do at St. Mary's. I've got no delusions about that, I don't see why you should. But we're on the edge here and we've only got one chance to keep this little start-up cosmetics company from being smothered by the painted ladies. And one chance to keep everybody who depends on Diagnostique from being smothered with it."

David pulled away from Mitch's grasp and strode out the door.

"You're the best in the business, David," Mitch called after him. "We'll talk. We'll talk later in the week."

11

∙∙∙

"Carmina was having boy troubles, that's all I know," Charlie Seppo said without looking at Amy. The photographer was adjusting lights around a silk backdrop in his SoHo studio. "Some Milanese greaseball who treated her like shit. I don't know what she was doing with him. Carmina had men falling all over her."

"That's probably why she picked him," Amy said. A psychiatrist she'd interviewed yesterday claimed that many gorgeous women grew sick of men always fawning over them and so they swung to the opposite extreme, falling for bullies and sadists— men who acted contemptuous of their beauty. "But is there any way this Italian could have followed her to Nairobi, Charlie?"

"I doubt it. I never saw him."

For the past week, Amy had been doing background interviews for her "Perils of Pulchritude" article. Just about every psychologist she'd talked to had a theory accounting for instability in gorgeous women, but Amy needed more details to make the theories stick—such as which theory explained why Carmina del Ray had suddenly decided to commit suicide.

"Did you detect any other signs of depression in Carmina?"

The photographer shrugged, shifted a light reflector a few inches. In the ten minutes Amy had been there, he hadn't offered much. Neither had Midge Krieger or any other of the models' agents she'd interviewed for the article. They were all too busy putting a pretty face on the beauty business to answer the questions Amy asked.

"Did she seem at all panicky about her looks? Afraid she had peaked, that she was about to start losing it any minute?" Another popular theory about high anxiety in models.

"I have no idea what was on her mind."

"Come on, Charlie," Amy said. "You were there the last night with her. You were one of the last people to see her alive. Tell me how she seemed, how she acted. What did she talk about? What was she worried about?"

Seppo turned and glared at Amy. He was a huge Viking-like man with a bushy brown beard and pale gray eyes.

"She talked about zebras," he said. "She said they looked 'unreal.' Listen, Amy, I'm telling you, I barely knew the girl. Now if you don't mind, I've got a shoot in here in about five minutes."

Amy didn't budge.

"Was she already stoned at dinner, Charlie?" she asked evenly, looking him straight in the eye.

"What are you talking about?"

"Look, everybody knows Carmina was a walking pharmacy, so tell me, was she stoned at dinner? Did she have anything to drink on top of it?"

Charlie Seppo suddenly leaned his large head in front of Amy.

"What are you going to do, rake this poor girl over the coals after she's been dead for a month? Don't you have anything more pressing to write about at *Femina?*"

Amy could feel his breath on her face. Instinctively, she pulled back, her pulse racing.

"As a matter of fact, I don't," she said, and stalked out of the studio.

12

Fairfield, Missouri. June 18, 5:45 A.M.

ALL UNITS: SALLY JEAN BAYLOR, EIGHTEEN, OF 14 PRINCE TER-
RACE IN FAIRFIELD WAS REPORTED MISSING BY HER GRAND-
MOTHER, EMMA T. BAYLOR, SAME ADDRESS, AT 5:35 THIS A.M. MISS
BAYLOR IS 5'10", 124 LBS., SHORT BLONDE HAIR, BLUE EYES. LAST
SEEN WEARING JEANS, RED "LUCKY BILL" T-SHIRT, AND BROWN
SANDALS. ⅛" MOLE JUST BELOW LEFT EAR. THE MISSING WOMAN
IS DESCRIBED AS UNUSUALLY ATTRACTIVE.

13

....

"They're such awful hypocrites," Amy steamed, shaking her head. "And so goddamned smug on top of it. Honest to God, I don't know how I've stood working with them all these years."

For the past fifteen minutes, Amy had been recounting the "Perils of Pulchritude" affair at *Femina* for her therapy group. The episode had raged through two consecutive editorial meetings with absolutely nobody—not even Pamela—siding with Amy. Every editor in the house thought that her article was in "questionable taste," especially the fact that she had exploited the untimely deaths of three international beauties to advance her theory that having a gorgeous face was risky.

"It's no accident that most of the top agencies in town are offering their models special seminars in self-defense and personal safety," Amy had written. "These aren't courses which your basic lady in the deli checkout line feels a desperate need to sign up for."

Amy had made an effort to keep her tone moderately light, but she managed to include every well-known horror story from the past ten years about great beauties who had been assaulted or who had died, who had become dissipated, suicidal, or had simply disappeared: that delicate young model with the flawless skin who'd been slashed from ear to ear by a rejected suitor; that lovely American beauty from South Carolina who fell under the spell of an Italian playboy-coke dealer and was now serving seven years for his murder in a Milanese jail; the French Elite model who had gone away to a weekend party in Surrey, never to be seen again. And then Amy had come back to Kelly Keane, Carmina del Ray, and Monique Le Fevre, the three magnificent ghosts on the walls of Tony Amato's photography exhibition: Kelly, burned out and careless, drowned off the Dover Cliffs; Carmina, high on drugs and low on self-esteem, taking her own life in Africa; Monique, naïve and narcissistic, abducted and apparently murdered right here in New York. One way or another, Amy wrote, every one of these women was a victim of her own beauty. That beauty stirred obsessive, venomous emotions in the men around them. Worse, that beauty made some of these women reckless, deluded them into believing they were invulnerable. And most dangerous of all, that beauty made many of these women feel unworthy of their gift, made them self-destructive.

"The article is simply not in the spirit of *Femina,* and I think you know that, Amy," Harriet Schwartz, the editor in chief, had argued in her patient, more-self-aware-than-thou voice. "People can read the *Atlantic* for dark, brooding thoughts, but that's not what we're all about here."

"My article's not brooding, it's informative," Amy had retorted. "It's a bloody public service. I don't get it. Are you actually afraid to let our readers know that life is sometimes far from perfect even if you have a perfect face?"

"That's hardly the point," Harriet had said. "I just don't see that particular kind of information as *Femina*'s mission."

"Our mission?" Amy had said. "What are we now, *The Watchtower?* What ever happened to our commitment to telling our readers the truth?"

"The truth, Amy, is that your article has a distinctly obsessive quality to it."

An awkward silence had followed and then Pamela had suggested that Amy put the article away for a month and see how she felt about it then. Pam's little speech had sounded remarkably pre-scripted.

"Sorry," Amy had replied coolly, "but I happen to think it's an important piece of journalism and if you don't run it here, I'll place it somewhere else."

It was her trump card. Her contract stipulated that if *Femina* refused anything she wrote, she could sell it to another magazine. Amy was confident that Harriet would be unhappy with the idea of seeing her by-line in *Glamour* or *Vogue* under any article, no matter how questionable its taste.

"Look, it's basically the tone of the piece that disturbs me," Harriet had said at last.

And so they had compromised on an edited version of "Perils of Pulchritude," which was a little more than half its original length and nowhere near as powerful. Monday, it had gone to the printers for July's issue.

"Christ, maybe Peter was right," Amy said to her therapy group. "He always said that there wasn't any room for any real probing truth at a glamour magazine."

Amy's group shook their heads supportively. The ten of them in the circle—all single, professional women between the ages of twenty-five and fifty—had remained silent during Amy's tirade. Tara, the woman sitting on Amy's right, now reached out and gave Amy's shoulder a sympathetic squeeze. Wendy, on her left, appeared about to do the same when Mary Goldfarb spoke.

"That's the first time I've heard you mention Peter in a long while, Amy. Have you spoken with him lately?"

Christ, hadn't Mary been listening to anything? Or was she on automatic-therapist, just tuning in to the last words spoken and turning them into a question?

"Yes, I've spoken to him," Amy said. "But I've been trying to talk about something other than men tonight, if that's all right. About my work . . . my career."

"We can get back to that in moment," Mary said. "But right now I seem to have missed something. When exactly did you see Peter?"

"Is it really necessary to go into this now?"

"I don't think it can hurt."

Amy took a deep breath.

"I ran into him at a gallery opening and it was a total disaster, okay?"

"What kind of a disaster?"

Amy hesitated a couple seconds, then told the whole story as quickly as possible, sketching her conversation with Peter, then describing the sudden appearance of Penny Twang's long arms reaching up around his neck.

"How absolutely infuriating and hurtful," Mary said. "I'm very sorry that had to happen, Amy."

"It's all right. I've gotten over it."

"I'm glad to hear that," Mary said. "Now let's get back to that article you were talking about. Tell me . . . how soon after your encounter with Peter and that model did you begin writing this 'Perils of Pulchritude' piece?"

Amy felt her face grow instantly warm.

"Come on, Mary, you know life's not as simple as that," Amy said.

"Before? After? A couple of days later?"

"All right, so I wrote a draft of the article that same night," Amy said, raising her voice. "But, honest to God, Peter had nothing to do with it. It was those pictures on the gallery wall . . . those poor dead girls."

"Is that the feeling you carried home with you that night . . . compassion? No pain? No anger?"

"Maybe a little of each," Amy said, her voice still loud. "But, listen, I hope you don't think that proves that this whole thing was just some exercise in displaced anger. That's what you want me to say, isn't it? That the article was really just my way of getting back at Penny Twang? Amy's revenge, the death of the pretties? Honestly, Mary, you can't explain away a good article that simply."

"Perhaps it doesn't explain it away, but it does put some perspective on your passionate involvement with the article, doesn't it?"

"Look, I'm a writer, damn it!" Amy burst out, her face flushing. "I write about what I see going on in the world. The world out there, not me in here. And three of the most beautiful women in the world have died in the last year. So I wrote an article about it. Is that so difficult to accept?"

For a long moment, nobody spoke. Beads of perspiration had sprouted on Amy's forehead.

"Well, I'm not a writer," Wendy began quietly beside her. "But I am a lawyer and I happen to know of four lawyers my age who've died in the past year and a half. I could name them for you. In fact, one of them was in my law-school class—he died in a car accident just two months ago. But the point is, I don't honestly think that four dead lawyers means that lawyers are at some special risk. I mean, everybody who meets an untimely

71

death is something—a lawyer, a Democrat, a redhead, a pretty model. So that doesn't really prove anything, does it?"

Tears abruptly appeared in the corners of Amy's eyes. Of course, Wendy was right. And Mary, too. Oh God, she was suddenly so tired of battling everybody. Tired of taking all her frustration out on Harriet and Pamela and all her sisters here. And, yes, by God, she was tired of taking it out on Penny Twang and all the other great beauties in the world. Amy's silent tears dripped onto her cheeks.

"Wouldn't it be wise to withdraw that article right now?" Mary Goldfarb asked at last. "So it doesn't end up an embarrassment to you?"

"It's too late," Amy answered quietly.

"There must be some way to stop it," Mary said.

"Afraid not," Amy said. "It goes on the stands tomorrow."

14

Sunday, out in Queens for his obligatory monthly visit with his parents, David remembered to ask for Mr. Wigglesworth just as he was about to leave. Amazingly, his mother knew exactly where to put her hands on the thirty-year-old stuffed brown bunny. In fact, Sophie Copeland seemed delighted that David wanted to take Mr. Wigglesworth back to Manhattan with him. She obviously took it as a sign that her thirty-six-year-old son was finally thinking seriously about marriage and children.

Nothing could have been further from the truth. Last night, David had fled Francesca's apartment, determined to put an end to that relationship.

During supper together at Cancun's, Francesca had talked at length about how losing the Mona Girl account was going to affect her career—entirely for the better, it seemed. Not only was Diagnostique paying her a considerable "kill fee," but her agent, Midge, already had another exclusive product representation lined up: Francesca would soon be the Intrepid Jeans Girl, at approximately twice what she'd been paid to be the Mona Girl.

"Sometimes these catastrophes turn out to be blessings in disguise," Francesca had said encouragingly. Familiar phrase, that. Mitch Papechki had used it just the other night to introduce his new approach to the Heat project.

"You're not making this easy for me, you know," Francesca had gone on, reaching her hand across the restaurant table and covering David's. "You seem so down, darling, as if what happened to Mona is all your fault. But you know that isn't so. This business is all fluke and caprice. Nobody understands that better than a model, believe me. I've seen careers crash on a badly timed pimple."

"That's comforting," David said, withdrawing his hand.

"I can't help you if you don't open up with me."

"Then don't try to help me."

David had barely uttered a word for the rest of the meal, then silently he had driven her back to her apartment. The moment they were inside her door, he put his hands on her waist.

"Let's go to bed," he whispered.

"Not now, David," she replied, gently pulling away. "Let's talk."

"Please, Francesca, I need solace tonight, not therapy."

Again he put his hands on her waist and again she stepped back from him.

"I'm sorry, but this doesn't feel right to me," Francesca said. "It makes me feel like I'm just some stress-release exercise for you."

"And this makes me feel like last month's account," David replied, turning away from her. "I think I want to go home now."

He strode to the apartment door and started to open it when Francesca's arms closed around his chest from behind.

"I just want you to share more of yourself with me, darling," she whispered, her mouth warm against his ear.

David shut his eyes. What a comfort it would be if he could talk with Francesca about what was really eating away at him: not Mona, but Mitch's scheme for coming up with Mona's successor. But at that moment at Francesca's door, he had finally realized why he'd been pulling away from her all night: He'd understood that he would never feel close enough to Francesca to share his most painful secrets with her. That simply wasn't the kind of intimacy he could ever have with her.

"Everybody's entitled to fail once in a while, you know," Francesca said, pressing her body firmly against David's back.

And that is when David had fled to the elevator.

"Christ, maybe it is all about failure," David said out loud in his MG, driving back to Manhattan from his parents' house. The worn velvet rabbit sat next to him under the safety belt of the passenger's seat. "First it was pure research and now I've failed in commercial research. I'm just spreading failure everywhere I go."

Mr. Wigglesworth stared at David with a benign smile on his pointed face. David smiled back at the stuffed animal. It was the first light moment he'd experienced in days.

David had not spoken a word to Mitch since Thursday. Friday, he had called his lab and talked briefly with Avi, his research assistant. All David had said was that he wouldn't be in for a few days. He didn't mention to Avi that Mitch's solution to the alpha-copulin problem was pilfering lab notes and test-subject blood samples from a competing laboratory. Industrial espionage.

Was that too grave a term for it? Was he being "precious" again? David knew firsthand that theft and fraud were rife in the world of pure research. He knew doctors at Mt. Sinai who had plundered data to be the first to publish, to clamber over colleagues' backs up the academic ladder. Compared to their vanity, making money seemed a far purer motive for research theft. And David certainly knew that espionage existed in the cosmetics industry; he'd frequently heard colleagues joke about "microfilm research." And once, half a year before Mitch had made his proposal, someone else had asked David to cross that line. On that occasion, the person making the request had been from a rival cosmetics company even smaller than Diagnostique. She was their director of research and her name was Sylvia Kronberg.

That had been in January, just months before Mona Eye Gel was launched. David had been seated across from Kronberg at the opening-night dinner of the Society of Cosmetic Chemists convention at the Ponchetrain Hotel in New Orleans. From the moment he met her, David had been powerfully attracted to Sylvia Kronberg. Not only was she extraordinarily lovely to look at—even at a convention devoted to beauty and its vicissitudes, men gaped at her like dumbstruck schoolboys—but she exuded a sensuality that pulled at all of David's senses. She reminded him of the Catherine Deneuve character in his favorite Buñuel film, *Belle de Jour*—cool and aristocratic on the surface but something animal throwing off heat from just beneath that surface.

"Dinner with the chemists," Kronberg said by way of greeting, smiling across the dinner table at David. "Sounds terribly dangerous, doesn't it? From the *chambre ardente*. Perhaps I should have brought my taster with me."

"Allow me," David replied, impulsively reaching out his knife, slicing off the corner of the butter patty on Kronberg's roll plate and then licking it off his knife. "But I should warn you, I have a high tolerance for toxins. To be absolutely safe, you should monitor my responses for a few hours."

Kronberg laughed.

"I'm much too hungry to wait for your responses, Doctor. I guess I'll just have to take my chances." Her green eyes glinted as she spread some butter on her roll. "My name is Sylvia Kronberg, incidentally. I refused to pin on that little name badge they gave me at the door: Somehow, wearing my name on a label makes me feel anonymous."

"I'm David Copeland," David replied, raising his wine glass to her. "And I can't believe you've ever felt an anonymous moment in your life, Sylvia."

They clinked glasses and drank, both of them ignoring the colleagues seated on either side of them. They continued to talk exclusively to each other throughout the rest of the meal. While the others talked about their problems with the recent FDA rulings, David and Sylvia talked about Europe's new fascination with basketball, the effect of socialized medicine on elective surgery, Altman's films, tropical fish—virtually everything but the cosmetics business. Halfway through the meal, Kronberg looked at David and said, "To think I almost decided not to come to New Orleans."

When the liqueurs were being served and the society's officers at the head table began to remove their speech notes from their coat pockets, David abruptly pulled his napkin from his lap and dropped it on the table in front of him. He looked into Sylvia Kronberg's eyes. She smiled and laid her napkin on the table, too. They rose in unison. Sylvia put her hand on David's arm as they made their way out of the dining room and directly to the elevator.

"I'm on the sixteenth floor," Sylvia said, and David pressed the button.

When they exited the elevator into the empty hallway, David turned and put his hands on Sylvia's waist. He kissed her quickly and softly on the mouth. Her lips were warm, moist. She put her hands on the back of his neck and pulled him to her again. They kissed a second time, longer this time, deeper. Neither of them closed their eyes. After the kiss, Sylvia sighed and said in an almost girlish voice, "Delicious," then, "It's been such a long time for me."

The moment they were inside her room, they kissed again. Sylvia took one of his hands and pressed it against her breast. David could feel her nipple hardening through the silk of her blouse. She unbuttoned the top of the blouse and David slipped his hand inside, under the top of her slip. She was not wearing a bra. Her breasts were firm and heavy and full.

Sylvia abruptly stepped back from him, her face flushed, her chest heaving. Her lips were parted and her light sensual eyes were fastened to his as she slowly released the second and then the third button on her blouse. She arched her back and let it slide from her shapely arms to the floor. David's heart was hammering. He made a slight movement toward her, but she raised her hand.

"Please wait," she whispered.

David remembered literally feeling his mouth salivate as Sylvia unzippered her linen skirt and let it drop to her ankles. She rolled down her panty hose and stepped out of them, then pulled her slip over her head and dropped it onto the floor. She stood naked and still in front of him.

"My God, you are the most glorious-looking woman I have ever seen in my life," David said, stepping toward her.

"Thank you, Doctor," Sylvia Kronberg said with a sultry smirk.

She walked to the bed, pulled off the blanket, and lay down under the top sheet. The mounds of her breasts and the slope of hips were outlined beneath it. David quickly undressed and slipped under the sheet beside her. He was already fully erect but he strained against his powerful impulse to immediately press himself hard against her; he wanted to savor her body, every inch of it. He put his lips to her neck, felt her fingers comb through his hair, tugging him gently against her as he licked his way down through the cup of her clavicle to between her breasts. Her skin was salty, her odor sweet, biting.

"My taster," she whispered.

David cupped his hand around her left breast. He closed his lips over the nipple, swirled his tongue around it, then sucked it hard and heard Sylvia cry out, "Yes. Oh, yes!"

Her hands were on his back, her nails sharp against his spine.

77

David slid down to her belly, the skin downy there, whiter, even softer. He darted his tongue into her navel, then slowly down the silky line of golden hairs that led to her thick reddish bush. Her odor was overwhelming there, like fumes from a tropical plant. His eyes smarted from it. He felt drugged by it.

His tongue slipped between her wet swollen labia. He pushed his tongue deeper into her, then out again and up along her slit to her clitoris. His tongue slowly circled around the base, then slipped up to the tip, flicked back and forth across it.

Suddenly, she grabbed the back of David's head and ground her pelvis against his face. Seconds later, she arched her back, her buttocks lifting off the mattress, and she cried out David's name, her voice now deep, guttural, a growl.

"David! Come inside me! Please, David!"

David slid back up the bed and Sylvia pushed him onto his back. She straddled him, holding herself on her haunches just above him, her hands on either side of his penis, cupping it like a sheath as she slowly lowered herself onto it. She clamped herself around it like a hot mouth.

David looked up at her. She looked even more beautiful than before, an elegant equestrian riding him. Her large breasts undulated softly as she rotated over him. He reached up to touch them, but Sylvia leaned back away from him.

"No. Just watch me, David. Just feel me," she whispered.

And so David dropped his arms back onto the mattress and gave himself over to just gazing at this vision of beauty that hovered over him and just feeling the currents of pleasure that flowed out from his groin along sensual meridians to his toes, to his fingertips, to the insides of his ears, to the tip of his tongue, to his own tingling nipples. When he finally came, it felt as if everything fluid inside him was flowing back along these same meridians into her.

Afterward, they lay together under the top sheet for several minutes, both of them staring at the ceiling, neither of them speaking. Then David heard Sylvia laughing softly.

"What?" David smiled.

"I am thinking of them downstairs," Sylvia said. She laughed again, a little more loudly. "They must be up to their third speech by now. Do you suppose we're missing anything important?"

David grinned.

"I don't think we've missed one thing this evening, Sylvia," he said.

She kissed his shoulder, then propped herself up on her elbow and looked down at him, her left breast brushing against the side of his chest.

"Wouldn't it be lovely if we didn't have to leave this bed for the entire convention?" she asked.

"We don't," David answered. "For the next three days, we'll have all our Cajun shrimp and biscuits delivered by room service."

Sylvia put her palm down on David's chest, spread out her fingers, then closed them, catching his chest hairs between them.

"I'm supposed to be busily finding out what's new in the world of cosmetics," she said.

"Cosmetics?" David repeated, deadpan. "I must be in the wrong hotel. I thought this was the pipe fitter's convention."

"No, truly," Sylvia went on, tugging again on his chest hairs. "The only reason I came down to New Orleans—the original reason, that is—is to find out what my colleagues are up to. That's what conventions are for, you know."

David turned his face toward her.

"I'm a colleague," he said, smiling.

"Isn't that lucky?" Sylvia laughed and kissed his shoulder again. "Then maybe you can tell me what's new in the world of suspensory mediums . . . the kind that are able to stabilize active enzymes. That's what I really need to know about."

David's pulse quickened. He turned his eyes away from hers.

"It seems everybody has a problem finding a medium that can hold together a whole spectrum of enzymes long enough for them to be absorbed by the skin," Sylvia went on, her fingers lightly tracing a circle around David's right nipple. "You know, finding the equivalent of calf fetal serum in something that behaves like a cold cream."

David took a long breath. Yes, he was certainly familiar with that particular technical problem. His solution to it for elactase is what had finally made it possible for Diagnostique to produce Mona Eye Gel.

"I'm afraid I can't help you, Sylvia," he said.

Sylvia laughed softly.

"Of course you can, David," she said.

79

David felt his chest and abdomen muscles tighten, his face suddenly grow hot. He looked at Sylvia. A long strand of gold hair hung over her right shoulder, half-covering her right breast. His whole body yearned to make love to her again. Right now.

"Please, Sylvia," he whispered. "Let's not spoil this."

"But we don't have to spoil anything," Sylvia said matter-of-factly, sitting up in the bed. "We're not competing with each other, David. I can guarantee you that the project I'm working on isn't even remotely similar to yours. But I do know that you've done some work on suspensory mediums, just as I have, and I don't see a reason in the world why we shouldn't be able to discuss our work with each other. I haven't overestimated you, have I? I mean, you certainly don't believe that what's happened in this bed should prevent us from treating each other as equals professionally, do you?"

"How do you know that I've done work on suspensory mediums?" David asked, his heart pounding.

"Don't be silly, David. It's a small industry. Everybody knows what everybody else is working on more or less. Certainly you know that."

"No, I don't know that," David said sharply. His temples throbbed.

Sylvia laughed.

"Preciousness doesn't become you, David."

"It's not preciousness, Sylvia," David said evenly. "It's disappointment. Deep disappointment."

He swung his legs over the side of the bed and sat there with his back to her, hoping in spite of himself that she would say something that could erase the last few minutes—that could bring him back into the bed next to her.

"So earnest," Sylvia said behind him. "You Americans are all so earnest in the end. What a shame. You showed promise of more than that, David."

David had put on his clothes as quickly as he had taken them off and let himself out of her hotel room. He hadn't spoken to her for the remainder of the convention, nor had he seen her afterward. In the six months since that evening in New Orleans, David had refused to even allow himself to imagine how his life would have changed if he had remained in Sylvia Kronberg's bed.

* * *

"Introducing Mr. Wigglesworth," David announced as he stepped into Examination Room A. It was Thursday again, afternoon clinic in child and adolescent endocrinology, an entire week gone by since David had spoken to Mitch Papechki. Last night, for the sixth night in a row, David had poured a beer glass of Absolut vodka down his throat as he stared at the tropical fish tank that glowed in the corner of his apartment bedroom. "Mr. Wigglesworth, meet Lisa and her friend Bobo."

"I told you he'd remember," Lisa Carlosso cried, grinning up at her mother. The five-year-old took Mr. Wigglesworth and hugged him against her large breasts.

David set Lisa's file down on the examination table. Clipped to the cover were the computer-generated results of RIA's of circulating thyroxine, gonadotrophin, and estradiol concentrations in the child's blood. Lisa's TH was normal for her age, as was her Gn, ruling out idiopathic or intracranial abnormalities. Similarly, her oestradiol and gonadal steroid numbers were within range, so there was virtually no chance of an ovarian tumor as the cause of her disorder. The radiologist's report confirmed this; the sonogram of Lisa's pelvic anatomy showed healthy ovaries, fallopian tubes, and uterus—healthy, that is, for the average young woman of fourteen or fifteen. In all, however, it was encouraging news; it meant Lisa's condition was reversible with monitored doses of gonadotrophin-releasing hormone.

"I'm going to give you some medicine to give Lisa every morning," David said to Mrs. Carlosso. "You can't miss a day if this is going to work properly. It's a hormone that stabilizes the other female hormones in her system. Brings them under control. Lisa is very quickly going to get a little girl's body back again. In just a few weeks, you'll see the hairs under her arms and in her pubic area start to drop out. And you'll see her breast tissue regressing and her nipples and areola diminishing in size. In five months, she'll look like any other five-year-old girl."

He smiled at Lisa as the youngster manipulated the two little bunnies like puppets. For David, the reversal of precocious puberty was always a wonder to behold. There were so many tiny incremental changes to track, not just pubic hair and breast changes but skin changes, scalp, hair, the shape of the brow, the expression in the eyes, the pucker of the lips, the tilt of the head. Like puberty itself, its reversal was a million little metamorphoses.

On the other side of the table, Mrs. Carlosso's small face was puckered. She looked worried.

"Lisa's going to be just fine," David assured her.

"If you say so," the woman answered anxiously, not looking at him.

"What are you worried about, Mrs. Carlosso?"

The woman shrugged, then bit down on her lip before speaking.

"Are they . . . ? You know, is she . . . going to look this . . . good . . . when she becomes a woman all over again next time?" Mrs. Carlosso stammered.

It took David a moment to realize that Mrs. Carlosso was talking about her five-year-old's perfectly-shaped breasts. David nodded his head slowly.

"Lisa is a naturally pretty girl," he said softly, smiling at Lisa.

Lisa smiled back and handed Mr. Wigglesworth to David.

"I'm going to keep this little bunny right here for when you and Bobo come back next month," David said. He pulled a pen from his jacket pocket and had started writing a prescription for a month's supply of GnRH when there was a sharp rap at the examination room door. "Who's there?"

"Ray."

"Be right with you."

David handed the prescription to Mrs. Carlosso, tweaked Bobo on the nose, and opened the door.

"Have you checked your box this afternoon?" Ray asked the moment David stepped into the hallway. Drops of sweat glistened on the black man's forehead. He was obviously trying to control his voice.

"What's the problem, Ray?"

"Memo from Art Malley. No, not a memo . . . a directive!" Kenworthy spat the word out. He held up a sheet of paper. "No more kids clinic. Two more weeks and that's it. Done with. The doors close. Part of St. Mary's saintly new austerity program. Children are expendable."

David grabbed the memo from Ray's hand.

"Read it and weep, boy," Ray said. "We're just the hired help here, not budget consultants."

David's jaw tightened as he scanned Art Malley's memo. It stated that the hospital's finance committee had unilaterally decided to close down the weekly public clinic in child and adolescent endocrinology as of the end of the month. It "saddened" them to come to this decision, but a "revised financial forecast" made it necessary.

"Bastards!" David's voice reverberated on the hallway tiles. Several feet away, a group of black adolescent boys and their mothers fell quiet and stared at David. "I'm not playing their fucking game."

"What game is that, David?" Ray asked, his voice pitched low as he placed his hand firmly on David's shoulder.

David pulled back uneasily from his friend's grasp. Ray didn't need to know about this.

"I'll take care of it," David said evenly and he strode off to the elevator. He'd let this whole goddamned thing go too long and now was the time to put an end to it. He got out at the third floor and headed straight for Art Malley's office. He pushed through the finance director's door before his secretary could stop him. Malley was hanging up his phone as David went in.

"Something I can do for you, Doctor?" Malley asked, his round face reddening.

"You're fucking right there is!" David threw the crumpled memo on Malley's desk. "Don't try this crap on me, Art."

Malley stood, walked to the door, and closed it before sitting down again. He straightened out the piece of paper and ran his eyes across it slowly, as if reading it for the first time.

"I'm awfully sorry about this, David," he said, not looking up. "But we suddenly find ourselves in one hell of a financial situation here. Cuts had to be made."

"Not this cut, Art! That clinic is the guts of my department and you know it."

"That may be so, Doctor, but that clinic of yours has become excessively expensive for us lately," Malley replied, as he pulled a manila envelope from the corner of his desk. "I was going to show this to you later, David. It seems your friend Ray Kenworthy has run up three hundred grand's worth of med orders that Medicaid is disputing. That would be one hell of a bill for us to be left holding."

"What do you mean? If Ray billed for it, we're covered, and that's it," David snapped. "He's the most meticulous physician you've got in this hospital, so don't try to sandbag me with that bullshit."

"I'm not trying to sandbag anyone," Malley said quietly. "I'm just trying to fight the good fight for St. Mary's. Trying to do my part to keep us afloat. I was under the impression that was what we were all trying to do here."

David couldn't hold himself back any longer. He leaned across Malley's desk and stabbed a forefinger against his chest.

"This is a goddamned squeeze, isn't it, Art?" he roared. "You worked it all out with Mitch, didn't you? You think all you have to do is threaten to close my clinic and I'll happily join his little extracurricular research party."

Malley pushed David's hand away and stood.

"I have no idea what you're talking about, David," he said.

"The hell you don't!" David roared. "You don't give a shit how Diagnostique makes money as long as its tax-free gifts keep pouring in. Well, it takes more than that to turn me into a sneak thief."

He turned and strode out of the office. He took the stairs down to the first floor. At the front reception desk, he had Ray Kenworthy paged.

"Ray? I'm going to be tied up for the rest of the day," he said into the phone. "Cover the Jonas boy and Zeda Stommer for me, will you? Their charts are on my desk."

"Of course," Ray said.

"And, Ray? Art Malley has a problem with some of your Medicaid med billings. You know what that's all about?"

"Oh, Christ, yes," Ray answered. "They're pestering me for some referral diagnosis dupes. Those people won't be happy until they've turned us all into bureaucrats."

"Just straighten it out, will you, Ray? I don't want Malley holding anything over us."

"No problem," Ray answered. "You can forget about it."

David's laboratory was dark save for a circle of light projected by the high-intensity lamp hanging low over his bench. Nobody home. Avi had probably closed up just minutes ago. In spite of himself, David felt the sweet calm of the laboratory descend on him. More than anything, he was going to miss the serene solitude of this place at night. The rage he'd felt in Malley's office was already subsiding. His decision was really quite simple in the end. He walked to the window and looked out at the Brooklyn Bridge—the pandemonium of the evening traffic looked benign from here. Scale. It was all a question of scale.

David turned and strolled to his bench. There actually wasn't that much to take home with him: his cardigan wool vest, his Rolodex, his copy of William's *Textbook of Endocrinology*. His lab notebooks would stay, of course. Diagnostique was entitled to keep those. David would tell Mitch exactly where he could find them. He'd make his exit like a gentleman.

David was fitting the textbook into his attaché case when he first saw the RIA printout on the bench directly under the spot of bright light. Blood hormone assays. Familiar stuff. Thyroxine concentrations—TH3's and 4's, Progesterone, Oestradiol, Luteinizing Hormone, Dehydroepiandrosterone. The usual endocrinological bloodwork of a female. But near the bottom of the page, an orange streak highlighted the words *Extrapituitary adrenal-androgen-stimulating hormone*. That was one of the newly isolated adrenal steroids recently written up in the *Journal of Reproductive Endocrinology*. One of the so-called missing links in the chemistry of the onset of puberty. Brand-new stuff. David pulled his reading glasses from his breast pocket and put them on.

"La Jolla Hemolabs, La Jolla, California" was printed in the top left-hand corner of the sheet and in the top right-hand corner was an HLA-typing code, the blood's genetic fingerprint. David picked up the sheet. There were eight more pages stapled to it and two more stapled stacks of RIA printouts on the bench beneath it. David ran his hand across his jaw. Of course, these were the assays of the three blood samples that Mitch's man Armand had delivered last week. Blood samples from three test subjects of another laboratory's experiment.

David turned to the second page. Christ, Mitch certainly hadn't spared any expense. This was the most comprehensive RIA David had seen since medical school, every hormone, steroid, enzyme, and enzyme precursor accounted for. Each complete RIA must have cost thousands of dollars. David flipped through to the last page. Near the bottom, there were six lines highlighted in orange: methylpropanoic acid, butanoic acid, methylbutanoic acid, methylpentanoic acid, propanic acid, acetic acid. All short-chain aliphatic acids. The six constituents of natural alpha copulin.

He sat down as he read the concentrations. These numbers were high, incredibly high. Top of the graph. Whoever's blood this was was generating the seductive pheromone at twice the average rate. Whoever's blood this was was literally oozing with the internal chemistry of sex appeal.

David turned back to the top sheet. There was no name or patient code number identifying the test subject, just the HLA code in the upper right-hand corner. He picked up the second RIA printout and flipped to the last page. Again, highlighted in orange were all the short-chain aliphatic acids. Again, the concentrations were phenomenally high. Only one in ten thousand women would have numbers that high in a natural state. David picked up the third printout. The same. Oozing with the precursors of alpha copulin. Oozing with sex attractants.

David abruptly returned all three printouts to the benchtop. He carefully straightened the little pile so that it was directly under the circular spot of light as he had found it. Time to get out of here. Time to go tell Mitch Papechki that he didn't work here anymore. David started to rise, then stopped and slowly sat back down again.

By God, somebody in some other laboratory somewhere had actually figured out how to stimulate superproduction of alpha copulin in corpus. Incredible! All these months, David had been diligently trying to synthesize the sex-attractant in vitro and here some genius had figured out how to stimulate a female hormone system to superproduce the natural perfume on its own. This scientist had worked backward inside the female endocrine system and found the hormone that stimulated the body's own production of the pheromone. Bloody brilliant, that's what he was. Who was he and how the hell did he do that?

David stood. He picked up his attaché case and sweater and strode directly out the laboratory door, then marched to the end of the hallway and rapped on the tank door.

"Come."

David pushed open the door and stepped in. Mitch was standing behind his worktable.

"David! How very good to see you," Mitch said, smiling warmly as he held out his hand.

David remained by the door. "Whose lab was that blood stolen from?"

Mitch dropped his hand but kept smiling. "Does this mean you're in, David?"

"I just want to know whose test subjects those are—whose research."

Mitch eyed David warily for a moment.

"All right, it's La Douce," he said finally. "Sylvia Kronberg's lab. She seems to be on to something, doesn't she?"

A sharp ironic laugh escaped David's mouth before he could stop it. Christ yes, Sylvia Kronberg was on to something. She was light-years ahead of him in developing a perfume that could pull a man by his nose into a woman's bedroom. David's head spun. It was perfect. Too goddamned perfect for words.

"Are you in, David?" Mitch repeated.

David could feel sweat prickle his scalp, slip down his temples and cheeks. He could almost see Sylvia in that hotel-room bed, still laughing. *Preciousness doesn't become you, David.*

"How soon would you resume contributions to St. Mary's?" David asked suddenly, his heart accelerating.

"Immediately."

"And the pediatric clinic would stay open?"

"That'd be up to Art."

"Bullshit. I need a guarantee from you, Mitch."

"I'll make sure your clinic stays open."

"And my part in this would be strictly interpretive, is that right, Mitch?"

"That and guidance," Mitch replied. "You'll have to tell Armand exactly what to look for and where he might find it."

David took a deep breath.

"And what if nothing comes of this, Mitch? What if all we ever find is tantalizing blood work but no answers?"

Mitch hesitated a moment.

"To tell you the truth, David, then we're all probably out of business."

It's for Lisa, David told himself later that night as he was going down Diagnostique's elevator. I'm doing this for Lisa and all of St. Mary's other little children.

15

....

"Honey, this is Mother at, let me see, at about six-thirty. I guess you're out to dinner with a friend or something . . ."

Amy, her raincoat still on, set the clear plastic container of salad on her kitchen table as she listened to her mother's voice on her answering machine.

"Listen, honey, I want you to consider something . . . just consider it. There're these people in Great Neck who've formed this very informal group to help young people meet each other. It's called Punch—Parents of Unmarried Children—and what they do is throw these sort of al fresco parties on Sunday afternoons when all you hardworking girls aren't doing anything anyhow . . ."

Amy hit the Off button on her answering machine. She wasn't up to listening to this just now. Bad for the digestion. She opened the refrigerator and pulled a stoppered bottle of Soave Bolla from the door rack, then picked a glass and fork from the dish-drying rack, slipped off her raincoat, and sat down in front of the spinach and watercress salad she'd bought at the Korean grocery.

The intercom buzzer rang. Amy shrugged. Just about everybody she knew was at Dot van Deusen's penthouse birthday barbecue. She paced to the wall phone and pressed the button.

"Who is it, Manuel?"

"A Miss Georgia O'Hearn," the doorman said.

Georgia O'Hearn, the Esprit Girl, coming by for an impromptu visit? This certainly set a new high in rising-young-model aggression. Amy barely knew the woman, had only met her once or twice at agency parties. No doubt, the model's agent had put her up to it—a little beauty editor schmoozing.

"Ask her what she wants," Amy said.

She listened to Manuel question O'Hearn; by the tone of his voice, she could tell that he was already smitten by the southern beauty.

"She says it's personal, Miss Martin," the doorman said, all earnestness. "She tried to call you at your office but you were gone. So since she just lives over on Seventy-second, she decided—"

"All right, Manuel. Send her up."

A minute later, Amy's bell rang, and she opened the door for Georgia O'Hearn.

"Good evening, Miss Martin," the young woman drawled as she entered. "I appreciate your seeing me like this, unannounced and all, but I do need to talk with you."

"I make a practice of never discussing business at home," Amy said coolly, still standing by the door.

"But it's not business," O'Hearn said quickly, her cornflower-blue eyes widening. "I told the doorman to tell you that. It's personal." She lowered her voice. "A personal problem."

Amy could just guess what was coming: a woebegone tale of a man who done Miss Georgia wrong. Every month, Amy received a half dozen letters in her "Beauty Bytes" mailbag requesting Lonelyhearts advice and invariably these letters began, "Dear Amy, I have a personal problem." Often, these same letters ended with a query about a new brand of eye shadow or lip blush, as if the correspondent's torturous love affair could be fixed at the makeup counter. However, Amy had never been approached for lovelorn advice by a model before. That's what models' personal managers were for.

"Can I get you a glass of wine?" Amy asked, starting back to the kitchen.

"Wine kind of dries out my skin," Georgia said solemnly. Like most gorgeous models, Georgia imparted this trinket of information about her body's reactions as if it was a gift, a beauty secret. "Do you have any Perrier or Evian or something?"

Amy smiled. Small-town beauties on the rise in New York could always rattle off the names of a dozen different brands of French mineral water, but if you mentioned Proust or Céline, they gave you blank stares. Céline? Isn't that a spring up in the Alps somewhere? Amy bit down on her lip. She'd caught herself again. Put-downs of gorgeous models—even just mental put-downs—were counterproductive. She'd already proven that once this month.

"All I've got is Canada Dry club soda, okay?"

"Sure. Thanks."

Georgia strolled over to the kitchen counter and sat down on a stool, leaning her heart-shaped face into both her palms. She was indeed a remarkable beauty with classic Grace Kelly-like features, yet something playful and kittenish in her big blue eyes. Just a year ago Georgia had been discovered by an Eileen Ford scout at a beauty pageant in Atlanta; now she was pulling in six figures for her Esprit ads alone.

"I read your article," Georgia said abruptly. "The one about the awful things that happen to pretty girls. It sure rang a bell, I'll tell you."

Amy took a long sip of wine, then immediately refilled her glass. Shit, here it comes again. *Femina*'s July issue had only been out three days and already everybody in the trade was talking about it. *Bad taste* were the usual words they used to describe it, although the word *subversive* seemed to be catching on rapidly. Amy had admitted to a few friends in the business that if she had it to do over again, she never would have written the article. But enough was enough. She was skipping Dot van Deusen's birthday party tonight just so she wouldn't have to go through another round of mea culpa. Pamela had said she thought the whole thing would blow over by the end of the week. It was still only Thursday.

"Listen, Georgia, that article was a temporary lapse in judgment." Amy stabbed her fork into her salad. "I was a little overwrought the day I wrote it."

"I bet you were," Georgia replied ingenuously. "I was pretty upset the day I read it. It's heavy. But, listen, there's a part I didn't understand; that's why I wanted to talk to you."

Amy felt a little shiver of uneasiness. She set her fork back into the salad container.

"What part was that, Georgia?"

"About Kelly Keane," the model said. "You wrote that she'd been shadowed by misfortune for a long time before she died in that accident over there in England. How did you mean that? That somebody had actually been following Kelly around?"

"Of course, not; it's just a figure of speech. All that was following Kelly was her personal demons and a bit of a drug problem." Amy gazed into the model's frightened blue eyes. "Whatever made you ask such a question?"

"Because somebody's been following me," the girl answered matter-of-factly. "Somebody who wanted to kill me."

Amy's heart thumped. She sat up straight and took a gulp of wine. Stay easy, she told herself. Don't jump any guns this time. She silently studied Georgia's face. Something in that face looked off, spooked. Was this another young model unhinged by the fast life? Maybe with a drug problem of her own?

"What makes you think somebody wanted to kill you?" Amy asked deliberately.

"I saw him," Georgia said. "Day before yesterday. I was out in San Francisco for my I. Magnin shoot and it was late and I couldn't sleep. That happens a lot to me. I get kind of wired after a long shoot and can't get to sleep. So I went out of the hotel for a walk around Ghiradelli Square."

"What time was this?"

"About quarter to one."

Amy shook her head. What was it that made these young models so foolhardy? They behaved as if they were immune to ordinary dangers, as if the whole world was a set for a perfume shoot. Familiar thought, that. It was one of the lines Harriet had cut from her article.

"Didn't that seem a rather late hour to be going out by yourself, Georgia?"

"I just went out in front of the hotel," the girl answered defensively. "And I only walked down to the pier. But that's when I saw him . . . in the shadows."

"Somebody you knew? A boyfriend?"

"No."

"But it was somebody you'd seen before."

"Not really."

"And you say this man was already in the square when you got there?"

"That's right."

Amy cocked her head to one side. "Then what exactly makes you think he was following you, Georgia?"

"I could just see it in the way he looked at me," Georgia answered, raising her voice defensively again. Her face had become flushed and the pupils of her eyes were dark with fear. "And then he started walking toward me, very slowly, and when I started to run away, he started running after me. And then he called to me. He knew who I was."

Amy leaned toward Georgia. "He called you by your name?"

"Yes. He said, 'Hey, Georgia, slow down.' He had some kind of an accent."

Amy closed her eyes a second, her mind racing.

"Listen, weren't you on the cover of *Seventeen* this month?" she asked, keeping her voice calm.

Georgia nodded.

"And I must have seen you in a dozen magazines in that Revlon ad that has your name under your picture," Amy went on. "Tell me, hasn't a stranger ever called you by name before?"

"Not the way this guy did," Georgia said, a tremor in her voice.

Amy shook her head.

"Georgia, isn't it possible that this man simply recognized you, Georgia O'Hearn, the cover girl, and he wanted to talk to you? Or maybe even in his wildest dreams he hoped to pick you up?"

"With a gun?"

"A gun?" Amy echoed the word automatically, her heart pounding, her face suddenly hot. "He had a gun?"

Georgia nodded.

Amy abruptly stood, one hand clutching the edge of the kitchen table. "Are you absolutely certain of that, Georgia? You were running away from him, weren't you? Did you actually see a gun?"

"You sound just like the police," Georgia grumbled.

"Did you actually see a gun?" Amy repeated, raising her voice.

"Look, he sure as hell was pulling something out of his pocket," Georgia said, her voice petulant yet still frightened, like a child's. "I didn't stop to ask him if I could take a close look at it."

"Yes or no, did you see a gun?"

"I couldn't swear to it, if that's what you mean. It happened so fast and a second later this midnight jogger came bouncing by—you know, in one of those glowing orange suits—and the guy coming after me freaked and ran away."

Amy sighed and slowly lowered herself back into her chair. Georgia hadn't seen any gun.

"Was that the end of it?" Amy asked.

"Yes."

"You got back to your hotel room all right after that?"

"Yes."

"And you called the police?"

Georgia shrugged.

"You did call the police, didn't you, Georgia?"

"Yes. But they said I'd have to come down to the station if I wanted to make a report and I didn't want to go through all that."

"Why not?"

"You know, the police always ask these insinuating questions like, What were you doing out by yourself? And what were you wearing? And then they show you these books full of pictures of really sick-looking guys."

Amy gazed at Georgia incredulously.

"You mean you've complained to the police before about being followed by men?" she asked.

"Well, that's the whole point, isn't it?" Georgia said, suddenly raising her voice quite loudly. "These scary things keep happening to me. I mean, I thought you, of all people, would understand that. Not like the others."

Amy hesitated. "Why? What do other people say to you?"

"You know." Georgia shrugged again. "That I've got an overactive imagination."

Amy couldn't suppress her smile. "Funny, that's what people say to me, too. Especially when I've been under a lot of stress. How about you, Georgia, have you been under much stress these days?"

"Sure, some. Comes with the job."

"How about men . . . any men troubles lately?"

Georgia lowered her eyes. "That comes with the job, too, doesn't it?"

Amy took a deep breath and let it out slowly.

"Georgia," she began softly. "I bet there've been men following you around ever since you were twelve years old. Men hounding you, whistling at you, trying desperately to pick you up. There are a million pigs out there and I'm sure you've had to put up with more than your share of them. But listen, if a man follows you around late at night, that hardly means he wants to

93

kill you." Amy paused, looked warmly into the young woman's eyes. "It sounds to me like this man out in San Francisco was just one pig too many and you let him get to you. And that's why you overreacted."

"But that isn't what you called it in the magazine," Georgia blurted in a brittle, still-angry voice. "You didn't call it overreacting there."

Amy was silent. Something inside her flinched.

"Georgia, exactly when did you read 'Perils of Pulchritude'?" she asked quietly.

"Your article? On the plane on the way out to Frisco, why?"

Amy looked down. Oh God, this was the ultimate irresponsibility of her article: It had triggered this small-town girl's big-city paranoia. Poor Georgia. The article had probably confirmed every hysterical warning her mother had stuffed into her gorgeous young head before she left home for New York: You can't be too careful, honey. There's horrible people out there and they're all out to do something awful to a beautiful girl like you. Wasn't that essentially the same message Amy had put out—gussied up with quotes from psychologists—in her article?

"Georgia, the reason I didn't call it overreacting in my article is because I was overreacting myself," Amy said softly. "And the reason for that is that not enough men have been following *me* around lately. Do you know what I mean?"

A sweet smile of relief started to appear on Georgia O'Hearn's perfect heart-shaped face.

"Look, I'm not saying you shouldn't be careful out there," Amy went on. "For one thing, I don't think it's such a smart idea to go walking around alone late at night in some strange city. But it's crazy to go around spooking yourself all the time. Life's too short to be frightened of everything and everyone."

For a few seconds, both women were silent. Then Georgia slid off the stool and walked over to Amy.

"I don't know," the young woman said, sounding almost shy. "Maybe I've been a little hysterical myself lately. Men, you know. They do make you crazy. They'll tell you anything, like they're going to get divorced any day now, anything you want to hear." A faint blush appeared on her cheeks. "Hey, I guess I should go now. I bet you'd like to finish your dinner."

"Such as it is." Amy laughed. She walked Georgia to the door.

"I hope you're feeling better. And look, if you ever need to talk again, give a call, okay?"

"Thanks," Georgia said. "Well, I'll see you. Maybe when I get back from Martinique. Or from Venice. I'm doing a Bergdorf's spread."

"Have fun."

Amy double-locked her door after the model had left. Then, on her way back to the kitchen, she hit the Playback button of her answering machine.

"Franny Hollander goes to these Sunday Punch parties all the time now and I understand that she met a very nice young man at the last one." Her mother's message droned on. "You remember Franny, Amy. Kind of a horsey girl."

P A R T

2

16

···

The reason Armand Diltzer had a perpetually runny nose, he explained to David, was because he spent nine hours a day, five days a week, going in and out of the cold room in the research unit of La Douce Laboratories. Armand was an assistant to a lab assistant there, a gofer and dishwasher for $3.80 an hour. David didn't ask Armand how much Mitch paid him for pilfering what he could from La Douce, but he imagined that it at least tripled Armand's meager income.

But if Armand was a second-level lab assistant, he was a third-rate thief. In the three weeks since David had painstakingly described to Armand exactly what he needed to determine the origin of the three vials of remarkable aliphatic-acid-laden blood, the sniffling young man had come up with nothing remotely useful. Instead of returning to Diagnostique with coded test-subject dosage books, he came back with Xeroxes of irrelevant lab notes and lab diary entries; instead of a printout of the medications inventory, he brought back a printout of the laboratory glassware inventory. It was not simply that Armand was inept, he was scared.

"You got to understand, it's not so easy like it was," he had protested to Mitch and David. "Like all of a sudden, everything's very tight over there. Everything's security, signing in and signing out. A different security guard at the door every day. It's that blood. Gotta be. They know some's missing."

"You take flasks in and out of that cold room all day long," Mitch had responded soothingly. "There's nobody but you keeping track of that inventory. We've gone over this before, Armand. Nobody's keeping tabs on you. I'm sure they have more important things to do."

"You don't know these people, Mr. Papechki," Armand said, wagging his pale pockmarked face. "That Dr. K, she just looks like a fairy princess, but she's the iron maiden. Like when Jasper dropped that one vial of blood, that was it. He was out. Done. Get your paycheck and go home, boy. I never saw him again."

Sylvia Kronberg often came up in Armand's excuses. He claimed she ran her laboratory like a military commandant with surveillance cameras in the corners of every room, random searches at the elevators, and, occasionally, Kronberg herself marching up to a worker and challenging her to explain exactly what she was doing at that moment and why.

In spite of himself, David took a grim satisfaction in hearing how paranoid and controlling Sylvia Kronberg behaved in her lab. He knew it to be the informed paranoia of an inveterate, self-justifying thief and, in some paradoxical way, it seemed to justify his own participation in this industrial-espionage game. Not that David very often found himself looking for justifications anymore. What amazed him more than anything was how effortlessly he had slipped into his new role. Sylvia would never accuse him of being precious now.

"They gotta be keeping those dosage books somewhere else, not in the lab," Armand was saying. "Like I looked everywhere in the lab. Nothing. No dosage books, no test-subject codes. All I could cop was another one of these."

Armand removed a small vial from his raincoat pocket and set it on Mitch Papechki's desk. Blood again. David picked up the vial and examined it, then held it to the light. On the fluid's surface, a thin ring of crystal diffused the light like a prism. Particles. Particles of cryoparticapates. This blood had been frozen and thawed. Sylvia Kronberg was obviously performing before-and-after treatment studies on her test subjects. The frozen blood was the base study.

"From the same cold room?" David asked.

"No, the other one, the one by her office door."

100

"Are there others like this? On the same rack?"

"Yeh, about twenty . . . maybe twenty-five," Armand said. "But listen to me, this has got to be the last one of these I'm copping. I almost fucking got killed grabbing this one."

David started to set the vial back on Mitch's table when he felt something grainy under his fingertip. He pulled his reading glasses from his breast pocket and put them on. Again, he held the vial to the light. Near the rim, a tiny piece of paper adhered to the hard plastic. Clearly, the rest of the paper had been ripped away. What was left had jagged ends of uneven black stripes printed on it. It was the remainder of a bar-code label.

David felt a tight hard smile pull at the corners of his mouth. This was a break. Kronberg was using bar-code labels to log her test subject's blood analyses in her computer. No doubt her dosage records could be accessed with those labels, too. It was the key into Kronberg's alpha-copulin experiment.

"Find the rest of this, Armand," David said, pointing at the ripped label, "and we're halfway there."

17

Therapy was finally working. For the first time in memory, dinner with her sister, Molly, didn't make Amy feel as if she was still fourteen years old and had cheeks covered with acne. Rather, she felt calmly, even playfully alert to all the decoys and sand traps that Molly inevitably set between them. Tonight, something that Mary Goldfarb had been telling Amy for years seemed perfectly obvious: *Molly* was the one who had the real problem. Big sister was the one who was desperately locked in the "I've got to be better than you are" game. But Amy didn't need to play that game anymore.

Molly had started in even before they sat down at their table.

"Is it the light in here or are your eyes turning blue?" Molly asked a little too loudly when they met at the bar in Marvin Gardens.

"I'm wearing tinted contacts," Amy answered. "I'm doing a story on them."

"You really don't need them, you know, hon. You've got such lovely brown eyes."

It was a quintessential Molly put-down disguised as a compliment, overdone reassurance when no reassurance was called for. Amy noticed that Molly reflexively had glanced in the smoky mirror behind the bar the moment she had said it. How obvious could it get that she was the one who needed reassurance? Molly was still as beautiful as ever; even in her "just little old me" worn French jeans and faded blue workshirt, she was a drop-dead beauty. But Amy felt a new awareness of her sister's need to use that beauty, to catch the eye of every man and to compare herself with every woman in the restaurant. The poor girl never gave herself an unselfconscious moment to simply enjoy the beautiful world around her.

"Are you seeing anybody in particular these days?" Molly asked over her Caesar salad.

"Not even anybody in general," Amy answered, grinning. She didn't feel any stomach-wrenching panic when Molly asked. No internal fits of jealousy because Molly always had a man, and two or three more waiting in the wings. But did Molly ever have a genuine relationship? Definitely not, according to Mary Goldfarb; Mary maintained that narcissists were incapable of experiencing true intimacy. Mary was convinced, however, that at the rate Amy was currently getting control of her life, she could look forward to a significant relationship in the very near future. That's the way it always happens, Mary said. First you do the hard work of learning to appreciate yourself from the inside out, instead of depending on what others think of you and the way you look. That work was the prerequisite for any relationship; after it, finding the right man was the easy part, merely the last detail. The marvelous irony was that when you genuinely felt good about yourself, when you accepted your inner beauty, you immediately became more attractive to men. "Beauty is as beauty feels about herself," Mary said. "In fact, beauty is psychosomatic."

In the last analysis, running into Peter at the gallery that night and all the craziness that followed—her jealous rage, her incendiary article, her conflicts with everybody—had turned out to be a significant growth experience, a crash course in reality. Seeing Peter for what he was—the lowest order of New Age macho hypocrite—had made it painless to cut her last threads of attachment to him. Most important, however, by acknowledging her jealousy of Penny Twang, Amy had finally been able to confront her deep-seated, self-destructive envy of all glamorous women, that insidious envy she had lived with ever since she was a little girl sharing her bedroom with Molly. Life was too rich to stay hung up on that absurd obsession.

When Amy said good night to Molly out on the street, she gave her sister a spontaneous hug.

"Good night, Beauty," she said, grinning.

"Good night, Brains," Molly replied with a surprised smile on her face.

It was an old routine they hadn't done since they were teenagers. It felt marvelous to laugh at it again.

The night was warm, with hundreds of people strolling Broadway. Amy stopped at the Häagen Dazs on Eighty-fourth and treated herself to a double chocolate-almond cone. It was easily worth an extra pound or two. She turned at Eighty-seventh Street and walked slowly to her building on West End Avenue.

"Buenas tardes, Manuel." Amy smiled at her doorman as she came in through the outside door. *"Como está?"*

Manuel shook his head.

"What awful times we live in, eh, Miss Martin?"

Amy licked her cone.

"I don't know," she replied. "It has its sweet moments."

"But your friend, I mean. That very, very beautiful girl with a face like a valentine. The one who visited you a few weeks ago. Josey O'Hearn."

Manuel took a keen interest in every good-looking woman who passed through these portals and frequently shared his appraisals of them with Amy. He apparently thought of himself as a professional colleague; both of them beauty mavens.

"Georgia. Georgia O'Hearn. What about her?" Amy said, waiting for him to open the inside door.

"My cousin, he work in her building," Manuel went on, not moving, his small eyes fixed on the tile floor. "The super told him about her. Awful, isn't it?"

Amy's face blanched. She felt dizzy. She leaned against the closed door.

"What's awful, Manuel?"

"I thought you knew," he said. "Miss O'Hearn, she's dead. Drowned. Down in the Caribbean. She fall off a boat and drown."

18

The tip of the monumental bat outside Yankee Stadium was just visible between the ancient water tank and the shiny aluminum air-conditioning unit on the rooftop of La Douce Laboratories. From his window seat in the Blimpie across the street, David could take in the entire front of the building. It was wedged between two other brick, four-story, turn-of-the-century factories: the factory on the left with the words HYCK'S THATCHED CHAIRS painted in bright yellow directly onto its bricks, an office-for-rent sign in one of its second-story windows; the factory on the right displaying a more modest plastic sign that read: BENT-NERR ENGINEERING. The sign hanging over La Douce's green glass front door was so small and in such poor repair that is was barely decipherable even from this short distance. Shabby. The whole building looked shabby. Ironic, that.

The only two La Douce products that remained on the cosmetics market—their flowery bath oil and *après bains*—were surviving because of their chic country-French packaging, pink satin-lined boxes tied with lavender bows like some picnic item in an Impressionist painting. Yuppie bathroom accessories manufactured in a Bronx slum.

But there was another irony that brought a wry smile to David's lips: how willing he had been to accept Armand Diltzer's

105

description of La Douce's quarters as some isolated high-tech armed camp surrounded by guards. It was that image which had brought David here this evening to look for himself. But this narrow Bronx street was hardly desolate; it teemed with people, most of them workers issuing from the doors of Hyck's, Bentnerr's, and La Douce Labs.

In twos and threes, they jostled out of the cosmetics company's front door, most of them women, chattering, laughing, looking happy to be done with another day's work—not at all as if they had just been released from some high-stress environment in which they were frisked and searched randomly throughout the day. It was becoming increasingly clear to David that Mitch's angry assessment was right: Armand Diltzer's TV-bred imagination was just churning out alibis for not doing what he was being paid to do. Another week and a half had gone by and Diltzer still hadn't managed to get out of La Douce with just a postage-stamp-size bar-code label.

David remained stuck. For the last three weeks, all he'd had to go on were those eight Xeroxed pages of laboratory notes Mitch had handed to him that first night. David had studied and restudied those pages, searching for a clue to Kronberg's methodology. The notes seemed to have been written in a stream of scientific consciousness, mixing established hormonal sequences with hypothetical links and precursors. Throughout, however, one postulate recurred: an imaginative stimulating hormone that was released from the hypothalmus at the onset of female puberty and that set off production of alpha copulin. Yet ambitious as Kronberg was, David was certain she would never even consider experimenting with a hypothalamic hormone for a commercial cosmetic. The hypothalamus—that master gland sunk deep in the brain—affected production of growth-hormone precursors, calcium regulators, and adrenal-cortical pigment-stimulating hormones. Tinkering with any part of the hypothalamic system would wreak havoc with the entire body, set off growth disorders, bone degeneration, skin disfigurement. The FDA wouldn't approve a hypothalamic-hormone cosmetic in a million years.

Yet there remained those three vials of blood indisputably oozing with the constituents of alpha copulin. They were real. They came from somewhere. Something had stimulated the pheromone's production in that blood.

David cupped his hand across his forehead to shade the evening sun that streaked down over the factory rooftops. Across the street, a last throng of workwomen and men tumbled out the door of La Douce Laboratories, jabbering, gesturing with their hands. At the center of the group, something gold glistened, a blond head that rose a few inches above the others. David pressed himself close to the window, felt his skin grow warm. An instant erotic sensation pulsed through him. It was Sylvia. The fairy princess among her loyal workers. David craned his neck to follow the group to the end of the street, where most of them descended into a subway entrance. Then he saw a shining gray limousine pull up at the corner and Sylvia Kronberg, smiling and waving, got inside.

19

"Of course, you're upset," Mary Goldfarb said, looking at Amy with her big brown cow eyes. "You're grieving. Something would be seriously wrong with you if you weren't experiencing a deep sense of shock and loss right now. A human being you knew is dead. In other cultures, mourners chant and wail; they have rituals for dealing with their grief. But we so-called sophisticated twentieth-century Americans are bereft of rituals. Someone dies and we don't know what to do. We don't know how to work through these feelings of loss. And that's how we end up so emotionally confused."

Amy took a deep breath and blew it out slowly. She had phoned Mary two nights ago, right after hearing about Georgia O'Hearn's death, and Mary had scheduled this special private session—even though she was officially on vacation.

"This girl's not just *dead*, Mary; there's a possibility somebody killed her." Amy stared at her therapist. "Why do you keep acting like that's a preposterous idea? You live in New York. I presume you read the newspapers. Even the *Times* reports two or three murders a day, if you get around to reading the B section."

"I don't find the *idea* of murder preposterous at all," Mary Goldfarb replied, calmly shaking her head. "But so far you haven't told me anything that makes me think this particular young woman was killed, rather than that she died in some sort of boating accident as it said in her obituary. Who else have you spoken to about this?"

"Just Midge Krieger," Amy answered. "Georgia's agent. Former agent. I talked to her yesterday, but it wasn't a very satisfying conversation."

"Did she say anything to make you doubt Georgia's death was an accident?"

"Midge didn't say much about anything," Amy replied, still feeling her annoyance with the agent. "Mostly, she was concerned about bad publicity. Georgia O'Hearn's life is over at the age of nineteen, and Midge is worried about how it's going to look in the trades."

"Maybe she was being particularly cautious with you because you write for *Femina.*"

"Of course that's why Midge would be closemouthed with me; she's still pissed about my 'Perils of Pulchritude' article. But under the circumstances, you'd think she'd make an effort to transcend that."

"She mentioned your article?"

"Oh yes, indeed she did. Brought it right up. I'm explaining to her how only last week Georgia was chased around Ghiradelli Square by some madman, and Midge cuts in with, 'I hope you're not going to drag Georgia's name through the mud the way you did Kelly's.' "

"Kelly?"

"Kelly Keane. One of the models I wrote about in that article. Midge immediately hauled out this whole story about how disturbed Kelly's family had been by my article. She said they thought I'd made it sound as if Kelly's accident was her own fault. I'm trying to explain to Midge that there's a possibility Georgia O'Hearn was murdered, and she drags out this 'you're blaming the victim again' guilt trip."

Mary nodded impassively. "So not even Midge—the young woman's agent—had heard anything suspicious about her death?"

"The point is, Midge wouldn't have told me if she *had* heard anything suspicious," Amy said deliberately. "She'd be afraid I'd write something about it."

Mary arched her heavy brows.

"So the fact that Midge *didn't* say anything about Georgia's death made you suspicious?"

"That's not what I said."

"But that's all you've spoken to—your elevator operator and Midge."

"That's all so far," Amy answered. "I tried to call the photographer who was on the shoot with Georgia in Martinique, but he's out of town. And I've been tempted to ask around the office to find out what's in the grapevine about Georgia, but I don't feel like putting myself through that abuse again."

"What abuse is that?"

Amy was silent.

"Do you think your colleagues would accuse you of seeing more in the Georgia incident than is really there?" Mary asked.

"Something like that."

Mary gazed silently at Amy for several seconds.

"Amy," she said finally, her voice pitched low, "why do you suppose it is so important for you to make this young woman's death your own responsibility?"

"I'm not trying to *make* Georgia's death into anything. She was in my apartment only a week ago, scared to death because somebody'd been following her around, threatening her. And what did I do? I told her that kind of thing comes with the territory, that she'd be nuts to go out in the middle of the night by herself again, but to stop spooking herself. Stop looking for things to be frightened of. I told her gorgeous girls always get followed around and—"

"And now you feel terribly guilty," Mary interjected.

"Of course I feel guilty!" Amy cried. "I *should* feel guilty! I didn't listen to my instincts and now she's dead!"

"And if you had taken your instincts more seriously, then what?" Mary asked. "Would you have made Georgia promise to wear a life vest if she ever got invited to a yachting party? Or signed her up for one of those personal-safety courses you wrote about? Or hired her a private bodyguard?"

Amy clenched her hands at her sides. "The very least I could have done is urged her to be careful, instead of convincing her she had nothing to be afraid of."

Mary pushed a lock of mousy-brown hair away from her forehead.

110

"And if you had urged Georgia to be careful, do you think she'd be alive today?"

Amy hesitated.

"She might be, yes," she answered quietly.

Mary leaned forward in her chair, looked intently into Amy's eyes.

"Amy, I'm not hearing any *facts* from you that suggest anything other than what was reported. Just that she fell off a yacht somewhere in the Caribbean and drowned. She could have been drunk or stoned, I certainly don't know, and from what you've told me, I don't think you can know, either. But I do see you intent on weighing yourself down with guilt. It feels like the flip side of your same old record. First you blamed all the beauty of these young women for every bad thing that ever happened to them, and now you're blaming yourself. You've swung from jealousy to guilt, but you're still living out your old obsession."

Amy lowered her eyes. She suddenly felt unbearably weak and tired.

"Amy, you've been doing well lately," Mary went on, her voice soft again. "You've started enjoying your work again, enjoying your colleagues and friends . . . even enjoying your sister. I've seen it in your face . . . you look so radiant lately, so ready to make yourself available to new relationships. Don't backslide now after you've made all this progress. Don't give in to the temptation to punish yourself again by letting your judgment be affected. Just let go of all the guilt you can and get on with your life, okay?"

Amy closed her eyes tightly. She felt very small, like a child.

"I'll ease back," she whispered. "I will."

20

The moment David walked into the examination room, he saw that Moire O'Brien was herself again. In the four months since surgeons had removed a tiny benign tumor from her anterior pituitary, the Cushing's patient had made a complete recovery. Moire's garish red beard was gone, her skin was pink and clear, her face had returned to its original oval shape, and silky blond hair again covered her fine-boned head.

"Hello, Miss O'Brien, I'm Dr. Copeland. Dr. Kenworthy's not in today, so I'll be examining you." David extended his hand to the young woman.

"I remember you, Doctor," Moire said brightly. Dressed in a hospital smock, she was sitting up perfectly straight on the examination table. "You were there the night before my operation. You came with that woman, the beautiful one. I still even dream about her sometimes. I've seen her in magazines, haven't I? The Mona Girl?"

"She *was* the Mona Girl," David said. Mona Eye Gel had been off the market for over three months now, approximately the same length of time since David had seen Francesca. "I should apologize for that evening, Miss O'Brien. I'm afraid it wasn't an appropriate time to bring a guest on rounds."

"Oh, I'm glad you brought her to visit me that night," Moire said earnestly as she lay back on the examination table. "I remember I kept trying to hold her face in my mind's eye when I was going under the anesthetic. It gave me something to hope for."

David shook his head in wonder. He remembered how painfully guilty he'd felt that night after taking Francesca on rounds.

"I'm glad to see you're making such an excellent recovery," he said as he warmed his hands against one another. He reached out and pressed his thumb and forefinger against the lacrimal bones in the patient's face; he could feel the soft tissue where calcium remodeling had recently occurred. He extended one hand under her neck and felt along her spine. Supraclavicular fat pads were gone, the humping eroded. David took one of her hands and stretched out her arm. Wasting had reversed; all her long muscles had returned smooth and firm. He walked to the foot of the table and examined her feet one at a time. No ulcers, no edema; the skin was again elastic and uniformly dense. All it had taken to bring Moire O'Brien back from the world of the grotesque was to remove a few cubic millimeters of tumorous tissue from her pituitary gland so that it could resume normal production of andrenocorticotrophic hormone.

"At first, I didn't think I was ever going to change back again," Moire said as David wrapped a sphygmomanometer sleeve around her arm. "My mother wouldn't let me have a mirror when I got home from the hospital, so I had to bribe my little sister to bring me one in my bed. Then all I did all day long was look at myself. Count the pimples on my cheeks and the hairs on my chin. I saw the first sign exactly three weeks after my operation . . . five hairs of that awful beard had disappeared."

David nodded, then pumped up the sleeve and listened with his stethoscope for pulse beats in the crook of her arm. Systolic, 120; diastolic, 78. Normal, healthy blood pressure.

"From then on, I could see tiny little changes happening almost every day," Moire went on. "Another pimple gone, another new hair on my scalp. But I'd have to look very quickly—kind of catch myself by surprise—to see the subtle changes. You know, like to see that my face wasn't quite so moon-shaped as before or my skin was a tiny shade pinker."

Moire suddenly averted her eyes and swallowed audibly.

113

David took a long step back from the examination table. He knew what was coming next; he had heard it countless times before from recovering Cushing's patients.

"Then, about three weeks ago, it stopped," Moire said quietly, no longer looking at David. "I wasn't changing anymore. I . . . I kept looking in the mirror and waiting . . . but it stopped. No more changes. I was just me again."

David pursed his lips but said nothing. Two small tears had formed in the corners of Moire O'Brien's eyes.

"Please . . . please understand . . . I'm very, very grateful to Dr. Kenworthy and you and . . . and everybody else at St. Mary's," Moire murmured. "It really was a nightmare, that awful disease, and I thank God it's over . . . but . . . but part of me keeps . . . keeps—"

"I know," David said softly. "It gets addictive, this watching for changes. That's not uncommon, Moire."

Moire brushed her tears against the sleeve of her smock. David bent over Moire's case folder a moment to allow her to regain her composure. Then he drew two vials of blood from her arm for the monthly assay of her pituitary, adrenal, and gonad hormone concentrations.

"I'll tell Dr. Kenworthy how well you're doing," David said. "He'll be disappointed he missed you."

David left the examination room with the RIA vials and fitted them into the wire pickup rack at the nurse's station. He peered over Sister Berzins's shoulder at the schedule book—a Mrs. Epstein was waiting in Examination Room D to have her estrogen patch changed; a Mr. Tilborn was waiting in Examination Room B for a glucose uptake.

"Hey, guy."

Art Malley smiled at David across the intake counter. The administrator had been acting gratingly familiar in the weeks since he had rescinded his order to phase out the Thursday-afternoon pediatric endocrinology clinic. Malley's retraction memo had appeared in David's box, as promised, only twenty-four hours after David had thrown in with Mitch's "interlaboratory research" scheme.

"Afternoon, Art." David glanced up for only an instant, then resumed searching for the Epstein file on Sister Berzins's desk.

"Ray out again?" Malley asked, stepping around the counter.

"He's got the flu," David answered. "He won't be in for a few days."

"Doesn't make your job any easier, does it?" Malley's smarmy face was next to David's now.

"We manage."

"Listen, David, I'm real pleased your department is back on track up here. That's gratifying for all of us." Malley placed his hand on David's sleeve. "But I'm afraid we've still got a little problem downstairs with Ray's Medicaid billings. He still hasn't produced those record dupes for us and we've got this god-awful auditor breathing down our necks. Give him a push, will you? We don't want this thing to turn into any kind of embarrassment."

"I'll take care of it," David said, pulling his arm away.

"I know he's a personal friend of yours," Malley went on. "Maybe you can give him a better sense of the urgency of this thing than I can."

"He's got the flu, Art. He's sick in bed," David said sharply, striding away. "I'll talk to him the minute he's back."

David crossed the corridor to Examination Room D, feeling both annoyed and vaguely disturbed. It was over three weeks since Ray had promised to take care of that Medicaid business; David had assumed it was already done. God knows, David had been preoccupied with some guilty adjustments in his own life, but now that he thought about it, he realized he'd seen very little of his colleague lately: Ray had been absent from their regular Wednesday-night basketball game twice in a row now and David didn't remember seeing him in the doctor's section of the cafeteria in the past week or so, either. And last Friday, Ray's wife, Glenda, had left a message on David's home answering machine canceling a long-standing invitation for a Sunday conch-fritter dinner with their family out in Montclair. At first, David had felt deeply disappointed—there was nothing he enjoyed more than a long afternoon with Ray and Glenda and their four bright-eyed, fast-talking daughters—but part of David had also felt undeniably relieved. Around Ray's fresh, fun-loving family, it might be too hard to ignore the dull ache of shame that David was just learning how to suppress.

It was almost six when David finished seeing both his and Ray's outpatients. That didn't leave enough time to go out for a decent dinner before he had to drive to Brooklyn. Armand was due at

Diagnostique at seven; he was coming directly from his job at La Douce. Armand had called Mitch early that morning and told him he'd finally made the breakthrough for which they all were waiting. He said he was finally putting it all together.

David took the elevator up to the hospital cafeteria and got in line. The menu board announced that they were once again featuring breaded pork chops in white sauce, ounce for ounce enough saturated fat to clog an Olympic athlete's arteries. Hospital cafeterias had a tradition of unhealthy food; interns joked that it was good for business. David was reaching for a plastic-wrapped deviled-egg salad when his beeper sounded in his jacket pocket. He stepped out of line and strode to the phone by the door. Mitch Papechki calling. The operator put him through.

"Our friend had to cancel tonight," Mitch said. "He says he's going to have the whole package for us by the end of the week. I think he's got it this time, David. Not a minute too soon, either. Talk to you tomorrow."

"Sure, Mitch."

David shook his head as he hung up the phone. Under its reflex, collegiate optimism, Mitch's voice had an edge of panic to it lately. This wasn't the first time Armand had called to say that he was finally putting it all together. What if the little pockfaced man was stringing them along? After all the anxiety David had put himself through before committing himself to Mitch's scheme, that would have a certain poetic irony, wouldn't it?

David started back to the cafeteria line, then stopped, realizing that he could go out to dinner wherever he liked tonight. How about grilled salmon at The Blue Mill while watching a Mets game? It was the kind of pleasure that men with a tenth his income enjoyed regularly. David took the elevator to the fourth floor and headed directly for his office. Inside, he put on his suit coat and grabbed his briefcase before switching off the light. He was just locking his office door when he saw Ray Kenworthy step out of the stairwell, a small, polystyrene insulated cooler in his hand.

"Ray? Aren't you supposed to be in bed?"

A startled smile appeared on Ray's broad face.

"One day in bed is a vacation, two's a punishment." Ray's basso laugh echoed in the empty corridor. "I actually missed St. Mary's hallowed halls."

David walked up to Ray.

"You're feeling better?"

"Not perfect, but a whole bunch better," Ray said. "Glenda's going to call you to reschedule our conch-fritter fest. My girls were heartbroken. They tell me you're the only white man I ever brought home who knows how to boogie."

Ray laughed again, then started to turn away. David put his hand on Ray's sleeve.

"Listen, Ray? Art Malley cornered me today. He says you still haven't turned over those record dupes for the Medicaid auditor. I'd like that taken care of before the end of the week, all right?"

Ray scratched at his jaw.

"End of the week would be calling it a little close," he said. "Tell him I'll have everything in a week and a half, would you?"

"You've already had two weeks, Ray. You aren't having a problem with this, are you?"

Ray held the plastic cooler tightly at his side. His eyes shifted from David's and David felt a ripple of apprehension pass through him.

"Look, if you're having trouble with this, I need to know about it," David said deliberately. "In this department, your problems are my problems."

"Really? And are yours mine?" Ray replied coolly.

David stared uncomprehendingly at his friend. "What the hell is going on, Ray?"

Ray looked back soberly, then abruptly broke into a boyish smile.

"Okay, I've got a little problem, but it's nothing to worry about," he said, leaning confidentially toward David. "What happened is Glenda glitched a few records on my computer. God love her, she pressed the wrong button and—zap—they were gone. She does all my billing, you know, but this time she screwed up royally. So, for the last two weeks, we've been up every night reconstructing everything she lost. We just need a few more—"

Suddenly, the door to Examination Room D swung open across the hall and a black boy of about twelve in a purple and black athletic jacket stuck out his head.

"Hey, coach, I been waitin' for—"

"Back inside, *mon!*" Ray called back sharply in dialect.

The boy looked sullenly from Ray to David, then closed himself back inside the room. Ray reached out his hand and grasped David's shoulder.

"Just give me five days, friend," Ray said quietly. "You know I'd never bring any shame on St. Mary's Hospital."

David hesitated.

"I'll see what I can do," he said finally.

Ray released his hand and David turned and walked to the elevator.

21

....

"Listen, I know it's a bore, but it's one of those de rigueur questions at *Femina:* Do you have any special beauty secrets to pass on to our readers?"

Amy smiled across her teacup at Aida, the lavender-eyed, raven-haired Roman model who was currently taking New York by storm. Aida grinned back at her.

"Well, first, of course, you must always avoid the sun. Not just at the beach, darling, but everywhere . . . in the deck chair, on the boulevard, those rays that come sneaking through the skylight of your lover's bedroom. The sun destroys your skin, indiscriminate of where it finds you. Next, you must never ever eat fried foods. Not *pommes frites,* not *vitello piccata.* Pimples live on fried foods the way morels live on loam. Third, always keep your face moist, *bella.* I spray with Evyan ten times a day absolute minimum. It makes the skin fresh like dew on a poppy. But most important . . ." Aida leaned forward, her light eyes sparkling mischievously. "To be absolutely sure you look beautiful, my friend, you must choose your relatives very, very carefully."

Aida burst into a throaty laugh and Amy immediately joined her. Amy was thoroughly enjoying herself this hot August afternoon. What a pleasure it was to do an old time glamour interview again. No product to critique, no suspicions to air, no axes to grind, just a charming chat over tea about the world of elegant clothes and exotic places and beautiful people. Mary Goldfarb was right, of course. Life did not have to be all Sturm und Drang. You can either focus on life's horrors or on its pleasures. It's your own choice, the most fundamental choice you have. Aida had obviously opted for life's pleasures. The Roman beauty exuded joy and confidence and warmth. But most refreshing of all, she was not another one of those international models who glided through the world mindlessly; rather, she was a discriminating and witty cosmopolite, a connoisseur of art and men and music and clothes. Aida's out-of-the-blue call to Amy offering her first exclusive New York interview was perfectly timed. God knows, everyone at *Femina* was thrilled. And as far as Amy was concerned, an afternoon like this was just what the doctor ordered.

"Before Robert comes for the 'at homes,' I need to fill in a few spaces, okay?" Amy said, glancing down at her notes. "Which do you call home—Rome or Lericci? You mentioned both."

"But I am from both, *bella*. And from New York and Paris and Buenos Aires, too. They all feel like home to me. I am a gypsy at heart, no?"

Aida leaned back her head and shook her mane of silky black hair. She was a remarkably dramatic-looking woman, her thick eyebrows constantly moving over her large intense eyes. In fact, all of her features were just a tad oversized—her full lips and mouth, her long aquiline nose. On another woman, these features might have seemed too much, indelicate, but on Aida they coexisted in stunning harmony. She was an example of what Amy had once called in her column, "The Loren Principle." If the bridge of Sophia Loren's nose were just a fraction larger, Amy had written, or her cheekbones just millimeters wider, or her lips only a touch thicker, she would cross that line that separates the exotic from the vulgar. Great beauty obeyed the laws of a finely tuned aesthetic principle.

"Are there any more at home like you? Any gorgeous younger sisters who we'll be seeing on the runways in a few years?" Amy asked, smiling. Over the years, it had become a standard question in her repertoire; it was the question to which every little sister who read *Femina* ached to know the answer.

"Not really," Aida answered.

"Last question, promise," Amy went on quickly. "Do you have some recent tearsheets I could take a peek at? A preview so I can let my readers know where they'll be seeing you next?"

Aida rose quickly and gracefully from her chair and paced to the bookcase by her living room door, where she took a stack of photographs from the bottom shelf. She returned and spread them on the tea table in front of Amy.

"For the *Times* magazine. They run in October, the twenty-something." The model uttered a clipped laugh, like a hiccough. "I always feel so . . . so natural in a de la Renta. So free, eh?"

Amy looked down at the photographs. They were stagy and slightly surreal in the current mode, although they were all taken at the predictable Venetian locales—Aida sitting at a café table in the Piazza San Marco, drinking champagne on the balcony of the Medici, leaning rather precariously against the rail of a *vaporetto*. The good life, courtesy of Bergdorf's.

A sudden shiver shook Amy's shoulders. Shit, this should have been Georgia O'Hearn's spread! The one she was supposed to do right after her shoot in Martinique. Amy felt a lump of anxiety swelling in her throat. Damn it, she had been doing so well at putting Georgia out of her mind, at fending off her obsessional guilt. On Mary's advice, she had abandoned the idea of calling Able Franke, the photographer on Georgia's last shoot, to quiz him about what he knew about her death. But for Christ's sake, this should have been Georgia's spread! She could be forgiven for being upset by something like that.

Amy squeezed her eyes closed for a moment. When she opened them, she forced herself to gaze down again at the *Times* tearsheets. A second tremor pulsed up her spine. In the corner of the *vaporetto* shot, a coarse-looking, stubble-faced Italian sailor was leering at Aida, his jagged teeth showing under his mustache.

"I hope you're always careful out there," Amy blurted.

"Careful of him?" Aida snickered, pointing at the leering boatman.

"Yes, of him. Of everybody. I've heard too many ugly stories lately."

"Ugly stories?"

Amy swallowed hard. Stop this right now, she told herself. She felt her pulse thumping in her throat.

"I happen to know there was a man following Georgia

O'Hearn around just before she died," Amy went on compulsively.

"Just before?"

Amy's face flushed.

"Not more than a week before," she protested, hearing how much weaker it sounded when she said it out loud.

Aida shook her head with a sardonic smile. She pointed again at the stubble-faced boatman in the photograph.

"*Bella,* this *ladro* charged us a thousand lire not to walk out of the frame," she said. "That's the biggest crime he's capable of."

Amy offered a contrite smile.

"My friend, I hope you aren't still carrying on about this perils of beauty business, are you?" Aida continued, wagging a long finger in front of Amy's eyes. "I mean, you're absolutely right, of course, this face of mine is a terrible burden. Especially because of all that money they keep throwing at me to take pictures of it. And all the men that I have to push away. So tiring, so boring. Not to mention one four-star restaurant after another, in Paris, Rio, Venice, New York. I know it's a terrible life, but somebody has to live it."

Again, Aida burst into musical laughter. Amy raised her head and managed to laugh with her.

The doorbell chimed.

"*Momente, momente,*" Aida sang out.

Robert Olinsky had arrived for some casual "at home" photographs of Aida to accompany Amy's interview. He had brought along Mitzi Bye, the stylist, and Barney Petersen, the makeup man, both of them top of the line. *Femina* was paying to get the best for this rising new star. Amy knew that Harriet Schwartz was already busy negotiating with Aida's agent for the fall fashions cover.

"I give you fifteen minutes, no more," Aida said to the photographer. She turned to Amy. "Do wait for me, *bella.* I have to be downtown at four . . . we can share a taxi."

"My pleasure."

Amy backed out of the living room as Mitzi and Barney descended on Aida with their little vinyl bags of brushes and powders and ribbons and lace. She paced along the unadorned walls of the apartment's main hallway. Clearly, Aida had made no effort to put her own stylish stamp on the place. The air was heavy back here away from the air conditioner. Amy stepped into the bathroom and closed the door behind her. She turned on the cold water and let it spray over her palms, then splashed some on her face. She already felt calm again, calm and cool. At least her recovery time was improving. Amy glanced briefly at herself in the mirror. Had she made a complete fool of herself before in the living room? Fortunately, Aida didn't seem to take it too seriously.

Amy swung open the medicine cabinet. She smiled. Both shelves were filled with glass containers of nail polish lined up like colorful toy soldiers. She pushed the door closed and twirled around, then took one long step to the bathroom closet and opened it. Here they were, all of Aida's creams and lotions and conditioners.

Amy Martin, the compulsive beauty snoop, started taking inventory. She had been prowling cosmetics closets ever since she was nine years old and began rifling though her sister Molly's secret makeup drawer in the table next to her bed. The cold cream, that's what does it, she would tell herself as she spread great gobs of the stuff on her pinched little face. And the blue eye shadow, that's it, all over my eyelids, and the blush high on my cheeks, just the way beautiful Molly does it—beautiful Molly who all the boys can't stop looking at.

But what a disappointment Aida's cache was: Johnson & Johnson baby oil, Almay cold cream, Maybelline mascara, Max Factor toilet-water spray, Clairol red hair dye. It was all about as exotic as a Lean Cuisine beef Stroganoff dinner. Not a single jar of Italian cleansing clay in sight. No Swiss placenta droplets to dribble on her throat, no Japanese caviar gels to rub under her eyes. Nothing but drugstore bargains. Amy sighed. Choose your relatives very carefully, right? Back in the hallway, Amy heard Robert's Rolli clicking away.

"That's it, darling. Yes, yes," he chanted. "Beautiful, yes, so beautiful. That's it. That's it."

Amy wandered into the kitchen and sat down at the table. God, it was hot back here. Next week in Montauk, she wasn't going to budge from her umbrella by the sea. Nothing but rest and recreation, Mary Goldfarb's strict orders. Amy lifted an Italian gossip magazine from the table and began to leaf through it, then closed it and fanned herself with it. A wine cooler would be perfect right now. A ginger ale would do.

"You're marvelous, darling," she heard Robert singing in the nondescript European accent he affected for international models he thought could help his career. "Give me just two more minutes, please. Please, darling."

Amy stood, walked to the refrigerator, and opened it. No wine, no ginger ale, just three bottles of Evian, a Perrier, a tomato, and half a dozen plastic deli containers. A model's refrigerator. Obviously, Aida got most of her nourishment from four-star restaurants. Amy was reaching for the Perrier when she noticed a handscripted label on the top of the nearest deli container.

"A.," it read. "Smooth on in the evenings."

Refrigerated night cream. Amy knew other women—most of them models—who also kept their skin creams in the refrigerator. The cold tightened up the pores, they maintained, a theory roundly countered by most dermatologists Amy had interviewed. Amy took out the container and set it on the counter. She pried off the cover. It was filled with a cream the color of tapioca. She lifted it to her nose and sniffed. Barely any fragrance at all. She dipped in one finger, then rubbed it against her thumb. The cream had a lumpy-pudding feel. Amy scooped out a dollop of the stuff and rubbed it against both palms. In symmetrical strokes, she spread it across her forehead, then down her cheeks and under her chin to her throat. Her skin seemed to drink it up. It barely left any film at all.

"So I see you found my little secret."

Amy spun around, her cheeks flushing. Aida was leaning against the kitchen doorjamb with her long legs crossed, a sly grin on her face. Amy lowered her eyes. Caught again, just like the first time when Molly had slipped unannounced into the bedroom and found little Amy smearing on her eye shadow. "You look totally ridiculous," Molly had sneered.

"I feel ridiculous," Amy murmured, offering Aida an embarrassed smile. "I'm afraid I'm a bit of a klepto when it comes to these things. Can't resist trying on other women's makeup. Especially beautiful women's. It's a professional obsession."

"I think it's a charming obsession," Aida said, strolling toward her. "Listen, if you wish to try some, please do. I can certainly spare a jar. Actually, it's my new favorite night cream. It took a week or so for my skin to get used to it, but from then on, it's been marvelous. Very gentle, very nourishing. It's not even on the market yet, but I have a friend in the business who let me have a little—what?—a little preview?"

124

"I really couldn't," Amy said as she fitted the top back onto the container. "I don't think I've ever realized how juvenile and rude this little addiction of mine is. I feel like I've invaded your privacy."

"Don't be silly, Amy, it's a gift. In this awful weather, it's deliciously cool on the skin." Aida lifted the container off the counter. "Of course, you mustn't write about it in your column yet—you know how secretive these cosmetics people are—but when it does come on the market, you'll have a lovely advantage over all the other beauty writers. You're getting two exclusives in one day, eh?"

Amy felt a surge of warm gratitude, not so much for Aida's little gift, but because this was the second time that afternoon that she had responded to one of Amy's neurotic habits with grace and good humor.

"Do you always reward thieves with gifts?" she asked. "Is that some sort of Roman custom?"

Aida laughed. She started to hand the container to Amy, then teasingly pulled her hand back.

"Two promises, my friend," Aida said, her lavender eyes flashing mischievously. "One, you must let me take you to my favorite restaurant next time I'm in New York. And two, please, no more crazy articles about how dangerous it is to have a beautiful face. I don't want my Papa worrying about me."

"Promise," Amy replied.

Out in the hallway, Robert, Mitzi, and Barney were jangling toward them to make their good-byes. Aida thrust the container into Amy's hand.

"Put it in your bag. Quickly, *bella*. It is our secret, yes? All beautiful women must have their beauty secrets."

....

Methylpropanoic acid	287
Butanoic acid	199
Methylbutanoic acid	305
Methylpentanoic acid	484
Propanic acid	356
Acetic acid	462

David pored over the RIA printout that had arrived at Diagnostique that afternoon. These were the results of the retest of the last blood sample Armand had pilfered from La Douce—the blood sample that had been frozen and thawed. After examining the numbers on the first assay the hemolab had done, David had ordered an assay of the reserve sample. These blood concentrations of aliphatic acids were high to be sure, every one of the six precursors of natural alpha copulin well above average, but the numbers didn't begin to compare with the concentrations found in the fresh blood Diltzer had delivered to them.

David pulled open the drawer of his bench and removed the RIAs of that fresh blood. Indeed, methylpropanoic-acid concentrations in the original samples were almost twice 287; in the second, it was even higher. As he started to turn the page,

David's eye flicked on the HLA identification code in the top right-hand corner of the sheet. For a split second, he didn't move, then he suddenly reached again for the RIA printout of the frozen and thawed blood sample and read its HLA code. He repeated the thirty-place numeral and letter combinations out loud to be absolutely sure he'd read them correctly. Then he smiled to himself.

The codes were identical. The blood was from the same test subject. The first—the once-frozen sample—was obviously the baseline, the subject before treatment. The second—the one brimming with the chemistry of sex appeal—was blood from the test subject after treatment—whatever in God's name Sylvia Kronberg's hormone treatment was.

David looked at his watch: 10:40. Armand had sworn to Mitch that he would be here tonight before nine. He'd even called Mitch a second time last night to assure him there wouldn't be any problem this time. He promised to have everything with him tonight: the test-subject names, the dates the blood samples were taken, the works.

"And he told me that bar code isn't what you presumed it was," Mitch had told David. "It's not Kronberg's, not part of her data system. He said we'd never guess in a million years where Dr. K had obtained that blood."

David didn't mind in the least if he'd been mistaken about La Douce's data-coding system, just as long as they were finally going to crack Kronberg's methodology, and he had a feeling that was going to happen at last. It was an exciting feeling, strangely similar to the excitement he'd felt a handful of times before in his life when, working alone in a laboratory, he'd been on the brink of putting together the pieces of a chemical puzzle on his own.

David impulsively rose from his chair and strode toward his laboratory cold room. He peered in through the small round window in the door. Row upon row of amber-colored flasks lined the shelves. All these weeks, Ari had plodded on with his original plan to culture alpha copulin in vitro, but that experiment wasn't any further along than it was half a year ago. For weeks now, David had stopped reviewing Ari's data. Sylvia Kronberg was very clearly so far ahead of them that Ari's research was just makework now, a charade.

A footstep in the hallway behind David. He immediately

turned his head and peered out the laboratory door. It was only Mitch in his sweat suit pacing down the hallway, pumping handweights at his side.

"Hang in there, David," he called over his shoulder, not stopping.

David looked down at his watch: exactly 11:00. Diltzer was now two hours late. David started back to his bench when his phone rang. He took two long steps and picked it up on the second ring.

"Dr. Copeland here," he said automatically.

"Armand there?" A woman's voice. Raspy, tired. Behind it, the faint whine of a siren or of a child crying in a closed room.

"There's nobody here by that name," David answered, choosing his words carefully.

"Come on, Copeland, is Armand there or isn't he? Just tell me."

David hesitated.

"Who am I talking to, please?" he asked.

"Alice Diltzer," the woman said. "Armand's wife. He's supposed to be there, right? So is he or isn't he, Dr. Copeland? Just tell me that, because he hasn't been home since yesterday."

David stared silently out the laboratory window for a moment before he spoke.

"I'm afraid I can't help you," he said flatly. And then he hung up.

It was after midnight when David finally went home. Armand Diltzer hadn't shown.

23

Mirror, mirror.

Amy spread the night cream under her cheekbones and along her jaw as she sat in front of the vanity mirror of the Montauk cottage bedroom she'd rented for the week. Her skin absorbed the cream instantly. It seemed to love this lumpy pudding, luxuriate in the feel of it. But, just like 99 percent of the ballyhooed new cosmetics that came across Amy's desk, this product's look and feel were all that was special about it. It hadn't made a particle of difference in the way Amy's skin looked or felt. If anything, her skin appeared a tad unhealthy these days. One incipient pimple was sprouting under her right eyebrow, another in the corner of her mouth, both of them the consequence of that Twinkie she'd devoured for lunch. Aida's favorite new night cream was no match for a Twinkie.

Mirror, mirror.

Amy worked the cream into the skin under her chin and on her neck. She had pink blotches here from the sun—simply because she'd been too lazy to re-cover herself with sunscreen after taking a swim. The sun was your skin's worst enemy, right? Beauty Rule Number One. Amy dipped her right forefinger into the plastic container and dabbed little dots of the cream along her hairline. While she was reading on the beach this afternoon, she had watched a sleek yacht sail by. On the foredeck, a paunchy middle-aged man in a silly-looking string bikini had stood with his arms around a pair of smiling, bare-breasted young women. When they saw Amy gaping at them, they had all simpered and toasted her with their martini glasses. Party, party. My God, is that the way it had ended for Georgia O'Hearn? Too many martinis on some millionaire asshole's yacht? Giggle, giggle, gasp, groan—the banal death of a party girl?

Amy stroked the night cream under her eyes and out to her temples, then closed her eyes and dabbed it on her lids. Aida had phoned her twice out here, once from Kennedy to fix a dinner date in a few weeks, when she would be back from Paris; then another call eight hours later from de Gaulle to make Amy promise yet again not to tell a soul about the night cream Aida had given her to sample. She'd been worrying about it the whole flight, she confessed to Amy. Her friend who was developing the cream would be devastated if she thought Amy Martin of "Beauty Bytes" had even mentioned the new product to anyone before it was fully perfected and on the market. Typical cosmetics-industry paranoia. Research and development people were forever beseeching Amy to sample the lotions and lipsticks and blushes they were developing, in hopes of getting some expert, consumer-sensitive feedback from her, but when she refused—as she always did on principle—they'd instantly begin begging her to forget everything they'd told her about their product and to swear not to breathe a word about it to anyone in the competition. Amy wondered vaguely what Aida's connection to the manufacturer of the night cream was. She was probably a candidate to be the product's media icon—the Tapioca Pudding Cream Girl.

Amy fitted the top back onto the container and pressed it tight. She turned her head to a three-quarter profile and sucked in her cheeks. This was her best angle. As long as she held her breath, her cheekbones looked high and mysterious, and with her head turned just this way, her eyes almost looked as if they actually were widely spaced, and if she squinted just a bit, her skin looked rather soft and delicate.

Gorgeous, right?

Wrong.

24

....

"Patient's name is Linda D. Fourteen years old, Hispanic, very bright, talented, graceful, attractive. A full scholarship student at the American Ballet School. The mother, who barely speaks a word of English, originally brought Linda to the walk-in on Twenty-third Street, concerned because her daughter hadn't begun menstruating yet and the walk-in referred her to us with a preliminary diagnosis of delayed puberty."

Dr. Lisa Chou paused to smile around St. Mary's cafeteria table at the new recruits—medical students on their first day of endocrinology rotation. Chou was leading a ritual round of "Name That Anomaly," a guessing game of the wildest hormonal disorders the department veterans had ever diagnosed. Traditionally, Ray emceed the quiz as Gil Gland, his hilarious parody of a hyperthyroid game-show host, but today Ray had excused himself as soon as introductory rounds had concluded.

Ray had looked exhausted this morning. He'd barely exchanged a personal word with anyone. Poor bastard undoubtedly had been up all night with Glenda reconstructing those lost case files for Medicaid. As promised, David had extracted a five-day extension for him from Malley. Two of those days were gone already.

"You say the patient was a dancer? Maybe we're looking at

131

marathoner's syndrome here?" Lynne Nyguen asked. Nyguen was clearly going to be the star of this rotation; the third-year student had already committed most of *Essentials of Endocrinology* to memory. "Let's say she dances three, four hours a day. That could put her over a seventy percent VO-2 max. Hyperathletic stress hormones. Overload of ACTH resulting in amenorrhea."

"A perfectly reasonable guess," Dr. Chou said. "But not even close. Do you want to go for the BMW convertible, Doctor? Or are you going to hold with the washer and dryer?"

David glanced at his watch. It was almost one o'clock and Mitch still hadn't returned his call, although Mitch's secretary had promised that he would get back to David by noon at the latest. David was hardly surprised though: The invincible Mitch Papechki was embarrassed. Mitch was finally admitting to himself that he'd been taken for a ride by Armand Diltzer, strung along all these weeks with promises of names and numbers and secret formulas. Armand hadn't shown up Thursday night, either. Hadn't even phoned. It was now abundantly clear that the runny-nosed little man had not come up with any alpha-copulin test-subject data or anything else. He had merely come up with a scheme for taking Diagnostique's money and David's time.

"What was the patient's estradiol concentration?" Hussad, an Iranian medical student, asked.

"You're jumping the gun, Doctor," Lisa Chou said. "Start with the clinical workup."

"Thyroid palpation?"

"Normal."

"Breast development?"

"Very slight. Just within normal range."

Chou looked around the table expectantly. Nyguen, who had squinted her narrow eyes nearly shut, now abruptly rapped her fork against the side of her Coke can.

"Hispanic. You said she was Hispanic, right? Where was Linda D. from? Where were her people from?" Nyguen's voice rose a few decibels with each question she asked.

Chou grinned.

"The Dominican Republic," she said.

"Got it!" Nyguen cried triumphantly, rising from her chair. "Alpha-reductase deficiency. Genetically inbred—there are pockets of it all over the Dominican Republic. She's a pseudohermaphrodite. Linda wasn't getting her period because she was finally developing a penis. Penis-at-twelve syndrome. Linda was a boy!"

"Bingo!" Dr. Chou said. "You win the car and the garage."

David made an effort to join in the laughter going around the table, but all he could muster was a faint smile. Now Dr. Chou was looking at him inquiringly. It was his turn to offer a case for "Name That Anomaly." David automatically cranked up the classic case of second puberty that he'd diagnosed as a resident, the case of a protein-starved POW who got to go through his adolescence all over again in middle age.

"Okay, next case: White, forty-two-year-old male who has been incarcerated for five years in a Vietnamese prison camp returns to the United States with signs of general malnutrition and is referred to the endo unit with complaints of abnormally low libido and loss of facial hair . . ."

David paused. Over Chou's shoulder, he saw a thin woman in a wheelchair enter the cafeteria and start wheeling toward their table.

"Virtually all the patient's body hair had also disappeared," David went on. "And his voice frequently fluttered in the upper registers when—"

David stopped. The woman in the wheelchair had come to a halt right next to him and was staring up at him, the pupils of her coal-black eyes radiating anger.

"You Copeland?" she asked. Her voice was raspy, aggressive—familiar.

David gazed down at her. Dr. Chou and the students watched him silently.

"Yes, I'm Dr. Copeland."

"Well, I'm Alice Diltzer," the woman in the wheelchair said. "Armand's wife. His widow."

David felt the blood drain from his head. Without uttering another word, he stood, put a hand on one of the wheelchair's handles, and, walking alongside it, guided her out of the cafeteria into the hallway. At the far end of the hall, he pushed open a red fire door and held it while the woman wheeled out into the air shaft. Only after the door was closed did he speak.

"What happened to Armand?"

"He's dead. That's what happened, Doctor."

"How did he die?"

"That's what I was going to ask you," the woman replied, raising one hand and spreading the fingers. There was something incongruously refined in the gesture.

"When is the last time you saw your husband, Mrs. Diltzer?"

"He never came home," she answered flatly. "Didn't call. Nothing. So after I brought the kids back from meeting—we're Witnesses—I called over there at La Douce. His real job."

David nodded. The woman had not taken her burning black eyes off of his.

"At La Douce, they told me Armand hadn't been in all day and they sounded pissed. They said Armand hadn't even called in sick or nothing."

"You're talking about Wednesday," David said.

"Yeh, Wednesday. In the afternoon. And he didn't come home for dinner that night, either. No call. Nothing."

"That's the night you called me," David said.

"Yeh, when I still hadn't heard from him after I got the kids in bed," the woman said. "Armand gave me your number over at Diagnostique a few weeks back. He said only to call you if anything weird happened. Like an emergency. I asked him what kind of emergency and Armand didn't say anything. Typical. He was always telling me there was nothing to worry about, but he was scared to death about something or he wouldn't have given me your number. I know Armand. He was scared and he was real excited. He told me he was going to pull one big bonus from your boss out there in Brooklyn. Your Mr. Papechki."

David felt a painful throb working its way up his neck. He pressed his thumb into a pressure point just below his skull for a moment before he spoke again.

"Do you know what kind of work Armand was doing for us, Mrs. Diltzer?" he asked quietly.

"Sure, I know. Not the scientific details, but I know he's been lifting stuff for you, if that's what you mean. We talked about it a lot before he got started. Read some lessons on it before we decided it was the right thing to do as long as we only spent the money from it for the kids."

David reflexively turned away. "For the kids"—a familiar justification.

"How did you find out Armand was dead, Mrs. Diltzer?"

"By looking at his body," the woman answered bluntly. "They

134

showed it to me downtown. In the morgue. They took him there direct from the subway. The doctor down there, Dr. Coviello or something like that, he said Armand had been dead for maybe four or five hours already when the cops brought him in. He'd been riding to Brooklyn and back on the D Train all night long, with everybody just thinking he was stoned. But he was dead."

David again gazed down at the woman. Her face was impassive, cold, even as her eyes blazed. David sucked in his breath and let it out slowly. Armand had never once mentioned that he even had a wife, let alone that she was confined to a wheelchair. The fact was, David didn't know for sure who this woman really was. And even if she was Armand Diltzer's wife, what reason did he have to believe that anything she told him was true? Considering Armand's past performance, it was even quite possible that he and his wife were working some elaborate blackmail scheme.

As if scanning David's thoughts, the woman abruptly reached into the side pocket of the wheelchair and drew out a long manila envelope. She held it up to David. In the upper left-hand corner it read, "Office of the Medical Examiner, City of New York." David took the envelope. He opened it and slid out a long pink piece of paper—a coroner's report. Stapled to the bottom was the coroner's photograph of a recumbent Armand Diltzer. David's eye skipped immediately to the second paragraph on the paper.

CAUSE OF DEATH: Mycardial infarc resulting from drug overdose. Fatal concentrations of cocaine found in blood serum 5–6 hours after cardiac arrest.

"That's a lie!" the woman hissed, jabbing at the paper. "Armand never touched drugs. He hated them, especially after what they did to his brother. Armand wouldn't even take a drink, except once in a while a beer. And since he's been working at the lab, he wouldn't even touch that. One beer only stuffed him up worse."

David slowly slipped the coroner's report back into the manila envelope. Alice Diltzer was telling the truth. For a long moment, he stood motionlessly in the warm still air of the air shaft.

"What . . . what do you suppose actually happened to Armand, Mrs. Diltzer?"

The woman shrugged contemptuously.

135

"Hey, isn't it obvious, Dr. Copeland?" she said, her voice rasping louder. "Armand found whatever it was you told him to go find for you."

She paused, again raising her hand and spreading her fingers. David stared at her.

"So Armand found it and then they caught him," she went on. "And then they killed him."

25

....

"So, what does a looker like you do on a hot Friday night?" the cabby asked, grinning into the rearview mirror.

"Take showers," Amy replied, avoiding the young man's sanguine gaze. "Very cold showers."

"Sounds boring."

"It's an acquired taste," Amy said coolly as she leaned back in her seat. Enough. The young man had been coming on strong since she got into his cab, asking his provocative, high school questions and punctuating them with winks in the mirror. He was attractive in a swarthy, Mediterranean sort of way and Amy felt vaguely flattered by his attention, but enough was enough.

It seemed like half the men in New York were on the prowl these days, not just Latin cabdrivers. Even seersuckered stockbrokers were chatting her up around the salad bar at the Korean grocery. End-of-summer syndrome, Pamela called it. She said that in the early days of September, the human mating instinct went berserk, as if it was two in the morning and the whole world was a bar that was about to close. Biology demanded that you pair off before the first frost.

But Amy liked to think there was more to it than that. In fact, she had decided that Mary Goldfarb was absolutely right: The moment you began feeling good about yourself, there were sud-

denly men everywhere. And, when there were men everywhere, you began feeling even better about yourself. It was altogether a delicious cycle. At moments, Amy was even willing
to believe that her mother's flea-brained fifties advice had
some truth to it: that—*Gawd!*—a smile was ultimately your best
feature.

No, that was going too far!

Amy grinned at her reflection in the cab window as they sped
up Central Park West. She had to admit she was looking pretty
damn good these days. There was obviously some truth in the old
saw that positive thoughts improved your looks. She'd been seriously considering writing an article on that, an analysis of the
effect of the emotions on physical attractiveness from a state-of-
the-art scientific angle. Maybe she could dig up one of those New
Age neurologists over at Rockefeller University who were always
tossing out quotable theories about mind over matter. She'd call
it "Mental Makeover."

Amy pulled her Filofax from her bag, turned to her "New
Articles" section, and jotted down the title idea next to a note
that read, "Think: pimples in Montauk."

For most of her week in Montauk, Amy had endured a horrid
case of acne. Pimples around her mouth, a few more on her chin
and along her hairline. She was certain they were an allergic
reaction to something, either to the sunscreen she'd been using
or the night cream Aida had given her, or, quite possibly, to all
the clams she'd been eating—loads of people were having horrendous allergic reactions to clams this summer. So Amy had
stopped everything: sunscreen, night cream, clams, Twinkies,
the works. But the pimples persisted. What's more, her sun-
drenched hair had grown frizzier than in memory—even her
eyebrows were suddenly terribly bushy-looking. Christ, she had
even sprouted a few wiry hairs on her upper lip. She hadn't been
plagued with those since puberty. It was a nightmare.

"Did anything else distressing happen on your vacation?"
Mary Goldfarb had asked at their first session after Amy returned
to Manhattan with her pimples. "Say, any unnerving run-ins with
men?"

"No run-ins with men of any kind," Amy had replied, reflexively touching her face. "Not much chance of that with me sporting these."

"How about your work? Were you able to leave the office in Manhattan?"

"Totally."

"And no more maudlin thoughts about that young model who lost her life?"

Amy hesitated. "Not many."

"But you're still battling some guilt feelings about her, aren't you?"

"I guess," Amy answered. "A yacht came sailing by one afternoon and my imagination started churning again, wondering about Georgia. It made me realize how little I still knew about how she died."

"And how did you handle those thoughts?"

"Well, instead of just sitting there letting my imagination run wild, I decided to make a couple of calls, and maybe that way put the whole thing to rest. So I phoned Able Franke again—you know, the photographer on Georgia's last shoot—but he was never in and didn't return my calls."

"Who else did you call?" Mary asked.

"Just the San Francisco Police."

"Really? What did you ask them?"

"I wanted to verify that Georgia had actually reported being chased by an armed man and if they'd ever done any follow-up on it. But some imperious sergeant told me they don't give out that kind of information over the phone, especially not to magazine editors."

Mary Goldfarb gazed silently at Amy for a long moment, then abruptly burst out laughing. "Do you honestly wonder where those pimples came from?"

Amy touched her face again. "Come on, Mary, don't tell me you think these are just worry zits."

"Worse, I think they're compulsive anxiety zits. Really, Amy, I thought you'd promised yourself to ease away from your preoccupation with that poor young woman. Instead, you go off on what's supposed to be a restful vacation and manage to work yourself into a frenzy over her. And look what it does to you."

"I can't believe all this is psychosomatic," Amy said.

"Want to bet?" the therapist asked, smiling warmly. "Listen, for one week why don't you completely stop these repetitious thoughts and compulsive phone calls about this young woman

139

and see what happens. Be firm with yourself this time. Distract yourself any way you like. Smile at interesting-looking men in elevators, eat all the clams you want, smear on lotions and creams to your heart's content—but no more guilty thoughts or anxious phone calls. Just try it for one week and see what happens, okay?"

What had happened was that by the end of that week, Amy's pimples were gone. Every damned one of them. And on Sunday morning as she was washing her face, she realized that even the hairs that had spontaneously appeared on her upper lip had just as suddenly vanished. Mind over matter. The undeniable fact was that once she gave all those guilty, obsessive thoughts a week of rest, her whole face cleared up, exactly as Mary had predicted. Bloody amazing, that's what it was.

"Ask Rockefeller docs about specific relationship of anxiety to condition of skin and hair," Amy jotted in her memobook.

It was even more remarkable than that, because once the pimples and stray hairs were gone, Amy actually began looking better than she had in years. All kinds of people said so, not just her therapist. People complimented her on her complexion— that certainly was a first—and several others made comments about her hair—how rich it looked, how thick. Even Francesca Levesque, who had been snubbing Amy ever since Mona Eye Gel prematurely expired, seemed impressed when they ran into each other at an agency cocktail party.

"Well, you're certainly improving with age, darling," Francesca had said, giving Amy a long, appreciative once-over just before a PR photographer snapped their picture. "I guess it was just a question of waiting long enough."

In the backseat of the cab, Amy smiled to herself. She drew a line under the words *Mental Makeover*. Fabulous title.

"Hey, pretty lady!" the cabdriver called. "You want me to take Eighty-fifth or Eighty-seventh? Or how about once through the park?"

"Eighty-seventh is fine, thank you."

They caught a red light at Broadway and Amy decided to get out and walk the rest of the way home. Crossing the street, she could feel the young cabdriver's eyes on her, looking her over from head to toe. She had to fight the impulse to turn and catch the expression on his face, but confident girls never did that, Molly had instructed her long ago; they didn't have to. Amy sailed down Eighty-seventh to West End Avenue, slowing at the bookstore window to catch her reflection.

"Miss Martin?"

A tall, worn but attractive-looking woman in her early forties called out from under the awning of Amy's apartment building. The woman had straight, streaked brown and blond hair and soft blue eyes. She was wearing an acetate apricot-colored blouse with Jordache jeans and espadrilles.

Amy halted. "Pardon me?"

"I'm Sarah Louise O'Hearn," the woman drawled, extending her hand. "The Spanish fellow at the door told us you'd likely be coming home around now, so we waited. We wanted to talk with you in person."

Amy stared uncomprehendingly at the woman for a second, then grasped her hand.

"You must be Georgia's mother."

"I am," the woman said. "I recognized you from your picture in that magazine, Miss Martin. You're doing yourself up differently, I see . . . your hair, I guess it is. Georgia told us you'd been very kind to her."

Amy swallowed hard. "I was terribly sorry to hear about your daughter."

"Thank you, Miss Martin," the woman replied softly. "It was God's will, I suppose."

Amy nodded uncomfortably. Over Mrs. O'Hearn's shoulder, she saw a middle-aged man with short-cropped salt-and-pepper hair coming through the outer glass door of her apartment building toward them. He wore a V-neck sweater that exposed a small triangle of black chest hair. Sarah O'Hearn flicked her eyes toward him and a slight twitch rippled across her lips.

"This is Mr. Louis O'Hearn, Georgia's father," Sarah said, as the man placed a hand on her waist, looping a thumb through a belt hole of her jeans. "Louis, this is Miss Martin."

Louis O'Hearn did not offer his hand.

"We came up with a truck," Sarah O'Hearn went on rapidly. "You know, to take Georgia's belongings back home. They wrote us we'd either have to pay another month's rent or they'd throw everything out. Put it all out in the street like trash, can you imagine?"

"That's awful," Amy said.

"Par for the course, wouldn't you say?" Louis O'Hearn said in a surprisingly adolescent-sounding voice. "That's mainly what people take an interest in up here, isn't it? Real estate? The quick turnover?"

"Not everyone," Amy answered defensively.

"Miss Martin, we wanted to ask for your help," the woman went on urgently. "We thought maybe working on the magazine and all, you'd know how to find out these things."

Amy felt her heart accelerate. From the corner of her eyes, she spotted Manuel gazing through her apartment building's glass front doors at the three of them. If she was going to walk away from these people, she knew she had to do it very soon.

"Find out what things?" she asked automatically, not moving.

"What really happened to our Georgia," Sarah Louise O'Hearn answered, a tremor in her voice. "Seems nobody wants to tell us the whole truth. Not even what happened to my baby's body."

Amy pulled her eyes away from the woman's pained face. Make your excuses and go home right now, she told herself.

"Who won't tell you the truth, Mrs. O'Hearn?" she asked.

"Nobody will. A lawyer told us to write the American Consulate's office down there, but this is all we got." Georgia's mother suddenly sucked in her breath, and in a quick, sinuous movement drew a square of folded paper from her front jeans pocket and presented it to Amy. Amy unfolded it, a letter typewritten on the stationery of the United States Consulate to the French Antilles which began with the United States government's heartfelt condolences and ended with a tangled sentence about how their powers were severely limited and circumscribed on foreign soil.

"Double-talk and bullshit," Louis O'Hearn said. "They all probably got themselves some business deals down there with the Frenchies. Investments to protect."

"Who else did you try?" Amy asked, looking only at Georgia's mother.

"We sent a letter down to the Martinique police—the gendarmes," Mrs. O'Hearn answered. "And they sent us back this three-page form to fill in, all tiny letters and spaces, the whole thing in French. We had to take it to the language teacher up at Rupert High to do it right. That was over three weeks ago and we haven't heard a word from them."

"What about your congressman?" Amy asked. "Have you tried—"

142

"You think some congressman's going to listen to us?" Louis O'Hearn cried suddenly. "Hell he will. Nobody wants to listen to me when I tell them that it wasn't the undertow that killed my little girl."

Amy stepped back from him, her heart pounding. "What did kill Georgia, Mr. O'Hearn?"

"I wish to God I knew," he said. "But it wasn't liquor and it wasn't the undertow, I can tell you that. My Georgia wasn't a party girl, no matter what that Krieger woman says. She wasn't like these New York girls who'll put any damned thing into their bodies. She wouldn't even drink a beer. And Jesus is my witness, she was the best girl swimmer I ever saw. That girl could swim a hundred yards underwater without taking a deep breath. She didn't just dive off the side of that boat and not come up. No way. Not my Georgia."

Amy swallowed hard. "That's how Midge Krieger told you it happened?"

"That's what she said."

Sarah O'Hearn abruptly reached out her hand and grasped Amy's bare arm just above the elbow. There were tears in the woman's eyes.

"Georgia sent us that article you wrote, Miss Martin," she said. "The one about all the awful things that can happen to a girl just because she's a beauty. Georgia'd been so scared, you know, ever since that man chased after her out in San Francisco, so we made her call home every night. She called us that very last night from her hotel room and she told us everything was going just fine. She was just going downstairs for dinner and then she was coming right back up and going to bed early. When Miss Krieger called us the next day, she said Georgia never even slept in her bed that night." A sob broke from Mrs. O'Hearn's throat. "God, if they'd only just find her body so we could give her a decent Christian burial—"

"I told Georgia not to go down there if she was feeling scared," Louis O'Hearn interrupted loudly. "But Georgia said I was over-reacting. She said that's what you told her, Miss Martin, that she was overreacting."

Amy suddenly pulled away from both of them, her face burning.

"I'll see what I can find out for you," she said.

* * *

143

Minutes later in her apartment, Amy again dialed Able Franke's number. It had been over two weeks since she'd sworn off phone calls like this. This time Franke was home.

"I can't talk about Georgia now," the photographer told her.

"Why not, Able?"

"It's not permitted in the program," Able lisped. "No death focusing. I'm doing a mind cleanse—'Peaceful Warrior Training.'"

"Whatever that is," Amy said coldly. "Refusing to share Georgia O'Hearn's last moments with me because you're in any kind of training is going to sound a little ugly to my readers."

A long pause and then Franke sighed loudly into the phone.

"I went through this a dozen times with those gendarmes and then another ten times for Midge," he protested.

"One more time," Amy said.

Franke sighed again and then finally began to recount his story.

He said he had suspended shooting that first day in midafternoon after the sky clouded over. The session had gone well and they still had the next day for fill-ins. Georgia had ridden back with him to the PLM Marina Hotel. They'd both gone up to their adjacent rooms on the second floor to change. Georgia told him that she'd meet him at the pool. When she still hadn't shown up after two hours, he phoned up to her room. No answer. He'd assumed she was napping. Later, when he returned upstairs to change for dinner, he'd rapped on her door. Again, no answer. He asked a hall maid if she'd seen the woman in Room 23–28 leave and the maid said that yes, she'd seen her leave an hour or so before in a T-shirt and miniskirt. Franke figured she'd met somebody and gone out for the night. Models had a knack for meeting men in strange hotels who wanted to take them out to expensive dinners, he said. That was all he knew until the next morning when the gendarmes knocked on his door while he was still meditating and reported that Georgia was dead, drowned in a drunken boating accident off Trois Islets.

"Did you know then that they couldn't find her body?" Amy asked.

"They said they were still looking for it," Franke answered.

"Did they tell you who Georgia was with when she went overboard?"

"No."

"Who reported that she had drowned, Able?"

144

"I don't know exactly. A woman, I think. Foreign. French isn't exactly my forte, you know, and they all talk like their mouths are full of coconuts down there, anyway."

"Was this woman on the boat with Georgia?"

"I really don't know."

"Is the woman still down there? Does she live in Martinique?"

"I honestly don't have the vaguest idea, Amy. Do you think we can end this conversation now? I'm starting to feel a tiny bit fragmented."

"Were they still searching for Georgia's body when you left?"

"I suppose so, but I can't be absolutely sure," the photographer answered wearily. "I flew back to New York early that afternoon and then had to fly out to Madrid the next afternoon. Like, thank God nothing crazy happened in Madrid, right?"

PART

3

26

"Sit down, David, would you? You're giving me acid indigestion hopping around like that."

Mitch Papechki gestured to the chair on the other side of his desk.

"You should be nervous, Mitch," David snapped, perching on the edge of the chair and leaning across the desk. "We all should be feeling damned nervous and guilty. A man is dead because of us . . . because of what we asked him to do for us."

"You really are full of crap, David. You know that, don't you? Completely and utterly full of it." Papechki smacked the top of his desk with his open palm. "Armand Diltzer was a cokehead who just happened to be in our temporary employ at the time he snorted his last line of cocaine. You do know what a cokehead is, don't you, Doctor? I imagine you only get about thirty or forty of them every night on St. Mary's doorstep."

"It wasn't an overdose."

"Is that a second opinion, Doctor? Did you do blood tests of your own?"

"Mitch, I know how Armand's blood tested; that's not the point. I'm just questioning how the drug got into his bloodstream. I'm just questioning—"

David abruptly stopped, feeling like he'd run out of air. Some separate place in his consciousness knew that if he ever allowed himself to acknowledge the enormity of his culpability in Armand's death, he'd be completely paralyzed. What he had convinced himself only two months ago was benign industrial espionage—just routine American corruption—had ended in murder. And he was a part of it.

"I wish to God I could believe it was only an accident," David finished in a half-whisper.

Mitch shook his head, a grim smile spreading across his boyish face.

"Boy! She sure as shit knew how to press all your buttons, didn't she, David? What did it? The wheelchair? The casually scattered references to the Good Book? That creepy thing she does with her hand? Or was it the totality of the widow Diltzer's performance that allowed you to so readily toss out the conclusions of the medical examiner of the City of New York?"

Mitch shook his head back and forth again.

"They should put her on 'Great Performances,'" he said. "First, she works me over for two thousand dollars' worth of 'bereavement' money and then—"

"You gave Alice Diltzer money?"

"Indeed I did," Mitch said, bending forward. "I owed Armand a little under a thousand, and I doubled it just because I felt a genuine stab of compassion for the lady in the wheelchair. She has a baby in diapers, a junkie husband who spent all their money getting high. I don't deny it got to me, too, even if at this point I was finally and painfully aware of the fact that my only relationship to Armand Diltzer had been as his mark, his stooge. He'd been stringing us both along for months. Let's not forget that part, okay? In the midst of our grief, David, let's not forget that Diltzer was the one who was yanking our chain."

David looked numbly back at Mitch.

"I didn't know Alice Diltzer had spoken to you," he said.

"David, she's a professional," Mitch said deliberately. "Look, I wasn't going to tell you this, but after I gave her the two thousand dollars, she looked up at me cold as ice and told me she wanted two thousand more. A real shakedown. I had the distinct feeling that she'd done this kind of thing before. I told her to take her money and get the hell out of here. I'll bet you anything she went straight from here to St. Mary's to work on you . . . before you and I had a chance to talk."

David rubbed his hand across his forehead. Mitch could be right. He'd probably been a little too guiltily eager to accept Alice Diltzer's version of her husband's death.

"But what if she is telling the truth, Mitch?" David asked evenly. "What if it's true that Armand never touched drugs? What if it wasn't an accident?"

Mitch looked earnestly into David's eyes.

"Listen, David, I know you've never been completely comfortable with what we were supposedly trying to accomplish here with Armand," he began in a low voice. "I know it never sat well with you, and now I wish I'd respected that more and never involved you in this. I also know that I'm the kind of man who wants to win so badly that I can step out of bounds sometimes without being aware of it. But let's be very clear on a couple things here, okay? First, nobody ever kills anybody for trying to steal some cosmetics company's new secret formula. There'd be corpses strewn all over the streets of New York if they did. And even that's beside the point, David. The point is, I do know there are boundaries, and if I had the slightest reason to suspect that Armand Diltzer's death was not accidental, I'd go straight to the police and tell them exactly what he'd been doing for us. I know full well what that would end up doing to Diagnostique and my career . . . and to your's too, for that matter. But I haven't lost all perspective. I still know the difference between some new brand of perfume and a man's life."

David nodded as Mitch went on.

"But I wasn't about to humiliate myself or you or anybody else until I had all the facts accounted for. That's why I immediately hired a private investigator, and there's one fact he turned up the first day: Armand Diltzer had been snorting coke ever since he got out of the army." Mitch offered David a tired smile. "And that is why the little asshole had such a runny nose."

27

It had been raining in Martinique since Amy landed that morning, a warm, hard rain that left the air thick and the skin sticky. Amy rolled open the taxi window to let the large drops splash on her face as they drove along the coast road to Trois Islets. Undoubtedly, Mary Goldfarb would call those sharp, stinging drops yet one more example of Amy's self-punishing behavior. But today Amy didn't give a good goddamn what Mary thought of her behavior or even how many stress pimples blossomed on her chin.

Saturday morning, Amy had placed a call to the American Consulate in Martinique, but no one picked up, not even an answering machine. Then, after half a dozen attempts, she finally reached the central office of the Martinique police in the capital, Fort-de-France. A young woman who spoke impeccable English informed Amy that to obtain a copy of a police report, she had to first write a letter to the Prefect of Internal Affairs, requesting Form US–9385. This morning, Sunday, she had phoned Mary Goldfarb from Kennedy Airport and left a message on her machine that she would have to miss Sunday-night group. Unexpected business trip, she told the machine. Amy wasn't about to explain the real reason why she was suddenly flying down to the French Antilles.

"Regardez! La maison Josephine," the taxi driver called over his shoulder. He pointed out his window. *"A gauche."*

He slowed as they bumped by a bright pink clapboard house overgrown with bougainvillea. A handpainted sign explained in French and English that in this humble cottage the future wife of Napolean had been born. He conquered Europe with his sword, the sign said, but Josephine conquered him with her beauty. An epigram on Gallic priorities.

Minutes later, as the taxi rumbled into the port village of Trois Islets, the rain thinned to a drizzle and then stopped altogether. They coasted past a patio restaurant called Poisson d'Or and came to a halt in front of the Hotel de Ville. The driver pointed at an outdoor side stairway, then asked whether Amy wanted him to wait for her. Amy said yes. She stepped out into the sudden bright sun, strode directly to the stairway, and climbed to the entrance of the Trois Islets Bureau des Gendarmes. On the flight down, she had reminded herself of a principle she'd learned in basic journalism: Don't go to the bureau that filed the report; search for the person who wrote it. She pushed through green-louvered, saloonlike swinging doors directly into a high-ceilinged room with a single desk and chair on the far side of a dark-wood counter. A slender, cocoa-colored man in a midnight blue long-sleeved uniform that had obviously been designed for cool Parisian nights smiled up at her.

"A votre service," he said.

"Merci," Amy replied. *"Je suis Americaine et . . ."*

"I speak a bit of English," the man said, rising. He gazed at her with pale sea-colored eyes. "Have you lost something? Your husband perhaps?"

Amy looked back at him. He was all charm, sexy French charm, the mother country's cultural gift to the colonies.

"A friend of mine drowned here about five weeks ago," Amy said evenly. "She was American, too. Georgia O'Hearn."

"I remember, of course," the policeman said. "This was very unfortunate. My sympathies."

"I'd like to see your report on the incident," Amy said.

The man hesitated, his eyes still fastened to hers.

"I'm afraid that is not possible, not just like this," he said, shrugging. "It is a matter of protocol. First, you must write a letter to the Prefect of Internal Affairs in Fort-de-France requesting—"

Amy abruptly turned and walked to the open window by the door. She could feel the officer's eyes following her, watching the bounce of her hair, the swing of her buttocks. She leaned one hip against the wall, her back still to him.

"Is there any way we can skip all that," she said softly. "I'm only here overnight."

For several seconds, neither of them spoke. Then Amy heard the policeman take three steps toward the back wall, followed by the roll and thump of a file drawer opening. She still had not turned back to him.

"I usually go out around this time for a cup of Nescafé," the man said. "I'll be back in four or five minutes, no more."

He was walking around the end of the counter and toward her now. As he came alongside her, his hand lightly touched her waist.

"Please take a seat while you are waiting for me," he said. Then he slid past her and was out the door.

Amy felt her cheeks flush. This is probably how Molly would have done it, she thought—that sudden twirl away from him, the strut, the long pause. Somehow it all seemed to come naturally to her today. She went around the counter to the policeman's desk and looked down. A blue file lay open on top of the blotter.

"O'Hearn, Georgia," it read along the top. *"Morte acciden-tale."*

Amy sat down. The entire report consisted of one typewritten page. Two years of Sarah Lawrence French were adequate to understand it.

At 7:18 P.M. on August 3, a red-haired woman in a wet bathing suit arrived alone at the Trois Islets station and said that a young American woman had drowned. The young woman was identi-fied by the passport and wallet in her bag as Mlle. Georgia O'Hearn, 310 West Seventy-second Street, New York, New York, U.S.A. The red-haired woman stated that she had only met Mlle. O'Hearn that evening when the two of them were the sole pay-ing guests on the calypso boat *Minoque.* She stated that after drinking a great number of glasses of planter's punch, Mlle. O'Hearn insisted on stripping down to her bikini and going snor-keling. They were then about two miles out, just beyond the reef.

Both the red-haired woman, Mme. Yolanda Carvaggio, an Ital-ian national staying at Hotel Flamande Blanc, and Henri Bouq-uard of Trois Islets, *Minoque*'s captain, tried to dissuade Mlle.

O'Hearn, but the young woman maintained that she was an experienced swimmer who could judge for herself when she'd had too much to drink. Grasping M. Bouquard's underwater torchlight in one hand, she had gone over the side wearing mask, snorkel, and flippers. She had been seen only once after that, waving from about fifty meters off the starboard foredeck. Five minutes later, Mme. Carvaggio had jumped into the water to try to locate Mlle. O'Hearn. A half hour later, Captain Bouquard had brought Mme. Carvaggio ashore to report the accident, then sailed back out to the reef to look for Mlle. O'Hearn. Other boats, including a police cruiser called down from Fort-de-France, joined in the search. The search was finally terminated at noon the next day. Only the underwater torch had been recovered, some five hundred meters farther out to sea.

State medical examiner, Albert Treloins; Chief of Police, Frederique Cossain; and Trois Islets officer, Alois Biloix, concurred in declaring the death an accidental drowning, which they attributed to the deceased's inebriation and the perilous Trois Islets undertow. Nonetheless, a magistrate's court in Fort-de-France found Henri Bouquard guilty of reckless endangerment and of operating a pleasure boat without a life raft. He was fined five hundred francs and stripped of his charter license for twelve months.

Amy raised her eyes to the open office window. She could see the lush Hotel de Ville garden and a trio of coconut palms just beyond it. The sea line cut through the center of the window, as in a child's drawing. Sky, sea, land—no jagged lines, nothing complicated. How many natives of Trois Islets felt the need to go to psychotherapy twice a week? Not a thing stirred outside the window, not even a palm frond. Why was it so difficult to believe that the best girl swimmer Louis O'Hearn had ever laid eyes on had gotten giddy on sweetened rum and fruit juice and misjudged her ability to swim against the evening tide?

Amy heard a footstep on the wooden stairs outside the door. She felt her cheeks grow warm, her pulse flutter with anticipation. She rose and faced the door.

"*Que fait-tu ici?*" A large black man in a gendarme uniform pushed through the louvered doors. He glowered over the countertop at her with protruding veined eyes.

"*Excusez, je—*" Amy voice quavered.

"You are looking for someone, Mademoiselle?" the black man

asked in heavily-accented English as he walked around the counter toward her.

"As a matter of fact, I am," Amy answered, forcing herself to glare resolutely back at him. "Two people, actually. An Italian woman by the name of Yolanda Carvaggio and a boat captain by the name of Henri Bouquard."

The policeman's eyes shot to the report that lay open on the desk blotter. He took one long step, grabbed the sheet, and held it behind his back.

"Jean Claude becomes stupid around American women," he said. "You do not belong here, Mademoiselle."

"I'm a reporter," Amy said quickly. "For an American magazine. Would you please tell me where I can find those two people?"

"For that, you must go to the Prefect of—"

"I find it hard to believe that the official police report of an accidental death doesn't include the addresses of the only two people who witnessed it," Amy said. Her heart was skittering in her chest.

"Monsieur Bouquard lives in this *commune* no more," the gendarme said. "He makes his home in Domenica now. He has family there."

"When did he move away?"

The policeman shrugged. "Some weeks ago."

"And the Italian woman, where is she now? What is her home address?"

Again, the large man shrugged.

"What about the *Minoque?*" Amy asked, raising her voice. "Is it still here in Trois Islets?"

The black man's bulging eyes darted from Amy to the window and back again.

"Yes, the *Minoque* is still here," he said, spitting out the words. "Henri's brother-in-law, Gerard, runs it now."

The policeman took another long step toward her and leaned his large moon-shaped face directly in front of Amy's. Amy stepped backward, banging her buttocks against the desk. The policeman reached out his arm and pressed his palm against the wall. A wet, lascivious-looking smile began to spread across his lips. Amy had no space to move. She was cornered.

"This Gerard," Amy cried loudly, aiming her voice at the open window. "Does he take passengers?"

The black man remained motionless for several seconds. His smile vanished and he dropped his arm to his side.

"Of course, Gerard takes passengers," he said. "He is here for your pleasure, Mademoiselle. All of us here in Martinique are here for your pleasure."

28

"Sure, I took your Mr. Papechki's money. He owes it to me. And the good Lord knows he owes it to our children. That money he gave me, plus a whole lot more. You tell me how I'm supposed to feed them."

David stood just inside the door of the Diltzer's two-room Brooklyn apartment. Behind Alice Diltzer, a blotchy-faced boy in Pampers played in a net playpen under a poster-size print of Jesus cradling an injured lamb in His arms. The television set in front of him was on without sound. Both of the toddler's nostrils were dripping; he looked remarkably like his late father.

"I'm sorry, Mrs. Diltzer, but I have nothing to do with your financial arrangements with Mitch Papechki," David said deliberately. "You said on the phone you had something to show me."

Alice Diltzer stared silently up at David, then abruptly wheeled her chair backward to the playpen, leaned over the side, and wiped her little boy's nose with the back of her hand.

"You still think Armand OD'd, don't you?" she said in a flat voice.

"I think there's a good chance you didn't know everything about your husband," David replied softly.

"I'm sure I knew a whole lot more about him than your wife knows about you," Alice Diltzer said, wheeling back to him. "Or did you tell your wife the kind of work you were doing with Armand?"

David put his hand in his jacket pocket and felt around for his car keys.

"Listen, Mrs. Diltzer, you said on the phone that you found something in Armand's clothing . . . in the clothes they gave you at the morgue. Something you thought I should see."

"That's right. I found it in Armand's shoe, wadded up under his arch support."

"Would you show it to me now, please?"

Mrs. Diltzer reached into the side pocket of her wheelchair and drew out a white square of folded paper. She clutched it against her thin chest.

"What if this is just what you sent Armand looking for?" she said, her voice rasping. "What if this is Dr. Kronberg's big secret?"

"I'm not working on that project any longer," David said evenly.

"Aren't you? Isn't that what you drove all the way out to Flatbush for, Dr. Copeland?"

"No, it's not," David answered.

The widow glared up at David with her fiery black eyes. He could feel her contempt pour onto him. Undoubtedly, she knew how desperately he wanted to keep believing that her husband was only a cokehead who'd overdosed himself.

"I'm almost through that two thousand dollars your Mr. Papechki gave me," Alice Diltzer said, the square of paper still pressed to her chest. "Half of it went just to bury him."

David hesitated only a second, then reached inside his jacket. He had come prepared. He took out a bank envelope and counted out ten one-hundred-dollar bills. Without a word, the Diltzer woman thrust the square of paper into David's hands and took the money. David unfolded the paper.

Scribbled in the upper right-hand corner in pencil was: "23 pts. serum / logged La Douce 7.17"

And below that, the notation: "Lex to 68 St. Enter 67."

David felt his pulse become rapid. Apparently, Armand had been following some kind of lead to the source of those blood samples. He hadn't been bullshitting about that much. David turned over the piece of paper.

This was it.

Xeroxed at the center of the sheet was a black and white bar code. David brought it close to his eyes. He could see the rip line through the bar code's center where Armand had painstakingly pasted the two halves of the original label back together. He'd found exactly what David had asked him to find. And then, God help him, just as Alice Diltzer had said, Armand had gotten caught with it; but they hadn't found the photocopy he'd hidden in his shoe.

David's neck throbbed.

"What else did Armand have on him when he died?" he asked.

"Nothing worth mentioning. Just the clothes on his back."

"When did you bury him?"

"Tuesday last week."

"Did they give you a police inventory with the bag of his belongings?"

"Yes." The Diltzer woman wheeled around and removed a small orange plastic bin labeled DO IT NOW off the top of the soundless television set. She pulled an envelope from the bin, returned to David, and handed it to him.

David scanned the short computer-generated list of Armand Diltzer's last worldly goods: shirt, pants, belt, socks, shoes, five dollars and change, two subway tokens, a Slim Jim, and a bottle of Afrin nasal spray.

"Did you keep the nose spray, Mrs. Diltzer?"

The woman shrugged.

"His Afrin bottle? Did you keep it?"

"It wasn't in the bag."

"Are you sure?"

"Yes, I'm sure. They must have thrown it out. I had no use for it, anyhow."

The boy in the playpen had pulled himself up onto his feet and now, clinging to the netting, began to softly sing a familiar cereal commercial.

"May I have another look at Armand's death certificate?" David asked.

Alice Diltzer reached again into the side pocket of her wheelchair and withdrew the long manila envelope from the medical examiner. She started to hand it to David, then pulled it back onto her lap.

"I'm not giving away any more money today, Mrs. Diltzer,"

David said softly. "I only want to look at it. I'm not going anywhere with it."

A quick grimace, like a flinch, crossed Alice Diltzer's face and then she shoved the envelope at David. He studied the death certificate silently for several minutes before giving it back and turning toward the door.

"I'll be in touch with you, Mrs. Diltzer," he said.

"God is my witness," the widow Diltzer said as he let himself out the door, "I only use the money for the children."

David had counted off twenty-two stoplights coming south on Flatbush Avenue to find his way to the Diltzer residence. Now, going back, he made it through five green lights before having to stop for a red. While he waited, he slipped his hand into his coat pocket and fingered the folded piece of paper Alice Diltzer had given him—rather, the paper she had sold to him for one thousand dollars.

He shifted his MG back into first and, resting his foot on the clutch, raced the motor as he watched for the cross-street light to turn amber. He'd take the Manhattan Bridge back into town and cut straight across to Chambers. He could be at the office of the Medical Examiner of New York City by three o'clock if the traffic remained this sparse. On his left, a cab inched into the intersection just before the light changed. David popped his clutch and as he shot past the cab, he glanced into his side mirror. A bottle-green Audi driven by a peroxide blonde wearing owllike sunglasses slid up alongside the cab behind him. The car seemed familiar—the bottle-green color was striking. He vaguely remembered noticing it when he turned onto the avenue.

As David sailed through the next five lights, he glanced several times into his rearview mirror and saw the Audi still behind him. The sixth light had just turned amber and David gunned from a third of the block away and sped through the intersection as it turned red. He braked to a quick halt at the next light. Reflexively, he looked into his rearview mirror. The Audi was gone. David sighed. His guilt about Diltzer had him on edge, imagining things. He inserted a Charlie Mingus cassette into his tape deck and punched it on—"Blue Mingus." Again, he slipped the MG into first, raced the motor, checked his side mirror. And that is when he saw that the Audi was right next to him. David felt his face grow hot as he raised his eyes to the driver. The peroxide blonde was turned toward him and now she hiked her sunglasses up on her head. Except for the cheap-looking hair, she was a remarkably attractive woman—fine alabaster complexion, aquiline nose, wide, generous mouth. Suddenly, she raised a small black object in front of her eyes. Instinctively, David ducked his head, his heart knocking in his chest. Just as he ducked, he saw the woman's finger flick, and in that instant he recognized the object in her hand—a Minox camera. She had just taken his picture.

David sat up straight, yanked his foot off the clutch. His car lurched straight ahead. He was halfway into the intersection when he hit the brake, twisted the wheel to the right, and turned onto the side street. For a good fifteen seconds, he sped down the left lane, heading directly toward an oncoming cab. He blared his horn. To his right, a van slowed. David twisted into the opening back into the right lane. He immediately shot his eyes to the rearview mirror. Gone. The Audi was gone. David swiped the back of his hand across his forehead. His whole face was sopped with sweat and he could not keep it dry for the rest of the trip back into Manhattan.

"Dr. Coviello? There's a Dr. David Copeland out here for you."

The receptionist continued to leaf through a travel magazine as she spoke into the speaker phone on the corner of her desk.

"What does he want?" a voice came back with the familiar blunt cadences of a Queens native.

It had been surprisingly easy to locate deputy assistant coroner Vincent Coviello; according to the medical examiner's office, his daily schedule did not often vary from these precincts. Before taking the elevator up to Coviello's province on the eighteenth floor, David had called into St. Mary's and told Sister Berzins where he was and to pass the word that he'd probably be late for rounds.

"Tell Dr. Coviello I'm the personal physician of Armand Diltzer," David said, aiming his words directly into the speaker phone. "Dr. Coviello signed Mr. Diltzer's death certificate ten days ago."

"Gladys will be happy to make an appointment for you," Coviello's voice came back.

"Could you give me five minutes right now, Dr. Coviello," David said. "I'm in the neighborhood."

"I'm smack-dab in the middle of a gluteal necropsy, doctor," Coviello replied, a trace of something like glee in his voice.

"I think I can handle it," David answered, trying to sound amused.

For several seconds, there was no reply. The secretary absently raised her hand to the speaker phone, apparently about to disconnect, when Coviello's voice issued from it again.

"P.M. Six A, second door on your left," he said. "Masks and suits are in the big box by the door."

The secretary gestured with her head toward the opaque-windowed swinging doors behind her. David walked to them, pushed through, turned to his left. Ten steps and he was in front of Post Mortem 6 A. He leaned over the cardboard box by the door, pulled out an apron—no sense in suiting up completely for this little conversation—and put it on, then tore open a surgical mask and taped it on. He rapped once on the door and opened it.

Two figures covered completely in green two-piece operating smocks, paper shoe slips, plastic gloves, masks, and surgery skullcaps stood on either side of a long, slightly sloping steel table that extended straight out from the wall opposite the door. Lying on the table, facedown, was a woman's body that weighed easily 250 pounds. The corpulent corpse flattened on the table like a snail to a rock. The head was turned to the side at an odd angle that suggested broken cervical vertebrae, but the two figures in surgical costumes hovered over the corpse's midsection, specifically over her mountainous buttocks—the gluteal tissue of the deputy assistant coroner's little witticism. One figure held tweezers in his hands. He glanced at David through aviator glasses.

"Is that with a C or a K, Dr. Copeland?" he asked in the same Queens-accented voice David had heard on the speaker phone outside.

"C," David answered through his mask.

He took a long step closer to Coviello. A trickle of blood slid down gutters on either side of the table, draining into twin polyurathane bags at the foot. A microphone hung by a cord over the table's center. Leaning over one gelatinous buttock, Coviello darted down his tweezers and plucked out a shiny sliver. He held it up to the light.

"Glass shard number forty-six, left buttock, lower-left quadrant. Two centimeters, plus or minus. Dry. No apparent hemo stains. F bag."

Coviello deposited the shard in a polyurathane bag attached to a hoop on the side of the table, then looked up again at David. It was impossible to read the man's expression behind his mask.

"Party girl," he said. "Died with her ass in the glass. A tray of champagne glasses. Crash landing."

Coviello's associate laughed appreciatively. The high-key laugh was the only clue that the associate was a woman.

"What did you say was the name of your patient?" Coviello asked.

"Diltzer," David answered. He pulled open his mask and let it hang from the side of his face. "Armand Diltzer. You performed the autopsy on the twelfth. Mycardial infarc attributed to overdose of cocaine."

"Sounds familiar." Coviello hunched over the buttock again. "So?"

"I was wondering if you took any scrapings of Mr. Diltzer's nasal membranes," David asked.

Coviello's tweezers darted down again.

"Shard number forty-seven. Left buttock, lower-left quadrant. Half a centimeter, if. Dry, no hemo stains. F bag."

Coviello did not look up.

"If I had taken a scraping, it would have been listed on the certificate, Doctor," he said.

"Apparently you didn't, then," David said in as neutral as voice as possible. He took another step toward Coviello. "What can you tell me about the bottle of nasal spray that was found on the patient?"

"I don't recall any nose spray," Coviello answered.

"It was an Afrin bottle," David went on. "Mr. Diltzer was addicted to monohydrochloride. Membrane rebound. A scraping probably would have shown that. It also would have shown whether or not he was a habitual cocaine user."

Coviello abruptly plopped his tweezers into the hollow of the corpse's back and ripped away his surgical mask, revealing a thick walrus mustache and a condescending smile.

"What are you, Copeland? An insurance dick?" Coviello asked, turning toward him. "Breaking a big money case with your incredible discovery that cokeheads stay happy on the job by sneaking the white stuff into their nose-spray bottles? Going to sue Afrin? Do you have any idea how many cases we see of that in one week down here?"

"I assume that if you found a spray bottle on an overdose victim, you'd have it analyzed then," David said.

"Only on special request. Say the DA's office, to pick a random example. Otherwise, if we already have a positive blood test, it isn't worth the trouble or the expense. I only do piecework on order." Dr. Coviello gestured at the corpse in front of him. "This one's father is a police sergeant. He's convinced somebody must have pushed her. He's also convinced she weighs a hundred and twenty-five pounds."

Coviello's appreciative assistant laughed again.

"Where do you suppose I could find that Afrin bottle?" David asked.

Coviello shrugged.

"It wasn't returned with the patient's belongings," David went on. "And I assume it wasn't disposed of."

Coviello turned sharply, his hip knocking against the autopsy table.

"Why don't you assume yourself right out of here, Copeland?" he barked. "You aren't happy with my report? Fine. Go ask for another one. No trouble at all. Ask your lawyer what a piece of cake that is. Or are you a lawyer, Copeland? You sure as hell don't sound like somebody's GP. All you have to do is take a few dozen depositions, petition the court, and then try and find a judge who'll give you the time of day. Twenty thousand dollars later, you might even get them to disinter this fellow Diltzer's body and then you can scrape hell out of whatever's left of his nasal membranes."

David had not withdrawn an inch while Coviello roared at him, and the moment the man stopped, he heard a soft, rhythmic, plopping sound between them. Both men looked down. The blood gutter of the autopsy table had shaken loose from the lip of the collection bag and drops of blood were dribbling onto the bottoms of David's pants and shoe tops. David stepped back. Coviello smiled.

"What are you, Copeland?" Coviello asked. "A friend of the deceased? A business associate? Have you got some personal reason to think this man didn't die of an OD? Some privileged collateral evidence you want to tell the judge about?"

David didn't answer. He suddenly turned and strode out the door. He pulled off the apron and swiped at the blood on his shoes but only managed to smear it. He dropped the apron and mask into the bin at the end of the hallway, then pushed through the door into the reception area. As he stepped into the elevator, a pretty young black woman in a green operating smock eyed his shoes.

"Lestoil," she said to David, smiling. "It's the only way to get it out of leather. Everything else leaves a stain."

David nodded numbly. His head was spinning. Coviello had certainly asked the right question: Was David ready to explain to some judge why he suspected that Armand Diltzer's death wasn't necessarily the result of a self-administered overdose? Was he prepared to ask Mitch Papechki to make a deposition about the nature of the work Armand was doing for Diagnostique?

The elevator bounced to a stop at the second basement and the doors slid open. David stepped out alone into the narrow corridor and pulled the heavy metal door that opened onto the parking garage. He looked at his watch. He felt a pang of urgent longing to be at St. Mary's, to spend an hour or two on the ward before he had to go home by himself and think about what to do next about Armand Diltzer. It was not even five o'clock. He could make evening rounds in plenty of time if uptown traffic wasn't too thick. David turned to his right. He could see the rear of his MG from here. Then he saw a man in a tan windbreaker standing next to it, his foot on the MG's rear bumper. When the man saw David, he removed his foot and started toward him.

"David Copeland?" the man called.

David stopped, his heart racing.

"Dr. David A-for-Aaron Copeland?"

The man was pacing quickly toward David now, one hand in his pocket, the other extended in front of him, his palm open wide. He was a few years older than David, an inch or two taller, and barrel-chested. He was wearing jogging shoes.

"The Sister told us we might find you here, Doctor," the man said.

David stared at the man only a moment longer, then spun around and started sprinting toward the door.

"Stop, Copeland! Stop right now!"

David kept running, one hand forward, ready to grasp the door handle. He could hear the heavy thudding footsteps of the

big man behind him. He grabbed the door handle, pulled. Nobody in the corridor, the elevator gone. A door marked EXIT on
his right. David yanked it open just as the big man came in
behind him through the other door.

"Stop, you fucker!" the man yelled. He was less than ten feet
away.

David started up the stairs three at a time. He made it to the
first landing in four giant steps. As he swung around the turn,
he saw the big man coming after him. His face was flushed and
dripping wet. David was almost a full flight ahead of him. One
more flight and he'd reach the door to the lobby. There'd be
other people there, a good chance there'd even be a policeman
in this building's lobby. Four more giant steps and David
grabbed the door handle, turned it, pulled. He stepped into the
lobby. It was full of people. David plunged into the crowd.
Home free.

"Stop that man, Officer!" The voice of the big man was suddenly shouting behind him.

A policeman appeared in front of David. He closed his hand
around David's arm.

"Okay, hold it right there," the policeman said.

People stopped on either side of them. One of them was pointing at David's shoes—at the caked blood on David's shoe tops.
The big man in the windbreaker was lumbering up to them,
breathing heavily. David felt dizzy.

"Officer, this man—" David began, then stopped. The man in
the windbreaker was holding a badge in front of the policeman's
face.

"Federal prosecutor's office," the man sputtered. He turned to
David. "Are you David Aaron Copeland, Chief of Endocrinology,
St. Mary's Hospital?"

David swallowed hard.

"I am. What the hell is this about?"

The big man reached inside his windbreaker and pulled out a
sheaf of paper folded lengthwise. He stuffed the papers in
David's hand.

"Federal warrant," the man said, no longer panting. "Department of Medicaid Fraud Control. You have twenty-four hours to
produce the case files of Dr. Raymond T. Kenworthy listed on
this document or you will be placed in custody. Kenworthy is
being served separately—if we can find him."

167

The policeman released his hold on David's arm. He looked at the man in the windbreaker questioningly.

"These docs don't make enough money," the big man said, shaking his head at the policeman as David started to turn away. "They have to bilk Medicaid to pay for their sports cars."

29

....

"Try the week of August third then," Amy said to the clerk at the Hotel Flamande Blanc's registration desk. *"Je vous en prie."*

The clerk, a willowy, dark-skinned young woman with a gold cross hanging from a chain around her neck, turned her eyes languorously toward the wall clock, slowly withdrew a Gauloise *filtre* from its blue package, lit it, inhaled deeply, and exhaled through her flaring nostrils before turning another page of the loose-leaf room register on the desk in front of her. Her eyes skimmed down the page.

"Non," she said at last, not looking up. "No Carvaggio."

Amy drilled her fingers on the counter.

"Maybe she checked in the week before that," she said. "The last week in July, whatever that was."

Another slender young black woman appeared alongside Amy, passed under the hinged section of the counter, then perched on the corner of the registration desk. The two young women immediately began chattering in the impenetrable island patois, the registration clerk suddenly so prettily animated that the contrast with the dull listless face she had offered Amy was almost comic.

While she waited for the young women to finish their conversation, Amy surveyed the open-air lobby of the small beachfront hotel. A heavy-breasted woman sat half-asleep behind a table under a Hertz car-rental sign. Amy had just learned that the Flamande only had twenty guest rooms; she wondered vaguely what the Hertz people could possibly pay someone to sit here all day in off-season. She turned and peered through the opaque glass windscreen at the beach end of the lobby. A dozen or so white sunbathers were lying on lounge chairs catching the last intense late-afternoon rays.

"We did not register anyone all summer by the name of Car-vaggio," a woman's voice said from behind the counter.

Amy turned back to the registration desk. The young woman perched on the corner of the desk was addressing Amy in crisp, lightly accented English.

"How can you be sure of that?"

"I would remember that name," the young woman replied with a somewhat patronizing smile. "It is the name of an Italian painter, no? Baroque, eh?"

"Yes, I believe it is," Amy answered, nodding her head in acknowledgment of the young hotel clerk's surprising erudition. "But the police have record of someone by that name who was registered here in August."

"Perhaps they are mistaken," the young woman said flatly, slipping off the corner of the desk onto her feet.

"I read the report myself," Amy said.

The woman shrugged.

"Perhaps it was the Hotel Flamande on St. Barts," she said. "It is not an uncommon confusion. We often get mail for guests in that hotel. I am sorry we could not help you."

With that, the young woman turned brusquely back to her colleague and again began speaking in patois. Amy remained standing at the counter for several seconds, then turned and started back toward the entrance. Her cabdriver had been doz-ing in his taxi in front of the Trois Islets Hotel de Ville when she exited the police department. This time, he stood waiting for her beside one of the bright, showy hibiscus bushes that lined the Hotel Flamande Blanc driveway. She started to raise her hand to get his attention when she saw he was talking to another man, who was partially obscured by the tropical bush. This man had a large round head and was wearing the familiar midnight blue uniform of the gendarmerie.

Amy yanked down her hand and took a long backward step through the entrance, her eyes remaining fastened on the policeman. He was smoking and now, as he flicked the ash off his cigarette into the gravel driveway, he turned his face slightly toward her. All Amy needed to see was one bulging eye in profile to recognize him. It was the policeman from Trois Islets and he was clearly following her. Amy's skin prickled. She sucked in her breath, spun around, and strode through the lobby onto the beach.

The sunbathers were almost all women ranging from teen to middle age, every one of them bare-breasted. Ah, the French. First, they convert the black population to Christian modesty, then they abandon it themselves for the sake of darkening their own skin. The pursuit of beauty was license for any contradiction—that was the gospel according to Coco Chanel. Amy's sandals started to sink into the sand. Bending her legs one at a time, she removed them, looped the straps together, and let them dangle from her hand. She started scanning the beach for the best way to get back to the bay road without being detected by the policeman when she noticed that a slickly handsome young man in his early twenties had twisted around in his chaise longue and was gazing avidly at her, his dark lusty eyes slowly tracing down her body. Incredible! Here the boy was on a beach full of bare-breasted women and he was mentally undressing *her!*

Amy laughed and wheeled away from the young man's gaze. She paced quickly down to the water and turned left toward the lowering sun. She hiked up her skirt and held it above her knees. After about twenty paces, she glanced up toward the hotel. From here, she could see around the corner of the hotel to the front driveway, could just make out the two taxis sitting in front. One of them was the taxi that was waiting for her. The warm clear water lapped over the tops of Amy's feet. She smiled. For some remarkable and wholly inappropriate reason, she felt quite marvelous.

Fifteen minutes later, wedged between a little girl with an elaborate maze of corn-rowed hair and a large woman with a chicken in her lap, Amy was riding in a bus named *Son Gout* back to the port of Trois Islets.

30

David carefully cut around the perimeter of the bar-code label that Armand Diltzer had pieced together and photocopied. Then David turned it over and stroked it with Elmer's glue, blew on it a few times, and applied the facsimile label to a 50-cc Plexiglas blood vial. He was holding it up to the light, slowly turning it back and forth, when there was a sharp rap on his office door.

"David?" It was Art Malley.

David held his breath, didn't move. He'd come up to the ward via the east stairway so he wouldn't be seen and as soon as he'd entered his office, he'd locked his door. Art Malley was just one of several people he didn't want to have to deal with at this point. He stared at the door handle as Malley turned it.

"You in there, David?"

David said nothing. The handle rotated back. Silence. David gently inserted the vial into his side coat pocket, stood, walked to the door, and listened. Malley was gone. David paced back to his desk and punched the redial button on his phone—Ray Kenworthy's number at his home in Montclair. It was the fourth time David had tried the number since he'd returned to St. Mary's that afternoon with the federal warrant in his pocket. Again, three rings and the Kenworthy answering machine clicked on with the recorded sassy voice of Ray's youngest daughter, Mahalia: "If I had known *you* were going to call, I'd have stayed at home, but—"

David hung up. Where the hell was Ray? On a plane to the Bahamas? His story about Glenda's computer glitch was obviously pure bullshit. The five days' grace David had pulled for him had come and gone and now here was this goddamned warrant for records of eighteen of Ray's outpatients. It was so clearly a scam, not some trivial computer error, and David was finally facing the fact that he'd been suckered into covering for Ray without having any idea what Ray was really up to. David could feel his stomach clench as he remembered his soulful-eyed friend assuring him that he could never bring any shame on St. Mary's Hospital.

But what the hell kind of scam was Ray up to?

The moment David had arrived at the hospital, he'd let himself into Ray's office and searched through his file cabinets for the names listed on the warrant. Not one of the names was there, of course. Ray had undoubtedly removed them weeks ago—that is, if those patients had ever existed in the first place. Obviously, their medical records did not appear in the hospital's central computer bank either, but there was one file from which the eighteen names had not and could not have been deleted: the central billing file. Every one of the names was there, from Armstrong, Carl to X, Abdul; and for each one of them, Medicaid had been charged an average of twenty thousand dollars for medications purchased from the Gentech Corporation. Ray had not even taken the trouble to vary the putative medications provider for his little fraud. Any Medicaid auditor with half a brain would have questioned $332,000 worth of medications from a company whose basic product was synthetic growth hormone, the biogenetically generated replacement hormone that promoted normal growth in pituitary dwarfs. Any auditor would know that a hospital St. Mary's size would annually treat five or six cases at the most of that rare hormone disorder.

Or was Ray's scam even more blatant and naïve than David at first suspected? Could Ray actually have been purchasing synthetic GH through Medicaid and then selling it on the black market? Ever since Gentech had discovered how to synthesize growth hormone—thus forever replacing the old method of harvesting pituitaries from corpses and milking the hormone drop by drop from the dead organs—mass-produced GH had become second only to anabolic steroids as the best-selling black-market hormone. It was especially popular among Yuppie parents who were happy to shell out twenty grand a year for three or four years to ensure that their young sons would have a significant height advantage on the playing fields of Andover and Yale and eventually, they fervently hoped, in the power corridors of New York and Washington, where, as a rule, only men over six feet tall made it to the chairmanship or, for that matter, to the presidency.

But why would Ray take a risk like that? Did he need money that desperately? He had occasionally complained to David about the cost of keeping four daughters in private school, but if Ray needed money that badly, he could easily make an additional hundred thousand dollars in part-time private practice instead of spending every minute of his extra time in free clinics and boys clubs. Goddamn him! Ray had been the one true moral heart David could depend on at St. Mary's; that's what hurt the most about this. Rising slowly from his chair, David started for the door. Christ, who was he to judge Ray Kenworthy? Ray didn't have the blood of a murder on his hands.

David unlocked his office door and opened it, peered out to the hallway, then strode quickly to the stairwell. He walked all five flights down to the second floor with his right hand cupped protectively over the empty vial in his coat pocket. At the blood-lab door, he knocked once and entered.

"Dr. Hunk, what a surprise. Something I can do for you, hon?" Imelda, the chief blood technician, winked at David from her stool in front of the component separator. She was a shapely Cuban in her early forties who always left her lab coat unbuttoned over tight-fitting sweaters.

"Yes, please," David said, gingerly withdrawing the vial from his pocket. "I wondered if you could run this through the ABO/RH scanner for me."

The technician took the empty vial from his hand, then cocked her head to one side.

"Is this some kind of joke? There's nothing in here, Doctor."

"I know. I just need to identify the label . . . where it comes from. I'm fairly sure it's from one of the major labs in town. You're programmed for all of them, aren't you?"

The technician nodded.

"What's the problem?" she said. "Sloppy lab work? Somebody lose a blood sample on you?"

"Something like that."

The technician slipped off her stool and brushed by David to a large olive-colored steel console in front of the window. She rotated a red handle, then set the vial in a slot on a metal conveyor at about shoulder's height. She sat in front of the console and quickly hammered a message into the keyboard. She paused a few seconds, then drilled in another instruction. The machine suddenly came to life with a low whirring sound and then, like a windup toy soldier, the empty vial marched into the scanner. Instantly, the printer on the technician's left spat out a line of letters and numbers. Imelda leaned forward to read them. She turned to David.

"Greater New York Blood Program," she said.

"What?"

"You know, the central blood-collection center. The label's off one of their blood bags. Somebody's donation."

David shook his head incredulously. Had Armand Diltzer been murdered for this? Because he had discovered that the serum samples suffused with the precursors of alpha copulin came from a few women's generous contributions to the Greater New York blood drive? That was it?

"Are you absolutely sure, Imelda?"

"This machine doesn't lie," the technician said as she tore off the printout and handed it to David. "It's inhuman."

David took the stairway down to the first floor and exited through the emergency entrance to the street. He'd decided to leave his car in the hospital garage; he felt safer on foot. It was too late to go uptown to the Greater New York Blood Program today. All he wanted now was to go home, lock himself inside his apartment with a bottle of vodka, and try to figure out why the world was crumbling around him.

He was crossing Tenth Street in the middle of the block when the first boy registered in the corner of his eye. The youngster had appeared from behind a small van double-parked near St. Mary's front entrance and there was something vaguely familiar about his purple and black satin athletic jacket. David had just stepped up onto the curb when he saw a second boy in the same purple and black jacket dribbling a basketball along the sidewalk toward him. The boy was twelve or thirteen, black, and unusually tall.

"That's our man!" A voice across the street.

David turned his head. Five more black boys in identical jackets were crossing the street toward him. Now David could see the insignia and name enbroidered on the back of one of the jackets: HARLEM GIANTS, JUNIOR LEAGUE BASKETBALL. The boy with the ball threw a bounce pass to one of his friends in the street, then moved toward David with his hands raised like a guard on defense. Up close, the boy had a surprisingly youthful face with smooth cheeks and the faint beginnings of a few wiry hairs along his upper lip.

"Just let him give us the shots and we'll leave you be, man," the boy said.

"What shots?" David took a long step to one side, but the boy stayed with him. He was at least David's height.

"Don't act like you don't know what I'm talking about, Doc," the boy said. "Dr. Ray's our main man. Keep the Feds off his ass. We missed one week already."

Two of the other boys had circled behind David, passing the basketball back and forth. David could feel the ball breeze past the back of his head.

"You're patients of Dr. Kenworthy?"

"We're his *team,* man," another boy said, his voice high, preadolescent. "We're the Junior Giants."

"Dr. Ray's shots gonna send me to college," said the boy directly in front of David. "Six-six and I'm over the top. Goin' get myself an ath-el-letic scholarship."

"You keep those Feds off Dr. Ray's ass," the boy behind David hissed. "You do it, man, or somebody's gonna to cut you real bad!"

David turned his head, saw the boy dig his hand into his jacket pocket, and in that instant, David finally put together what was going on here. Ray Kenworthy wasn't an embezzler, he was a philanthropist. He wasn't selling growth hormone to Yuppies on the black market; he was giving it away to these Harlem black boys, boys who showed natural potential for posting up, for slam dunks and Alley Oops, the Michael Jordans of the future, who had everything but a guarantee of the necessary height to get a basketball scholarship to college. A couple of years of weekly GH injections and they'd be assured the extra five or six inches they

176

needed. Ray had turned Medicaid into his personal extra-inches scholarship fund. It was fraud, big time. Ray had to know he was in serious trouble. Even if he turned himself in tomorrow, St. Mary's would still be out the more than three hundred thousand dollars Ray had injected into the Junior Giants.

"Listen, I don't have any control over federal agents," David said, trying to keep his voice cool, reasonable. "I work with Ray. Fact is, I'm in this jam with him."

"Fuck you are!" barked the boy behind David. "I saw you in the hallway last week. I heard you pushing Ray."

The boy suddenly yanked his hand from his pocket and David glimpsed a flash of silver in the corner of his eye. He turned, stared: It was a switchblade. David suddenly feinted to his left, then darted to his right, charging around the boy in front of him.

"Don't look back, asshole!" one of the boys yelled. " 'Cause we're gonna stay on your ass wherever you go 'til Ray's in the clear."

A split second later, the basketball whacked against David's side. The blood vial in his pocket instantly shattered and as David sprinted on, a shard stabbed through the lining of his pocket, through his shirt, and cut into his skin.

31

....

"I am sorry, Mademoiselle, I wish I *had* been on board the *Minoque* that night," Gerard Bouquard said, glancing up at Amy from his perch on a dock post where he sat mending a fishing net. "Perhaps if I had been . . ."

Gerard's voice trailed off in a Gallic shrug as he lowered his eyes over the fishing net again. The current proprietor of the calypso boat *Minoque* was a native Martinique white of indeterminate age—fifty at the very least. He was a tiny man with a bony, jug-eared head that was probably the result of a dozen generations of island inbreeding. His florid face, wizened from sun and rum, looked like a sun-dried tomato.

"Did your brother-in-law keep a log of his passengers?" Amy asked. She had to squint to look at Gerard against the setting sun.

"Henri?" Again, the little man shrugged, this time adding a crooked smile. "Henri cannot write, and if he could . . . well, he would get it wrong anyhow."

"Did he tell you anything about the other woman who was on his boat that night? An Italian woman. Yolanda Carvaggio. She's the one who reported the accident to the police."

For several seconds, the little man remained hunched over his fishing net without replying. There was a light breeze coming off the water that felt refreshing after Amy's hot bus ride back into

178

Trois Islets. For the last few miles of that ride, she had repeatedly glanced back through the bus's rear window, but all she had seen were tourists driving brightly colored Opels, no dark blue police Peugeots.

"Henri told me nothing about the accident," Gerard said finally. "Not one thing. And the day after they took away his charter license, he was gone. To Dominique, his brother said, but who knows? I had to pay Henri's fine myself to sail the *Minoque*. A waste that was."

"Why was it a waste?"

"She is jinxed," Gerard replied, gesturing to the *Minoque*, moored at the end of the dock. "No tourists come anymore. That boat even scares fish away."

Amy gazed at the *Minoque*. A tattered canvas awning flapped pathetically over the small boat's helm. It looked like a Price cartoon version of a pleasure boat; Amy couldn't imagine even the most economy-minded tourist choosing the *Minoque* for a sunset cruise. God knows what had brought Georgia O'Hearn onto it.

"How far out did Henri go on his sunset cruises?" Amy asked.

"To the reef," Gerard said.

He turned and pointed out toward the setting sun. He might have been pointing to the end of the earth.

"How far out is that?"

Gerard shrugged.

"A kilometer? Two?" Amy asked. The question was, was it too far out for the best girl swimmer in all of Georgia to make it safely back to shore?

"It costs me fifty francs just in petrol to go out there," Gerard said. "I need at least two passengers to make it worthwhile."

Amy continued gazing out at the horizon. The water looked still. Louis O'Hearn had been told that his daughter was pulled out to sea by the undertow.

"I could take you out there for a hundred francs," Gerard said.

Amy hesitated. The little man shrugged.

"Eighty francs," he said.

Amy turned and looked back at the sleepy town. She could see several people now sitting at tables on the terrace of the Poisson d'Or Restaurant. She gazed up at the Hotel de Ville a hundred yards away. Leaning against the stair railing outside the police entrance was a large black man in a gendarme uniform. Amy squinted. Her body tensed. It was the bulgy-eyed officer who had followed her out to the hotel. He was back, and he was looking straight at her.

"Fine, eighty francs," Amy blurted. "But now, I want to go immediately."

Gerard rose off the dock post.

"It is the most beautiful time of day to go out to the reef," he said, leading the way to the *Minoque.* He pulled in the boat, then offered Amy his calloused hand as she stepped over the rail. Amy looked up. The gendarme was lumbering down the stairs, his eyes still on her. Gerard untied the mooring and scrambled to the helm, which consisted of a spoked Deux Cheveaux steering wheel and a key dangling from the ignition. The engine coughed to a start like a grass mower, then lurched away from the dock at a surprisingly rapid clip. The gendarme had come to a stop and now, putting his hand to his cap, he smirked and saluted Amy.

Amy turned away from him. A rusted steel drumhead rested on a tripod at the center of the narrow deck. She rapped her knuckle against a hexagonal dent labeled A# and it made a dull ping sound. This entire so-called calypso boat reeked of decay. She sat down on the wooden deck bench and lifted her face to the spray as the *Minoque* raced toward the dropping sun.

"Planter's?" Without turning his bony head, Gerard held an unlabeled bottle of coral-colored liquid out at his side. He gestured at a pink plastic bathroom glass on the chrome-rimmed shelf across from Amy. The glass was probably reserved for delicate guests, those who didn't drink their planter's punch straight from the bottle.

"Merci." Amy took the bottle and poured an inch of the viscous liquid into the glass. Could this be the same glass from which Georgia had drunk? Had the Carvaggio woman shared the glass with her?

Amy handed the bottle back to Gerard. His open shirt fluttered behind him, revealing ridges of gray scar tissue along his rib cage. Amy turned back toward the sun.

It was indeed impressive out here in the clear turquoise water, the pale blue sky becoming rosier by the second; yet something about it was almost too vivid, like one of those retouched sunset posters with inspirational messages by Fritz Perls scripted along the bottom—the kind of poster that Amy could easily imagine Georgia O'Hearn hanging on her bedroom wall. Perhaps Georgia had met someone in her hotel lobby who told her about this quaint native boat that sailed off into the gorgeous pink sunset every evening. Very unpretentious and untouristy. Why don't you come along?

If that person had been a man, Georgia would have certainly declined, but what if the stranger had been a woman? Say, a sophisticated woman with a European accent?

Glass in hand, Amy paced over the vibrating deck to the rear of the boat and gazed back at Trois Islets. Already the small port village was barely recognizable; it could have been an outcropping of rocks glazed pink by the late sun. Amy guessed they were at least a mile out already. Could the best girl swimmer in all of Georgia have made it back to shore from here?

Amy put the plastic glass to her lips and took a taste of the syrupy punch—the kind of quick sip she imagined Georgia taking—then started back to her bench seat. Suddenly, she came to a halt, the boat bouncing under her feet. Something odd had registered on her retina. For a moment, she could not identify what it was, just that she had this unsettling "something's wrong with this picture" feeling. An instant later, her eye found it: a piece of cloth rolled into a ball in the open cubby at Gerard's feet. This rag had faded to pale lilac and green, but Amy was sure she recognized the pattern: it was a de la Renta. From this summer's cruise collection. Somebody had left her brand-new six-hundred-dollar Oscar de la Renta frock behind on the *Minoque*.

Amy took a deep breath and ambled toward Gerard.

"May I—?"

She stopped as Gerard turned to her with an inebriated smile.

"May I have some more?" she blurted, holding out her glass.

Gerard handed her the bottle. Amy poured some punch into her glass, then deliberately jerked her hand, spilling some onto her tan linen culotte.

"Shit!" In one quick movement, she pushed the bottle back into Gerard's hand, grabbed the lilac and green cloth from the cubbyhole, and began mopping her culotte with it. She spun around and paced to the rear of the boat with the rolled-up dress in her hand. She said shit several more times for good measure. Gerard had not turned again from the wheel and the setting sun.

Amy quickly unrolled the dress in her lap. A good half of the hem was missing—ripped off for rags, perhaps—and there were oil stains all along the left front of the garment, yet the dress remained unmistakably the product of a haute couture designer: The faded colors on the thin fabric were still rich, what was left of the line still classic, all of it perfectly cut and sewn. Wouldn't it make an arresting photo for *Femina,* Amy thought automatically—this elegant rag lying on the deck of this barbarous boat, a testament to the endurance of classy goods.

But whose classy goods? Quaint as the *Minoque* might seem to some, how many women owning six-hundred-dollar de la Renta cruise frocks would wear them on board this grimy boat?

And how many would leave them behind?

Amy pursed her lips. The hotel maid had told Able Franke that Georgia was wearing a miniskirt when she left her room. And the police report had said that Yolanda Carvaggio arrived in the Trois Islets police station in a wet bathing suit after having searched for Georgia in the water. The report also said that Henri Bouquard sailed back out to the reef to continue his search immediately after dropping Madame Carvaggio ashore to report the accident and that Henri continued his search through the night. Had the Italian woman ever returned to the boat?

Probably not.

Could she have left her dress on board?

Possibly. In fact, quite likely.

Amy turned the dress over in her lap. Just below the waist on the right was a shallow and buttoned credit-card pocket, a practical touch de la Renta had recently added to his cruise collection for the woman who couldn't be bothered with a handbag when she hopped ashore for some quick portside shopping. Amy unfastened the button and slipped a finger inside. She felt a coin and an edge of paper. She pulled out a single centime piece and a ripped triangle of blotterlike paper. She brought the paper up to her nose. It had a potent almondy fragrance, like those scent-impregnated paper inserts the perfume companies stuck in their magazine advertisements. Written on it in pencil were the numbers "23–28."

Amy's heartbeat began to race automatically. She sucked in her breath. She remembered writing down that same number sequence in her notebook during her conversation with Able. It had been Georgia O'Hearn's room number at the PLM Marina Hotel.

The boat suddenly veered sharply to the right, pitching over its own wake. Amy looked out into the water. They had arrived at the edge of the reef. The boat stopped, its engine idling noisily in three-quarter time. Gerard slowly turned around. His lips were drawn back in a stiff grimace. The rose-colored light reflecting off the water gave his bony face the look of a carnival mask. He was walking toward her, his hands behind his back.

"What do you want with that rag?" he said.

"Nothing . . . I—"

Amy felt the blood drain from her face.

Oh God, what had she expected? Henri Bouquard had been the last man to see Georgia O'Hearn alive and Gerard was his brother-in-law. He had not brought Amy out to the edge of ocean at the end of the day simply to make eighty francs.

Amy jumped up, the de la Renta dress slipping from her knees to the deck. Her hands trembled. She took a long sideways step toward the rear rail. She quickly darted her eyes from Gerard's face to the shore. It was barely visible, a thin pink line along the horizon. There was nothing but sky and sea as far the eye could see. She was a dot on that line. She was the vanishing point.

This is how it ended for Georgia, Amy thought. Out here beyond the reef in a glorious Caribbean sunset with no one in sight. Just Henri Bouquard and Yolanda Carvaggio—if that was the red-haired Italian's real name. They had pushed Georgia over the rail, just as Gerard was about to push her now.

But why? Why would anyone have wanted to kill Georgia? Jealousy? Did Yolanda Carvaggio have a husband who had fallen for Georgia's magnificent face? Georgia had said something about problems with married men. Did jealous wives ever really murder their pretty young rivals? Could Amy imagine killing Penny Twang because she'd stolen Peter from her? Could she imagine meticulously premediating a murder on a remote Caribbean island and then reporting it as an accidental drowning?

But why report it at all?

After secretly luring Georgia out to sea, why come back to shore and announce that she was dead? Why not just let people gradually discover that she was gone? Wouldn't that arouse fewer suspicions?

"You wish to snorkel, m'mselle?" A snorkel mask suddenly appeared dangling from Gerard's outstretched hand.

"No!" Amy took another long step away from him.

His face still frozen in a masklike grimace, Gerard brought his other hand out from behind his back. It held an underwater spear gun and it was swinging toward Amy.

Amy leapt back from him. She felt the cold metal of the boat rail at the back of her knees, and then she was in the air, somersaulting backward over the rail, the world upside down, the sun setting into the sky. She hit the water headfirst, her eyes still open. Just inches in front of her face, the shining steel blades of the propeller turned in slow motion. She swung her arms and head back toward her buttocks, completing the somersault in an attempt to push clear of the blades. And in that instant—her heart pounding with fear, her half-empty lungs already straining for air—she noticed with some other calmly observant consciousness that her right hand was still clutching the triangle of paper which she had removed from the pocket of the abandoned de la Renta frock. Except now, instead of seeing Georgia's room number written in pencil on it, through the clear blue water she saw the ink-scripted words *Wash and Cut—7.19—$95.* Somebody's receipt from a beauty salon. Somebody only five weeks ago in the world of the rich and the safe who had paid ninety-five dollars to make herself look pretty.

The paper left Amy's hand in a whirl of bubbles. She pulled against the water with both arms. Next to her, the propellers were spinning at full speed, a disk of silver. Amy fought her instinct to swim to the surface and gasp in air; she dove deeper, away from the boat and Gerard's lethal spear gun. In a matter of only seconds, she pulled herself down to the coral, the iridescent yellow and orange shapes like bright miniature cactuses all around her. A sudden stab in the palm of her right hand. A pink cloud erupted in front of her face. Blood. She'd cut her hand on the coral.

Amy twisted her head, peered upward. The rose stream of her blood was already reaching the surface. The whole world above her glowed a magnificent pink. Amy could not hold her breath a second longer. In two big fanning strokes, she pulled herself up. Was this it? Either drown or be shot with a spear? Would she feel anything when the spear pierced her skull? Just a stab of pain like the one she'd felt in her hand . . . and then nothing? She pushed her face through the water's surface and gasped in a great lungful of air, then pulled her head back underwater again.

God! How many times could she do this before Gerard got her? Before his spear gun was perfectly set and aimed, just waiting for her face to bob above the water one last time? For the first moment since her feet had left the deck of the *Minoque,* Amy felt the full force of her terror. Above her, the pink world was shading into purple.

But that was all that was above her. No dark shadow. No spinning propeller. Nothing but sky. Again, Amy pushed her face through the surface of the water, her eyes opened wide. No Gerard! She twisted her body around and around until she saw the *Minoque.* It was now just a flash of spray disappearing in the distance.

"Oh God!" she cried, tears of relief springing from her eyes. "Oh God!"

Her voice was tiny, no louder than the little lapping sound made by the caps of water slapping her face.

Oh God! Suddenly Amy was seized by a terror even more horrible then the one that had just released her. She was absolutely alone. She was miles from land. It was getting darker every second.

Don't panic, she told herself. Just swim, slowly and steadily. She pointed herself toward the shore, closed her eyes, and began the long arcing strokes of the crawl. She imagined herself in her health-club pool back on Fifty-second Street. How many laps would it take? Thirty? Fifty? She counted her strokes, said the numbers aloud. Eighty-one, eighty-two, eighty-three. Don't open your eyes yet, she told herself. Not yet. Her shoulders had already begun to ache. Her breaths began to come closer and closer together. She was sure she had done twenty laps by now. She opened her eyes and stared straight ahead.

She could barely see the land at all. If anything, she was farther from shore than when she had started; and now she was sure she felt the tug of the undertow gently pulling her farther out to sea.

So this is how it ends. Not with a quick stab of pain followed by nothingness, but drifting slowly and ineluctably into this blackening void, mind fully alert, knowing that before she ever slept again, her lungs would fill with water and she would sink to the bottom of the ocean.

Amy rolled over and floated on her back—to conserve energy, she thought. Conserve energy for what? To do what? To live another hour out here? She stared up at the now deep purple sky. It was—right now, at this particular moment—magnificently beautiful.

"I am living now. Still living," Amy said out loud.

Tears filled her eyes, rolled from the corners along her cheekbones into the water.

"Right now," she whispered, "I'm still here."

The cloudless sky was changing every second, every fraction of a second. Now a shade deeper purple. Now a streak of crimson at the horizon. Now a glinting point appearing directly above her. Venus? How sad to die now, just when life had started to open up. Just when she'd begun to feel confident and attractive and ready to look in earnest for a man with whom to share her life.

A faint humming sound in the water. Amy sucked in her breath and held it. Was it only inside her head? An autonomous mantra? No, the sound was coming from behind her. Her heart pounding, Amy flipped over, turned in the water toward the sound. She saw a boat speeding toward her, foamy white spume flying up on either side of its bow, a blue, white, and red flag streaming behind it. The French tricolor.

Amy lifted her head out of the water. She could see a figure clad in blue standing at the boat's rail scanning the water. She recognized him even at this distance: It was the handsome police officer with the sea-colored eyes. He was coming for her, coming to save her. Amy raised her right arm out of the water and waved at him, her savior. The police boat sped straight ahead, farther out to sea.

Holy God! Hadn't he seen her? Was she a figure without ground in this infinite black sea?

"Here! Help me! *Au secours!*"

Amy was shouting with all her might, but even to herself, her voice sounded lost, like a bell tinkling in a hurricane. She turned in the water, keeping her eye on the police boat as it began to dip at the edge of the horizon.

"Help! Help! Save me!"

Let him see me, dear God. Please!

Nothing. The boat was gone. Salty tears ran down Amy's face into the salty sea.

Suddenly, her body felt as if it had turned to stone, her legs sinking uncontrollably, dragging her deeper into the water. Now, only her shoulders and head were above the surface, her arms flailing to keep her afloat, arms so tired the muscles in them tore, searing pain shooting into her chest. And then she was under, kicking, pushing, reaching for an invisible handle above the surface to pull her back up. Her face pushed through the surface, choking, water deep in her throat gagging her. She gasped for air, knowing the next time she went under would be the last.

And then, a few degrees to the right on the horizon, the boat appeared again. It was arcing back toward the shore. Amy ripped off her blouse. She raised it above her head and began waving it back and forth.

"Help!"

The boat seemed to hesitate in the water, then its nose shifted and it resumed speed, but now it was coming toward her. It was definitely coming straight at her. Amy could see the officer on the deck waving at her. She released the blouse and waved back at him. Then, pulling her hand down, she pushed her hair away from her forehead, ran her fingers through it like a comb.

Better. Wet hair always looks better pulled straight back from the face.

32

....

Just as he was exiting the front door of his apartment building, David saw a figure in satiny purple flash between two parked cars across the street. David jumped back inside, his eyes scanning the street. The Junior Giants had threatened to stay on his ass until their Dr. Ray was clear, but as far as David knew, Ray hadn't even been located by the federal investigators yet. Several minutes passed without spotting anyone in a purple jacket before David finally walked outside and hailed a cab.

Now, that cab turned left on East Sixty-seventh Street, past a rubble-filled, fenced-in corner lot and came to a halt opposite the brick facade of Julia Richmond High School. Chiseled in stone over the graffiti-covered front steps was the school motto: KNOWLEDGE IS POWER—BACON. Directly across from the school was the Greater New York Blood Program. No motto, just rules: DONOR HOURS 8 TO 6. ALL VISITORS OTHER THAN DONORS MUST REGISTER AT DOOR. David surveyed the area as he paid the driver. It was only eight in the morning and the schoolyard was still empty.

Stepping out of the cab, David felt a dull ache just below his rib cage where the broken blood vial had gouged his skin yesterday. He straightened up quickly and climbed the steps, swinging his attaché case at his side. He made his way directly to the registration desk, his St. Mary's ID already out of his pocket.

"Good afternoon, I'm Dr. David Copeland, Chief of Endocrinology at St. Mary's Hospital," he said to the uniformed guard at the desk. "I'd like to talk to somebody in donor records, preferably the director."

"Are you expected, Doctor?"

"No," David said, leaning over the desk. "But we've got the possibility of a Code Three situation downtown. That's why I came here personally."

David saw the guard wince at the mention of Code 3, the code word for donor blood contaminated with hepatitis or AIDS. Code 3 was a blood bank's most dreaded nightmare. At some point in the middle of his sleepless night, David had decided that this lie, ugly as it was, was necessary; he didn't have the time to try to penetrate standard donor-confidentiality protocol. The guard had already dialed an in-house number and was now speaking rapidly into the phone.

"Miss Hawkins will see you," the guard said to David.

Hawkins, a handsome black woman in a tailored tweed business suit, met David solemnly at the door to the Donor Records Office. She shook his hand without speaking. As soon as they were inside the office, she asked, "Have we had transmission, Doctor?"

"Possibly," David said. "We'll need to test the donor as soon as possible."

"HIV?" Hawkins said, panic in her eyes.

"No, not HIV," David answered. He was already feeling guilty for putting this earnest, hardworking health official through this anxiety. Just one case of AIDS transmitted through the blood bank would make front-page news; heads would roll at the New York Blood Program, and worse, scores of patients would die because they would refuse transfusions rather than risk contamination with the bloodborne AIDS virus. "We believe it's viral thyrotoxicosis, but we can't be certain. We've decided not to call the CDC in on this yet. We want to check it out ourselves first."

David opened his attaché case and removed the ABO/RH printout of the bar code Armand Diltzer had stolen from La Douce Laboratories. He set the printout on the counter. The Records director scanned the identification number.

"We have a rigid confidentiality protocol here, you know, Doctor."

"Yes, I know," David said. "I thought we'd cut this thing off at the pass. Find our donor, run some tests on her. Maybe it can all stop right there."

Hawkins hesitated only a moment, then picked up the printout, walked to her desk, and sat down. She began typing rapidly into her computer. At the desk beside her, a slim Asian woman with silky black hair hanging to her waist looked up from her computer and smiled flirtatiously at David. David smiled back. That was one part of his life that had come to a complete standstill: He could barely remember what it was like to spend time with a lovely woman.

Ms. Hawkins stared at her display screen, frowned, and banged a new set of instructions onto her keyboard. The screen went blank for a second, then a new message pulsed at its center. The Records director turned in her chair to look at David.

"You must have the wrong ID here, Doctor," she said. "No donation with this number was ever logged here."

"My people are sure it came through the NYBP," David said.

"Look, it's obviously coded with our prefix," Hawkins said defensively. "But what I'm telling you is that we never received a donation with this particular identification number. I don't know where you got it, but it's not logged here, and every drop of blood that comes through our doors is automatically logged here."

David rubbed his hand across his jaw.

"Who puts the bar-code labels on the blood bags?" he said.

"The nurse in charge of the collection at the point of origin," Hawkins answered.

"What point of origin?"

"We make collections all over the metropolitan area, Doctor. The labels are pasted on the bags wherever the blood is taken."

"And where does the nurse in charge get the labels?"

"Off a roll." Hawkins rose and returned to the counter, reached under it and placed a roll of peel-and-stick bar-code labels in front of David. "Some get torn, some get lost or thrown away. There's no reason for us to keep track of any of those. The only labels that mean anything to us are the ones that come back here identifying a bagful of blood."

David put on his reading glasses and picked the roll of labels off the countertop. The first four digits were the same on every label—clearly the prefix identifying the NYBP—but the next seven identification numbers came off the roll sequentially.

"Do me a favor, would you, Ms. Hawkins?" David said softly, leaning both hands on the counter. "Run the five numbers that came before and after the one I gave you through your log."

Again, the Hawkins woman hesitated, then lowered her eyes, shaking her head.

"I am truly sorry, Doctor," she said deliberately. "But I can't pull donors' names out randomly for you. That's a breach of confidentiality I cannot make."

David looked beseechingly into the woman's eyes.

"Please," he said. "I have reason to believe that somebody's life is at stake."

"I'm sorry," Hawkins said. "You'll have to take this to the program director."

David was about to continue pleading when he saw the pretty Asia woman behind Hawkins furtively pantomiming to him, her long fingers pointing from her eyes to her computer to a window that faced out on the front of the building; then she pointed to her watch and flashed five fingers. Five minutes.

"I'll speak with the program director then," David said softly. "Thank you for your help, Ms. Hawkins."

He turned and walked out the door.

Ten minutes had already passed and Hawkins's attractive assistant still had not appeared. David huddled just inside the entrance to the Blood Program building. Students had begun to congregate in front of Julia Richmond High across the street, several wearing colorful satin athletic jackets. David scrutinized their faces warily while he waited. He was slowly becoming convinced that he had misinterpreted the young assistant's gesture. Now what? Could he actually plead his case to the Blood Program's director? What exactly would he say? That someone who had been doing industrial espionage for him at a cosmetics company had traced some pheromone-laden blood back to the Blood Program and now David wanted to find out whether this spy had been onto something critical—something, say, worth murdering him for? Somehow, that didn't quite sound like an explanation that opened bureaucratic doors.

A woman brushed past David and pushed through the front door. It took him a moment to realize that it was Hawkins's assistant. She immediately turned left on the sidewalk and paced quickly out of view without once looking back. David waited a beat, then pushed out the door and started after her. He trailed about twenty paces behind her, his eyes anxiously sweeping around him. Any gangly black teenage boy could easily be a Junior Giant with a knife; any overweight man in a windbreaker could be a federal agent with an arrest warrant; any cheap-looking blonde could be the woman who'd followed him from Alice Diltzer's apartment. In only forty-eight hours, David had acquired a varied retinue of pursuers. The Asian woman turned left on Second Avenue, then entered a coffee shop. Relieved, David followed her to a booth at the rear of the shop and sat down across from her.

"Claire Ling," the young woman said, reaching her slender hand across the table.

"David Copeland." David took her hand and shook it briefly.

"I told the boss I was going to the bank," Ling said, smiling. She was even lovelier close up, her skin a deep gold color, her eyes jewel-bright. She was a testament to the cultural universality of sexual attractiveness; David could not imagine any man, be he from Bejing or Oslo, who would not find Claire Ling attractive.

"I don't know exactly what you're looking for, Doctor," she said, lifting a computer printout from her handbag. "But if there's been any contamination, it was some time ago. The label you're looking for comes out of a sequence from about thirteen months ago. Exactly a year ago July seventeenth."

David reached for the printout. Frozen blood could be thawed without damage for up to eight years.

"Funny thing is, I scanned twenty-seven numbers and could only pull nine donors," Claire Ling went on. "That's a hell of a lot of labels to be lost. Especially when I figure they're all missing from the same collection."

"What collection is that?" David asked intently, leaning across the table.

"Big celebrity collection," the pretty Asian replied. "A mobile unit they set up at the Waldorf Astoria last summer. The city was in the middle of the worst blood shortage in years, so these celebrities decided to set an example. I remember all these models and actresses lying in the lobby of the Waldorf donating blood while the cameras rolled. Around the Program we called it 'The Beauty Bleed.' All the glamour magazines covered it."

"And every one of these labels is missing from that particular collection?"

"Right, and that really doesn't make any sense at all," Claire Ling said, lowering her voice. Her narrow black eyes flicked momentarily to the front window of the coffee shop. "I ran this thing through my PC a dozen times and all I came up with is nine pints of blood logged for that whole collection. I remember seeing the setup on the Channel Five news that night and there were at least twenty-five of those gorgeous models in there. I mean, there has to be more than just labels missing."

David stared at the pretty young woman. There was not a doubt in his mind that the blood donations were not simply missing, they had been diverted to La Douce Laboratories.

"I double-checked on our collection prep sheet," Claire Ling continued, pulling another printout from her bag and handing it across the table to David. "Twenty-seven women signed up for the 'Beauty Bleed.' We even got their confidential releases ahead of time so they wouldn't have to deal with the paperwork, you know, on camera."

David scanned down the sheet. The prospective donors were listed alphabetically, previous donors starred and pledged organ donors double-starred, their HLA codes listed alongside their names.

"As you can see, most of them had made donations with us before." Ling shrugged and lifted her spare, fanlike eyebrows. "Who knows? Maybe that's how they stay so thin."

David smiled faintly, then popped open his briefcase and pulled out the manila folder that held the hormone assays of the four vials of blood Armand Diltzer had smuggled out of La Douce. He placed the list of Beauty Bleed donors on the table next to it and traced his index finger down the HLA codes. In less than one minute, he had a match.

The blood of a woman by the name of Kelly Keane had turned up in the cold rooms of La Douce Laboratories twice in the past year. Once frozen and once fresh.

"May I keep this?" David asked, gesturing to the printout.

"Of course."

"Can you give me a number where I can reach you privately if any other questions come up?"

The young woman offered David an openly inviting smile. Oh yes, how very nice it would be to go off with this Asian beauty right now and make love for the rest of the morning. Forget about La Douce's stolen blood and Armand Diltzer's death. Just spend an hour or two in sweet oblivion. Still smiling at him seductively, she jotted a telephone number on the corner of the donor-list printout. David was just picking it up when three quick beeps emanated from his jacket pocket. He pulled out his electronic pager, clicked it off, and read the number off the bottom. It was Ray Kenworthy's home phone number.

"Excuse me a moment." David rose, walked to the pay phone by the door, and dialed Ray's number. Ray picked up on the first ring.

"David?"

"Ray, where the hell have you been?"

"Busy, very busy," Ray said. His tone was flat, controlled. "Listen, David, I'm terribly sorry about that warrant they hit you with. It shouldn't have happened. I never really expected this to go that far."

"What *did* you expect, Ray? You're way out of line with this, you know, not just with Medicaid, but with those boys and with our depart—"

"But it's all going to work out, Dave," Ray interrupted soothingly. "That's what I wanted to tell you. We've just about solved this awful mess I got us in."

"Solved it? How, Ray? How the hell do you solve eighteen cases of illegal prescription, not to mention three hundred thousand dollars' worth of fraud?"

"You just solve it," Ray said, his tone flat again. "Now listen to me David, the clock is still ticking on those case warrants, so Art wants us both to stay out of sight for the next twenty-four hours while he hammers out all the details of the deal."

"Art? What kind of deal could you possibly—?"

David heard the line go dead as he spoke. He hung up the phone, then slowly made his way back to the booth at the rear of the coffee shop, but he did not sit down. "You've been very helpful," David said, taking Claire Ling's hand. "Maybe we can get together sometime."

33

··

"Will you be watching the movie?"

"Beg your pardon?"

"The movie. Earphones. There's a four-dollar charge."

"God no," Amy said, smiling wearily up at the stewardess. "No movie today, thank you. In fact, if I fall asleep, don't wake me for lunch."

Across the aisle, a heavily tanned man with a gold chain around his neck laughed.

"Busman's holiday, eh?" he said. "No movie, I mean."

Amy glanced at him quizzically.

"You're in the business, right? I figured you for either an actress or a model the minute you walked on board," the man went on, leaning his head into the aisle. "I've sort of got an eye for these things."

Amy leaned back her head and squinched her eyes closed without responding. In her mind's eye, she once again began rerunning her rescue by Jean Claude, the handsome blue-eyed officer who had hoisted her out of the water with one lean-muscled arm.

"Voilà, I caught myself a mermaid," the officer had said as he hefted her onto the police-boat deck.

He'd immediately thrown a towel around her and then tugged

her to him, his hands rubbing up and down her back. Above her waist, Amy was wearing only a bra—the blouse she'd ripped off to wave as a semaphore was already floating over the horizon—and under her bra's sopping, sheer fabric, her nipples began to tingle as they pressed against his khaki shirt.

"Thank you, thank you," Amy repeated in a half-whisper, her lips almost touching the man's warm golden-brown neck. She shivered against him. "I went down twice already. One more time—"

"It is my duty, Mademoiselle," the officer answered softly, one hand pressed firmly in the small of her back as the other continued to dry her shoulders. "It is my pleasure."

Amy closed her eyes. Her body was covered with goosebumps from the cold water, yet just under the surface her skin felt hot. Her heart was still thudding with the remnants of her terror and now, as it gradually slowed, it seemed to pump even more powerfully, her blood coursing through her in a warming current. Her entire body felt grateful to be alive and she had never felt so vibrantly vital in her life.

"We should do something about that cut," the officer murmured.

As he led her slowly down into the cruiser's cabin, Amy glimpsed the narrow back of the man at the helm. The motor revved and roared and the boat lurched forward just as Amy came off the last step of the stairs. She braced herself against the tall officer, then sat on the edge of the bunk, hugging the towel around her shoulders. In a matter of only seconds, the officer produced a bottle of iodine and began dabbing at the coral cut in the middle of Amy's right palm. It stung sharply, yet the sudden burn under her raw skin was somehow thrilling. Now the officer knelt in front of her and began gently wrapping a gauze bandage around her hand. Amy gazed at his intense sea-colored eyes while he worked. He ripped the end of the gauze in short lengthwise strands, looped them under the bandage, and tied it off neatly. Finished, he remained on his knees, his eyes looking up at hers. He gradually lowered his eyes to her mouth, then traced down her neck to her breasts. Only at that moment did Amy realize that the towel had slipped from her shoulders and her breasts were uncovered save for her bra, which she now saw was virtually transparent from its soaking. Somehow it felt much too small, barely containing her heaving, full, and, she thought, looking down at herself, beautifully shaped breasts. Had it taken a near brush with death for her to appreciate what a wonderfully womanly body she possessed?

"Forgive me," the officer said softly. "You are magnificent."

"There is nothing to forgive," Amy whispered.

She did not reach for the towel, did not move at all, and when she saw him extend his hand toward her, his long fingers gently touching the side of her right breast, she leaned toward him. Both his hands were suddenly behind her, finding the clasp of her bra, unfastening it, the bra springing loose, her breasts seeming even larger once released, her nipples hard, pointing, aching for him to touch them. The young officer parted his lips, leaned forward, and closed his mouth around her right nipple, his tongue flicking in a circle as he sucked on it. A jolt of sensation, like an electric charge, shot straight from her breast to between her legs, hot, burning. She felt herself become instantly slippery wet inside. She grasped the back of his head in both her hands, parted her knees, and pulled him closer. Above his head, she saw the last underlit purple cloud of the day through a high porthole. Next to it, the ship's clock struck once. Seven-thirty.

Seven-thirty? That was about the same time that Georgia O'Hearn had been reported missing to the Trois Islets police station. And yet half a dozen boats, including two police boats, had been unable to find the best girl swimmer in all of Georgia in the tropical twilight.

"Let me help you out of these," the officer was whispering, his hands now on the waistband of Amy's culotte.

Amy hesitated, her heart pounding. Somewhere deep inside her head, she could hear Mary Goldfarb and every woman in her therapy group imploring her for once in her life to abandon herself to the moment, and God what a gloriously sexy moment it was. "Be here now!" her group cried.

"Were you on one of the boats that searched for Mademoiselle O'Hearn's body?" Amy said out loud, both her hands firmly on the officer's shoulders as she sat up straight.

Jean Claude looked up at her startled, then nodded his head gravely.

"Yes, I was," he said softly.

"There was still some light and none of you could find her?"

"She must have been pulled down by the undertow already by the time we got out there," he said. His hands had dropped from her waistband to the bunk, but now he turned his wrists and cupped his palms around the sides of her thighs. "Was she a very dear friend of yours?"

"Very," Amy answered, an effortless lie. She closed her eyes. She felt Jean Claude's hands slide under her thighs and then gently begin to tug her legs apart. Amy abruptly flashed open her eyes, drew in her breath.

"It wasn't just the undertow," she blurted, crossing her arms over her bare breasts. "Gerard tried to kill me, too."

"Petit Gerard?" The handsome young officer on his knees cocked his head to one side, an unsuccessfully suppressed smile turning up the corners of his lips.

"Yes, Gerard, Henri's brother-in-law. He attacked me with a spear gun. That's how I ended up in the water, just like Georgia. And he left me out here to drown, too."

"Perhaps that is the way it seemed," the officer said, his supercilious smile creeping back again.

"That is the way it happened," Amy said evenly. She grabbed the towel off the bed and wrapped it around her torso.

"We saw Gerard's boat come in," the officer said. "We met him at the dock. He said you jumped out of the *Minoque* and never came up. Only blood came up, he said. Our people are very superstitious, you know."

"Gerard tried to kill me!" Amy shouted. "What do you think he'd tell you? No wonder somebody can disappear down here and you don't have a clue what happened to her or to the only two people who were with her on that boat."

The officer shook his handsome head back and forth.

"You have been through so much," he said soothingly, reaching for her hand. "So much sea, so much sun. So much exposure."

"You're goddamned right—too much exposure!" Amy stood furiously, her shins barely missing the kneeling officer's chin. "Take me back to shore. Right now, Monsieur."

For the rest of the ride in, she had only spoken to Jean Claude once, to request a shirt with which to cover herself. She took a taxi from Trois Islets to a motel next to the airport and she boarded the first Martinaire flight out in the morning.

Opening her eyes, Amy saw that the NO SMOKING and FASTEN SEAT BELTS signs had flashed off. She clicked open her safety belt, pulled her handbag from under the seat in front of her, and stood.

The man across the aisle looked up from his *Business Week* and smiled.

"Back to civilization," he said, wagging his eyebrows at her.

Amy marched back to a bank of toilets, found a vacant one, slid inside the door, and locked it behind her. She looked at herself in the mirror. Jesus Christ, there was nothing like an attempt on your life and a lousy night's sleep to make you look absolutely radiant. Her skin glowed this morning; her eyes sparkled. She almost could pass for a model—well, maybe a Spiegel-catalogue model. Mary Goldfarb's prescription for letting herself shine was only half right. Amy's blood was flowing and her skin glowing because she was doing something about Georgia's death instead of hanging back and feeling guilty about it. That's what had changed. That look of hesitancy was gone from her eyes; those guilt creases were gone from the sides of her mouth. She looked like a woman who met life head-on and, damn, she looked good. Camus was right: After thirty, you are responsible for the way your face looks.

Amy opened her handbag and pulled out her contact-lens case. She sat down on the toilet-seat cover, leaned forward, sprang out her lenses one at a time, and set them inside the case. That felt a whole lot better. She'd forgotten to take them out last night. She stood and pressed down the cold-water lever and let the cool water run over her wrists. Then she splashed some on her face. She dug into her bag and pulled out a small round plastic container that had once held some takeout wasabi and now was her traveling case for the night cream Aida had given her to sample. The rest of the cream—what little remained—was home in her refrigerator. She had neglected to put the cream on last night, which was a mistake, because the stuff really was wonderfully soothing at bedtime; she might have slept better. She'd have to ask Aida to get her some more of the cream when they had dinner this week. Amy dipped her finger into the little container, dotted the cream across her forehead, and smoothed it in. After sea and sun and dry cabin air, her skin seemed to drink the stuff in gratefully. It was quite a promising product, actually, a high eight or nine on the A.B.Q. She'd tell Aida to tell her research friend he was on to something. She put another dollop on each cheek and stroked toward her chin, then closed the container and stuffed it back into her bag. She was just about to unlock the door when, unable to resist, she reached for the courtesy bottle of cologne on top of the sink and spritzed her neck with it. Almond. It smelled of almond.

Amy cupped her hand over her forehead. The scrap of paper with Georgia's hotel room number on it had smelled of almond, too, even after weeks of sitting in the pocket of the de la Renta dress in the cubby of the *Minoque.*

Amy closed her eyes. For the first time since it had happened, she remembered that triangle of paper still clutched in her hand as she had hit the water beneath the boat. Something else was written on it. Amy rubbed her lids with her thumb and forefinger. A receipt. Right, a receipt for a wash and cut. High ticket. Ninety-some dollars. In July sometime. Only about five weeks ago, she remembered thinking. But where? It hadn't said. The torn scrap hadn't even said in which city this woman had paid over ninety dollars to have her hair washed and cut. But that almond smell—there was something familiar about it. Amy stood, grabbed her handbag, opened the door, and went back to her seat.

"Hi," the man with the gold chain around his neck said. "All freshened up?"

Amy pushed on the reading light, pulled her Filofax from her bag, then searched its side pockets for her reading glasses; as part of her positive-image program, she'd forsworn glasses for the last few weeks. She found them, slipped them from their case, and started to put them on. Ouch! The stems of the glasses scraped against her cheekbones. She tugged at the stems, stretching them, then finally pulled them over her ears, only to discover that they weren't any use anymore at all; the outer rims of the glasses cut into her scope of vision: it was as if they had shrunk. They must have been damaged somehow during her little Caribbean adventure. Amy stuffed the glasses back into their case, opened her memo book to her *A* list of beauty salons and makeover artists, and squinted down at it.

Adams, Flip; Alquist, Jimmy; Andre, Pierre; Arden, Elizabeth . . .

She turned the page and scanned to the bottom, then the next page and the next.

Clay, Cal.

That was it.

The almond smell. Cal Clay's honey-almond scrub. His salon reeked of it. His stationery, his card, even his receipts were impregnated with the scent. It was Cal's signature.

34

....

"This doesn't have what I'm looking for," David said, handing the July issue of *Glamour* back to the clerk. In the Yellow Pages, he had located a newspaper and magazine back-issues store on lower Broadway, not far from his apartment, and he had taken a cab directly to it from the coffee shop where Claire Ling had handed him the "Beauty Bleed" donor printout. "Do you have last August's issue?"

"Listen, Mack, this isn't a browsing library. I'm selling magazines."

David rapped his knuckles against the side of his attaché case. Inside it was proof positive that someone at La Douce Labs had stolen blood donations intended for the New York Blood Program. Now he wanted one more piece of information before he took this proof to his old college friend Frank Oxnard in the DA's office—information he believed would link that bizarre blood theft to Armand Diltzer's death. He wanted to find the model blood donor by the name of Kelly Keane and ask her whether she knew that she was being used by La Douce in their pheromone treatment experiments. David was certain she did not. He was convinced that La Douce was conducting hormone experiments without knowledge or consent of any of their test subjects. High-risk experiments. And that is what Armand Diltzer came too close to discovering.

"Tell you what," David said to the clerk. "Give me all of last year's *Glamours*, *Vogues*, and *Feminas*."

"The whole year?"

"Right."

"You want 'em in a box or in a bag?"

"Use your own discretion."

"What?"

"A box. Give them to me in a box."

David paid the man in cash, hoisted the cardboard box under his arm, and flagged a cab. He gave the driver his address on Tenth Street. He considered stopping for a General Tze chicken to go at Wok Two's on the corner, but he was already feeling too visible in the street; better to go straight home and lock the door. He was pretty sure there were still some cold sesame noodles that were under a week old left in his refrigerator. He lugged the box of magazines into his apartment elevator, set it on the floor, and stabbed the button for the sixth floor. When the door opened at his floor, he pushed the box out into the hallway with his foot, then stepped out, leaned over, and picked it up.

He was less than two yards away from his apartment door when he suddenly stopped, his heart pounding.. There were three deep gouge marks in the jamb next to the lock of his door. He set down the box and his briefcase, then stood perfectly still, listening. Not a sound. He stepped soundlessly to the door, turned the knob, and pushed. The door swung open. The lock bolt was not simply broken, it was gone, excised. David stepped into the front hall, stopped again, looked toward the living room, cold sweat slipping down his face. Not a thing was out of place. No tables upturned, no drawers left open. He heard a dripping sound coming from the other end of the hall. It sounded like a leaky faucet. David turned, creeping on the balls of his feet down the hall. The dripping sound was coming from his bedroom. He nudged the door with his knee, then stepped back with both his hands raised as it swung open.

He smelled it before he saw it. The sickening acid smell of dead fish. David's eyes shot to the corner of his bedroom. There was a hole the size of a softball at the bottom edge of his tropical-fish tank where the last trickle of water seeped onto the floor. The fish, glazed and slimy and perfectly still, lay scattered on the rug, where they had been sucked out with the current of released water. David took a long step into the room, his heart thudding. Lying next to a blue and gold angelfish, soaked, its corners curling, was a color photograph. He leaned over and picked it up. It was a photo of himself looking out the driver's seat window of his MG. His heavy eyebrows were arched and his blue eyes opened wide; he looked to himself like a startled boy, naïve, foolish. Of course, he knew immediately who'd taken the picture: the blonde in the Audi. David turned the photograph over in his hand. On the back, written with a laboratory grease pencil in a left-slanted European cursive, it said:

It was a mistake to send Armand on a fishing expedition. Stop right now, Doctor. It's starting to smell.

35

Nothing seemed to fit right. Her favorite Moschino tweed skirt kept riding up, cutting her at the knee instead of just below it. She could feel blisters developing on both her heels as they kept slipping out of her oldest pair of flats. And her bra strap was putting the sunburnt skin on her back through some exquisite new form of torture.

Too much exposure, Amy thought, just like the blue-eyed officer had said. Her body was paying for all that sun and saltwater, swelling here and shrinking there. But remarkably, none of this seemed to deter men on Madison Avenue from smiling at her admiringly as she strode uptown. A fashion forecast in there somewhere: short skirts and cleavage were about to make a comeback.

Amy entered the lobby next to the KLM office and took the elevator up to Cal Clay's penthouse studio. She hadn't been here since her makeover last April, and the reception area had been completely renovated since then: Now it looked like an Art Deco set for a 1940s musical, all potted palms and scrolled chaise longues. A severe-looking society blonde sat rigidly on the edge of one of these chaises reading *Vogue,* obviously pissed at having to wait for Cal's ministrations.

"Ms. Martin, I almost didn't recognize you," the receptionist said, smiling up at Amy. "You look like you've just been some-place fabulous."

"Yes, fabulous." Amy's nose twitched. She already smelled Clay's signature honey-almond scent rising from the reception-ist's desk. She had no doubt about it—it was the same scent she had smelled on the torn receipt she'd discovered in the pocket of the de la Renta frock.

"I don't think we're expecting you today, are we?" the recep-tionist asked, anxiously scanning her appointment book. Every A-level salon receptionist in the city knew Amy by sight, read her column religiously, and knew that the writer of "Beauty Bytes" was to be accommodated whenever possible. "But maybe Cal could squeeze you in for a touch-up if—"

"No, no," Amy said, her raw right heel slipping painfully out of her shoe again. "I just wanted a couple of words with him if he has a moment between sessions."

Amy was improvising, and not very elegantly, either. She probably should have slept when she returned from the airport this afternoon instead of just stopping at her apartment for a shower and a change of clothes. What exactly was she going to ask Cal, anyhow? If he remembered clipping the locks of a woman by the name of Yolanda Carvaggio? Or perhaps that wasn't her real name, Cal, but she had an Italian accent and she was a redhead and she came in for a wash and cut about five weeks ago. Do you know her? Where she lives? Do you know if she vacationed in Martinique recently? Christ, she should have planned this out better. For one thing, Cal certainly wasn't about to divulge his clients' names to *Femina*'s gossipy beauty colum-nist. God knows, there were still many women out there who were as secretive about their makeup artists as they were about their psychiatrists. They still clung to the delusion that their husbands and lovers were willing to believe that their makeovers had somehow come about naturally.

The receptionist's phone buzzed. She lifted it, listened a sec-ond, then set it down without uttering a word.

"We're ready for you, Miss Van Ardsdale," the receptionist called, rising, then she turned to Amy and said sotto voce, "I'll see if Cal has a moment for you."

The impatient socialite clicked across the marble floor, then disappeared with the receptionist through the gilded door to Cal Clay's private studios.

Amy hesitated only a second. She grabbed the appointment book off the receptionist's desk, spun it around right side up, and began flipping backward through the pages. September 4, September 3, September 2. She pinched several pages between her thumb and forefinger and turned them together. July 22. About right, just a day or two under five weeks ago. She squinted. "Lauren Buckley—Makeover—11:30; Isabelle Steinberg—Wash & Cut—1:30; Trudi Jessel—Touch-up—3:00." Amy scanned down the page. It was a regular Who's Who of society women, media types, models, actresses, diplomats' wives; Cal probably gave them all smoky eyes and trompe l'oeil hollows under their cheeks, his famous chanteuse look. But there was no one on July 22 named Carvaggio; in fact, there wasn't one Italian-sounding name on the page.

Footsteps on the other side of the wall. A woman's voice.

"She wouldn't tell me," the voice was saying.

A man spoke, his voice too low to make out.

"Fabulous," the woman replied. "She looks absolutely fabulous."

Footsteps again. Louder. Amy started to return the appointment book to the receptionist's desk, but it caught under the desk's marble overhang and slipped from her hands. The book glanced off the side of the desk and smacked loudly onto the marble floor. Amy froze. The footsteps stopped just behind the door. Impulsively, Amy leaned over, scooped the book off the floor, and raced toward the ladies room. She pulled the door open. Shit! It wasn't the ladies room anymore; it was a utility closet. The door to Cal's private studies was opening. Amy hesitated for only a fraction of a second, then stepped inside the closet and closed the door behind her.

Pitch-black in here save for a pencil-thin line of light at the bottom of the door. Outside, the sound of heels tapping against the marble floor. Amy held her breath. Her shoulders trembled. She slowly let out her breath, then sucked it in again. Acidy sweet fumes stung her nostrils. Honey-almond fumes. Amy fumbled in her handbag, pulled out the penlight attached to her key chain, and clicked it on. The shelves of the utility closet were loaded with plastic two-gallon bottles of murky brown liquid.

Outside the closet, the footsteps had stopped. Amy pulled open the appointment book. July 19. She ran the penlight down the page. "Harriet Schwartz—Wash & Cut—4:30." How about that, Harriet, her venerated editor in chief? Harriet who always acted like beauty salons were only for *Femina*'s readers, not for the truly sophisticated women who wrote the magazine. Amy's eye scanned down the page. A couple more familiar names. Xoli, the Balinese model. Katherine de Jong, the gallery owner. Someone who was inscribed simply as "A." who also had come in for a wash and cut that afternoon. But no Carvaggio. No Italians.

Amy turned back a page. July 18. Again, she scanned the penlight down the column of names; then, halfway down, she stopped.

"Pola di Cenzio—Wash & Cut—2:30."

Amy's pulse accelerated. She knew that name from the society columns, knew that Pola di Cenzio was Italian through and through, spoke with an Italian accent. And Pola was a redhead, a real Roman redhead. She was the wife of Alfredo di Cenzio, a member of the Italian delegation to the UN, a dapper man who was frequently photographed dancing at fashionable clubs with gorgeous women half his age.

A sudden metallic squeak. The door handle to the closet was turning. Amy abruptly closed the appointment book and stuffed it behind the top row of plastic bottles.

And then the closet door swung open.

"Gotcha!" Cal Clay burst into uproarious laughter.

Amy's face burned.

"Really, darling!" Cal said, catching his breath. "I'd heard you snoop around in people's vanity closets, but this takes the prize!"

And then the makeover artist burst into uproarious laughter all over again.

36

It looked like a Breugel painting, a diptych titled, say, *The Virgins and the Bloodletters.* The two-page wide-angle photograph in the center of the year-old copy of *Femina* magazine had a slightly satiric, surreal quality—all these gorgeous women lounging about with blood-intake tubes emanating from the crooks of their arms, leading into donor bags. MODEL CITIZENS, the magazine headline read, but David preferred the nickname Claire Ling had passed on to him: "The Beauty Bleed."

David was sitting up in his bed fully dressed, his shoes still on, a glass of vodka in his hand, the thirty-six dog-eared past issues of *Femina, Vogue,* and *Glamour* spread out around him. The rank smell of dead fish still hung heavily in the air even after he'd gathered them all up and flushed them in twos and threes down the toilet. His bedroom rug was soaking in Lysol in the bathtub.

It had taken him less than fifteen minutes to find the "Beauty Bleed" spread, and now he began counting the smiling perfectly-shaped faces in the photograph: the fragile Grace Kelly-like blonde in a filigree peasant blouse; the sculpted ebony North African beauty in a shimmering pink body suit; the sultry, sloe-eyed brunette in blue pajamas opened halfway to her navel. A couple of the faces seemed vaguely familiar, from ads, he supposed. And one was intimately familiar—Francesca. She was near the front of the spread, looking directly into the camera with a smile that bordered on the lascivious; no doubt Francesca sensed something primal in this mixing of blood and glamour. She was wearing beige linen pants and a soft lavender blouse that clung to her breasts. David took a long swallow of vodka. For an instant, he remembered what it had been like to cup those beautiful breasts in his hands, remembered the silkiness of her skin, the scent she gave off when they made love. Life was orderly then: He did an honest day's work at St. Mary's and Diagnostique, and then he rewarded himself by making love to a beautiful woman. David shook his head. That must have been somebody else's life.

David counted twenty-seven beautiful faces in all, twenty-seven model citizens who had donated blood a year ago July 17. That checked—it was exactly the number of women who had signed up. It meant that exactly eighteen of those donations had never made it back to the cold rooms and freezer stores of the New York Blood Program.

Now David looked at the caption beneath the photograph. Kelly Keane was the fifth name listed. David flicked his eyes back up to the photo. Keane was identified as the sloe-eyed brunette in the scanty pajamas. The caption said nothing else about her. David lifted the Manhattan phone directory from his bed table, flipped through it—scores of Keanes, but not a single Kelly or K. Who said she lived in New York? Or maybe Kelly Keane was only her professional name. David dialed Information: There is indeed a Kelly Keane, the operator informed him, but she had an unlisted number. Of course. Any woman who looked like that wouldn't make herself easy to find.

David considered phoning Sara Huffey, head of publicity at Diagnostique—she'd certainly know how to go about locating Kelly Keane—but talking to anyone at Diagnostique seemed unwise at this point. David was now certain that Mitch had lied to him with his story about hiring a private investigator who had "confirmed" Armand Diltzer's cocaine habit. How far would Mitch go to hide his connection to the late Armand Diltzer? All Mitch had left was his cosmetic corporate image.

But who else could David call—Francesca? She certainly knew everyone in the modeling world. But she could also be tricky to deal with, might ask too many questions. Francesca had been at the "Beauty Bleed," too; she might very easily be one more unwitting subject of La Douce's hormone experiments.

Impulsively, David reached for the Yellow Pages, turned to Modeling Agencies. Several familiar names here: Elite, Ford, Marquessa. He emptied his glass and refilled it, then dialed the Ford Agency. A cheerful actorish voice picked up: "Ford Agency. Good afternoon. May I help you?"

"Yes, please," David said. "I'm with . . . Coronet Productions and there's a particular model a client of ours is interested in seeing. We believe she's with Ford, but we're not absolutely sure."

"I can check for you. What is her name, sir?"

"Keane. Kelly Keane."

A short pause, then: "Listen, I don't know who you are, but that's not very funny."

"What do you—" The phone abruptly went dead. David slowly hung up. What had that been all about? Was his impersonation of an advertising man so transparent?

Suddenly, David heard the rattle of the elevator cables through the wall behind his bed, then the thud of the elevator carriage coming to a halt and the whistle scrape of its doors opening. He waited for the sound of voices. He heard nothing, not even footsteps. The locksmith had told David that he'd need a new door before he could get a new lock and the building superintendent had said he couldn't get David a new door for a day or two. All that was between David and the hallway was a broken door held closed by an upended kitchen table, like a child's play fortress.

Stop right now, Doctor. It's starting to smell.

David swung his feet over the side of his bed. Some vodka swirled out of his glass and spilled onto his shirt. Half a dozen magazines cascaded onto the floor. David set his glass down on his bed table and started for the bedroom door. His hands were numb cold. The superintendent had told him he would need a copy of the police report on the break-in for the building's insurance company. David did not tell him that he had not informed the police about his broken door and vandalized fish tank. When David was ready to go the police, it would not be to report dead fish.

He walked on the balls of his feet toward the table braced

against the door. He paused a moment to listen again. Nothing. He swung one leg at a time over the table's jutting legs, then leaned his head to the door and fitted his eye to the peephole. Directly across the hall, two middle-aged men were locked in a silent embrace: David's gay neighbor had once again scored an afternoon's companion.

David slowly returned to his bedroom. He poured himself another glass of vodka and drank it down, then sat down on the edge of his bed. He was about to lean back against the headboard when, from the corner of his eye, he saw a familiar image floating below him. It was the same beautiful brunette he'd seen in the "Beauty Bleed" spread: Kelly Keane. She was smiling up at him from the open page of one of the magazines that had dropped onto the floor. David leaned down, picked it up. There were photographs of two other beautiful women next to Keane's, women he also recognized from the "Beauty Bleed" spread.

THE PERILS OF PULCHRITUDE, the headline beneath the photographs read. "By Amy Martin, Beauty Editor."

David flipped back to the magazine cover: July. He rolled the cool glass across his forehead and set it on the bed table before he returned to the picture of Kelly Keane.

"Why do the glorious young beauties keep dying on us?" the Martin article began. "Is there something dangerous about having a gorgeous face?"

The magazine began to flutter in David's hands.

"In the last year alone, we've lost three of the world's prettiest faces: the incomparable California beauty Kelly Keane in February, the exotic Brazilian redhead Carmina del Ray in March, and now the magnificent Monique Le Fevre is gone . . ."

David's heart thudded in his chest.

February? Kelly Keane dead eight months ago?

Impossible. Only three months ago, Armand Diltzer had delivered a vial of Kelly Keane's fresh blood.

37

They caused quite a sensation, both of them, as the maître d' led Amy and Aida through Le Cirque's sumptuous dining room to a plush corner banquette. Amy took in every little response—the ripple of evanescent hushes as they passed each table, the quick, envious glances of the women, the slow, grateful gazes of the men. A spontaneous regal smile had appeared on Amy's face the moment she entered the exclusive restaurant, and now she sailed through the dining room like a princess.

It was the dress that did it, of course. The shimmering Herrera evening dress she'd bought at Bergdorf's this afternoon, that and the touch-up Cal Clay had insisted on giving her after catching her snooping in his utility closet. "Just a couple of snips to prove that I forgive you, darling," he'd said.

The dress had been Aida's idea. When she'd phoned Amy that afternoon to tell her that she was back in town and had made reservations for them tonight at Le Cirque, she had insisted that Amy try on this gorgeous dress she'd spotted at Bergdorf's.

"The instant I saw it, I thought of you, *bella,*" Aida told her. "Why don't you treat yourself to something truly elegant just this once?"

It hardly seemed an appropriate time for Amy to be treating herself to a fifteen-hundred-dollar evening dress, but Aida's phone call had caught her at a vulnerable moment, a moment when she'd realized how desperately she needed a friend in whom she could confide. Only minutes prior to Aida's call, Amy had returned to her apartment from Cal Clay's studio and phoned her lawyer, Brenda Pannopolis.

"I want to see you as soon as possible," Amy had said.

"How's next Tuesday?" her lawyer had asked.

"How's tomorrow?"

"That important? What's this about?"

"A friend of mine who was killed a few weeks ago."

Brenda had been silent for a moment; when she spoke again, her voice was edged with professional excitement.

"Are you in some kind of trouble, Amy?" the lawyer had asked. "Were you involved in this death in any way?"

"Not directly," Amy answered. "But I'm investigating it."

Suddenly, the lawyer began laughing into the phone.

"God, you had me worried there for a moment," Brenda said. "Why didn't you say this was for a story?"

"But it's no—" Amy had cut herself off, abruptly aware of the fact that she wasn't really ready to tell her lawyer why she had flown down to Martinique the day before yesterday. Brenda's tone already sounded so skeptical and disapproving—*Amy and her stories.*

"Actually, all I need from you is the name of a good private investigator," Amy had said finally, and the conversation had come to an end soon after that.

Remaining at her kitchen table, Amy had then tried to think of whom she could talk to about what had happened in Martinique. Certainly not Mary Goldfarb or anyone in her therapy group; and there was no sense in even trying to confide in any of her colleagues at *Femina,* not even Pamela. The "Perils of Pulchritude" affair was months old, but everybody on staff still treated Amy as if she was a borderline paranoid. So who did that leave—Molly? Tell big sister that she had personally been investigating Georgia O'Hearn's death because she felt so guilty about not having taken the gorgeous young model's fears seriously? Molly wouldn't have the vaguest idea what she was talking about. Guilt? What's that, Brains?

It was then that the phone had rung and Aida, her throaty voice full of enthusiasm and warmth, had set their dinner date for tonight. At that moment, the vivacious Italian had sounded exactly the friend Amy needed—cosmopolitan, open, sympathetic. Still, that hardly seemed sufficient reason for running off to Bergdorf's and buying a Herrera dress to wear to dinner, simply because Aida recommended it. It took trying on every outfit in her closet for Amy to be convinced that she'd have to buy *something* new if she was going to make an appearance in front of the fashion-conscious guests of Le Cirque. Not a single one of Amy's dresses fit properly, not even the Linda Allard gown she'd bought in June. She must have lost a good ten or twelve well-selected pounds in the past few weeks alone, not that she'd been eating all that carefully. There was definitely an article somewhere in that: "The High-Anxiety Weight-Loss Program."

When Amy had finally gone down to Bergdorf's to look for something to wear to dinner, she had decided to at least try on the shimmering silver and black Herrera Aida had urged on her. Instantly, all hesitations vanished. It was as if the dress had been made for her. And standing in front of the tripartite mirror in Bergdorf's fitting room, Amy felt all the anxieties of the last few days momentarily lift away. She looked fabulous. She smiled at herself with her newly acquired regal smile. My God, what if she turned out to be one of those lucky few who came into their own in their thirties? Why not? She had the same parents as Molly, was bred from the same genetic pool. Maybe she was just on a different biological timetable. Molly had certainly been less than a spectacular-looking child up to the age of thirteen, but at adolescence, she had blossomed as no other girl in all of Great Neck Junior High had. Not just her breasts and hips, *everything* blossomed—her hair, her eyes, her skin, her cheekbones. Maybe Amy was just a very late bloomer.

"Tonight we celebrate," Aida said as the maître d' seated them in the corner banquette of the main dining room. "Pierre, bring the champagne *immédiatement.* You do like champagne, *bella?*"

"Love it," Amy smiled, noticing a third place setting on their table. "Are we expecting someone else?"

"Yes," Aida said. "A surprise. A friend is joining us later. To help us celebrate."

"What exactly is it that we're celebrating?"

"Ourselves, *bella.*" Aida laughed. "The joy of being beautiful women. It is worth a celebration, no?"

Aida's large eyes flicked to a nearby table where a distinguished-looking silver-haired man still gazed admiringly at the two women.

"I do almost feel beautiful tonight," Amy said, smiling self-consciously. "I guess anyone would in this dress."

"Your beauty's always been there, darling," Aida replied. "It just needed a little nudge."

The champagne arrived and the two women clinked glasses.

"To the lucky few," Aida said.

"Yes, the lucky few," Amy echoed softly, then sighed. Automatically, she found herself again thinking about Georgia, one of the lucky few whose luck had run out.

Aida set down her glass.

"There is something upsetting you, *bella*," the model said. "I feel it."

Amy nodded uncomfortably. Aida reached across the table and touched the back of Amy's hand with the tips of her long fingers.

"If you wish to talk about it," Aida said. "I am here."

Amy closed her eyes a moment. She had known since Aida had phoned that she would be having this conversation with her, yet now it was hard to begin. She took a deep breath.

"Somebody I know has been murdered," Amy said quietly. "And I think I may be the only one in the world who knows about it."

Aida's large eyes fastened on Amy's. She nodded silently.

"I know I have a tendency to overreact at times," Amy went on, remembering her outburst about the leering Venetian sailor in Aida's photo spread. "But this isn't in my head, Aida. It's real. I'm absolutely certain of that."

Again, Aida nodded and she continued nodding silently as Amy unfolded the entire story: Georgia O'Hearn coming to her apartment with her account of being followed in San Francisco, the first word of her accidental drowning in Martinique, the confrontation with Louis and Sarah Louise O'Hearn, the Trois Islets police report, the sudden disappearance of Henri Bouquard and his mysterious Italian passenger, Amy's near-fatal sunset cruise on the *Minoque,* the de la Renta dress with the torn salon receipt in its pocket. Aida listened keenly, her large eyes widening as Amy went on. She didn't utter a single word until Amy came to her discovery of the name Pola di Cenzio in Cal Clay's appointment book.

"My God, I know Pola," Aida interrupted, her voice low. "Not well, but I've met her a few times in Rome, a few times in New York. She and her husband turn up at all the parties, although they usually end up leaving separately. Alfredo has a weakness for leggy American models. In fact, I distinctly remember seeing him dancing with Georgia O'Hearn at one of those affairs . . . and Pola throwing one of her tantrums. She has serious emotional problems."

"What kind of emotional problems?"

"Temper problems, jealousy problems." Aida shook her head in disgust. "Fits and mad scenes and breakdowns. She's always disappearing for a week or two for a rest cure somewhere."

"To Martinique?"

"I wouldn't be surprised. I remember hearing that Pola was off somewhere sunny a few weeks ago and now she's back in Rome acting crazier than ever. Very crazy. I heard she actually physically attacked some pretty young woman at an embassy reception just because Alfredo was chatting the girl up."

"Jesus God." Amy closed her eyes for a moment, her heart thumping. She remembered Georgia's lament about married men who were always promising to get divorced. "That's it, you know. It's got to be her . . . Pola di Cenzio. She's responsible for Georgia's death. She probably killed her herself."

"I'm afraid it sounds very much like you may be right," Aida said, shaking her head. "Poor Pola, crazy woman."

"Not crazy, jealous," Amy blurted, a little too loudly.

"Jealousy makes people crazy," Aida replied softly, again reaching across the table and touching Amy's hand. "These things happen more often than we like to think. Perhaps more often when Italians are involved."

"No, more often when beautiful women are involved," Amy said, suddenly angry. "Jesus, Georgia was a victim of her beauty exactly as I warned in my article. And she knew it. She knew her beauty was going to kill her somehow."

"Perhaps so," Aida said. "Forgive me if I was one of those who didn't take you seriously enough. But the tragedy probably had more to do with Georgia's naïveté than with her beauty. She didn't realize what a dangerous game she was playing when she became involved with Pola's husband."

Amy drew in her breath.

"But I do take you seriously now, *bella,*" Aida went on quickly. "And I will do what I can to help. I have a friend in Rome who is a lawyer. I will call him first thing in the morning and tell him our suspicions. Ask him what the appropriate step is to take now, and where. In Italy? In Washington? I am sure it will have to be handled delicately."

Amy looked up at Aida, chagrined at having lashed out at her.

"I can't thank you enough, Aida," she said quietly. "There was really no one else in the world I could have told this to. I honestly didn't know what to do."

"I'm glad if I can help you. It was too much of a burden to carry by yourself."

Suddenly, Amy found herself smiling broadly with gratitude and pride and immense relief. By God, it really was amazing how perfectly on target her suspicions had been: a faithless husband, a jealous, unstable wife, and poor Georgia, the naïve young victim of the crazy wife's jealousy. Ultimately, it was so terribly banal: jealousy and revenge, the stuff of tabloids.

"Let's wait and hear what my lawyer friend says before we talk to anyone else about this, don't you think?"

"Yes, of course," Amy replied. She took a long sip of champagne and sat back in the banquette. Her sense of vindication was still spreading through her like a warm current. She really did feel like celebrating now.

"Then it's done," Aida said, raising her gaze over Amy's shoulder. "Perfect. My surprise guest has just arrived."

Amy knew without turning her head that a beautiful woman was being led to their table. She could tell by the familiar ripple of hushes that moved through the dining room behind her. Aida rose from her seat and now Amy stood, too, and turned to greet Aida's surprise guest: Sylvia Kronberg. The Swiss scientist looked even more stunning than Amy remembered her. She was dressed tonight in a black crepe St. Laurent dress with a simple string of pearls around her stemlike neck. Pierre, the maître d', stood by proudly as Kronberg and Aida exchanged a total of four kisses on each other's cheeks.

"You two have met before, I believe," Aida said.

"All too briefly," Kronberg replied, putting her hand on Amy's shoulder and leaning forward to kiss her cheek, too.

For a fraction of a second Amy resisted self-consciously. It wasn't that multiple kissing was too intimate a greeting to exchange with a virtual stranger—Amy was around Europeans enough to know that ritual was hardly a sign of intimacy anymore. It was the familiar face-aching self-consciousness of standing in the middle of a room with beautiful women on either side of her that made her hold back. It seemed everyone in the restaurant was gazing at them. But, by God, it *was* the three of them they were gazing at, a glittering trio—blond, raven-haired, brunette. Kronberg kissed Amy's right cheek and then her left. For one giddy moment, Amy felt as if she was being initiated into an exclusive sorority.

"How long has it been since we met at that awful photo exhibition?" Kronberg asked Amy after they sat down. "Five months? Six?"

"It must be close to that."

"You're even lovelier than I remember you," Kronberg said, studying Amy's face with her brilliant green eyes.

"Thank you," Amy replied graciously. "And so, I must say, are you."

"I don't know about either of you, but I'm famished," Aida said, signaling the waiter.

"God yes, starved." Sylvia Kronberg laughed.

For the next two hours, the three women ate: luscious glazed oysters with champagne hollandaise, a succulent roast pheasant with red currants that Aida had ordered in advance—and they consumed another full bottle of Dom Perignon champagne. And all the while, they told one another an endless round of stories, almost all of them about men—the pestering men they couldn't get rid of, the absolute "perfect" men they somehow couldn't turn on to, the devastatingly sexy ones who got away. Aida told one long and deliriously funny saga about a German viscount who had followed her in his Lear jet from Rome to New York to Rio just to ask her out to dinner and how she had refused him simply because she hated his shoes. "Horrible little pointy alligator shoes," Aida said, sipping her champagne. "Enough to ruin any girl's appetite." Amy began telling the story about her affair with Peter, but halfway through, she realized that she didn't like telling this story anymore, especially not the part about her self-mocking little jokes and Penny Twang's long arms around Peter's neck. Perhaps I have more to thank Mary Goldfarb for than I give her credit for, Amy mused. Not only have I gotten over Peter but I've finally gotten over the compulsion to tell humiliating stories about him.

"He sounds absolutely dreadful," Sylvia said. "Was it difficult to finally send him on his way?"

"Not too," Amy replied, smiling. She was thoroughly enjoying herself this evening. She hadn't had such charming and witty company in years; God knows, gossiping with her colleagues at *Femina* had long ago grown stale. Only once during the entire dinner did Amy think about Georgia O'Hearn again—when Sylvia made some passing reference to meeting a "delicious" Italian tenor at a party in Rome—but Amy managed to push the thought away.

With their coffees, the waiter brought grand snifters of cognac, compliments of the house. The three women raised their glasses in unison.

"To us," Aida said.

"Yes, to us," Amy repeated, and she took a long swallow of the sweet liqueur.

"We have marvelous plans for you, *bella,*" Aida said, smiling. "We intend to make you very rich and very happy."

"Rich would be nice." Amy laughed. "At least I could afford to pay for this dress."

"Richer than that," Sylvia Kronberg said softly.

Amy felt uneasy. She looked from Sylvia's radiant face to Aida's and back again.

"What did you have in mind?" she asked.

"My night cream," Sylvia said. "You know, that Aida let you sample. We're preparing to market it now."

Amy's face burned. She was furious. Christ, she should have known this whole evening was too good to be true. It was a goddamned setup to get Amy Martin to plug Sylvia Kronberg's new night cream in her column. Give it high marks on the A.B.Q. Shit, she would have given it a good review anyhow. But Kronberg wasn't taking chances. Obviously, La Douce was in too precarious a condition to take any risks. But make Amy rich? What the hell was that all about? Did Kronberg actually think she could buy her with payola?

"I think you're making a terrible mistake," Amy said evenly.

"Not at all," Aida said. "You're ready to make a move, *bella.* I know it, you know it. It's time you joined us instead of standing on the outside criticizing us in the beauty business. You're talents are wasted at that magazine."

"You're one of the most gifted people in the business," Kronberg went on, smiling. "We want you on our side, Amy. Helping us target our product, marketing it. Our people are prepared to make you a very good offer. Several times over what you're making at *Femina.* A senior vice-presidency."

"You can't be serious," Amy said, an irrepressible smile appearing on her lips.

"Absolutely serious," Kronberg said. "Your office will be next to mine."

"I never expected this."

"You're made for the job, darling," Aida said.

"I'm surprised no one else stole you from that magazine earlier," Kronberg said.

Amy pursed her lips. It was true that in the months since her "Perils" article, she'd grown gradually less enthusiastic about *Femina.* The incident had made her aware of something so restrained and inhibited about the atmosphere of the office. God knows, she couldn't begin to imagine an evening as sparkling as this one with any colleague at the magazine. Maybe it was time for a switch, a fresh start somewhere new.

"What exactly would I be doing for you?" Amy asked.

"A number of things," Kronberg answered. "Targeting markets. Evaluating potential customers. Making personal contacts at the highest level. I'll give you a more complete job description when you come by my office. Run you through our whole operation, all off the record, of course. Let's set a meeting up while Aida's still in town so we can all talk together. Would Friday be too soon for you?"

"I'll need some time to think about this," Amy said.

"We've had our eyes on you from the start, *bella,*" Aida said, smiling. "You simply can't refuse us."

38

··

"Ms. Martin?" A man's voice, low, urgent.

Amy froze. Instinctively, she stepped back, turned toward the cab that had just dropped her off, but it was already cruising through an amber traffic light half a block away.

"Please. I have to talk to you."

A dark figure emerged from the shadow of the canopy in front of her apartment building. He was tall, unshaven, with unkempt black hair and bloodshot eyes. Something cylindrical in his outstretched hand. A gun? He took a long step toward her. Amy backed off the curb, her pulse racing. She looked up and down West End Avenue. Not another person within two blocks of her. Not a car in sight.

"You know me, Ms. Martin. We met once. At St. Mary's hospital. I'm—"

In that instant, she recognized him. The blue-eyed prince from Diagnostique, David Copeland. But he barely resembled the handsome, confident doctor who had strutted up to the lectern in that hospital lecture hall six months ago. Copeland's mouth hung open, his eyes looked half-crazed. Christ, that was it: He'd come for revenge, another bitter researcher who blamed his failure on Amy Martin's "Beauty Bytes." That's what he was doing in front of her apartment at one in the morning. Amy sucked in her breath, grasped the lapels of her coat, and closed them over the open neck of her new evening dress.

"Come by my office tomorrow morning if you have something you want to talk about, Doctor," she said, deliberately trying to keep her voice neutral, devoid of fear.

Copeland took another step toward her. His eyes darted up and down the street.

"It can't wait," he said in a hoarse whisper.

Amy did not move.

"What do you want?" she asked.

"Information," Copeland said. "About some women you wrote about. In here."

He raised his hand, the one with the cylinder in it, and Amy cowered away from him. Then, from the corner of her eye, she saw that all he held in his hand was a rolled up copy of her magazine.

"What kind of information do you need at this time of night, Dr. Copeland?"

"Information about how these women died," Copeland answered flatly.

A car suddenly appeared at the Eighty-eighth Street corner. It turned toward them, flashing on its high beams. Copeland jumped to the far side of the canopy. He looked terrified. The car roared past them. Copeland raised his terror-stricken eyes to Amy's.

"Somebody's trying to stop me," he murmured. "They broke into my apartment today, left a warning."

"Trying to stop you from what?"

Copeland clenched his muscular jaw. He looked as if he was in pain. "Please, it's not safe here. Can we talk inside?"

Amy peered at Copeland. She had no reason in the world to trust this man. "Not tonight. I'm sorry."

"Please, Ms. Martin." Copeland's voice broke. "You have no idea how important this is. It's bigger than any story you can imagine. Just two minutes, that's all I need."

Amy hesitated. Copeland's pain was genuine, of that she had no doubt. She stared at him, her pulse racing.

"Two minutes, no more," she said curtly.

She took a step around him and headed straight for the front door of the apartment building. Copeland followed her inside, staying a full step behind her until they were inside the elevator.

As the doors slid closed, he raised his bloodshot eyes to hers in the harsh fluorescent light.

"I tried to call you several times this evening," he said softly. "I left a message on your machine. But I couldn't wait. I decided to take a chance and come up here. I've been out there a couple of hours. I didn't even know if I would recognize you."

A faint smile appeared on Copeland's haggard face.

"I didn't recognize *you*," Amy said, smiling back in spite of herself. Indeed, Copeland looked infinitely softer than when last seen. No arrogance tonight, no macho strut. She lowered her eyes.

The elevator door slid open and Amy led the way to her apartment. As she unlocked the door, she was struck by the thought that this desperately frightened doctor was the first man to enter her apartment in half a year. Inside, Copeland helped her out of her coat and then, for a long moment, he gazed with a look of undisguised surprise and admiration at her in her shimmering Herrera evening dress. Amy turned away uncomfortably.

"What exactly is it that you wanted to ask me, Dr. Copeland?" she asked.

Copeland hesitated, then again held out his tattered copy of *Femina* as if it was an offering.

"Last July, you wrote an article about three models who had died," he began, his voice pitched low, as if he was still afraid of being overheard. "I need to know everything you can remember about how each one of these women died. In particular, the one named Kelly Keane."

Amy stiffened, stepped back from him.

"Please try to remember, Ms. Martin," Copeland went on quickly, looking steadily into Amy's eyes. "I have reason to believe that Kelly Keane is still alive. In fact, there's a possibility that all three of those women are still alive."

Amy felt the blood drain from her face. She groped behind her for the wall, leaned back against it.

"What in the name of God are you talking about?"

Copeland stepped toward her. He was now holding out another tattered copy of *Femina,* this one opened to a two-page photo spread. Amy stared down at it. The headline read, MODEL CITIZENS. She vaguely remembered it—some kind of celebrity blood donation that the media had fussed over on a slow news day.

"It began with this, I'm almost certain," Copeland was saying. "All three of them were there. Keane, Le Fevre, del Ray. All three of them donors. This is when the experiment started. When they stole their blood, tested it for the first time."

"What makes you think Kelly is alive?"

The words came out of Amy's mouth in a dead monotone. She hadn't taken her eyes off the photograph Copeland held in front of her. She was staring at Georgia O'Hearn's heart-shaped face smiling out from the upper left-hand corner.

"Her blood," Copeland answered. "A vial of it turned up in my laboratory less than three months ago. I had it tested and it was fresh. Fresh blood."

"How did you know it was Kelly's blood?"

"The HLA typing. It matched."

Amy nodded numbly. She didn't really understand anything Copeland was saying, but a feeling of dread was spreading through her like a numbing poison.

"Please tell me everything you remember about the circumstances of Kelly Keane's death. Was it an accident?"

Amy looked up at Copeland. She swallowed twice before speaking.

"Kelly drowned." Amy pushed the words out of her mouth. "The English Channel. Dover. They said she slipped off some rocks on a late-night walk. She'd been taking drugs."

"Was her body recovered?"

Amy was shaking. She opened her mouth to speak but no sound came.

"Do you remember if they buried her, Ms. Martin?" Copeland's voice was loud, insistent.

"No! No body!" the words suddenly burst out of Amy. She was quaking uncontrollably. "They never found Kelly's body. And they never found Carmina's, either. Or Monique's. Or Georgia O'Hearn's!"

"Georgia O'Hearn? Who is she? Is she in this photograph? Was she also reported dead?"

Amy's head was spinning. Her knees suddenly buckled under her and Copeland grabbed her around the waist with both hands. She leaned all her weight against him, trembled against his chest.

"Who—" Amy swallowed hard and started again. "Who's doing these experiments with these women?"

"A cosmetics company."

Amy closed her eyes. She knew that if she did not strain against it, she could faint, drop into a blessed oblivion of unasked questions. She forced her eyelids up, her mouth open.

"Which cosmetics company?" she whispered.

Copeland was silent.

"Please," she cried, her lips against his ear. "Tell me. I need to know."

"La Douce," Copeland said. "La Douce Laboratories. Their research director. Her name is Sylvia Kronberg."

A sob burst from Amy's throat.

"Oh God."

Amy Martin trembled in David's arms. Her breathing was labored; she was clearly in shock. But why? What did she know about any of this? David tightened his grasp on her, pressed his palm against the soft warm skin where her dress dipped down in the middle of her back. She felt light in his arms, yet he sensed a current in her body that made her feel surprisingly substantial. He lightly brushed her hair away from her face and looked down at her. It was remarkable how different she looked from the high-gloss beauty editor who had taunted him with smartass questions at the Mona press conference. Amy Martin was an extraordinarily attractive woman—a genuine beauty.

She gently pushed herself away from him. Her face was flushed.

"I . . . I'm part of it," she said, her voice cracking.

David's jaw went slack. He stared at her, felt panic rising in his throat. Jesus Christ, so she was part of it, too. That's why she was frightened; she'd been found out. His eyes darted to the door. It was only ten steps away. He could be out of here in a minute.

"She's using me," she said in a monotone. "Kronberg's using me in her experiment somehow."

She abruptly twirled around, the hem of her gown rising like a dancer's, and strode away from him into the hallway. David hesitated only a second, then followed her into her kitchen. He watched from the kitchen door as she went directly to her refrigerator and opened it. She pulled something out, closed the door, and turned to face him.

"Kronberg gave me this," she said, holding out a plastic deli container. "Or rather she had somebody give it to me. To try it. To test it."

David took the container from her. A handwritten label on the top read, "A. Smooth on in the evenings."

"How long ago was this?" he asked.

"Six, seven weeks ago."

"What did they tell you it was?"

"A night cream. A skin cream. A new product they were developing."

"And did you try it?"

"Yes."

"More than once?"

She closed her lovely almond eyes before replying.

"Every night," she said quietly, a tremor in her voice. "I spread it all over my face every night."

"For the last six weeks?"

She nodded.

"Do you know what it is, Doctor?" she asked. Her body had started to tremble. "Is it dangerous? Can it do anything to me?"

"I don't know," David answered quietly.

He pried the top off the container. A quarter-inch layer of pale yellow cream covered the bottom. He dipped in his forefinger, rubbed some against his palm, sniffed it. No odor. His skin absorbed it almost immediately. Was this it? Sylvia Kronberg's secret pheromone preparation? Her hypothalamic hormone-stimulating cream?

"Have you observed any unusual reactions or symptoms since you started using the cream?" David's tone was automatically neutral, his doctor's voice.

"What kind of symptoms?"

"Anything," David said. "A change in your appetite, in your sleep patterns, digestion. A missed or late period. Sudden mood swings, temper tantrums."

She shook her head no.

"What about skin eruptions?" David continued. "Hair loss? Appearance of new body or facial hair?"

She hesitated.

"Nothing that lasted more than a few days," she said.

"Any sudden weight gain or loss?" David went on. "Change in shoe size? Clothing size? Bra size? Rings or glasses that no longer fit? New bone growth or soft-tissue growth in the skull? Change in the breadth of your nose? The thickness or length of your jaw?

The color or texture of your skin? Any noticeable changes in the shape of your face?"

As David recited the litany of clinical hypothalamic-disorder symptoms, he flicked his eye from Amy Martin's elegant face to her long sculpted neck to her perfectly rounded bare shoulders, then below the hem of her dress to her shapely calves and finely turned ankles. With every question, Amy Martin nodded her head up and down. Now tears began to form in the corners of her wide-set brown eyes and drip onto her cheeks.

"Has anyone who knows your body well remarked on any changes in your physical appearance?" David went on. "Is there anything at all that seems unusual to you when you look at yourself in the mirror? Your breasts? Your abdomen? Your legs?"

"Yes. God yes," she whispered. She was weeping freely now. "My face . . . my breasts . . . my legs . . . changes . . . hundreds of them. . . . They all seemed so natural, Doctor. . . . They all seemed so perfectly natural."

"Can you describe these symptoms to me, Ms. Martin?" David asked softly.

"My symptoms . . . my symptoms—" For a moment, her lips continued to move but no words came.

David took a step toward her. He wanted to comfort her, but she raised her hand, signaling him not to come any closer.

"You . . . can . . . examine . . . them . . . for . . . yourself . . . Doctor."

As Amy choked the words out, she reached a slender hand to her side and pinched open the catch of her dress, pulled the zipper down to her waist and over her right hip. She gave a quick twist of her hips and the dress slid down to her ankles. She raised her feet one at a time out of the gown, then kicked it to the side on the kitchen floor. Her limpid sorrowful eyes gazed directly into David's as she pulled her half-slip over her hips and down to the floor. Now she was only wearing a strapless bra and a pair of pink satiny panties. He gazed at her silently, his heart thudding. He didn't dare to move. She unfastened her bra in the front where the two cups joined and it sprang open, revealing rose-colored nipples on her high rounded breasts. She flung the bra to the floor and immediately began to roll the satin panties over her hips and down her long smooth thighs. They dropped to the floor. Stark naked, Amy Martin turned up her palms at her sides, a trembling patient ready for examination.

"You're incredibly beautiful," David blurted, gazing at her.

She stared back at him. Her tears had stopped, but the wrenchingly sad look remained in her eyes.

"Not six weeks ago," she said in a half-whisper. "I didn't look like this then. Six weeks ago, I didn't have any of these symptoms, Doctor."

David inhaled deeply. He felt dizzy.

"Who else knows about this?" he asked.

"A woman named Aida who works for Kronberg," she answered, shifting her weight to her right foot and gracefully turning out her left, like a dancer. For a moment, it seemed as if she had forgotten that she was naked. "There are probably others, too, but I couldn't tell you who they are."

David nodded.

"I didn't know myself," she went on softly. "Not consciously. I never once questioned why . . . how all this was happening to me. Can you believe that?"

"Yes, I can believe that." David ached to touch her. He took a slow step toward her, but again she raised her hand and again he stopped. Tears were once more silently flooding down her face. For several seconds, neither of them spoke. Then a soft sob issued from her throat.

"Will I stay like this?"

David gazed at her, overwhelmed with wonder and pity and lust.

"I really don't know," he answered softly. "I don't have any idea how the cream works . . . other than that once it's absorbed, it works directly on the endocrine system."

"Then it could all fade . . . all disappear?"

"I imagine the symptoms could reverse under certain conditions, but I don't really know. I have no data to go on."

Amy closed her eyes. David could see her entire body straining not to tremble.

"Why . . . why do you think they did this to me?" Amy whispered, her eyes still closed.

"I suppose it's part of an experiment," David answered.

"Maybe it's something else, too," Amy said, suddenly opening her eyes again. "A bribe . . . a diversion."

David looked at her questioningly.

"And it almost worked—I was almost blinded by my own beauty." She smiled a painful smile. Her voice was low and full of feeling when she spoke again. "I've always wanted to look like this, Doctor. Can you possibly understand that?"

"Of course, I can," David replied softly. "I don't think there's a woman in the world who wouldn't want to look the way you do right now, Amy."

Amy gazed back at him, tears dropping from her face onto her breasts.

"Dr. Copeland?"

"Yes?"

"Would you hold me, please? Right now, hold me very tight."

David's arms closed around her before she could finish.

She felt drugged, crazy, on the edge of a dreamscape. What was she doing in this man's arms? All she knew was that she could not stand here alone and naked one second longer. The two of them had just penetrated an incredible secret, a mad secret, and they were alone with it. This man, this doctor, this David Copeland, was the only person in the world who could have any idea of the wild and frightening feelings that were pounding through her. She raised her face to his, looked up into his deep-set blue eyes. He lightly touched the side of her face with his fingertips, then leaned his face down, brushed her cheeks with his lips. Then she kissed him, softly on the lips, folding in to him, pressing her breasts against his chest. She clutched the curly hair on the back of his head. Then she kissed him again, parting her lips, opening herself to him. I shouldn't be doing this, she thought—a distant thought, as if it were coming from a different mind in a different body.

"We shouldn't be doing this," she whispered.

"I don't think we have any choice," he whispered back.

Amy smiled, then silently took his hand and led him down the hallway to her bedroom. She lay down on her bed and watched as he quickly kicked off his shoes, pulled his shirt over his head, slipped off his pants, then stripped away the rest. He walked toward her, his body a hard shadow in the dimly lit room, then hovered above her. His eyes moved up her legs, lingered at her waist, then up across her breasts, and finally rested on her face. His eyes were intense, powerful, and as they looked deeply into hers, a dream memory suddenly poked through her consciousness; she remembered David Copeland studying her naked body on a hospital examination table in that long-ago dream. The memory startled her.

"What about Kelly? What about Georgia?" she was suddenly whispering. "We have to—"

"Not now . . ." David touched his fingers to her lips, then lowered himself onto the bed beside her. He lay on his side, ran his fingers through her hair. When she turned to face him, she felt the tips of her breasts tingle and burn as they brushed against his chest. Now her whole body tingled. His hand slowly traced up her side, slid from hip to waist, then gently cupped the side of her breast.

This is me. All of this is me.

He pushed his face closer, licked a circle around her lips, his hand pressing against her breast.

This is me and no one else. This feels more like me than I've ever felt in my life.

She touched his cheek with the back of her hand, smiled into his wonderful blue eyes, started to kiss him, then stopped.

"David?"

"Yes?"

"If . . . if I didn't look like this . . ."

His hand slid down her back and over her buttocks, pulled her against him. Amy closed her eyes. Her question evaporated, incomplete, irrelevant.

The searing sound shot through David like an electric shock. He sat bolt upright in the bed, his heart racing, his brain still dream numb. For a moment he was lost. Then he saw the brown hair cascading on the pillow next to his, saw the achingly delicate outline of Amy Martin's brow and cheekbone.

The searing sound again. David swung his feet over the side of the bed, stood, searched for his trousers. They were in a pile at the foot of the bed. David swooped them up and pulled the electronic pager from his pocket just as it shot another high-pitched beep into Amy Martin's bedroom. He clicked it off, read the number off the bottom: St. Mary's Hospital, Art Malley's extension.

David's eye went to the clock-radio on the bed table. Eight-forty, later than he'd stayed in bed in months. They had made love through most of the night, gently, then urgently, then gently again. The last time he had looked at the clock, it had been after five in the morning.

He tiptoed out of the bedroom to the hallway and into the kitchen. Amy's panties lay in front of the sink like a giant pink butterfly. He found a wall phone next to the door, dialed. Art Malley answered himself.

"David Copeland here."

"Good. Glad I caught you before you tried to come in. You need to stay clear of the hospital another couple days, David. Lay low. We're still working on our settlement with the Medicaid people, but until it's a done deal, that warrant stays hot."

"What deal is that, Art? Is St. Mary's coming up with the three hundred grand?"

David could hear Malley take a few breaths before he answered.

"Three hundred grand and a whole lot more, Doctor," Malley said finally. "Thanks to your friend Ray Kenworthy. He's a good man, David. A hundred percent loyal to St. Mary's."

"Ray? Where's he getting the money?"

"Don't worry about it, David. Now that Diagnostique is out of the picture, none of this is your problem anymore," Malley replied, an edge in his voice.

"Look, I've got Feds on my ass and punks chasing me with knives, so it's still one hell of a problem for me," David said angrily into the phone. "Just tell me, who's paying our bill?"

David could hear Malley trill his fingers on his desk.

"Well, you'll be meeting them soon enough anyhow," he said, his voice soft again, soft and arrogant. "In fact, you're going to be working with them, David. They're called Sportsplex. They're a major sports-management consortium. And they're going to be making some very generous contributions to St. Mary's Hospital once we iron out all the details."

A short laugh, like a bark, erupted from David's mouth. Christ, it was all the same to these people: eye gels, a six-inch height boost, Sylvia Kronberg's transfiguring hormone-cream. It was all cosmetics.

"What kind of details are you ironing out, Art?" he asked. "How to guarantee Sportsplex the agenting options on Ray's Junior Giants once the boys turn pro? After Ray's shot them all over six foot ten with growth hormone? Is that the sweet new deal you're working out for good old St. Mary's Hospital?"

232

Malley remained silent several seconds. When he finally spoke, his voice was low, menacing.

"Listen, David, this is one deal you're not going to fuck up," he said. "So I'd be very careful if I were you. You're in deeper shit than you know. I know people all over this town who'd like to get their hands on you right now, Doctor."

With that, Malley hung up the phone and David felt a tremor pass through him. He hung up, too, then slowly turned around. Only then did he see Amy Martin standing behind him in the hallway. She had a bed sheet draped like a toga over her voluptuous body, and a look of dread on her gorgeous face.

"We have to find them, you know," she said softly. "Kelly, Monique, Carmen, Georgia. We have to find all of them."

"I know," David answered.

"It's fabulous, Sylvia. I still can't believe it. It's the most incredible hormone cream ever created. When can we talk?"

"I was beginning to wonder when it would finally click for you. But I knew you'd be pleased. Very pleased. Why don't you come by tomorrow at two, Amy?"

P A R T
....

4

39

"First slide, please."

A photograph of Amy smiling self-consciously next to Francesca Levesque appeared on the screen at the front of the office.

"Do you remember when this was taken?" Sylvia Kronberg asked.

"At that awful Tony Amato show, wasn't it?" Amy laughed, squinting at the screen. "What are those ridiculous smudges doing around my eyes?"

"I believe you'd just had a makeover that afternoon," Kronberg said, smiling across her mahogany desk at Amy. "André Sybert."

"God, yes, André Sybert," Amy said. "He said he was giving me a face full of wit and irony. Somehow I ended up looking like Stan Laurel."

"Not quite that bad." Aida laughed. She was sitting in the Barcelona chair beside Amy's. "But it's certainly not you, *bella.*"

"No, not you at all," Kronberg murmured. "Next photo, please."

A second photo of Amy appeared on the screen next to the first, this one taken at an agency cocktail party. Amy tried to remember exactly when it was taken. The third week in August, she calculated. The week after she'd come back to Manhattan from her vacation on Montauk. Two weeks after starting to use Sylvia Kronberg's "Makeover Cream."

"I remember," Amy said. "I'd just gotten over a horrible case of acne."

"Yes, probably a bit of facial hair and a few other indignities as well," Kronberg said. "That happens the first week or so. Kind of a mini-reprise of puberty before the new synthetic hormones mix in with your system and take hold. It's a shame we didn't manage to get any photos of you during that period. We could use documentation showing that part's only transient. That's going to be one of the most demanding aspects of your job, you know, Amy—getting clients to continue using the cream during this period of regression—but I'm confident you'll be able to reassure them. Your clients will all be women who've put their faith in you for years. They know how skeptical you've always been of phony medical cosmetics. They trust you."

Kronberg smiled.

"And besides," she went on, "you're their 'Makeover Girl,' Amy. Always have been and always will be."

Amy nodded graciously. She had been rehearsing these modest nods and eager smiles in front of her mirror for the last twenty-four hours. So far, she seemed to be carrying off her role as grateful acolyte convincingly.

"You can see some difference in your eyes already," Aida said, looking up at the screen. "More luminosity. More depth and variation in color. May we have a close-up of her pupils, please?"

A whirring sound as a single eye in each photograph enlarged and filled the screen. The extent of the difference between the two eyes *was* remarkable. The eye on the right was still brown, of course, but it was flecked with glints of gold and, indeed, it was much more luminous. It seemed to shine with some inner light.

"It's absolutely amazing!" Amy said. She had no problem delivering that line with conviction.

"It's certainly not an effect one could even hope to approximate with tinted contact lenses," Kronberg said.

"Or with cosmetic surgery," Aida said.

"But of course not, darling," Kronberg said reprovingly. "None of this can be affected with plastic surgery, none of it.

Plastic surgery manipulates the outside only. It's unnatural. It can't begin to deal with the components of genuine beauty."

Kronberg abruptly turned to Amy and peered deep into her eyes. Amy felt her heartbeat increase. Was she really fooling Kronberg or just fooling herself? Amy forced the most gloriously impressed-looking smile she could manage.

"May I see the photos in full face again?" she asked.

"Certainly," Kronberg replied.

Both projections zoomed back to full-face photographs of Amy.

"You've always been the most celebrated before-and-after girl in the world," Kronberg said, smiling. "That part won't change, will it? We'll include the complete series of these photographs in your sales portfolio. Your clients will like that. They already identify with you completely."

Amy responded with what was meant to be a conspiratorial wink, but she immediately wondered whether it was too much, whether it looked to Kronberg like overacting. Amy again focused her attention on the screen that hung in front of floor-to-ceiling file cabinets on the far wall. She studied the side-by-side photographs of herself.

"I think my skin had started to change already, too," she said seriously.

"Definitely," Kronberg said. "It's much less dense, much softer. You can see that clearly in the way it drapes your lacrimals. Your skin has actually begun to grow thinner there. Softer, suppler. Nothing else can come close to doing that. Not the highest-priced so-called hormone cream on the market."

Kronberg uttered a soft self-satisfied laugh.

"There's certainly never been anything like it," Amy said with a tone of utter admiration. "It's the ultimate cosmetic."

"Yes, it is," Kronberg said. "So many products have made that claim before, but this time it's true, isn't it? Next photo, please."

A third photograph appeared on the screen next to the second. It obviously had been taken on the street in front of the *Femina* office building, but Amy couldn't remember who took it or when.

"Candid Camera," Aida said. "I was across the street with my telephoto lens. We didn't have any other opportunity to record your progress that week. Something comic about the pose, wouldn't you say?"

Amy's heart was thudding again. They were both so open about spying on her all these weeks, so confident that she'd find nothing reprehensible in it. Didn't it enter their minds that she might resent this invasion of her privacy even if she didn't resent their manipulation of her bones and skin? Probably not. And, ultimately, they were right. If this were all Amy really did know about their operation—that they'd been secretly monitoring her progress as Kronberg's hormone cream metamorphisized her into a beauty—she'd probably be so overwhelmed with gratitude that she wouldn't resent a thing.

And to be perfectly honest, didn't she genuinely feel that gratitude now anyhow? Even knowing that spying was the least of Sylvia Kronberg's crimes?

Amy turned her head, tried to refocus her thoughts. Kronberg's people had been following David, too, tracking his every move. Like fish in a tank, as David had said. Amy could not even be sure that Kronberg was unaware of David's visit to her apartment. All Amy was certain of was that both Sylvia and Aida were in the cab that had dropped her off after dinner and that the cab had been a block away before David appeared out of the shadows. All the rest was guess and hope, the initial calculated risk that this whole day—and night—was built on.

Amy stared at the new photo on the screen. Aida's lens had caught her straining to button her blouse after it had popped open across her bosom.

"What week was that?" Amy asked, offering an amused smile.

"Your fourth," Aida replied.

"Obviously, you'd already begun to outgrow your wardrobe," Kronberg said. "But you were still far from guessing what was going on, weren't you?"

"Very," Amy said. "I thought I was looking prettier because I was thinking pretty thoughts. Beautiful illusions. Ridiculous, eh?"

"Not at all, it's quite natural," Kronberg replied. "You would have been crazy to question why you were becoming more beautiful. We only really look closely when our looks fail us. And for people like you, the realization that you're turning into a beauty is especially slow . . . you were so unwilling to believe that Amy Martin was entitled to be beautiful. Your self-image was hard to crack. But that is precisely the way I wanted you to experience your makeover—gradually, with doubts. I wanted you to grow into it, not to be shocked and uncomfortable with it the way women so often are with cosmetic surgery. Now, you'll be able to explain to our customers how natural the transformation feels, not just how natural it looks."

"Yes, how very natural it feels," Amy echoed.

"And it truly is, you know," Kronberg went on earnestly. "Makeover Cream releases the beauty that was meant to be yours all along. Supplies you with the hormone you were deprived of in adolescence. Like any hormone treatment, it simply rights an imbalance in your endocrine system."

Amy nodded. How pure Kronberg made it sound, as if lack of beauty were a dread disease for which she had found the cure.

"Next photo, please."

The fourth photo appeared to the right of the third. It showed Amy, Aida, and Sylvia Kronberg seated at their banquette at Le Cirque just two days ago. Pierre, the maître d', had insisted on taking the photograph before they left—"as a souvenir of the most beautiful trio of women who ever graced my dining room."

"Super the grid," Kronberg said.

Fine grids were simultaneously superimposed over each of the four photographs of Amy's face. Some of the lines bled over the edge of the screen and glinted on the steel file cabinets that surrounded it.

"This helps us pinpoint new bone growth and calcium remodeling," Kronberg said. "You can see the repositioning of your eyes more clearly. There's additional separation of more than half a centimeter. Not much, really. But it's a critical difference, wouldn't you say? 'The Loren Principle' I believe you once called it in your magazine . . . the difference between the ordinary and the sublime."

"God knows how many times I've been told that my eyes could never be separated," Amy said. "I must have asked every plastic surgeon in three continents that question."

Kronberg smiled. She signaled for the grids to be removed.

"Look from left to right, one photo at a time," she said softly. "It's as if your face was coming into focus. You do have the perfect face for Makeover Cream, Amy. You were an almost-but-not-quite girl, just like all those almost-but-not-quite girls who spend thousands every year on phony makeup."

Amy drew in her breath slowly. Kronberg was right about that: Her face did look as if it had gradually come into focus like an autodeveloping Polaroid picture, what was beautiful in her face sharpened, highlighted, emphasized.

"I guess I can understand why I didn't see what was happening to me," Amy said. "But why didn't anybody else notice, Sylvia? My friends, my sister? Why didn't anybody say anything?"

"But I'm sure they did notice," Kronberg replied. "They simply couldn't put their finger on precisely what it was that was changing. The changes are so subtle, you see, so gradual, and there are so many of them. Heaven knows, half the time, people don't even notice when you're wearing new glasses or that their husband shaved off his mustache a week ago. But they are aware that *something* is different, *something* has changed. I'm confident a great number of people have commented on how lovely you're looking lately, Amy. How very attractive. And I'm certain men have started to behave quite differently toward you. More attentive. More quickly aroused."

Amy nodded, then lowered her eyes. Yes, very quickly aroused, she thought. She felt her cheeks coloring, then started to panic, confused. She couldn't keep track of which responses were appropriate and which were dead giveaways? Could a mere blush connect her to David?

Aida was laughing.

"That part can be a serious problem," she said.

"It's the pheromones," Kronberg said. "One of the side effects of hypothalamic Sex-Attractant Hormone is that you start putting out this subliminal odor that attracts men like moths to a flame. Actually, we feel that effect is too strong. Women want to be admired, not mauled. I'm looking in the lab for ways to modify the pheromone effect of SAH."

"That's probably a good idea," Amy said. David will certainly find that detail supremely ironic, she thought. He had confessed to her exactly why he had started investigating La Douce's experiments, that the object of Armand Diltzer's espionage was to find out how Kronberg was getting her test subjects to produce a pheromone called alpha copulin. But pheromones, it seems, were simply a somewhat annoying side effect of the Kronberg treatment.

"Hormones—synthetic or natural—are always risky, of course, and you'll undoubtedly find customers worrying about that,"

Kronberg went on, peering down at her notes on the table. "They know that you can stimulate production of one hormone and easily end up throwing a dozen others out of balance. But you know from your own experience, Amy, that that's not true with Makeover Cream. Of course, we've tested it on other subjects without any problems whatsoever, so you can promise our customers that our product is perfectly safe. No side effects, no organ damage. You can assure them that our product is bio-genetically engineered under the most hygienic conditions."

"Good. Perhaps I should take a look at your production process sometime," Amy said, trying to sound curious, nothing more.

"Certainly," Kronberg answered crisply. "We'll have to take you to Basel one day to look over our facility. It's impressive."

"That's where Makeover Cream is made?"

"Where SAH is synthesized, yes."

Amy held her smile. Basel? Jesus Christ, could she and David be about to risk their lives searching in the wrong place—*on the wrong continent*—for the source of the Makeover Cream process? And couldn't Kelly and Georgia and Monique and the other missing models be in Basel, too?

"The point you'll want to stress most, of course, is that Makeover Cream is organic in the purest sense," Kronberg continued. "It becomes part of the body's system. You can assure every customer that our product is perfectly natural."

"Very good. It will be a pleasure to use that much-abused word *natural* and actually mean it," Amy said. The ironies were starting to make her head spin. In recent years, almost every beauty product was pitched as "perfectly natural"; it's what cosmetics customers wanted to hear. The makeup myth had always held that the customer's beauty was innate, just lurking beneath the surface waiting for a "natural" product to nudge it out. And oh God yes, Kronberg's Makeover Cream was a natural product.

"It's really quite miraculous how much power SAH has to affect our appearance," Kronberg said. "Until recently, we attributed ninety percent of beauty to our genes, the rest to diet and hygiene. But I never really believed that, not in my heart. Not since I was a little girl. I grew up with a beautiful sister, too, Amy. My genes came from the same gene pool hers did, and yet she was beautiful and I was not."

"We have that in common, too," Aida said softly beside Amy. "We all have beautiful sisters."

The pencil slipped from Amy's hand, bounced from the table to the floor. She blushed. Aida was laughing again.

"Yes, we're all makeover beauties here, my friend," Aida said.

Amy tried to regain control of herself by staring at the picture of the three of them on the screen. The beautiful trio. Somehow she could imagine how each of the other two must have looked before their transformation: Aida, a horsey young woman with features too crowded on her long face; Sylvia Kronberg, a doughy-faced, washed-out blonde with bland peasant features. Made over. All made over. Why did the idea of their transformation seem any more artificial than her own?

"But it's the hormones, not the genes," Kronberg went on, raising her voice. "It's the mix, the apportionment, the balance of the genetic material that counts. It's the orchestration, not the notes."

Kronberg waved her hand and the four photographs vanished from the screen and the lights in her office came up. Kronberg stood, paced to the window, and looked out for several seconds before she continued.

"Medicine has always been predicated on negativity," she said. "It focuses on disease, not health; on deformity, not beauty. There are hundreds of medical atlases crammed with pictures of patients who have been disfigured by hormone imbalances. But no respectable medical man would imagine in his wildest dreams a hormone that creates beauty, that *in*figures. Their only aesthetic model is *dis*figurement. Heaven knows, our professors in Basel laughed at the very proposition of a master aesthetic hormone."

Kronberg smiled at Aida and the elegant Italian model smiled back. Amy's head reeled. So Aida had been a student at the Basel Institute, too. Another brain turned beauty.

"But that is precisely what I had isolated in my laboratory—an infiguring hormone, SAH," Kronberg went on. "God knows nothing would have come of it if I hadn't found American investors. People with vision."

Abruptly, Kronberg turned and looked directly at Amy.

"Tell me exactly when you realized that my cream was causing your metamorphosis?"

This was it, Kronberg's big question, her test. Amy strained to remain calm. She grasped her hands together under the table.

"Wednesday night, after I'd left you," she said, turning up her palms in an expression of modesty. "I mean, it must have been clear to you at dinner that I didn't actually have the foggiest idea why you wanted me to work for La Douce. I know I enjoy an estimable reputation as a beauty writer, but that hardly seemed to justify the offer you were making to me."

Kronberg nodded tentatively.

"The truth is, I stopped really looking at myself in the mirror long ago," Amy went on. "Stopped giving myself the once-over from head to toe years ago when I realized how terribly depressing it always made me feel. The inventory always came up short, if you know what I mean. But that afternoon when I was down at Bergdorf's trying on the Herrera, I found myself gaping at my reflection like Narcissus. Enjoying it immensely in spite of myself. And so that night, when I was getting ready for bed, I removed the robe that I usually leave hanging in front of the full-length mirror inside the door to my bedroom closet and undressed very slowly in front of it. It was almost like a striptease, teasing myself."

Amy paused and looked seriously at Sylvia Kronberg.

"And suddenly standing in front of that mirror, everything that I'd been explaining away all these weeks couldn't be explained away any longer," Amy said. "It wasn't my new diet that had made my hair so thick and lustrous. It wasn't positive thinking that was making my bust burst out of my bra. It wasn't some lucky new phase of natural maturation that was making my eyes look more aesthetically spaced at the age of thirty. At that moment, it was perfectly clear. It clicked. It was the cream, the tapioca-colored cream that Aida had given me to try. I'd been made over and the cream did it."

"Perfect," Kronberg said, smiling.

"Perfect? I was furious!" Amy said sharply, looking Kronberg straight in the eye. "I felt deceived and manipulated."

"I know, I'm sorry," Kronberg said, her face softening. "But I felt it was important for you to have the experience of changing naturally, unself-consciously. We knew that ultimately it would make you a better representative for our product."

"Tell me, had you planned on my sneaking that container of cream out of your refrigerator?" Amy asked, turning to Aida. "Or did that just make it easier?"

"Of course, we planned that," Aida replied, shrugging. "After all, your reputation preceded you."

"But somehow you survived your fury?" Kronberg asked, pushing on seriously. "You put it behind you?"

"Not right away. After the fury came a kind of delirium. I felt crazy for hours. And I barely slept that night," Amy answered softly, every word of it true. "But by morning, I realized that more than anything, I felt incredibly happy. Happy and very, very lucky. I'd admitted the truth to myself: There's nothing I ever wanted more than to look like this."

"Of course," Aida said simply. "Everyone does."

Kronberg abruptly turned back to the table in front of her. She flipped open a folder and pulled out a sheet of paper. Amy's test—if that's what it had been—appeared to be over for the time being at least.

"The price for a year's supply of Makeover Cream is one hundred thousand dollars," Kronberg said matter-of-factly. "Right now, it's still extremely expensive for us to manufacture. But more to the point, that price is easily within reach of the customers we've targeted. These people spend many thousands on plastic surgery and cosmetics and makeovers every year as it is. And you'll be able to tell them that this is the only makeover they'll need for the rest of their lives."

Amy nodded.

"Obviously, we're not going to advertise Makeover or stock department-store shelves with it," Kronberg went on. "This product is in a unique category, totally exclusive. We're going to rely entirely on personal sales. Private, confidential sales. I'm sure you realize that it's in everyone's interest that the general public not have any knowledge about our product, not an inkling. The beauty industry is far too competitive to risk letting word out that SAH even exists. As it is, we've taken every security precaution against industrial espionage."

Kronberg looked at Amy steadily. Was this another test? Or was it a warning?

"Yes, I saw the surveillance cameras in the hallway," Amy replied earnestly. David was sure that Kronberg's security precautions had included Armand Diltzer's murder, but Amy couldn't allow herself to think about that now.

"And quite frankly, this allows us to avoid any hassles with the FDA," Kronberg continued. "They'd make us test SAH for years, the way they did minoxidil and Retin-A. We can simply postpone all that nonsense for the duration of our start-up and get on with capitalizing our venture. You don't have any problem with that, do you, Amy?"

"None at all," Amy answered. "As long as you can assure me that it's perfectly safe."

"Absolutely," Kronberg said. She smiled. "Anyway, I know this is the way our customers want it. They'll want their makeover to appear a natural development, as natural to the world as it does to themselves. That's why we dose it out in a cream instead of a pill . . . somehow that makes it feel more natural. And heaven knows, all our customers will be happy to keep Makeover a beauty secret for the select few. Sort of a secret sorority. We've been very careful to eliminate every woman from our customer list who might have difficulty keeping that secret. And we'll have them all sign confidentiality agreements as well, so there's no misunderstanding about our policy. I'm sure none of them would want to risk discontinuing treatment before it's complete."

Again, Amy nodded.

"Now let's get down to how much money is in this for Amy Martin, shall we?"

Amy laughed.

"I'd be lying if I said I wasn't curious," she said.

"And I'd be lying if I said that we didn't want you working for us very, very much," Kronberg said. "Every woman who's ever wanted a makeover knows who you are. They trust you. When you call a woman on our list, she'll be eager to see you. When you show her your before-and-afters, she'll want to do exactly what you've done. You're our seal of approval, Amy. You're the only Makeover Girl we've ever wanted to represent us."

"Thank you," Amy said, lowering her eyes in a show of modesty.

"We're offering you a base salary of two hundred and fifty thousand dollars a year," Kronberg said, again looking down at the sheet of paper on the table in front of her. "On top of that, you'll get a ten-percent commission on all sales. That's ten thousand a customer per year, and each customer will need the cream for three years, so that's thirty thousand per sale."

"Three years?" Amy repeated, her pulse accelerating.

"Yes, it takes approximately three years for the changes to set, to guarantee permanence," Kronberg responded. "It basically mimics first puberty in that respect, too . . . three years for the transformation to fix. Female beauty is usually affected between the ages of thirteen and sixteen."

Oh God, three years! Amy automatically touched her hand to her face, traced her fingertips across the smooth skin that covered her cheekbone.

"And if a customer stops using the cream before those three years are up?" she asked. She knew the answer before Kronberg opened her mouth.

"Reversion begins within a matter of weeks," Kronberg replied flatly. "She'd gradually go back to looking exactly the way she looked to begin with, no better, no worse."

"Of course," Amy whispered. She felt a dizzy panic swirling inside her head. Last night, she'd spread the last of the cream Aida had given her onto her face. As of tonight, she was in reversion.

"Your own three-year supply will be free, of course," Kronberg said. She smiled. "It's obviously in our best interest to keep Amy Martin looking perfectly gorgeous."

"That's certainly a relief," Amy said, forcing a gracious smile, though it truly was relief she felt at that moment. But a fraction of a second later, she was slammed with depression. Sylvia Kronberg certainly wasn't going to keep Amy Martin looking perfectly gorgeous if David's plan to uncover La Douce's secret operation worked. Behind bars for kidnapping and murder and who knows what else, Kronberg wouldn't be dispensing Makeover Cream to anyone.

And how would it feel to look like the old Amy Martin again? No doubt infinitely worse than it had felt before she'd ever looked like this. And how would other people react as she reverted? Would Amy's brief episode of beauty even be remembered a few weeks after it had faded away?

"As a matter of fact, you must be just about running out of Makeover Cream around now," Kronberg said. "We'll have to get you some more very soon. Perhaps we can make it part of a celebration for your first sale."

Amy felt a tremor pass across her shoulders. Kronberg had thought through every step.

"You'll hold it out as sort of an incentive," Amy said, her bitter tone flowing naturally.

"I think of it more as a response to your commitment than as an incentive. We took a calculated risk when we chose an investigative reporter as our Makeover Girl; your commitment means a great deal to us." Kronberg smiled. "Let's take a look at our first customer, shall we? Slide, please."

Amy took a deep breath and let it out slowly. She reminded herself that the important thing was to get out of this office alive, no matter what she looked like. She raised her eyes to the screen. A photograph of a thirtyish, sandy-haired woman with small heavy-lidded eyes had appeared on it.

"Her name is Beverly Todd Freye, daughter of Elliot Todd of Boston. She's thirty-two, divorced, and worth approximately eleven million dollars. She's had consultations with half a dozen plastic surgeons in the past year alone, but none of them, of course, was able to assure her that he could do anything significant about those eyes or that protruding windpipe or that skin, for that matter."

Amy stared at the face on the screen. With larger eyes and a longer face, with depth and sparkle in those eyes, with definition and glow in that face, Beverly Todd Freye would look quite lovely, even stunning. How easy it would be to sell her a three-years supply of Makeover Cream. Three hundred thousand dollars, thirty thousand of them for Amy. A tidy sum for an afternoon's work over tea. And then Amy's little bonus: her next jar of Makeover.

Reversion begins in a matter of weeks.

"Ms. Freye has been a loyal subscriber to *Femina* for the past six years," Aida went on. "She not only reads 'Beauty Bytes' regularly but she's had makeovers with five out of eight of the makeover artists you've recommended."

Kronberg was right, of course. Amy was perfect for the job, perfect in every way—including her ability to delude herself. Amy gazed up at the screen. God knows, once she'd begun feeling attractive—even if she hadn't known how or why she'd become that way—it had been remarkably easy for her to stop one question too soon in her thinking about Georgia's death; to be diverted from her suspicions over and over again. Aida and Kronberg had counted on the power of vanity to delude and they had been absolutely right. If David Copeland had never appeared at Amy's door, what would she be doing now?

Would I actually be accepting this job?

Amy swallowed hard. The answer was as plain as the lovely aquiline nose on her perfectly proportioned face.

Aida concluded her presentation of Beverly Todd Freye and handed Amy a sheet of paper with Freye's curriculum vita and her unlisted phone number.

"Why don't you see if you can set up something for the next day or so?" Kronberg said.

"I'll do my best," Amy replied.

The lights came up and all three women stood. Kronberg clasped Amy's hand in both of hers, then kissed her twice on each cheek.

"How very lucky we all are to have each other," she said, smiling.

Aida accompanied Amy out to the hallway.

"That went very well, I thought," Aida said.

"Me, too," Amy said, pressing the button for the elevator.

"Listen, *bella,* I wanted to tell you, I spoke to my lawyer friend in Rome. He promised to look into that Pola di Cenzio business for us, but he says it will have to be handled delicately because these things are so hard to prove. You know, with it being out of the country and no corpus delicti. He says it might take some time."

"How long?"

"He couldn't say. Some months perhaps."

"Whatever," Amy said, shrugging. The elevator had arrived; the doors opened.

"Let's have dinner again soon," Aida said.

"Yes, let's," Amy replied. She stepped into the elevator and blew Aida a kiss. "Ciao."

"Ciao, *bella.*"

Amy put her thumb on the Close Door button as the elevator doors slid closed. Then, counting slowly to thirty in her head, she continued to hold it there. At thirty, she pulled her thumb away and the doors slid back open on the same floor—the top floor—but Aida was gone. Amy stepped quickly back into the hallway, darted her eyes back and forth, then raced bent at the waist to the end of the hallway. She turned right, jogged ten more steps to the entrance to the ladies room, and pushed the door open. No one at the sinks, no stall doors closed. She raced to the last stall, entered, closed the door, and latched it. She put one foot on the toilet-paper dispenser and the other on the plumbing behind the toilet, her body wedged, suspended in the corner of the stall.

And then she waited.

40

Renting an office at Hyck's Thatched Chairs had been easy. All it took was money, six months' rent, cash in advance to Mr. Hyck himself. Hyck hadn't even inquired what David wanted the office for, nor did he seem concerned about the possibility of David roaming around in his building after everyone else had left for the evening. The safe in Hyck's office was locked, he'd informed David. It seemed there wasn't much worry about industrial espionage in the thatched-chair business.

David checked his watch: 5:22. He pressed himself to the office wall and peered down through the front window to the street below. Workers were already streaming out of Hyck's and Bentnerr's Engineering, but not a soul had yet emerged from La Douce's doors. Apparently Sylvia Kronberg kept her workers to a strict timetable even on Friday evenings.

David paced back to the metal desk at the center of the office, unscrolled the blueprints that lay on top of it, and once again studied the floor plan of the A. C. Wilbraham Building, built in 1910 as a chocolate factory, sold seventy-five years later to a startup American cosmetics company incorporated under the name of La Douce Laboratories. The blueprints, purchased for a fee of twenty-five dollars from the Department of Engineering, were the only help David was going to get from the City of New York.

Thursday morning at precisely ten, David had phoned the District Attorney's office from Amy's apartment and asked for Frank Oxnard, the First Assistant DA. Oxnard's secretary had taken David's name and seemed about to jot it down on her boss's *B* callback list when David said, "I need to talk to Frank right away. Just tell him it's about the Princeton game. Bubriski wants him to suit up."

Oxnard, a Quincy House hallmate of David's at Harvard, had missed the cut for varsity basketball four years in a row. Now, he picked up his phone, laughing.

"Copeland, you bastard, you're fifteen years too late. I'm up to a hundred eighty pounds and get winded walking in from the parking lot. How the hell are you doing? I was actually thinking about you just a few months ago. Beth—my wife—saw your picture in *Femina* magazine next to some unbelievable-looking young thing. You're in the cosmetics business, am I right?"

"I was," David answered. "Listen, Frank, I need your help."

"What can I do for you?"

"I've . . . I've kind of stumbled onto something incredible. Incredible and horrible. A criminal operation that's being run out of New York. From the Bronx, actually."

Oxnard was quiet for a moment.

"What kind of operation is this, David?" he asked finally.

"Theft, illegal medical experiments on human subjects, murder." The words came out of David's mouth as if he'd recited this list a hundred times.

"I assume you've got something in the way of evidence for all of this," Oxnard said.

"When can I see you, Frank?"

"Why don't you come down right now?"

Not taking any chances—only an hour ago Art Malley had warned him that there were people all over the city searching for him—David had left Amy's through a basement exit and flagged a cab on Riverside Drive. He was inside Oxnard's office before eleven. Oxnard shook David's hand warmly, but David already sensed something distanced and critical in his old classmate's eyes.

"Tell me everything you know and how you know it," Oxnard said, removing a legal pad from the middle drawer of his desk.

David sat in the Harvard chair across from Oxnard. He took a deep breath and let it out slowly.

"Sometime last March I agreed to participate in some industrial espionage of a cosmetics company called La Douce Laboratories," he began.

Oxnard jotted down a few words, then nodded benignly, not looking up. David continued. He described how he'd learned about Armand Diltzer's death from a cocaine overdose, the Xeroxed bar code Diltzer's widow found hidden in his shoe, and David's confrontation with Assistant Coroner Coviello, pushing his doubts that Armand's overdose was accidental.

"Did you petition for a review of Coviello's autopsy?" Oxnard asked.

"No."

Oxnard raised his eyebrows.

"Why not?"

"I guess at that point, I wasn't entirely convinced that Armand had been murdered," David said.

Oxnard removed his glasses and peered at David.

"Is that it? Or is it that you weren't quite ready to admit to anyone that you were involved in industrial espionage?" Oxnard said. "You can lose your medical license for something like that, I'm told."

David winced. He wondered why Oxnard was coming on so strong.

"Let me finish, Frank, okay?" he said. He quickly recounted how he had discovered that blood donations were missing from the NYBP's "Beauty Bleed" and then described coming home to find his fish tank vandalized and the photograph with the threat written on it.

"What precinct are you in?" Oxnard asked. "Do you have the name of the policeman you reported the break-in to?"

David shook his head. Oxnard furrowed his eyebrows.

"You did report the break-in to your local precinct?"

David hesitated.

"Not yet," he said.

"Not yet?" Oxnard repeated incredulously. "Why not, David?"

"I wanted to determine a few more things on my own before I involved the police."

Oxnard abruptly stood up behind his desk, the legal pad in his hand.

"I think that'll be enough, David. I don't need to hear the rest of this story . . . whatever it's supposed to be about. It's not in your best interest and it's not in mine, either." Oxnard tore his two pages of notes off his pad and began ripping them in half. "I guess I should have told you this before . . . *Femina* magazine isn't the only place I've seen your name recently. It also turned up on my desk a week ago on a warrant for a Medicaid investigation."

"Jesus, Frank, I had nothing at all to do with—"

"I phoned St. Mary's Hospital while you were on your way down here," Oxnard went on quietly, now standing directly over David. "I spoke with a top administrator over there, a man named Malley, Arthur Malley. He told me that you'd recently been dismissed from the hospital. He also said that he'd been personally concerned about you for some time now. That you seemed to be having personal problems of some sort ever since you were dropped from your research position at Diagnostique and—"

"That's bullshit, Frank! All of it bullshit!"

Christ, Malley would say anything to keep the District Attorney away from St. Mary's while he worked out his deals with Sportsplex and Medicaid. But how did you explain that to Frank Oxnard without sounding totally paranoid? David took a deep breath. Hell, maybe it was best that Oxnard had cut him off in the middle of his story. It only got more unbelievable as it went on—fresh blood from supposedly dead women, a pleasant-looking magazine editor who had metamorphosed into a transcendent beauty. The whole thing was indistinguishable from the rantings of some bitter, addled, once-promising doctor who didn't seem to be able to hold on to a job anymore. David reached his hand into his jacket pocket and touched the plastic container holding the last drops of the experimental night cream Kronberg had passed on to Amy Martin. It was the only thing remotely resembling hard evidence that he could produce right now, but he seriously doubted that the cream would reveal anything incriminating under standard RIA analysis.

"Frank, listen to me," David began again, trying to keep his tone reasonable. "You know who I am. I haven't changed very much in fifteen years. And I'm telling you that I have good reason to believe that the people at La Douce are responsible for the disappearance of at least four young women. If you get a warrant to search their plant, I'm certain I can lead you to the scene of some very dangerous and illegal medical experiments . . . and probably a whole lot more."

Oxnard stared at David incredulously.

"You just don't get it, do you, David?" he said. "There's a warrant out for *your* arrest, my friend. A federal warrant. You're in extremely serious trouble. No judge in his right mind would grant a search warrant based on anything you said, let alone this absurd story of yours."

David drew in his breath, then laid both hands on the arms of his chair and pushed himself onto his feet.

"That doesn't leave me too many options, does it, Frank?"

Oxnard abruptly grasped David by the shoulder. It felt like the grip of a cop.

"I'd watch where I went the next few days if I were you, David," he said, his voice low, almost a growl. "And for one, I'd keep far away from this La Douce Laboratory. I'm talking here as an old friend, and I have to tell you that I'm under a legal obligation to report to the federal investigators that I've had contact with you and that I have a pretty good idea of where they might look for—"

David shoved away Oxnard's hand and strode out of his office without looking back. What a fucking mistake this little trip had been. He changed taxis three times on his way back to Amy's apartment.

David again looked at his watch: It was exactly 5:30. He rushed to the window, peered down. A throng of women was just bursting though La Douce's doors. David edged his head closer to the window frame, and craned his neck. There she was. Even from this angle, David recognized Sylvia Kronberg, her shining gold head rising above the others. At her side was another tall woman, who had raven-black hair and a long stride. Aida, no doubt. The Italian beauty Amy had described to him. Keeping close to the wall, David followed Kronberg and her workers with his eyes as they walked to the subway entrance at the end of the block. Then he saw the silver-gray limousine arrive and Kronberg wave her royal good-bye before she and the raven-haired woman entered the car and rode away. David gazed after them. From where he stood, he could see the sun just dropping behind the giant bat in front of Yankee Stadium.

David paced back to the desk. He pulled open the bottom file drawer, removed a canvas gym bag, unzipped it, and took out a pair of black sweat pants and a black turtleneck. He took off his jacket, tie, shirt, and pants, rolled them together in a ball, and stuffed them into the file drawer. He slipped on the black clothing and sat down, then reached again into the gym bag. His hand touched a flashlight and under it, a small automatic camera that he had loaded with black and white ISO 1000 film. He moved his hand to the left until his fingers touched the barrel of the automatic revolver he had purchased that morning on Forty-first Street. He pulled all three items out, put the camera into his left pants pocket, the gun in his right. He placed the flashlight on the desk in front of him, then drew in his breath and looked down again at the blueprints.

The exterior of the A. C. Wilbraham Building had changed very little in seventy-five years. The only significant renovations David could see were the steel front door and the huge aluminum air-conditioning unit on the building's roof. The rest of the edifice was identical to the drawings, the same large granite-framed, five-to-a-row windows on each of the four floors, the same decorative Victorian cornices. From the outside, at least, the building didn't seem like an easy place to hide anything; but who knew how much the interior had changed since La Douce had taken over ownership. The only constant David was betting on was the plumbing; he knew it was usually cheaper to tear down a wall than to reroute a pipe. David put his feet up on the desk and watched the shadows slowly stretch across the length of the office and then vanish.

The Blimpie across the street closed up at seven-thirty. The last office light at Bentnerr's Engineering went out at quarter to eight. At 8:45, the street had been completely empty for more than a half hour. David waited another forty-five minutes before he lifted the flashlight off his desk, walked out to the hallway and onto the stairwell. He climbed two floors, crossed the hall at the top floor, and went up another half-flight of metal-runged stairs to a steel door. He gingerly pressed against the steel rod-latch. The door swung open and David stepped through it quickly. He was on the roof of Hyck's Thatched Chairs.

For a moment, David crouched perfectly still in front of the door, like a sprinter listening to the countdown to Go. When he was a boy, he'd often gone up to his family's apartment roof at night and sat alone in the shadows listening to the city. Now he listened. All he heard was the hum of distant traffic. He looked up. He could just make out his reflection in the huge aluminum air-conditioning unit directly across from him. He took a deep breath, rocked onto the balls of his feet, and dashed across the rooftop to the two-foot brick crest at its edge, put a palm down on the crest and swung both legs over, landing with a soft thud on the tar roof of La Douce Laboratories.

Again, he crouched. Again, he listened. A dog was barking a block or so away. He waited until it stopped and listened again. Nothing.

Remaining on his hands and knees, David crawled diagonally to the far corner of the front wall. He edged to the parapet, raised his head just above it, and looked down: not a car on the street, no one. He raised himself onto his knees, leaned his chest against the top of the parapet, craned his neck down, and peered at the window below him. If his theory of plumbing was correct, the bathroom was directly below him.

David pulled the flashlight from his pocket. He stood, straddled the parapet, and leaned forward, hugging himself against the overhang with his right arm, extending the flashlight down with his left. It didn't reach the window. He stretched, the brick digging into the palm of his right hand as he extended his left hand lower. Still short by a few inches, he worked the flashlight to his fingertips, his fingers straining to keep a grip on it. He made it. He touched the top of the glass. He tapped it twice with the flashlight, then quickly withdrew his hand, still clinging to the overhang. He waited, suspended there like a toy monkey hanging from the edge of a child's bed table. But nothing happened: no movement, not a sound. Shit! His whole goddamned plan was wrong.

A soft screech, like a thumbnail against a blackboard. David looked down. The glass was moving. The window was grinding open on a side hinge. Thank God! David waited until it was fully extended, then loped his other leg over the parapet and began slowly lowering himself toward the shallow sill. No contact. He pointed his toes like a dancer. Not even close. David closed his eyes. He took a deep breath, opened his eyes again. Then he let go. His feet literally bounced on the sill and David was suddenly tumbling forward, his ribs scraping against the edge of the glass, his hands touching the cold floor before the rest of him crashed onto the tiles of the executive ladies' room of La Douce Laboratories.

Amy Martin was standing over him with a mixture of terror and concern on her lovely face. She leaned down, touched his cheek with her fingertips.

"Anything broken?" She mouthed the words.

David shook his head. He pointed at the window and Amy rushed over and rolled it closed. He slowly pulled himself onto his feet. Amy returned to him, put her lips to his ear.

"I missed you."

David kissed her quickly. She offered him a frightened smile.

"Kronberg claims they don't manufacture the cream here," she whispered. "She says it comes from Basel."

"Maybe. But I'll bet anything that fresh blood wasn't flown in from Switzerland." David's guess was that the fresh blood had been drawn from test subjects right here in La Douce, where Armand Diltzer had found it.

Amy nodded but continued to look unsure and frightened. She had insisted on being part of this mission despite David's warnings. Tonight, at the very least, David wanted to find Kronberg's records of the putatively dead women's blood samples. He was confident that Kronberg, whatever she had to hide, was enough of a meticulous research scientist to keep records of all her experiments. And he was counting on these records to lead them to the missing women. But Amy had argued that even if Kronberg did keep those records, she'd have them under tight security; to gain access to them, David would need Amy's help. David didn't have experience pulling data through a computer security system; the writer of "Beauty Bytes" was a past master at it.

"Not a single computer in Kronberg's office," Amy whispered. "Just file cabinets."

"We'll try the lab."

Armand had described to David a glassed-off computer cubicle in the corner of the lab from which he'd stolen the blood. It was on the second floor. David looked at Amy questioningly: Was she too terrified to continue with this?

"Let's go," Amy whispered, grasping his hand.

David squeezed back, then led the way to the door. He slowly pulled it open. Dim yellow light issued from eye-level sconces at ten-foot intervals along the hallway. David traced his eye along the wall to where it met the ceiling. At the corner, his eye stopped. A small security camera was slowly pivoting toward him. David pushed the door closed.

He lowered himself to his hands and knees, then signaled Amy to do the same. He reached up and pulled the door open again. Like well-behaved puppies, they crawled single file along the wall to the door under the EXIT sign at the end of the hallway. David reached up, turned the knob on the door, pushed. They crawled one at a time into the stairwell. The door swung closed behind Amy. It was suddenly black. That meant no security cameras, either. David stood, pulled his flashlight from his pocket, and flashed it on. Amy was standing too, now leaning against him. He could feel her heart pounding against his arm. He raised two fingers: two flights down. David put Amy's hand on the railing, his own just in front of hers, and then he turned off the flashlight.

They took the stairs slowly, pacing their steps in unison, pausing after each two or three to listen. At the first half-landing, David took Amy's hand and squeezed it before they took the turn and continued down. At the door to the third floor they stopped again, listened. All David could hear was their breathing and the hum of the air conditioning. He took a step toward the next flight of stairs, then suddenly stopped. Froze. A sharp click above them. Then a flash of light. Someone had entered the stairwell at the fourth floor.

David held his breath, instinctively reached behind him for Amy, grabbed her arm just above the wrist and squeezed hard. The clap of a single footstep echoed against the stairwell walls, then another. Someone was coming down the stairs behind them. David suddenly turned, pulling Amy around, and pushed the latch-rod on the third-floor door. The door swung open and he yanked Amy through after him. He looked up and down the tiled passageway, then dashed toward a half-open door directly opposite them. He squeezed through the door into a long dimly lit room; Amy was just behind him. He pulled the door closed after them, then put his ear to the door and listened. He could still hear the footsteps in the stairwell. Abruptly, the footsteps stopped. David waited. He heard the stairwell door open only a few feet away from him. Again, silence. David felt his face grow moist, then his sweat turn cold in the air-cooled room. He heard the footsteps start again, pause, then gradually fade as they continued down the passageway away from them.

David covered the end of his flashlight with his hand, snapped it on, let the beam shine through a slit between his fingers. He turned the thin line of light slowly around the room. There were boxes stacked to the ceiling on the far wall, a long packing table parallel to it, conical spools of twine hanging overhead. An industrial scale sat at one end of the table, transparent plastic bags of Styrofoam packing chips at the other. Shipping and receiving. On the opposite wall, enclosed in an open ironwork cage was an antique freight-elevator shaft, no doubt the elevator that had transported boxes of raw cocoa and trays of fresh-baked chocolate up and down the interior of this building three-quarters of a century ago. David turned the beam to the other side of the room. A double row of tall white plastic drums stood like shiny half-pillars against the near wall, a distinct, sweet, acidic odor issuing from them. David identified the smell immediately: La Douce's putatively French *après bain,* the one that came packaged like a gift from Monet. The lids were off a few of the drums and he could see sulfur-yellow beads inside—fragrance beads, undoubtedly the primary ingredient of the product. David heard Amy moving behind him. He swung the beam around. She was standing in front of an antique oak desk to the left of the elevator shaft. On the desk's top sat a Zenith hard disc computer, cables snaking out the back and into the wall, clearly connecting it to a mainframe.

Amy switched the computer on immediately, then sat on a folding chair in front of the screen as it blinked on. David walked up behind her. She was already scrolling through the document list: "Inventory," "Accounts Receivable," "Payroll." As expected, every accessible document referred to La Douce's legitimate cosmetics trade, their *après bain* and bath powder. Amy cleared the screen, hesitated a second, then drilled a series of instructions into the keyboard. Last night, she had explained to David that breaking through a computer's security system was like a game of chess: There were conventional opening moves and gambits, then increasingly more complex countermoves and countergambits as the program tested the user's right to reach further inside its secret recesses. The last time she'd broken through one of these systems, she'd said, she'd penetrated to some damaging research data about a cold cream that produced allergic reactions in some women. At the time, it had seemed as if she'd uncovered something momentous. Now, Amy drilled a counterresponse onto the keyboard. Suddenly, eight underlined spaces, each separated by a space, appeared at the center of the screen like the start of a game of Hangman. The program was asking for an eight-symbol password to get through to the next level. Amy shook her head, then typed in the word *Makeover*—eight letters exactly. The program rejected it. Too easy, too obvious. She tried letter combinations of names: Keane-Kel; Le Fevre—M; del Ray—Ca; O'Hearn—Ge. She tried S-Hormone. Kronberg—another perfect eight. All shots in the dark. All misses.

David leaned down to her ear. "Could it be a number?"

Amy nodded.

"Try 5-7-7-7-3-4-1-8," David whispered. He knew that number by heart: It was Kelly Keane's blood donation bar-code number, beginning with the NYBP prefix.

Amy typed the numbers in. The instant she typed the 8 into the last underlined space, the screen went blank. A split second later, a file appeared on the screen: File 57773418. This was it—the blood records of Kelly Keane.

David crouched in front of the screen. The first forty some lines were a complete hormone assay, including the short chain aliphatic acids that comprise alpha copulin. After all the hours he'd poured over Kelly Keane's RIAs, some of these numbers were familiar, particularly the pheromone constituents. David nodded and Amy scrolled down. She stopped. The letters *SAH*, had rolled onto the screen. After it appeared the number 247, and then, Modal Selection Factor: +98.7

"SAH . . . that's the hormone in Makeover Cream," Amy whispered. "Sexual Attractant Hormone."

Suddenly, the word *SELECT* began pulsing at the center of the screen.

Select?

Jesus Christ, was it that simple? That simple and orderly? Kelly Keane had abnormally high natural-blood concentrations of this hormone that Kronberg had isolated. Keane's numbers apparently put her somewhere in the ninety-ninth percentile of natural producers of SAH. The initial RIA of the blood sample stolen from the "Beauty Bleed" had determined that, and so Kelly Keane had been "selected."

Amy scrolled on.

A new series of SAH numbers rolled up from the bottom left of the screen, each one dated in a column on the right: SAH 256—March 24, SAH 301—March 30, SAH 325—April 12, SAH 343—April 24 . . . .

David shook his head. Since Kelly Keane's disappearance, her blood concentrations of Sex Attractant Hormone had risen steadily.

"It's coded for an adjunct file," Amy whispered, again typing a series of instructions into the machine. A window suddenly opened on the right half of the screen:

"Donor Selection," it read at the top. Then:

```
12.14—Ft. Lauderdale—Chevy
Op: Nt. Swim: 2–3 A.M.
Facilitators: A & R
   ABORT: 3 party
1.3—Lamar, Col.—Arpége
Op: autopyro—1–2 A.M.
Facilitators: A & K
   ABORT: Reschedule
2.25—Dover—St. Laurent
Op: Nt. Walk—12–1 A.M.
Facilitators: K & R
EFFECTED
```

Ship: Brit Air Courier # 104982: 2.26: 11 A.M./Rec'd:2.27: 1 P.M.

"That's the day Kelly supposedly died," Amy whispered.

David nodded.

"Is that all there is?" The file revealed everything except where Kronberg's "selection" had been received on February twenty-seventh and where she was now. David pulled his camera from his pocket, focused on the screen, and snapped; then he returned the camera to his pocket. "Try Carmina del Ray's number. It's 5–7–7–7—"

David didn't finish. The elevator cables dangling in the open shaft next to them had abruptly started to snake upward. Amy snapped off the computer; David turned off his flashlight. Suddenly, the gold crown of the elevator cab appeared, rising through the floor. Neither of them moved.

A cloud of coffee aroma wafted toward them.

A woman's voice, Spanish accent: ". . . ask for Thursday off, but she say with the beds filling up, she need me every night this week."

The car sailed up less than ten feet away from them, a dim, yellow-lit ghost ship. Two women in white nurse's uniforms on board. Trolleys stacked with trays. The smell of toast and eggs mixing with the odor of coffee. Then it was gone.

"Jesus, what was that?" Amy grasped David's arm.

"Smelled like breakfast."

"Let's get out of here, David. We've got enough," Amy whispered, nodding at the computer.

"Enough for Frank Oxnard?" David could imagine Oxnard simpering incredulously as he showed him snapshots of La Douce's "Donor Selection" data. It didn't prove a goddamned thing.

Amy turned away, took a step toward the door. Then she froze. David saw a crimson flush rise on the back of her neck.

Footsteps. David heard them now, too. Footsteps outside the door. He grabbed Amy's hand, pulled her toward the wall, then down to the floor. He crouched behind one of the white chemical drums, his knees against her back as she crouched in front of him. The footsteps grew louder, then stopped. David sucked in his breath, held it. The door swung open.

A man's voice, deep, full of the Bronx: ". . . not a slump, he's finished. He's got one hit in fifteen at-bats."

Fluorescent lights blinked on. Peering through a narrow space between the drum and the wall, David saw jeaned pant legs moving into the room.

Now another man's voice, black, ironic: "A man gets paid that much, who's going to retire? He'll hang in as long as they let him wear a uniform. What have we got?"

"Air Express . . . Special Handling . . . A dash P dash, twenty-five, thirty-eight. From Lisbon, Portugal. Should be over here. Came in this afternoon."

"Yeh, here it is. Call upstairs, would ya? We'll send it up in time for breakfast."

A rattling sound. Something rolling across the floor toward them. Amy's body trembled in front of David. He reached out, touched her waist with his fingertips, his other hand slipping into his pocket, closing around the grip of the revolver. Through the narrow opening, he saw a hand truck roll toward a white drum at the end of the row.

"Katrina?" The deep voice again. He was apparently talking into a phone or a walkie-talkie. "It's me, Bailey. Send the car down to shipping, would you, angel? We got a package for you upstairs."

"Got Portugal here," the black voice said. "Give me a hand."

"Sure thing."

David could see the white drum rolling on the hand truck toward the elevator door. Soft whir of the elevator motor, black cables slinking down eellike. The bottom of the elevator car appeared through the ironwork cage.

"Hold it, man . . . what's that?" Deep voice.

"Huh?"

"Over there, by the wall."

"Shit!"

Now David saw what they saw: a shank of Amy's shiny dark hair hanging out from the side of the drum. David's heart raced. Footsteps pounding toward them. Ten feet away. Five.

Suddenly, Amy was rolling forward, somersaulting out from behind the drum directly in front of the two men. Reflexively, they both bent over her.

"Jesus!"

David jumped up, pistol high, and whacked down on the back of the bigger man's neck—a direct hit on the cervical plexus. The man collapsed backward, dropped with a thud ass-first onto the linoleum floor. The black man's hand dove to the police holster at his side. A burst of yellow sprayed into his face—sulfur-yellow fragrance beads Amy had scooped and flung from an open drum. It gave David all the time he needed for another well-placed whack, this one between the third and fourth vertebrae of the black man's neck. This man fell more gracefully than his co-worker, rotating as he dropped like a top toppling.

Still bent over, Amy gaped up at David, her face red, her eyes wide, brilliant with excitement. David dashed to the shipping table and removed a roll of nylon tape, then returned to the two men lying at right angles on the floor. Working together, David and Amy bound both men's legs at the ankles and their arms to their sides. They were rolling tape across the black man's mouth when they heard a dull clanking sound behind them. David peered over the top of Amy's head. The elevator had arrived—empty, waiting.

Amy straightened up, raced toward it, grabbing the folding

chair from in front of the desk along the way. She pulled open the elevator door, planted the chair half-inside to hold it open. She gestured with her head at the drum that the workmen had rolled in front of the elevator.

"Open it." She mouthed the words.

A packer's shears hung by a hook from the side of the shipping table. David shoved his gun back in his pocket, grabbed the shears, and raced to the drum. He snipped the twin metal bands that fastened its lid, then sliced the plastic tabs under the rim. He gripped the rim and yanked the lid off.

Beads. More yellow fragrance beads.

Amy dug in with both hands, paddled the beads out like a dog digging in sand. In a few seconds, she hit bottom—a false bottom only six inches down. David opened the shears, inserted a blade into the rim, and sliced around the perimeter. Then, using the shears as a lever, he lifted; out came a dummy tray of yellow beads. Underneath was blue-speckled, white Styrofoam casing with grips like bowling ball holes at its center. David inserted his fingers and pulled.

"Holy God!" Amy gaped down, dumbfounded.

They saw hair first—gorgeous thick red hair fanning out through the circular opening at the top of the Styrofoam packing case. The hair was rather dry and brittle-looking, but that was to be expected of hair that had been subjected to the abuses of air freight for the past fourteen hours. David reached down. A tremor shook his arm. The moment his fingers made contact with the warm, pulsing scalp, he knew it was alive.

He waited a moment to steady his hand, then began cutting around the opening at the top of the case, gradually revealing the face beneath the hair—the long forehead, the thick high-arched eyebrows, the closed almond-shaped eyes, the bridge of the long aquiline nose. Amy stared down, dumbstruck. It was the face of a superb natural beauty.

"My God!"

Now using his hands only, David began carefully breaking away the rest of the Styrofoam casing that surrounded the bottom half of the woman's head. As he reached her nostrils, he found the nose clip he expected. Plastic tubing extended from it through holes in the casing to either side of the drum. David traced one to a round vent the size of a quarter on the outside of the drum where the passenger exhaled carbon dioxide. The other tube undoubtedly connected to an air-supply tank clamped in a compartment beside her, probably a blend of oxygen and nitrous oxide for a safe, unconscious journey. There was a third tube hooked over the woman's lips inside her mouth, this one dripping in water for hydration with perhaps a touch of sucrose for low-metabolic sustenance. She was probably catheterized and diapered, too. A neat life-support package for express shipment to La Douce Laboratory. *Shipping and receiving.*

"Mr. Bailey?"

The name issued like a parrot's squawk from where the two men lay on the floor. David started to reach for his gun, then realized the voice came from the walkie-talkie in one of the men's pockets.

"Mr. Bailey," the voice repeated with a soft middle-European accent. "We're still waiting for that package up here. And they're waiting for you down in the laboratory."

Amy looked into David's eyes, then put her mouth to his ear.

"Sounds like they send these packages upstairs solo," she whispered, gesturing at the drum. "If we're ever going to find out what's happening up there, this is it."

"Let's do it."

Without another word, they tilted the drum onto the floor. David planted his foot on the rim of the drum, then they both reached inside the top of the packing case on either side of the woman's head and pulled. For a second, there was no give; then, with a little whosh of air, the entire Styrofoam case began to slide out. It was actually two fitted halves that had been held together by the drum. They lifted off one half, like the top of an expensive doll case, exposing the rest of the passenger's body and her life-support apparatus—the two air-supply tanks, the water drip-bag, the urine bag. The woman was wearing a body stocking made of thick quilted material. She lay embryolike in the negative relief of the other half of the packing case.

Leaving her lying there, they rolled the empty drum onto the elevator. David ran back into the room and grabbed the insert tray of yellow fragrance beads. Racing back, he nudged the chair away from the elevator door with his foot and the door swung closed. Amy hoisted herself inside the drum first. Then David swung his feet one at a time over the side, planted them in the space where the two gas tanks had stood, and lowered himself slowly, holding the tray of beads over his head like a huge wedding cake. He fitted it into the rim above them. Total blackness. David crouched next to Amy like a twin in the womb.

"Good luck, Amy," he whispered.

"Same to you, David," she whispered back.

A second later, the elevator shuddered and began to rise.

David squirmed his hand into his right pocket, tugged out the gun. He settled his weight onto the balls of his feet, preparing himself to jump—a coiled jack-in-the-box with a loaded revolver. He counted silently. At seven, the elevator rattled to a halt; then no movement, nothing. For several seconds, all he could hear was Amy's breathing and his own, but then, gradually, he began to separate the layers of sound that filtered in from outside the drum. First, a vaguely familiar hum, mechanical, electric. On top of that, the flat drone of a woman's voice, amplified, artificial— the voice of a television actress: "Don't be absurd, Philip thinks it's still 1978 and he's Central's star running back. . . ." Somewhere behind that sound, there were other voices, real women's voices. Now footsteps padding toward them. David sucked in his breath, tightened his grip on his gun.

"He's slow and he's inefficient. I'll never understand why Dr. K hires people like that." It was the crisp middle-European voice they'd heard over the walkie-talkie. She seemed almost on top of them. "Put her over in Discharge and Entry. We've still got breakfast to get under control here."

Suddenly, the drum was tipping and David slid against Amy, shoulder to breast, knee to thigh. Now the rattle and thump of a hand truck—they were being rolled off the elevator—and then, just as suddenly, the drum was upright and still again.

"Dr. K's not back yet," the woman was saying, her voice beginning to recede from them. "We'll process this one in few minutes, eh? She's already kept all the way from . . . where was it . . . Portugal?"

A short laugh, then the low droning sounds from outside returned—the humming machinery, the television voices, the chatter—all a notch lower in volume than before. David counted in his head backward from ten, then searched for Amy's hand and squeezed it tightly. With the gun still in his left hand, he put his right palm squarely under the center of the false-bottom tray that covered them. He pushed up with a slow steady pressure. A crescent of light sliced into the drum above them as the tray cleared the rim. David moved the tray several inches to his left, then gently lowered it, resting it on the rim with a one-foot margin. Slowly, heart hammering, David raised the top of his head through that space and peered out.

For several seconds, David just blinked his eyes, unable to process what he saw. The sheer size of the room was overwhelming. This was not some anteroom hidden in the walls behind Kronberg's office; it was a sprawling, low-ceilinged, hangarlike room the dimensions of an entire floor of the building. Just like the false-bottomed tray set inside the drum, this room had to be set somewhere between the fourth floor and the roof of the building. Yes, that was it: The room was fitted into the air-conditioning unit—a dummy—on top of the roof.

It was a clinic—a mammoth one-room ward with parallel rows of beds along windowless walls. There were at least thirty beds in each row and occupying all but three of these beds, seated upright with breakfast trays in front of them, were women in blue-striped hospital smocks. Even from this distance—David guessed that this Discharge and Entry area for new arrivals was just to the right of the elevator—he recognized the clinical symptoms of critical hormone disorders in almost all of these women's faces: the wispy beards and mustaches, the progressive baldness, the plethoric complexions, the bloated moon cheeks, the acne. With the sole exception of two attractive young women sleeping in a row next to the three empty beds, this was a locked ward full of endocrinological freaks—close to sixty of them.

A white medical jacket flashed in the corner of David's eye, already close and moving closer. All David could see was the figure's midsection: pale, square hands, a pistol in a shoulder holster against a white shirt. David bit down on his lip, drew up his gun, and jutted the barrel over the top of the drum alongside his eyes. He held his breath. The white jacket paced to within five feet. Inside the drum, Amy's leg pressed against David's. The man in the jacket came to a halt directly in front of them, and David aimed his gun at the man's groin. He waited. A beat, and the white jacket glided to his right and out of sight. David let out his breath.

Still pointing his gun over the drum's rim, he again scanned the ward. In three of the four corners of the huge room, he saw oversized projection TV screens of the type found in sports bars. All three screens were simultaneously broadcasting a soap opera at full blast and most of the patients stared blankly at one or

269

another of the screens while they fed themselves breakfast. Their eyes—most of them protruding hyperthyroid eyes—had the glazed-over look of long-term hospital patients who'd been confined to bed for months under continuous sedation.

A good dozen nurses and orderlies in starched white uniforms circulated in the room, some distributing and collecting breakfast trays, others straightening bed sheets or mopping their charges' distorted faces. David noticed that almost all the personnel, men and women alike, were fair-skinned and blond, with decidedly European-looking faces. One of them stepped out from behind a pleated canvas ward screen at the head of a bed and now bent over a patient's arm, checking the flow of her IV tube. David's gaze abruptly stopped and he squint-focused on this patient. He searched for the IV stand next to her bed but couldn't find it. The tube emanating from the crook of her elbow ran over the top of the canvas screen behind her bed. Then he spotted the second tube snaking out from behind the screen into the patient's other arm. This tube was a clear line of crimson—blood-red. At that moment, David finally identified the familiar mechanical hum in the ward; he knew exactly what was behind that screen: a plasmapheresis machine. The disfigured young woman in the bed was a blood-component donor.

David shot his eyes up and down the ward. How had he missed it? Every sixth patient had blood–uptake and return tubes emanating from her arms. God, yes, this was a hormone clinic all right—a hormone-production clinic. Kronberg's hypothalamic hormone—her SAH—was being filtered out of these women's blood as it circulated out and back into their bodies. And, predictably, the more the hormone was sucked from the patients' blood, the more their hypothalamuses strained to replenish that loss, forcing it into constant overproduction. That is why Kelly Keane's SAH count had risen steadily after she had been "selected." It was also why all the women on this ward—all these living hormone-production plants—were so grossly disfigured. No doubt it was not so very long ago that each one of these grotesque women had been a world-class natural beauty. But now their endocrine systems had been turned upside down and were perpetually unbalanced as they vainly tried to compensate for the relentless drain. David lowered his head and reached into his pocket for his camera. One picture of this ward was all he'd ever need.

The slap of footsteps sounded directly behind the drum. David froze, swiveled his eyes, fastened them on Amy's eyes glowing next to him.

"... Dr. K's car coming ..." The voice of the nurse in charge again. "Let's get this one unpacked and prepped before she gets up here. She likes to be here for the EKG. ... *Mein Gott, who opened this?*"

In unison, as if they'd rehearsed it a hundred times, David and Amy sprang straight up, their heads simultaneously banging the tray off the rim of the barrel, flipping it off and over, the yellow beads flying, the revolver in David's hand rising shoulder-high, swinging in a half-circle, his forefinger looped over the trigger.

"I have a gun," David blurted, his voice flat. "Don't anybody move."

The head nurse, white-streaked blonde hair, white dress, a look of terror on her white face. Next to her was a tall, blond man with wire-rimmed glasses in a white medical jacket, the holster at his side.

"Take his gun, Amy."

Amy stepped quickly to the blond man's side, reached for the handle of his pistol. To his right, David heard the whine and whistle of the elevator cables, the clank of the elevator car rising.

"David! Behind you!"

A sharp blow cut between David's shoulder blades. Even as he gasped for air, he willed his hand to hang on to his gun, keep it trained on the blond man in front of him. But it was too late—a second blow from behind sent David sprawling forward, the gun sailing out of his hand. He hit the floor with both palms, rolled to his side, then scrambled onto his feet. From the corner of his eye, he saw the tall blond man draw his gun. Beside him, another man, muscular and black, also drew a pistol and aimed it at him.

Where the hell was Amy?

David was running half bent over, like a sprinter just off the blocks. He raced down the center of the ward, a blur of florid faces atop blue-striped smocks on either side of him, oblivious to him, staring stuporously at the soap opera on the television screens.

"Idiot!" The shout rang out behind him. "Stop!"

David spun, dove to his right, belly flopped onto the linoleum floor, and slid under a bed.

"Where's the girl?" The head nurse.

271

"I thought you—"

"Where did she go?"

Panting, David peered out from under the bed, scanned the six-inch-high world of bed legs and food-trolley wheels. The mattress creaked and groaned as a lump of human flesh shifted above him. Now, black leather shoes raced into view, stopped at the foot of the bed.

"The idiot is under the bed. Not to worry. He's not going anywhere."

David pushed himself backward, belly glided feet first toward the head of the bed, toward the vibrating hum of a plasmapheresis machine behind the maple legs of the ward screen. White-clad knees dropped onto the floor at the foot of the bed, one arm dangling, gun in hand. David swam backward on the slippery floor. His legs were just emerging from under the bed when something cold and hard rammed against his rump.

A woman's trilling laugh, high, operatic.

"That's a gun, *dottore*," the woman said. "I suggest you back out very slowly."

Temples throbbing, heart pounding, David did as he was told. As his head emerged from under the bed, he glided past a pair of elegant ankles in patent-leather pumps.

"Now, *bello*, very sweetly onto your knees," the woman said.

David raised himself onto his knees, lifting his eyes along a pair of long legs to the hem of a crepe miniskirt. He had to tilt his head back in order to see the face of his captor towering over him. It was a long face framed with silky black hair, feral, ferocious-looking and sublimely beautiful. The Italian, Aida. He'd been almost this close to her once before, but that time, she was wearing a blond wig and was pointing a camera at him. Now she was pointing a blunt-nosed service revolver directly at his forehead.

"Karl, bring the wheelchair over here," she barked.

The blond man drove a wheelchair between the beds. The patient in the bed under which David had hidden now turned her head, glanced at David blankly, then gazed back at the television screen in the corner of the room. The blond man locked David's right arm behind him in a half nelson, yanked him up into the wheelchair, handcuffed his left wrist to the arm of the chair, then wheeled him to the center of the ward, a gun pressed to the back of his neck.

"Hello, David." The familiar voice of Sylvia Kronberg. She was walking toward him from the open elevator, smiling radiantly. "Doing more research?"

Amy pressed herself flat as she could under the covers, huddled against the mammoth body next to her. She gripped David's gun alongside her cheek, felt the cold of the metal seep into her skull. She had snatched the gun while it was still spinning on the floor, then run with it while the others went after David. And then she had heard a hoarse androgynous voice calling to her from one of the beds.

"Amy? Over here."

It came from an orange face as big as a jack-o'-lantern, pig eyes, hoary corkscrew hairs sprouting from her chin. Yet there was something in that face that was intensely familiar.

"It's me, Carmina. Quick, come."

Jesus God, it was Carmina del Ray—the erstwhile Latin bombshell. Amy didn't hesitate. She had slipped in beside Carmina, pulled the sheet over her head, sunk in against Carmina's warm gargantuan flesh, tried to merge with it, to become part of a single mound under the covers. And now she waited.

"You're a better spy than I gave you credit for," Kronberg was saying loudly. Then, in an urgent half-whisper, "The elevator's secured. She's got to be in here. Find her."

"Right away." The black guard.

"Yes, *dottore.*" Aida.

"So tell me, Doctor, does my clinic surprise you?" Kronberg went on, her voice light and loud again.

"I don't understand how you can do it, Sylvia." David's voice sounded reasonable, remarkably steady. Amy guessed he was no more than twenty feet away.

Kronberg laughed.

"I do it because it's doable, David. Precisely the same reason anyone else would do it. That is, if they'd been persistent and fortunate and clever enough to discover SAH as I did. It's the product that all of us were ultimately searching for . . . all of us who take beauty seriously, that is. And that includes you, of course. You could have been part of this, you know, if your tender masculine pride hadn't gotten the best of you. It's a shame, really . . . all the fuss you made about your precious research on hormone-suspensory creams. It did no one at Diagnostique any good at all; your eye cream was doomed from the start. But it might have

273

saved us some time here . . . a month or two. Working together might have been pleasant."

"I could never have been a part of this."

"Are you quite sure, David? I remember lying with you in a hotel-room bed in New Orleans less than a year ago and hearing you protest you could never share data with a researcher from another cosmetics company, let alone participate in industrial espionage. Not for love or money. And yet, only months later, you were sending that unfortunate Diltzer man prowling around my laboratory. We surprise ourselves, don't we?"

The gun trembled against Amy's cheek. David had only told her about his conversation with Sylvia Kronberg at the New Orleans convention, not that it had taken place in bed.

"She's not in the cold room or the utility closet," Aida called, her voice now coming from the other side of the ward.

"Try under the beds," the guard named Karl called back.

"Or in them," Kronberg said. "Amy has always been clever at blending in."

Amy's whole body trembled under the covers.

"I regret with all my heart sending Armand on that mission," David was saying. "I never believed I was sending him to his death."

"How could you have known that, David?" Kronberg said, her voice soothing, almost motherly. "It's rare that we know the implications of any of our actions. We simply do what appears appropriate at the time. We operate out of personal necessity. Armand had his needs, you had yours, I had mine. Armand went too far and he had to be stopped. As we see now, he should have been stopped sooner. Perhaps if he had been, we'd all have more options tonight."

"You have to know when to stop yourself, Sylvia," David went on, his voice still steady, revealing no fear.

Without warning, Carmina del Ray yawned and turned her hulking body away from Amy, drawing some of the covers with her. A tiny tentlike triangle opened, exposing half of Amy's right eye. She could see David in a wheelchair only ten feet away from her, Kronberg and the blond man walking in tandem behind him, the guard holding a gun against the back of David's head. But Aida was nowhere in sight. Amy did not dare move, not even blink.

"Your discovery is remarkable," David went on deliberately, still amazingly calm. "More than remarkable; it's astounding. We've all speculated about an aesthetic organizing principle that guides human morphology . . . even Aristotle entertained the idea of an internal golden mean. Now you're the one who found it. You're the one who isolated SAH. But Sylvia, you must know that you cannot use human beings in this way."

Kronberg stopped only yards away from Carmina del Ray's bed. Amy's heart pounded. She held her breath as she watched Kronberg rest her hand on David's shoulder, then grip it tightly.

"Tell me, Dr. Copeland, exactly where do you think medicine would be today if we didn't accept donations from healthy, strong bodies—*gifted* bodies—and pass these precious donations on to the less fortunate . . . to patients who are in need? What do you suppose would happen to bleeders who were denied the gift of fresh plasma? Burn victims who were denied graft tissue? The child dying of uremia who was denied the gift of her sister's kidney? Would you be standing over her wasting body, wringing your hands, worrying about the proper use of human beings while she dropped into terminal coma?"

"Come on now, Sylvia, you don't really think you can compare these poor women's donations with kidney transplants?"

"Not entirely," Kronberg replied, arching her eyebrows. "This procedure is far safer."

Kronberg's face shone with satisfaction. Even with one half-curtained eye, Amy could see how much Sylvia was enjoying her colloquy with David, as if she were matching wits with him across a university high table rather than with a gun at his head. It seemed that for all her divine beauty, Sylvia Kronberg still yearned to be the smartest girl in the class.

"The difference is need," David answered, his eyes flicking quickly from bed to bed. "You're not depleting these women to save patients from their deathbeds."

"You sound like the claims attorney for a health-insurance company," Kronberg replied with a light laugh. "Is it so clear to you which procedures are necessary and which are not? Are you the last doctor in America still clinging to the notion that medicine's sole mission is survival of the patient and not the quality of her life?"

"Nurse!" It was Aida close behind Amy, maybe three or four

275

beds away. "Give me some help with this sheet. Very slowly, please."

Amy stared straight ahead without blinking, her heart racing as Kronberg stepped in front of David and leaned her face down to his.

"I work only with need, Doctor," Kronberg declared, all the lightness suddenly gone from her voice. "Desperate need. The kind of need that must be satisfied for life to be worth living. The women I work with have reached the point in their lives where they cannot face the world another day without treatment with SAH."

David remained silent. For a fraction of a second, it seemed to Amy as if he was looking directly into her eye through the tiny opening in the sheet.

"But what about the needs of the women here?" he asked finally, quietly.

"It's a question of equitable distribution," Kronberg said. "The same question we face about every medical resource that's in limited supply. Out of the hundreds of thousands who need it, who will get that kidney that's available for transplant right now ... today? Someone has to make that decision or no one will get it. Today, Sex Attractant Hormone is in very short supply; perhaps one woman in ten thousand naturally still produces the hormone in detectable amounts. The lobe in the hypothalamus that secretes SAH has atrophied in the rest of us. My guess is that a few millennia ago it was a survival characteristic that ensured male attraction and reproduction but, alas, evolution proved it unnecessary. It turned out that there were always enough males who needed little encouragement to reproduce with just about any woman regardless of her appearance."

Kronberg paused a moment. Amy heard Aida and the nurse move one bed closer to her. Her heart pounded.

"I'm a pragmatist," Kronberg went on quietly. "A utilitarian. I've always been comfortable with the idea of the greatest good for the greatest number. Every woman in this room has enjoyed years of incredible beauty. Perhaps *enjoyed* is the wrong word; there are too many women here who were spoiled by their beauty, squandered it without appreciation. That's something I can assure you will never be the case with the recipients of my SAH treatment. Listen, David, the arithmetic is simple ... each

276

donor can support ten women with a three-year supply of SAH. Ten beauties for one. I can assure you, David, I don't find it a difficult decision to make at all."

"But you've turned them into freaks, drugged-out freaks," David said. "You're not just taking their hormones, you're taking their lives."

"Not so," Kronberg said flatly. "What you see here is only a temporary solution, the same solution that's always been the first step in hormone-replacement therapy. We start with extracted natural hormones and work toward synthetics. But research toward that end takes a great deal of money, as you know. Millions and millions. We're self-supporting here at La Douce. That's why we went into production of Makeover Cream as soon as we were able. In a sense, these women are working toward their own liberation."

Amy watched David's face. His only response was to raise his eyebrows. He didn't really accept anything Kronberg was saying, did he?

"All these women will reverse, if that's what you're concerned about," Kronberg was saying. "Preliminary tests indicate that after only two months off of plasmapheresis they'll return to normal. They may not ever be quite as brilliantly beautiful as they once were, but they certainly will not be dismayed to look at themselves in the mirror in the mornings."

"You intend to let them go, then?" David asked benignly.

Kronberg shook her head.

"It's too late for that, of course," she said. "But every one of these women is still capable of leading a productive life. There's going to be lots of work for all of us at La Douce as we grow. We're planning to move to larger production quarters in the Caribbean quite soon. My staff up here is all Swiss, you know, trained at the Basel Institute . . . and we all grew up dreaming of tropical climes. I intend to make ours a very pleasant community for us to live and work in."

Still facing David, Kronberg again put a hand on his shoulder. Amy heard Aida searching the bed next to hers. Amy sucked in her breath, held it.

"There are people here who were adamant about wanting to give you more than a mere warning last week," she said softly. "But I resisted that idea. You know how rare a good endocrinologist is, one with imagination. Synthesizing SAH is going to require a great deal of imagination. I've never completely abandoned the idea of working together with you, David."

Amy saw David hesitate, then saw a smile spread across his handsome face.

"As you probably know, I'm recently out of a job," he said, gazing into Kronberg's eyes. "The truth is, I haven't gotten very far playing by the rules; in fact, after what I've been through at St. Mary's and Diagnostique, I'm not sure what the rules are anymore."

As Amy watched David offer his free hand to Kronberg, she felt the sheet lifting above her head. She clutched the gun tightly. Her head was spinning.

"I would consider it a privilege to work with the endocrinologist who discovered Sex Attractant Hormone," she heard David say as the sheet pulled away from her face.

"Now!"

David's wheelchair shot backward, a handle ramming into the blond man's groin, the man collapsing onto the floor. David yanked Kronberg's arm, pulled her stumbling across the front of the wheelchair onto the floor beside him.

"Now, Amy! Now!"

Amy pointed her gun at Aida's hand, pulled the trigger as she rolled off the bed. Aida screamed something in Italian as she pitched forward onto Carmina, blood squirting from her wrist, her own revolver dropping to the floor. Amy landed on her knees, instantly saw the black guard on the other side of the ward with his gun in front of him, searching in the confusion for his target. Amy fired again, saw the guard spin away and fall, crashing into a plasmapheresis machine. Every nurse and orderly seemed to have disappeared. Could they be armed, too? Ten feet in front of Amy, Kronberg was still struggling to free herself from David's grasp. Behind her, the blond man was just pulling himself up. Amy held her gun stiff-armed in front of her. She rocked onto her feet without losing her bead.

"I am pointing my gun directly at Dr. Kronberg's heart," she said loudly and deliberately as she walked toward Kronberg. "I want every one of you in front of me right now."

Kronberg stopped struggling. The blond man slowly began to raise his hands over his head. Not a sound, not a movement anywhere else in the ward.

"Everybody out here!" Amy shouted. She was directly over Kronberg now, her gun only inches away from the Swiss doctor's chest. "Believe me, I'm not afraid to pull this trigger again."

"*Schnell! Heraus!*" Kronberg spat the words out. Instantly, all the nurses and orderlies came filing out from behind the ward screens, their arms over their heads.

"Release Dr. Copeland," Amy said.

Kronberg nodded and the blond man pulled a key from his pocket, unlocked the handcuff from David's wrist. David stood, took two steps, and picked Aida's revolver from off of the floor. He looked at Amy.

"And now we're all going downstairs and calling the police," Amy said. "I count fifty-eight corpus delicti we have for them."

41

David injected five milligrams of Valium into the young woman's arm, then signaled an orderly to bring a wheelchair over to the bed. Together, they eased the patient into the chair. The orderly planted a pair of plastic sunglasses over the young woman's eyes and began wheeling her toward the elevator. The patient hadn't seen sunlight for seven months.

David made a checkmark on the second sheet on his clipboard next to patient number thirty-six—Baylor, Sally Jean—then started walking toward the next bed in the row. At Frank Oxnard's request, David was supervising the team of doctors and orderlies who were transferring Sylvia Kronberg's selected hormone donors to the Public Health facility on Staten Island. David offered the patient a smile. She was completely bald. Red spots covered her neck and face.

"Hello, I'm Dr. Copeland and I'm going to be giving you a little injection before we take you to a hospital."

Out of the corner of his eye, David saw Lisa Chou pacing toward him. David had insisted that Chou accompany the FBI agents who were inventorying La Douce's laboratory downstairs. Dr. Chou held a small plastic cooler at her side as she approached him.

"Well, it certainly looks like they were working hard on some kind of synthesis of their aesthetic hormone," Chou said. "I have no idea how far they got. We're taking a few flasks down for lab analysis immediately."

"Thank you, Doctor."

So Sylvia really had expected to go legitimate, synthesizing her SAH, perhaps eventually even getting FDA approval for it. And who's to say it couldn't have happened that way? Sylvia had believed she could keep her donor factory a secret until then; by that time, her lie to Amy would be true. She might have pulled it off. God knows, she'd kidnapped nearly sixty women before getting caught. David watched Lisa Chou walk with her package to the elevator. Frank Oxnard was just getting off.

"State of Washington just responded on the FBI computer to patient twenty-three," Oxnard said, smiling broadly as he lumbered toward David. "Presumed dead in an airplane accident over the Pacific Cascades. That's twenty-three for twenty-three, my friend. We've already set some kind of a national record for turning up living presumed deads."

David nodded. Not once had Frank Oxnard offered any words that even resembled an apology for the way he had treated David in his office two mornings ago; and judging by Oxnard's attitude this morning, he'd probably be claiming responsibility for cracking this case by the end of the day. That was perfectly all right with David. All he wanted now was to get these women safely on the road to recovery, and for Alice Diltzer and her son to receive some kind of official apology and recompense from the City of New York. And after that, David wanted to get as far away from all of this as possible.

"I'm going to press for more than just kidnapping and murder, David," Oxnard was saying. "We've got a chance to set a precedent here. There's a law on the books for illegal sale of organs—the 'body parts bill.' I'm going to prosecute for theft of hormones. What do you think? Of course, I'll need your help on some of the technical aspects of—"

David turned back to the patient without responding.

"Make a fist, please," he said softly to the red-spotted young woman. "This will only hurt for a second."

Two floors below, Amy led the young FBI electronics specialist to the computer terminal in La Douce's shipping room. He was an intense, red-haired young man with horn-rimmed glasses who seemed to blush every time he looked at Amy. Once they were inside the shipping room, the agent opened his aluminum attaché case and removed a floppy disc. He inserted it in the computer's *A* drive before turning it on.

"It's my own patented security breaker," he said, grinning. "It pulls directly out of backup without a strain. Want to take a look-see at anything before I start copying the whole works?"

Amy sat down on a stool behind the young man and pushed a lock of her hair away from her forehead.

"Yes, there is," she said. "Can you call up Carvaggio? It's a woman. Yolanda Carvaggio."

"Two *g*'s?"

"That's right."

The agent's fingers flew across the computer keyboard like a concert pianist's. The word *searching* pulsed for several seconds in the corner of the screen and then the name Yolanda Carvaggio appeared highlighted in the first line of a letter written in Italian and addressed to the Italian Embassy in New York.

"Request for a duplicate of a lost passport," the agent said, scanning the screen. "The Italians pass them out like party favors."

He scrolled back to the return address on the letter. No surprise; it was Aida's Manhattan apartment. Apparently, Aida had traveled to Martinique with the passport of one Yolanda Carvaggio to flash to the gendarmes. It was Aida as herself, however, who had approached Georgia O'Hearn in the lobby of her hotel and invited the young Southerner to accompany her on the twilight cruise; Georgia couldn't have resisted the invitation of the glamorous Italian model, no matter how frightened she might have been feeling. And then somewhere out at sea, Georgia had been drugged and transferred to another boat before being shipped in a chemical drum to La Douce Laboratories in the Bronx. Henri Bouquard's price had probably been no more than a couple thousand francs, more than he'd make in a year of sunset cruises. There were undoubtedly people like him all over the world who, for a small fee, had assisted Sylvia Kronberg's efficient Swiss staff with their kidnappings.

"Anything else?" the FBI agent asked Amy.

"Just a sec." Amy closed her eyes, searched her memory for the name of the deputy coroner David had told her about. "Coviello—Dr. Vincent Coviello."

"Two *l*'s?"

"I think so."

Again, the young computer expert typed furiously on the keyboard. A few moments later, Vincent Coviello's name appeared highlighted on the screen on a billing receipt for fifteen hundred dollars. The date was listed, but the service rendered was not. Assistant District Attorney Oxnard would at least have to do a little bit of legwork to pin the fraudulent autopsy charge on Coviello. God knows, Sylvia Kronberg's meticulous record keeping left little else for the prosecutor to do.

"Anybody else?" the agent asked.

Amy thought about it.

"I guess I can wait for the rest of this," she said, slipping off the stool.

She had taken only three steps toward the door when she stopped and turned around.

"I . . . I suppose she kept a file on me, too," she said.

"M-A-R-T-I-N?" the agent asked, not looking up.

"That's correct."

It took only a couple minutes for the agent to pull Amy's file onto the screen. At the top of the document, next to her name, Social Security number, birthdate, and address, were the words *Makeover Girl.* It was dated over three years ago. Amy sighed. Somehow it was a relief that Kronberg really had had her eye on Amy from the start, not just since she'd begun investigating Georgia's death. Under the top heading was a paragraph that began, "Patient: age 31, 5'6", 132 lbs. Onset of menstruation: 12 yr/4 mos . . ." and an exhaustive medical history followed for several pages. Kronberg's people had managed to get ahold of her medical records going back to her birth. Next came Amy's curriculum vitae, beginning with her Great Neck High School academic record and going through Sarah Lawrence and every job she'd held since, including confidential performance evaluations by her superiors at *Ms.* and *Femina.* Last came a section headed "Psychological Profile": it began with a brief history of the entire Martin family and was followed by a page-and-a-half report written by a counselor Amy had seen briefly in college. Finally, there were thirty odd pages that began, "The patient presented with characteristic post-thirty single-female anxiety, exacerbated by a long-standing history of low self-esteem and negative self-image. . . ." The author of this case history was Mary Goldfarb.

A highlight started pulsing over Mary Goldfarb's name.

"What's that?"

"Cross-reference. Means there's a separate file somewhere in here on this Goldfarb woman."

"Pull it up, please," Amy said automatically.

A minute later, a file on Mary Goldfarb, Ph.D. appeared on the screen. It was dated just a little under a year ago, well after Kronberg had started tracking Amy's career. The FBI agent began slowly scrolling through the document. Amy stared, reading every word. There was no mention of any fees paid to Mary by Kronberg. However, beginning on page two of the file was a detailed account of a personal relationship that Mary had maintained for several years with a young woman by the name of Mia Parks. Ms. Parks was described as a beautiful model who worked regularly in the garment district. The relationship, it said, was unknown to Mary's husband. No money needed. Kronberg had used blackmail to get Mary's help.

Amy abruptly turned and strode quickly out the door into the hallway, her face flushing. That Mary was a part of this was not really a surprise. The therapist had worked so consistently at trying to deflect every one of Amy's suspicions, not just about Georgia's "accident" but also about Amy's own changing face. Mary had done everything in her power to convince Amy that she was a victim of self-destructive impulses, that her worst enemy was herself, that self which yearned to be as beautiful as her sister Molly. A sudden rage burned in the pit of Amy's stomach as she opened the stairwell door.

"Mind holding that for me?"

A round-faced, blue-eyed policewoman called to Amy from inside the hallway. She was carrying six cardboard cartons that stacked up to just below her chin, each carton carrying a red and black stick-on label with the word *Evidence* on it. Amy held the door for the young woman.

"Hey, you're the lady from *Femina*, aren't you?" the blue-eyed officer said, smiling as she entered the stairwell. "Amy Martin, right? I read your column every month. This is some story, huh? You covering it for your magazine?"

Amy didn't answer immediately. She was staring down at the open top carton in the officer's hands. It held an even dozen plastic deli containers, the near-yellow color of their contents visible through the translucent tops. Three of those cartons composed a three-year supply exactly.

"Yes, I'm covering the story," Amy said, smiling as she let the door swing closed behind them. "Here, let me give you a hand with some of those, Officer."

E P I L O G U E
....

From Amy Martin's **"Beauty Bytes"**
FEMINA MAGAZINE, November

Remember blackheads? That B-word seems to have slipped out of fashion lately, but the little fellars still have a way of popping up— especially along the lip-line and in that oily little spot where nostril meets cheek. (You always meet the cheekiest types in those oily little spots.) Blackheads are your pores' way of saying, "Hey, let's try to be more open with each other," and I've found nothing that does that better than La Prairie's deep cleansing Cellular Balancing Treatment. Blackheads beware. . . . Seems everybody's talking about aroma-therapy—the art of healing through fragrance. Apparently, certain scents evoke certain memories—say, the smell of pine trees calls up happy Christmas memories and along with those memories come healing feelings. Makes scents. At least that's the theory behind Maxie's new line of aromatic foaming baths. I soaked in one called Spring Rain last night, but the only memory it triggered in me was the time I was crossing Broadway after an April shower and got splashed all over my white linen GianFranco by a passing taxi. . . .

As many of you know, this is my last "Beauty Bytes." I'll miss all of you terribly, but my husband has taken a job with a Los Angeles hospital and I'd rather miss you than him. Pamela Ross will be taking over this page with the next issue of Femina. In fact, as I write these words, Pam is downtown having a makeover at a marvelous new salon she's discovered.

—Amy

ACKNOWLEDGMENTS

....

I wish to thank a number of people who generously gave of their knowledge and time in helping me research this novel: the endocrinology department of Mt. Sinai Hospital in New York, especially Robert McEvoy, M.D., and my old Harvard classmate Edward Merker, M.D.; also the chief of Mt. Sinai's blood bank, Dr. James Louie; Rosario Noto, M.D., and Bruce Schickmanter, M.D., both of the Berkshire Medical Center; Tom Herman, M.D.; and Harry Solas of the New York Blood Center.

My good friend Dan Bucsescu, of Pratt Institute, and his class of unusually talented design students helped me work out the "hidden room" problem.

The book *Being Beautiful,* on cosmetics and the consumer, prepared by Katherine Isaac and Ralph Nader of the Center for the Study of Responsive Law, was a great eye-opener; I recommend it to all who are interested in the subject.

My good friends Lee Kalcheim and Julia Lord, and Elena Latici, offered me encouragement at a point in this project when I needed it very much; they know how much I appreciated that. Likewise, my friend Martin Jacobs.

My agent, Mel Berger, was a model of patience; my editor, Jared Kieling, was a model of thoughtful and meticulous editorial guidance, a rarity.

I also want to thank Beverly and Kim Kimball, whose Art-Colony-Over-Sears on Main Street in Great Barrington is by far the best place to work I've ever found.

Finally, as always, I thank my very good friend Freke Vuijst, who helps me do everything.

—DMK

ABOUT THE AUTHOR

Daniel M. Klein is the author of two previous medical thrillers, *Embryo* and *Wavelengths,* and of an autobiographical novel, *Magic Time.* Mr. Klein lives with his wife, Dutch film producer Freke Vuijst, and their daughter, Samara, in Great Barrington, Massachusetts.